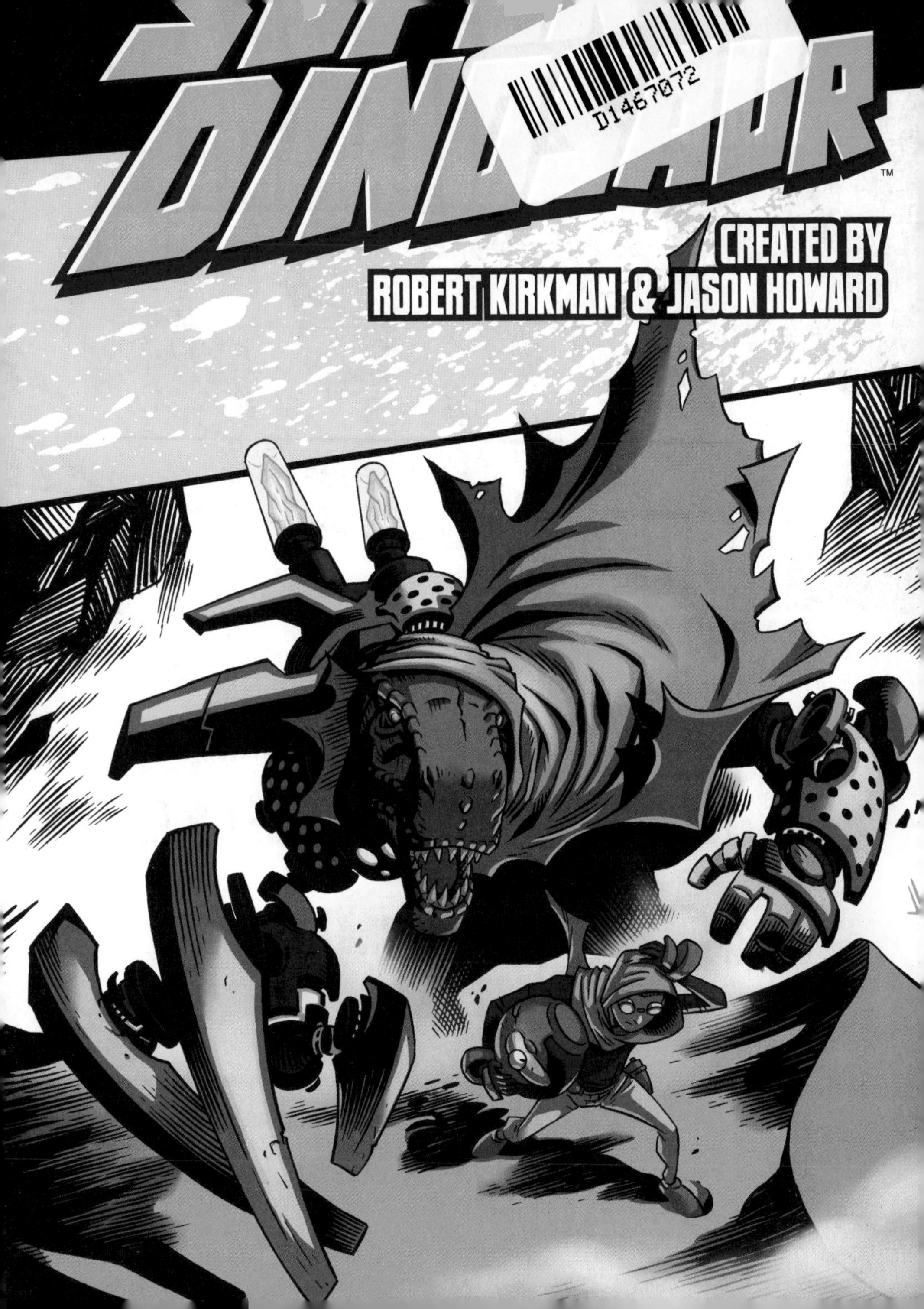
CREATED BY
ROBERT KIRKMAN & JASON HOWARD

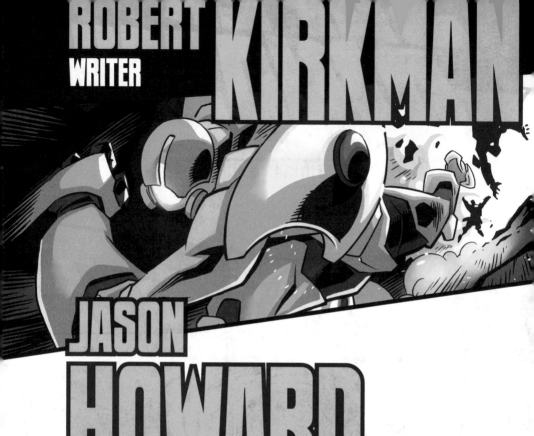

ROBERT **KIRKMAN**
WRITER

JASON **HOWARD**
ART & COLORS

CLIFF **RATHBURN** INKER

RUS **WOOTON**
LETTERER

SEAN **MACKIEWICZ**
EDITOR

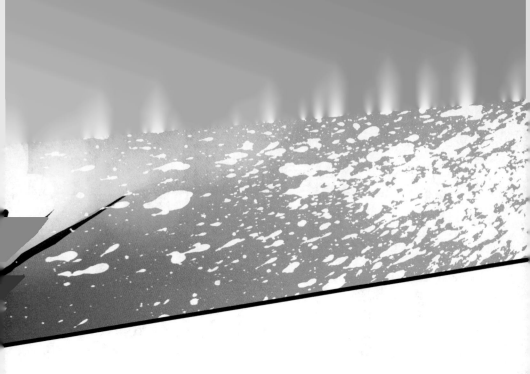

SUPER DINOSAUR, VOLUME 4
ISBN: 978-1-60706-843-3
First Printing

IMAGE COMICS, INC.
Robert Kirkman – Chief Operating Officer
Erik Larsen – Chief Financial Officer
Todd McFarlane – President
Marc Silvestri – Chief Executive Officer
Jim Valentino – Vice-President

Eric Stephenson – Publisher
Ron Richards – Director of Business Development
Jennifer de Guzman – Director of Trade Book Sales
Kat Salazar – Director of PR & Marketing
Corey Murphy – Director of Retail Sales
Jeremy Sullivan – Director of Digital Sales
Emilio Bautista – Sales Assistant
Branwyn Bigglestone – Senior Accounts Manager
Emily Miller – Accounts Manager
Jessica Ambriz – Administrative Assistant
Tyler Shainline – Events Coordinator
David Brothers – Content Manager
Jonathan Chan – Production Manager
Drew Gill – Art Director
Meredith Wallace – Print Manager
Monica Garcia – Senior Production Artist
Addison Duke – Production Artist
Tricia Ramos – Production Assistant
IMAGECOMICS.COM

SKYBOUND

For SKYBOUND ENTERTAINMENT
Robert Kirkman - CEO
Sean Mackiewicz - Editorial Director
Shawn Kirkham - Director of Business Development
Brian Huntington - Online Editorial Director
June Alian - Publicity Director
Rachel Skidmore - Director of Media Development
Helen Leigh - Assistant Editor
Dan Petersen - Operations Manager
Sarah Effinger - Office Manager
Nick Palmer - Operations Coordinator
Lizzy Iverson - Administrative Assistant
Stephan Murillo - Administrative Assistant

International inquiries: foreign@skybound.com
Licensing inquiries: contact@skybound.com

WWW.SKYBOUND.COM

PRINTED IN THE USA

OUR FAVORITE KID

DEREK DYNAMO

HAD BEEN CAPTURED BY...

THE EXILE

II

A REPTILOID

FRIENDS

TO THE RESCUE!

SUPER DINOSAUR

ERICA KINGSTON

ELLIOT CASEY

ERIN KINGSTON

ALONG WITH

WHEELS ARMOR

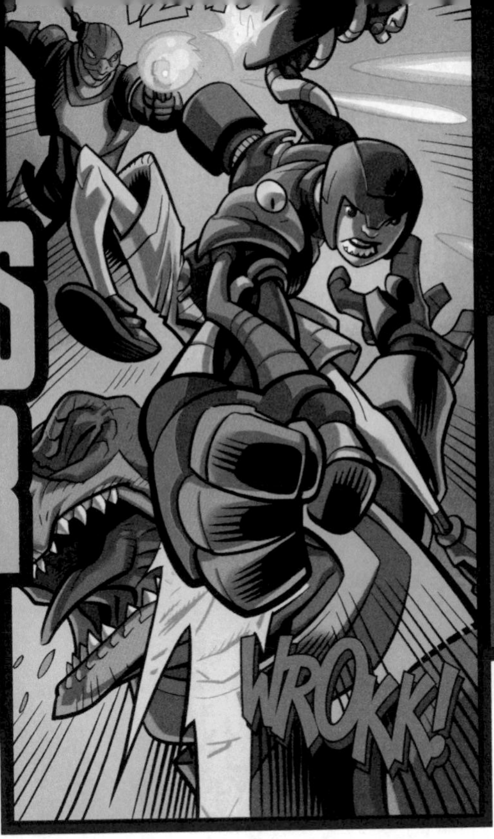
WROKK!

MEANWHILE

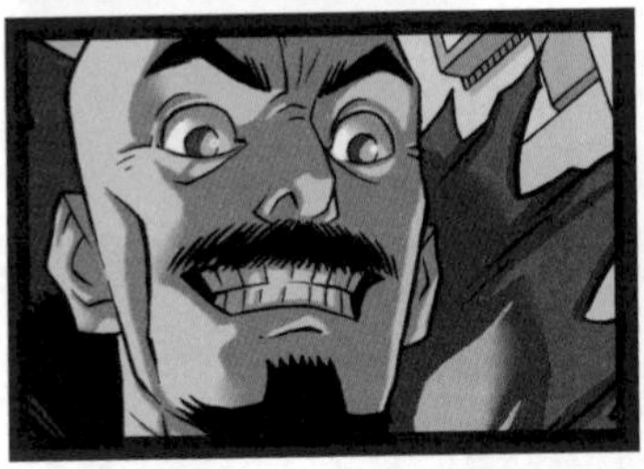

MAX MAXIMUS

INJECTED HIS CLONE WITH DYNORE

(IT'S COMPLICATED)

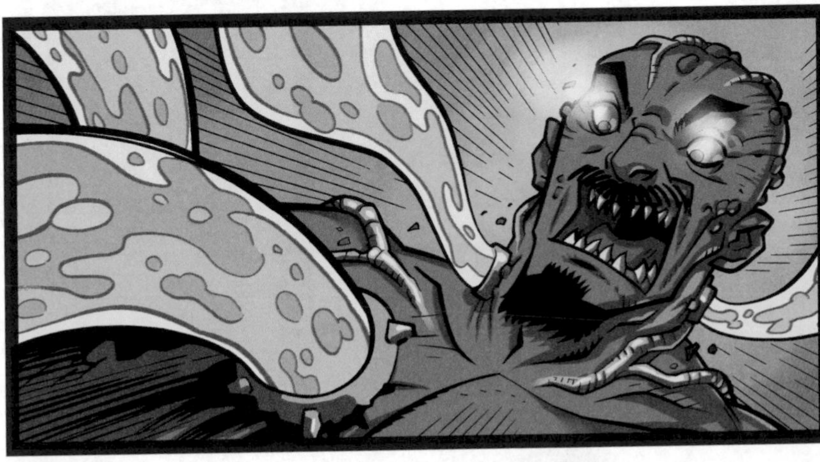

MINIMUS

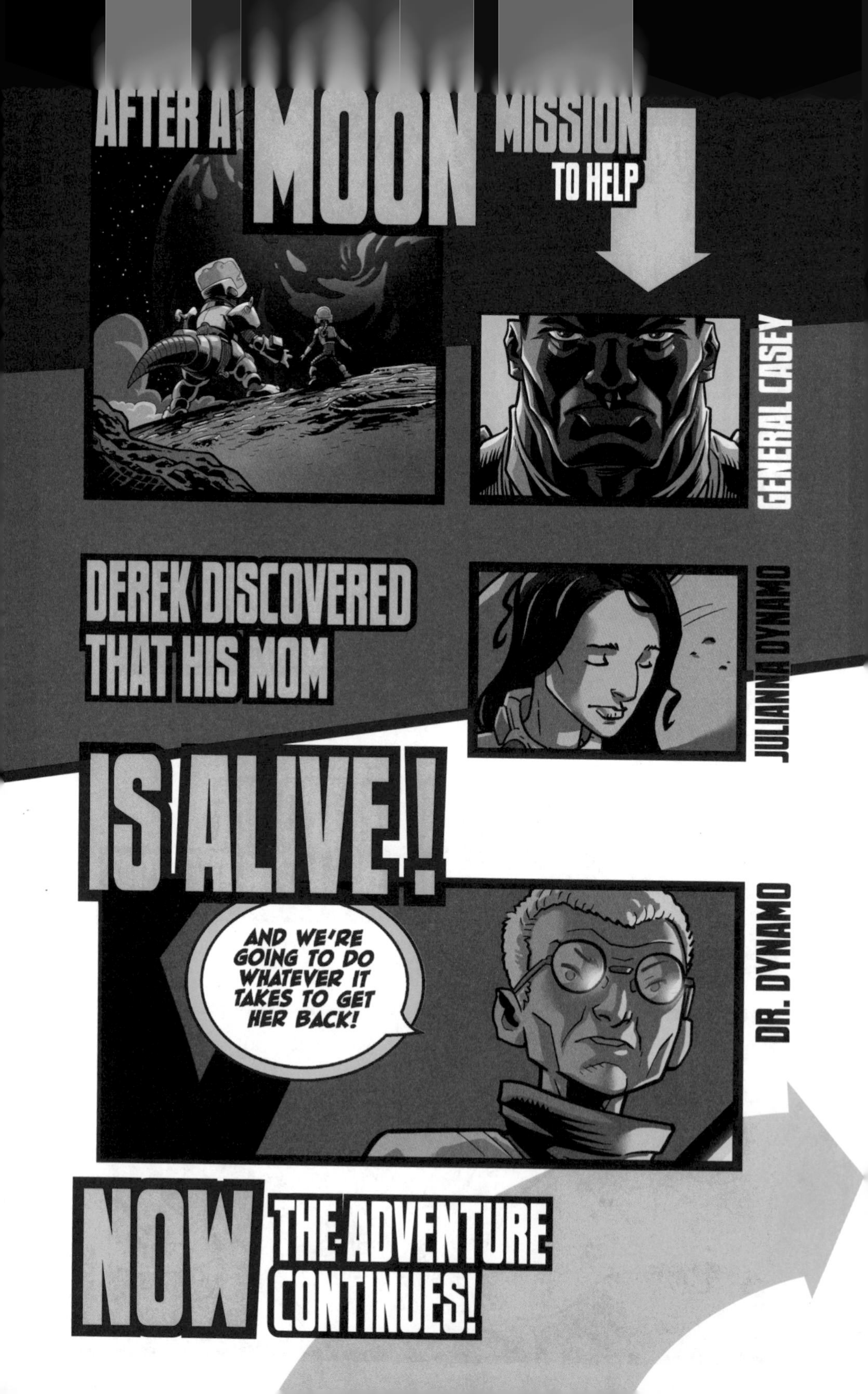
AFTER A MOON MISSION TO HELP
GENERAL CASEY
DEREK DISCOVERED THAT HIS MOM
JULIANNA DYNAMO
IS ALIVE!
AND WE'RE GOING TO DO WHATEVER IT TAKES TO GET HER BACK!
DR. DYNAMO
NOW THE ADVENTURE CONTINUES!

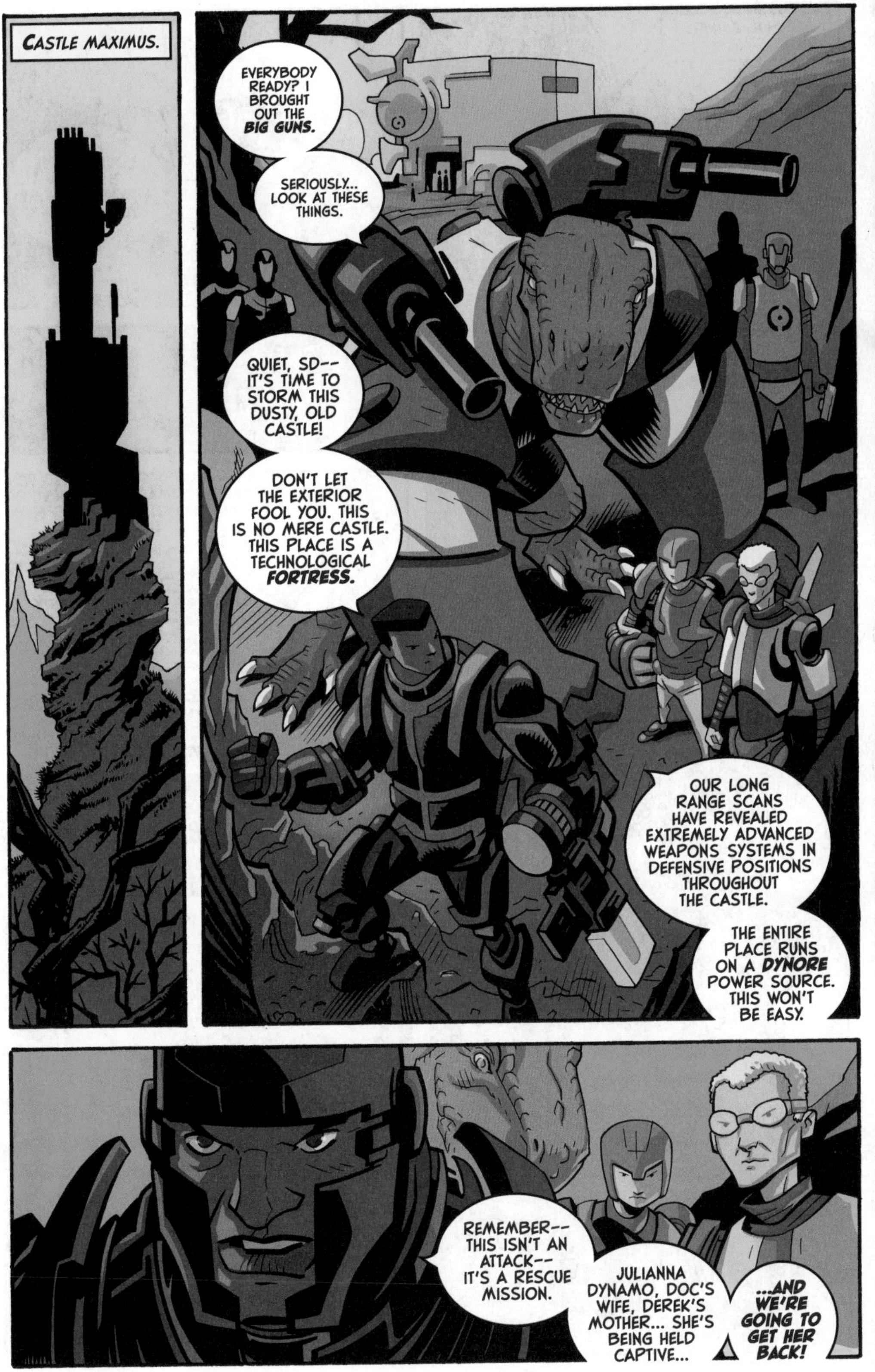
CASTLE MAXIMUS.
EVERYBODY READY? I BROUGHT OUT THE BIG GUNS.
SERIOUSLY... LOOK AT THESE THINGS.
QUIET, SD-- IT'S TIME TO STORM THIS DUSTY, OLD CASTLE!
DON'T LET THE EXTERIOR FOOL YOU. THIS IS NO MERE CASTLE. THIS PLACE IS A TECHNOLOGICAL FORTRESS.
OUR LONG RANGE SCANS HAVE REVEALED EXTREMELY ADVANCED WEAPONS SYSTEMS IN DEFENSIVE POSITIONS THROUGHOUT THE CASTLE.
THE ENTIRE PLACE RUNS ON A DYNORE POWER SOURCE. THIS WON'T BE EASY.
REMEMBER-- THIS ISN'T AN ATTACK-- IT'S A RESCUE MISSION.
JULIANNA DYNAMO, DOC'S WIFE, DEREK'S MOTHER... SHE'S BEING HELD CAPTIVE...
...AND WE'RE GOING TO GET HER BACK!

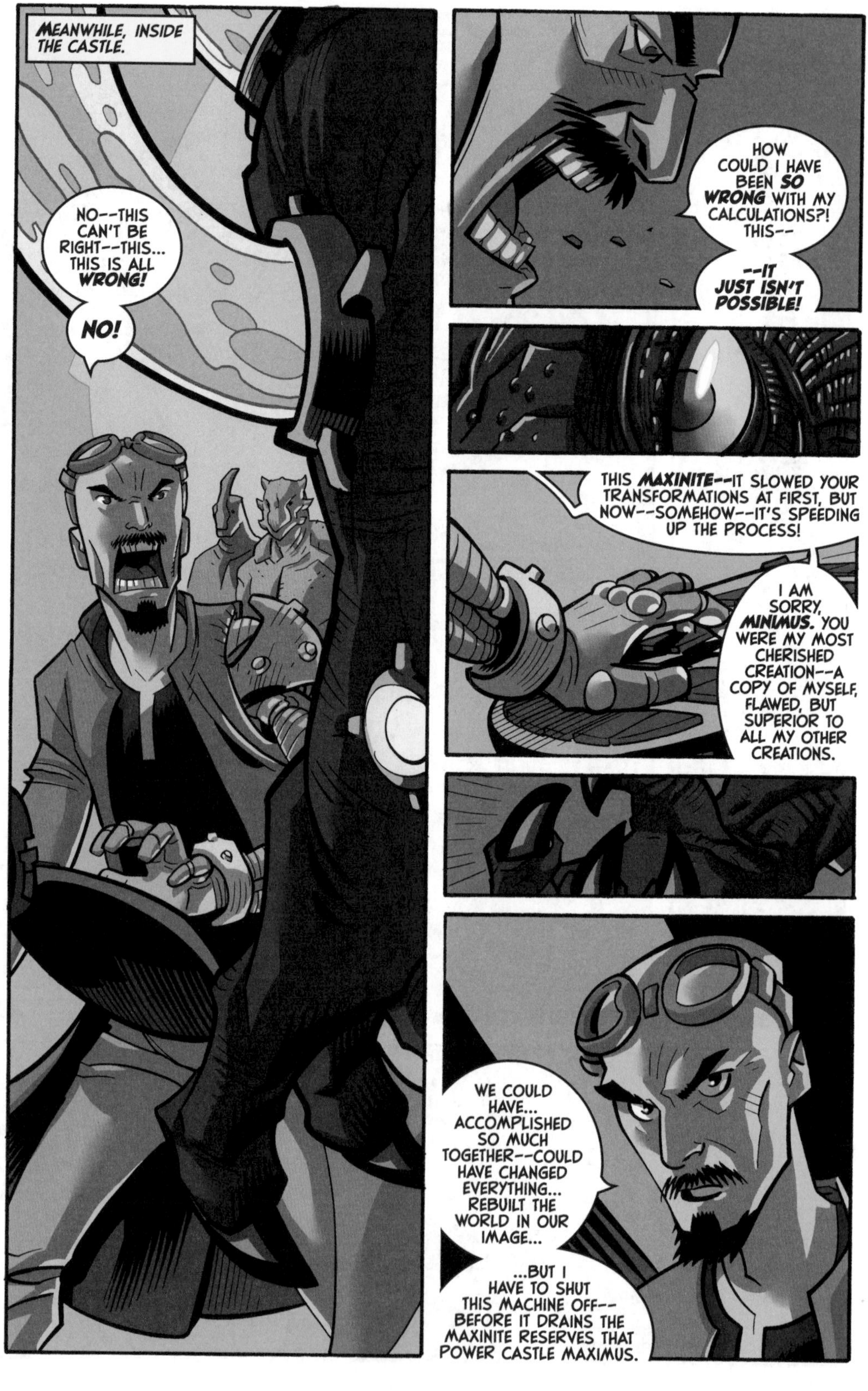
MEANWHILE, INSIDE THE CASTLE.
NO--THIS CAN'T BE RIGHT--THIS... THIS IS ALL WRONG!
NO!
HOW COULD I HAVE BEEN SO WRONG WITH MY CALCULATIONS?! THIS--
--IT JUST ISN'T POSSIBLE!
THIS MAXINITE--IT SLOWED YOUR TRANSFORMATIONS AT FIRST, BUT NOW--SOMEHOW--IT'S SPEEDING UP THE PROCESS!
I AM SORRY, MINIMUS. YOU WERE MY MOST CHERISHED CREATION--A COPY OF MYSELF, FLAWED, BUT SUPERIOR TO ALL MY OTHER CREATIONS.
WE COULD HAVE... ACCOMPLISHED SO MUCH TOGETHER--COULD HAVE CHANGED EVERYTHING... REBUILT THE WORLD IN OUR IMAGE...
...BUT I HAVE TO SHUT THIS MACHINE OFF--BEFORE IT DRAINS THE MAXINITE RESERVES THAT POWER CASTLE MAXIMUS.

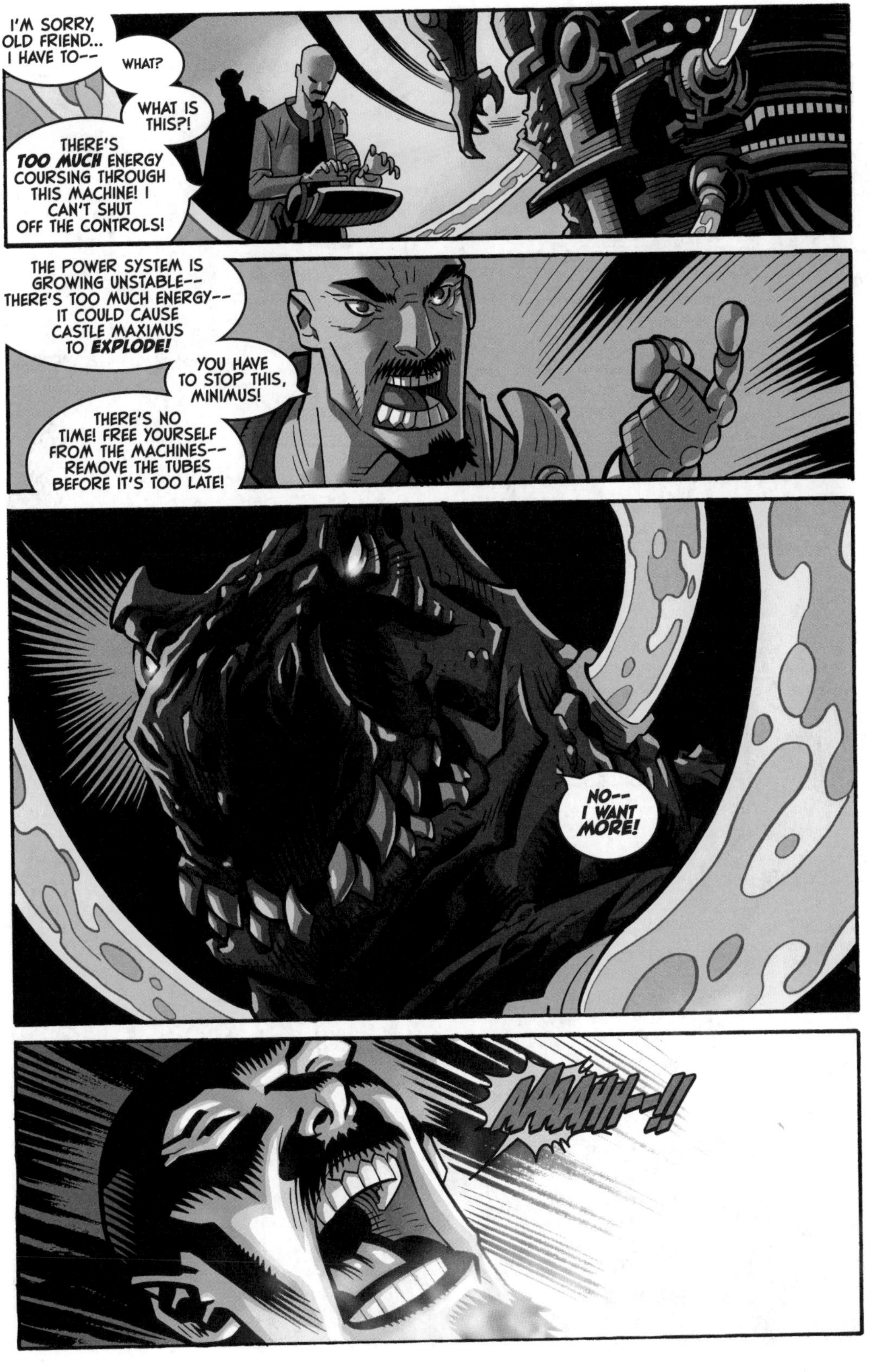

I'M SORRY, OLD FRIEND... I HAVE TO--
WHAT?
WHAT IS THIS?!
THERE'S TOO MUCH ENERGY COURSING THROUGH THIS MACHINE! I CAN'T SHUT OFF THE CONTROLS!
THE POWER SYSTEM IS GROWING UNSTABLE-- THERE'S TOO MUCH ENERGY-- IT COULD CAUSE CASTLE MAXIMUS TO EXPLODE!
YOU HAVE TO STOP THIS, MINIMUS!
THERE'S NO TIME! FREE YOURSELF FROM THE MACHINES-- REMOVE THE TUBES BEFORE IT'S TOO LATE!
NO-- I WANT MORE!
AAAAHH--!!

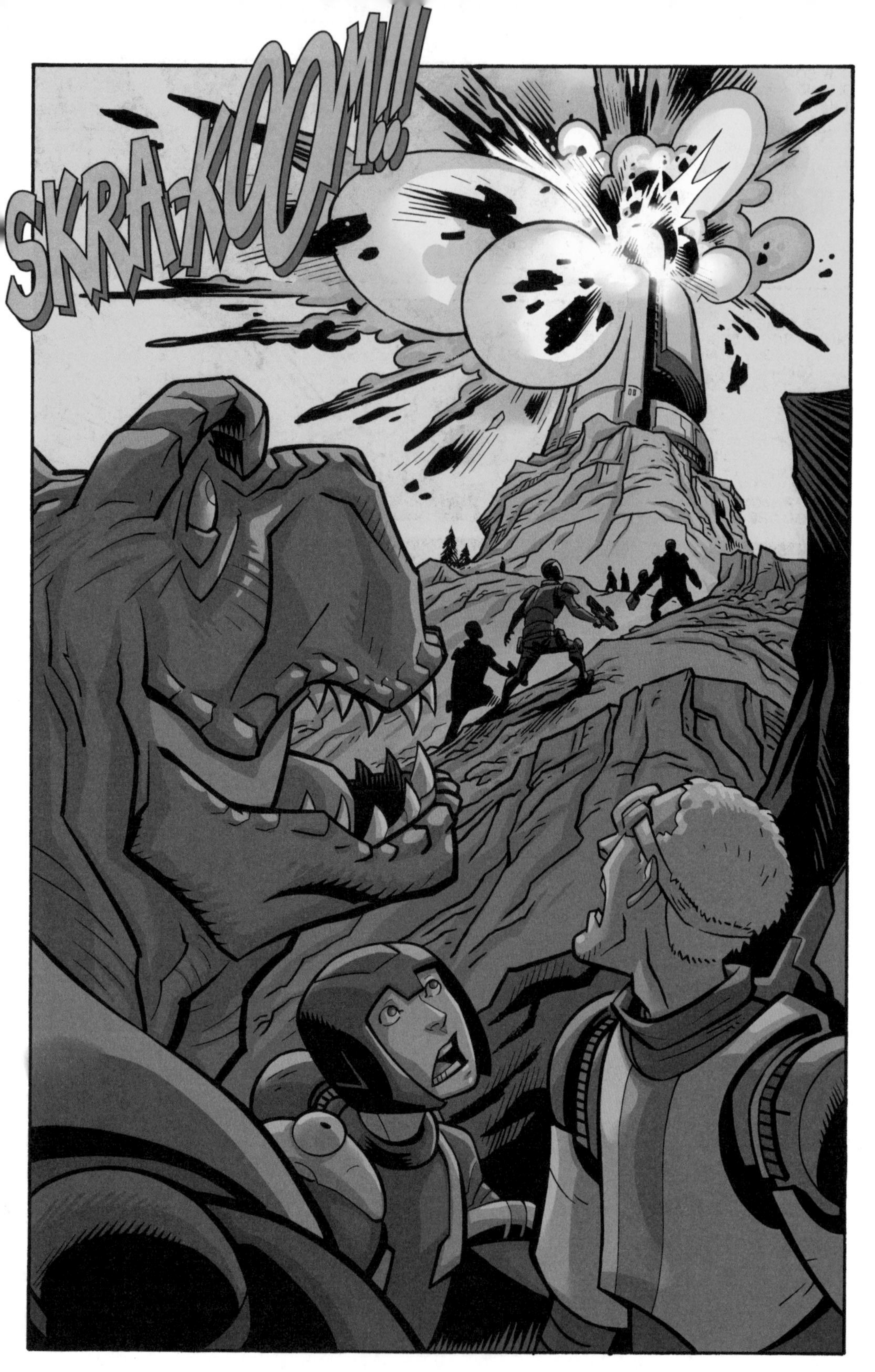
SKRA-KOOM!!

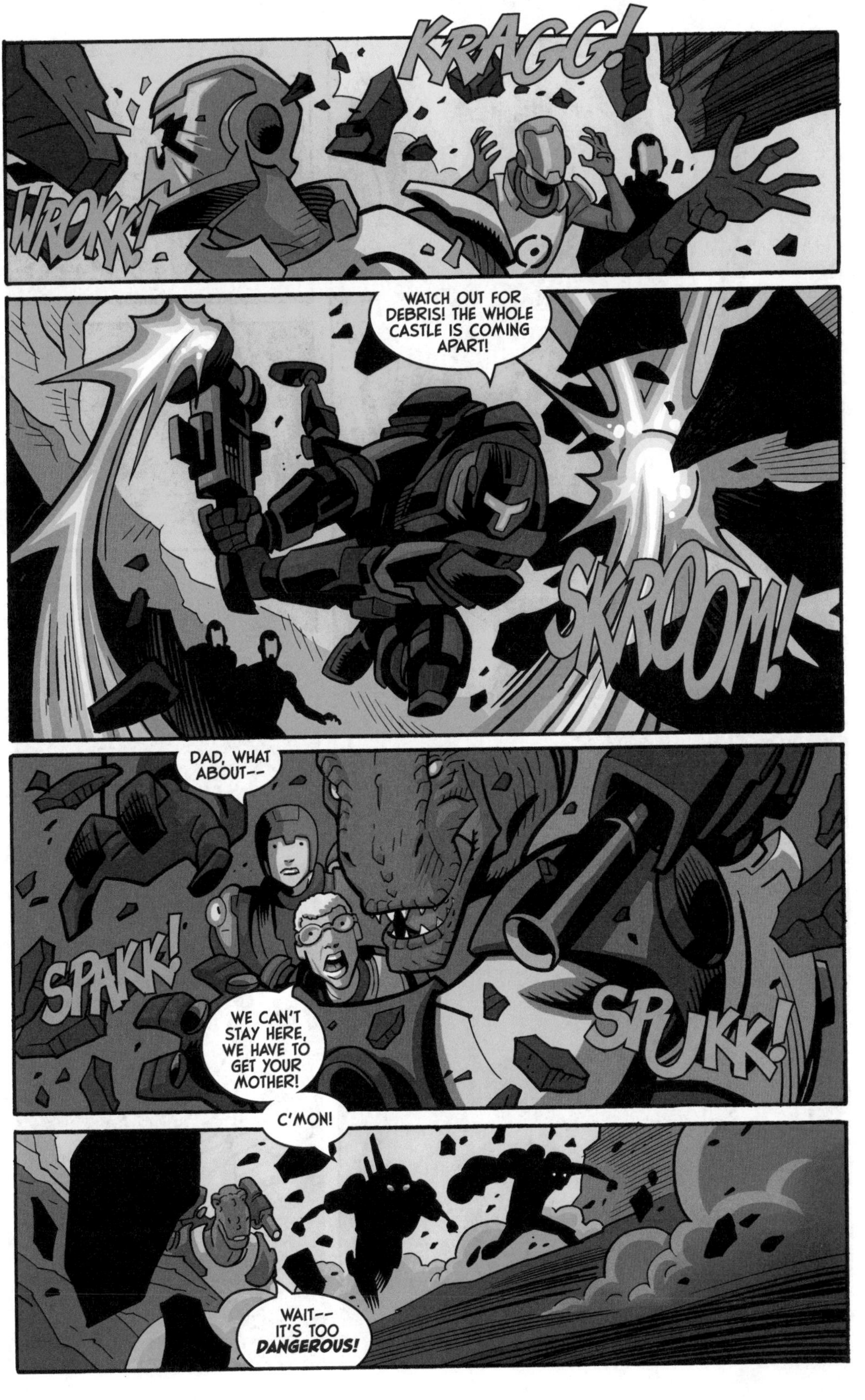
KRAGG!
WROKK!
WATCH OUT FOR DEBRIS! THE WHOLE CASTLE IS COMING APART!
SKROOM!
DAD, WHAT ABOUT--
SPAKK!
WE CAN'T STAY HERE, WE HAVE TO GET YOUR MOTHER!
SPUKK!
C'MON!
WAIT-- IT'S TOO DANGEROUS!

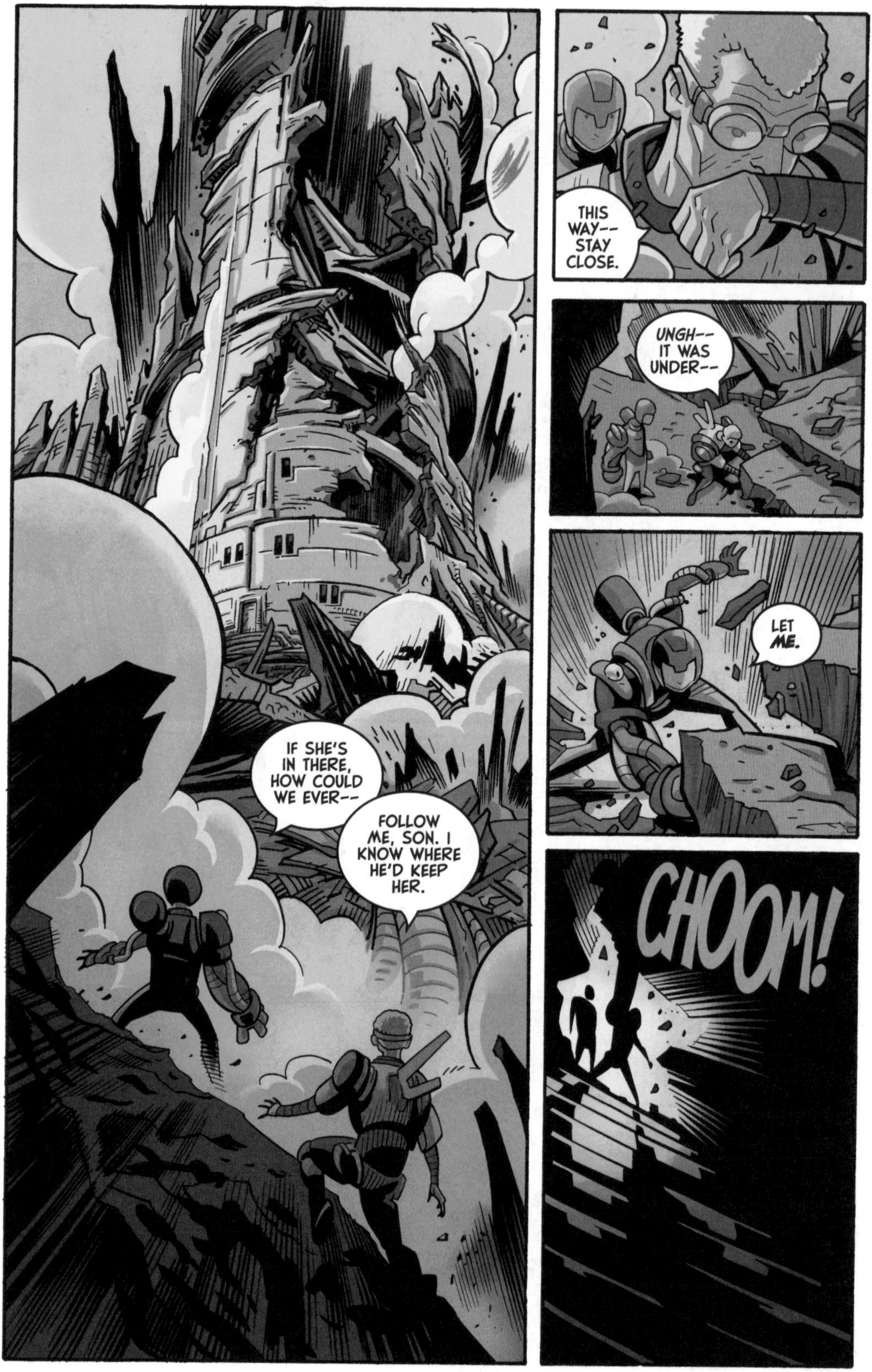
IF SHE'S IN THERE, HOW COULD WE EVER--
FOLLOW ME, SON. I KNOW WHERE HE'D KEEP HER.
THIS WAY-- STAY CLOSE.
UNGH-- IT WAS UNDER--
LET ME.
CHOOM!

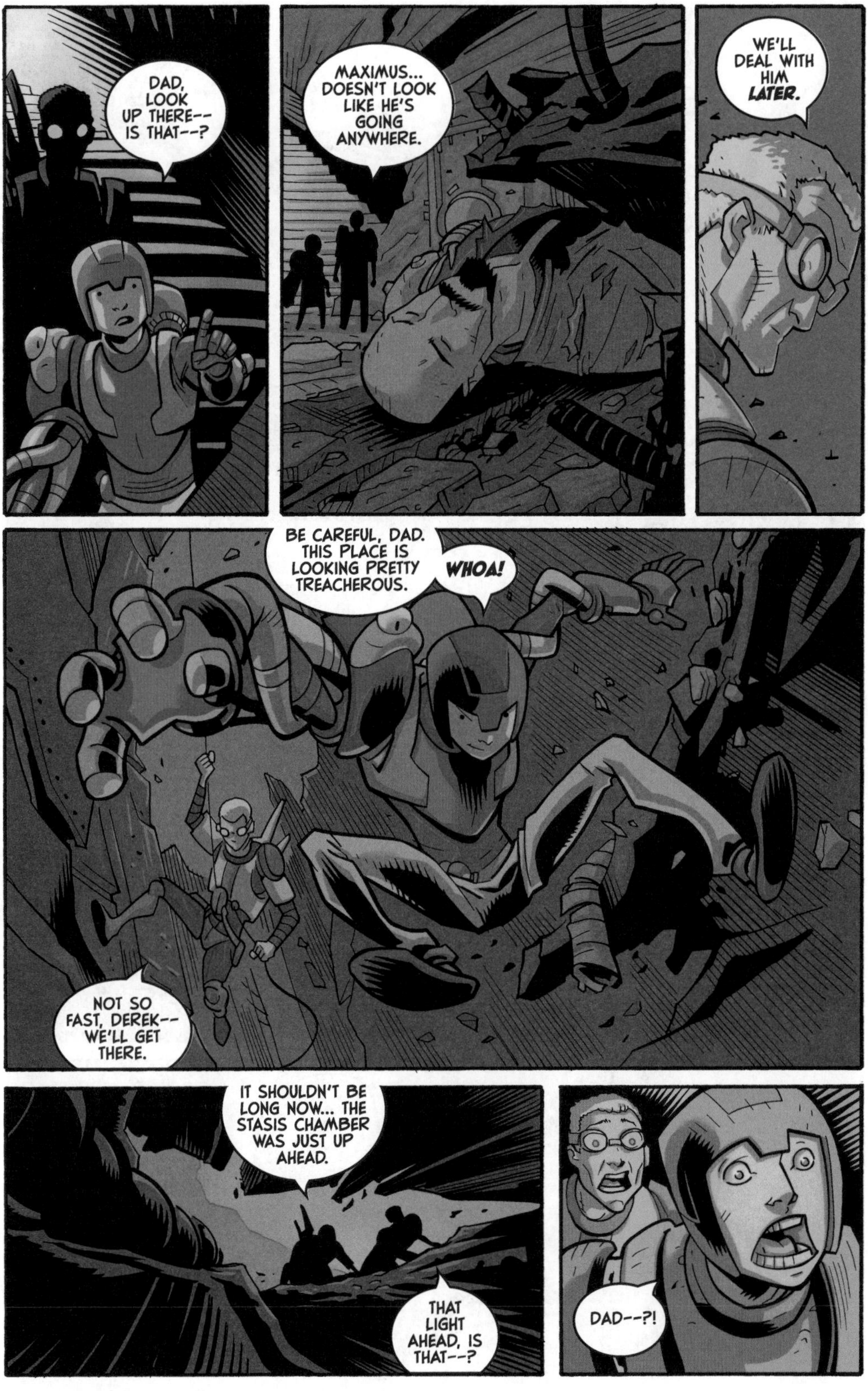
DAD, LOOK UP THERE-- IS THAT--?
MAXIMUS... DOESN'T LOOK LIKE HE'S GOING ANYWHERE.
WE'LL DEAL WITH HIM *LATER.*
BE CAREFUL, DAD. THIS PLACE IS LOOKING PRETTY TREACHEROUS.
WHOA!
NOT SO FAST, DEREK-- WE'LL GET THERE.
IT SHOULDN'T BE LONG NOW... THE STASIS CHAMBER WAS JUST UP AHEAD.
THAT LIGHT AHEAD, IS THAT--?
DAD--?!

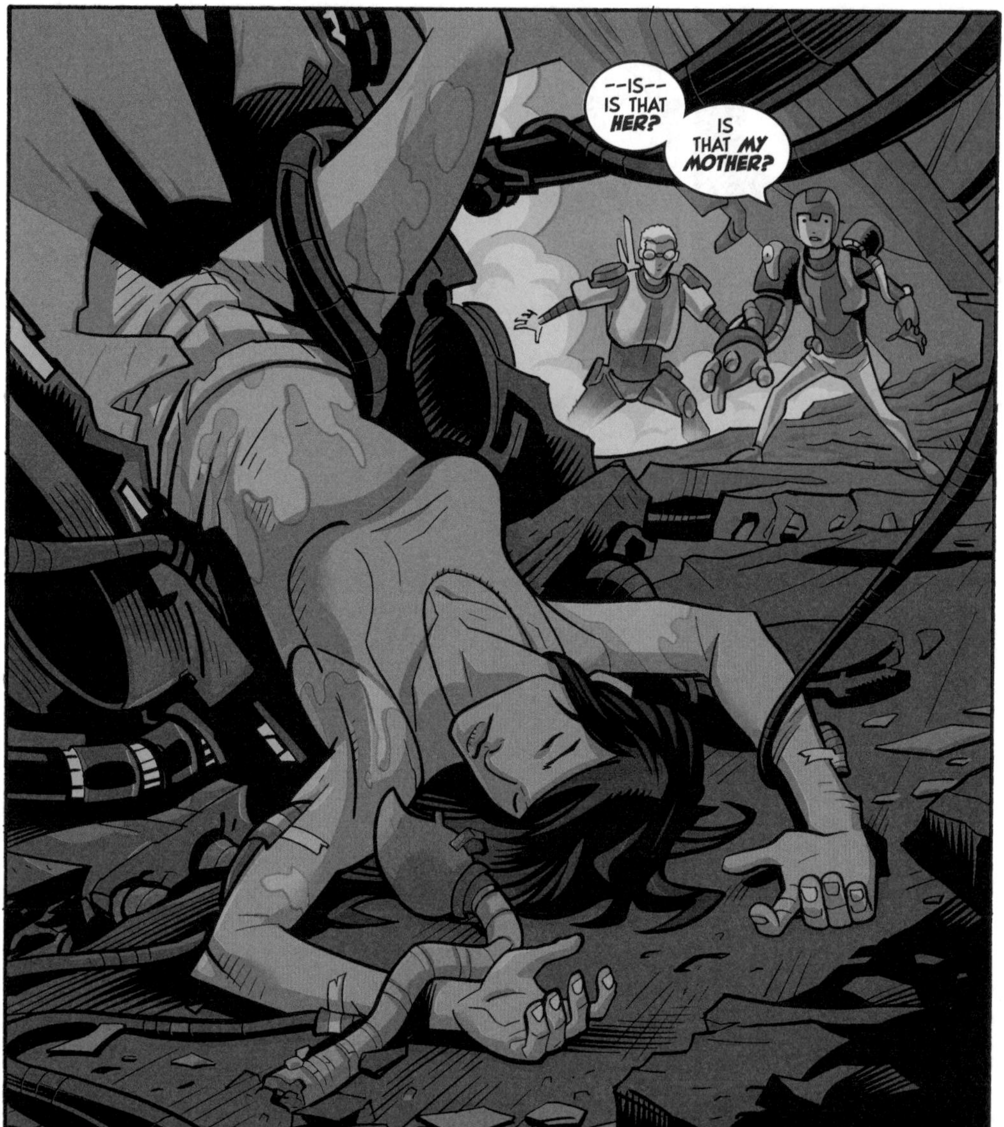
--IS--
IS THAT *HER?*
IS THAT *MY MOTHER?*
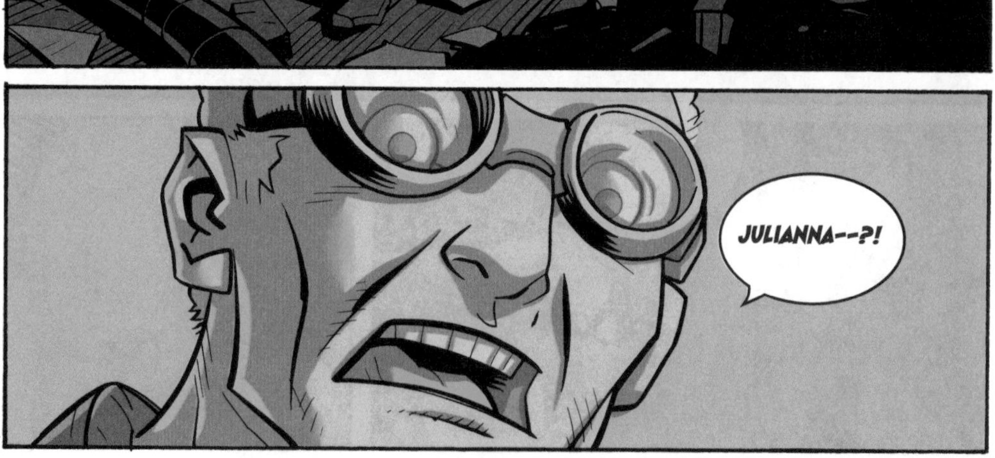
JULIANNA--?!

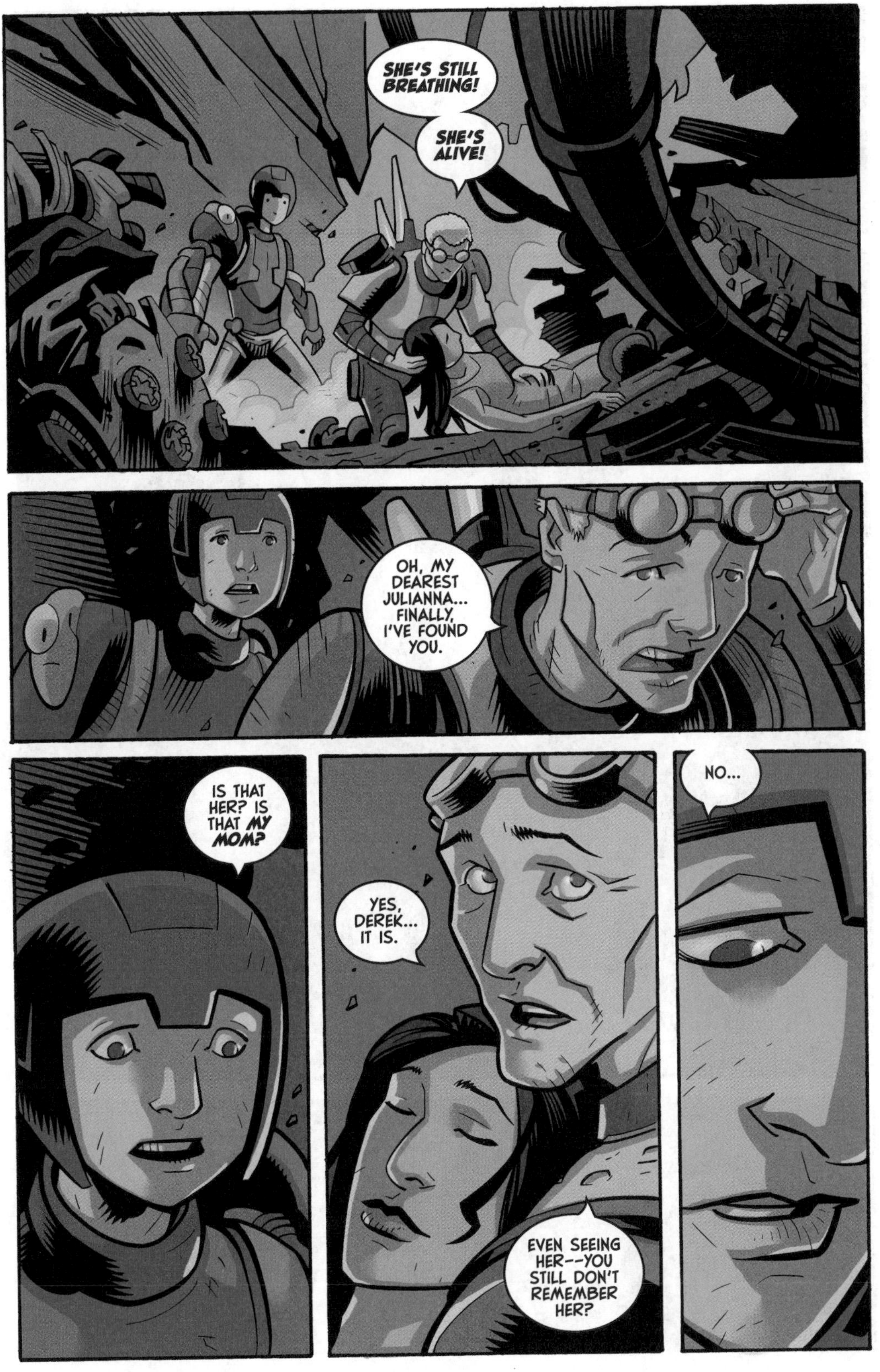
SHE'S STILL BREATHING!
SHE'S ALIVE!
OH, MY DEAREST JULIANNA... FINALLY, I'VE FOUND YOU.
IS THAT HER? IS THAT *MY MOM?*
YES, DEREK... IT IS.
NO...
EVEN SEEING HER--YOU STILL DON'T REMEMBER HER?

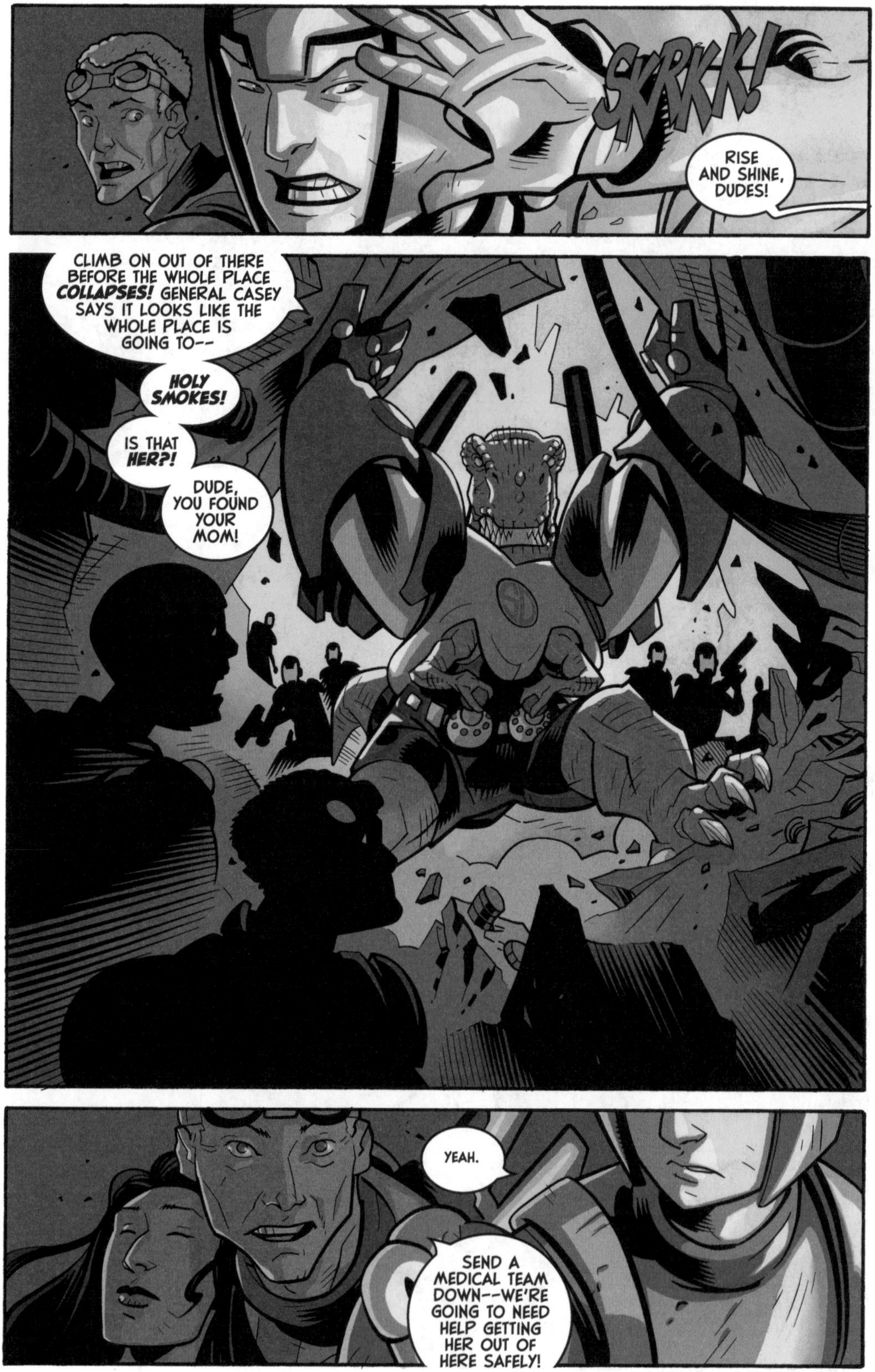
SKRKK!
RISE AND SHINE, DUDES!
CLIMB ON OUT OF THERE BEFORE THE WHOLE PLACE COLLAPSES! GENERAL CASEY SAYS IT LOOKS LIKE THE WHOLE PLACE IS GOING TO--
HOLY SMOKES!
IS THAT HER?!
DUDE, YOU FOUND YOUR MOM!
YEAH.
SEND A MEDICAL TEAM DOWN--WE'RE GOING TO NEED HELP GETTING HER OUT OF HERE SAFELY!

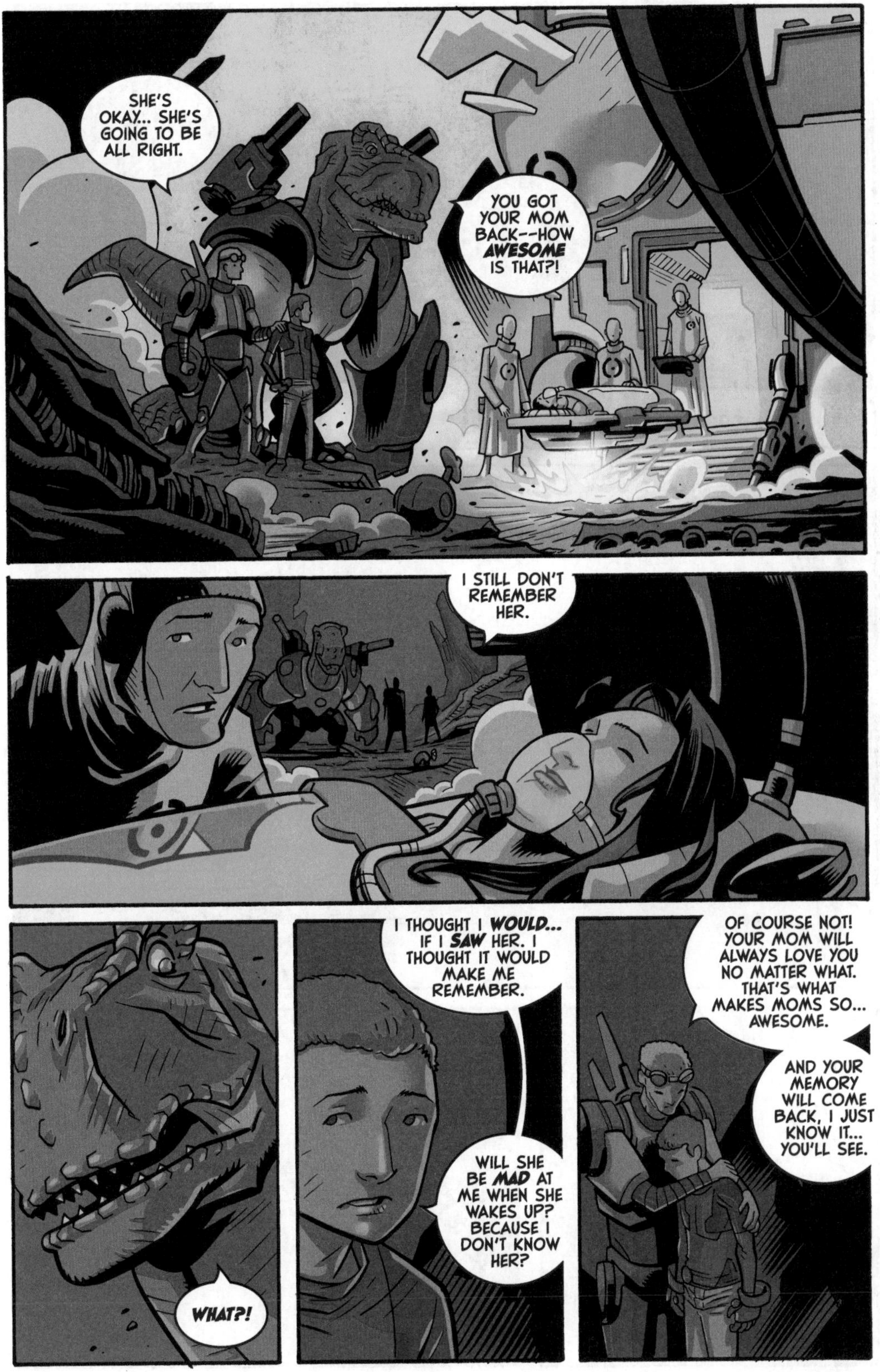
SHE'S OKAY... SHE'S GOING TO BE ALL RIGHT.
YOU GOT YOUR MOM BACK--HOW AWESOME IS THAT?!
I STILL DON'T REMEMBER HER.
WHAT?!
I THOUGHT I WOULD... IF I SAW HER. I THOUGHT IT WOULD MAKE ME REMEMBER.
WILL SHE BE MAD AT ME WHEN SHE WAKES UP? BECAUSE I DON'T KNOW HER?
OF COURSE NOT! YOUR MOM WILL ALWAYS LOVE YOU NO MATTER WHAT. THAT'S WHAT MAKES MOMS SO... AWESOME.
AND YOUR MEMORY WILL COME BACK, I JUST KNOW IT... YOU'LL SEE.

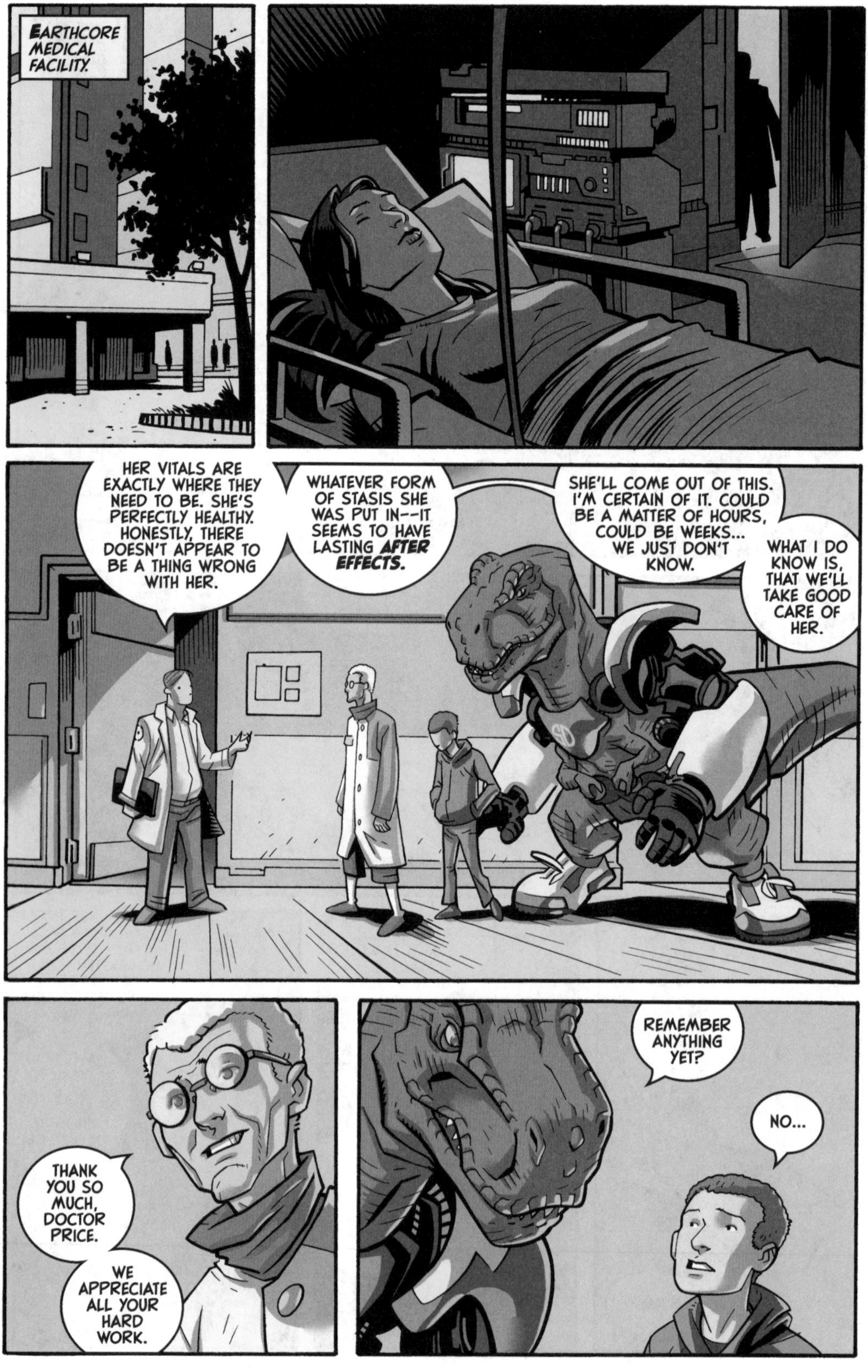
EARTHCORE MEDICAL FACILITY.
HER VITALS ARE EXACTLY WHERE THEY NEED TO BE. SHE'S PERFECTLY HEALTHY. HONESTLY, THERE DOESN'T APPEAR TO BE A THING WRONG WITH HER.
WHATEVER FORM OF STASIS SHE WAS PUT IN--IT SEEMS TO HAVE LASTING AFTER EFFECTS.
SHE'LL COME OUT OF THIS. I'M CERTAIN OF IT. COULD BE A MATTER OF HOURS, COULD BE WEEKS... WE JUST DON'T KNOW.
WHAT I DO KNOW IS, THAT WE'LL TAKE GOOD CARE OF HER.
THANK YOU SO MUCH, DOCTOR PRICE.
WE APPRECIATE ALL YOUR HARD WORK.
REMEMBER ANYTHING YET?
NO...

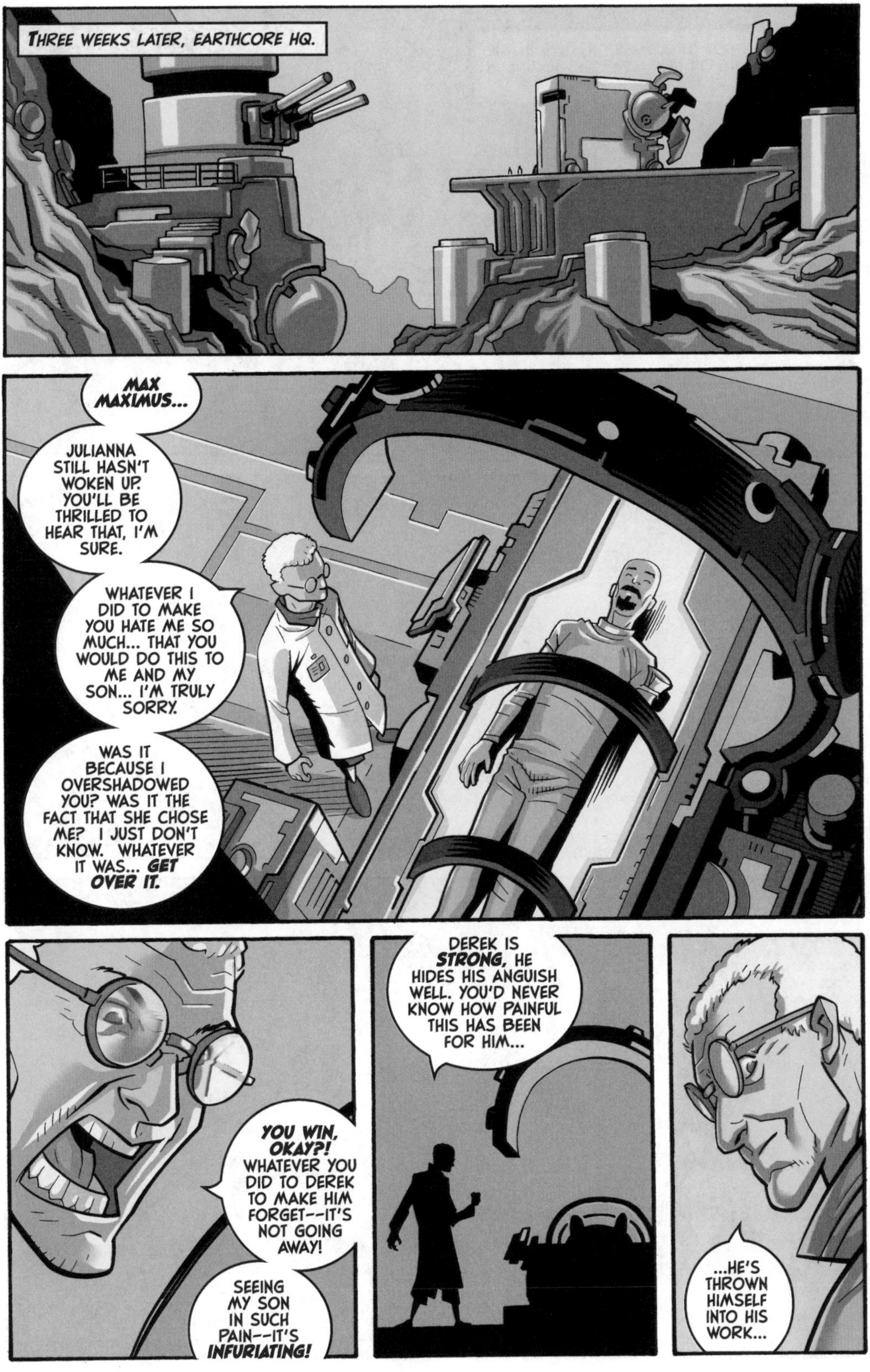
THREE WEEKS LATER, EARTHCORE HQ.
MAX MAXIMUS...
JULIANNA STILL HASN'T WOKEN UP. YOU'LL BE THRILLED TO HEAR THAT, I'M SURE.
WHATEVER I DID TO MAKE YOU HATE ME SO MUCH... THAT YOU WOULD DO THIS TO ME AND MY SON... I'M TRULY SORRY.
WAS IT BECAUSE I OVERSHADOWED YOU? WAS IT THE FACT THAT SHE CHOSE ME? I JUST DON'T KNOW. WHATEVER IT WAS... GET OVER IT.
YOU WIN, OKAY?! WHATEVER YOU DID TO DEREK TO MAKE HIM FORGET--IT'S NOT GOING AWAY!
SEEING MY SON IN SUCH PAIN--IT'S INFURIATING!
DEREK IS STRONG, HE HIDES HIS ANGUISH WELL. YOU'D NEVER KNOW HOW PAINFUL THIS HAS BEEN FOR HIM...
...HE'S THROWN HIMSELF INTO HIS WORK...

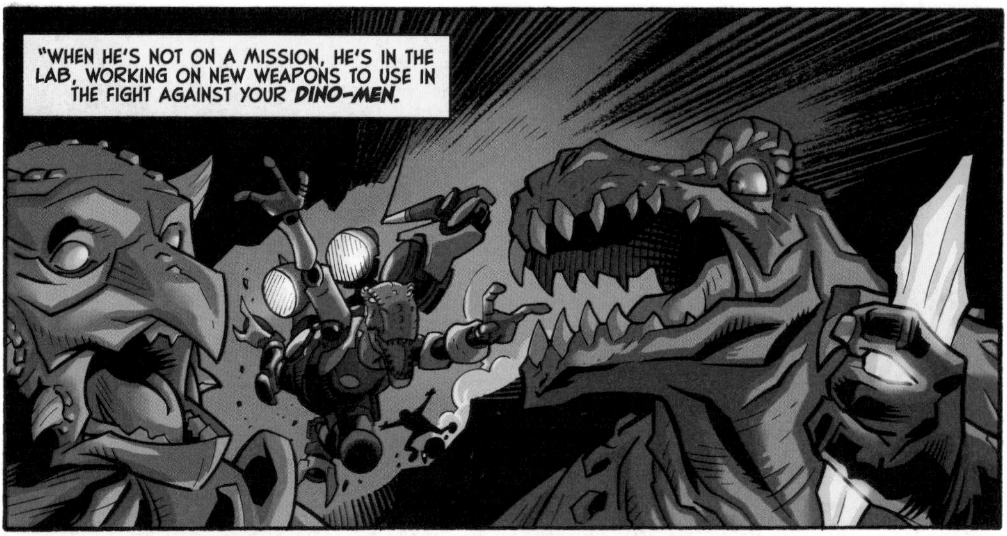
"WHEN HE'S NOT ON A MISSION, HE'S IN THE LAB, WORKING ON NEW WEAPONS TO USE IN THE FIGHT AGAINST YOUR DINO-MEN.

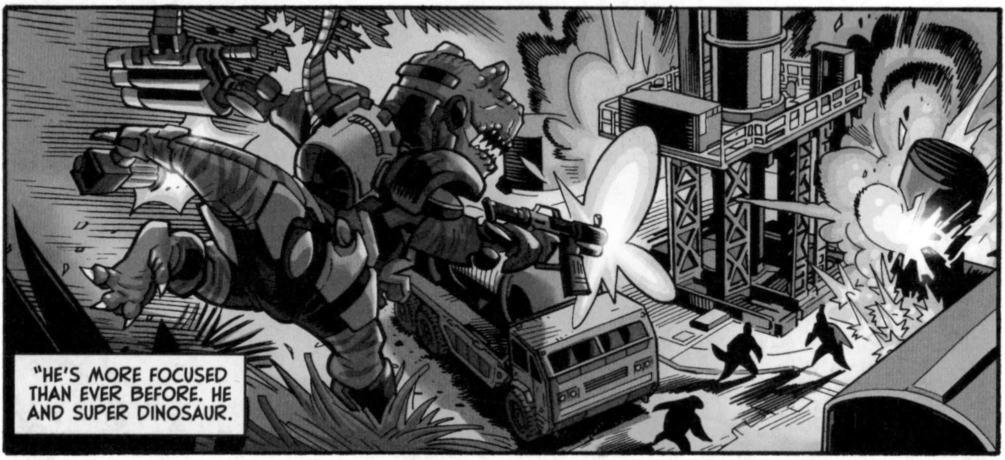
"HE'S MORE FOCUSED THAN EVER BEFORE. HE AND SUPER DINOSAUR.

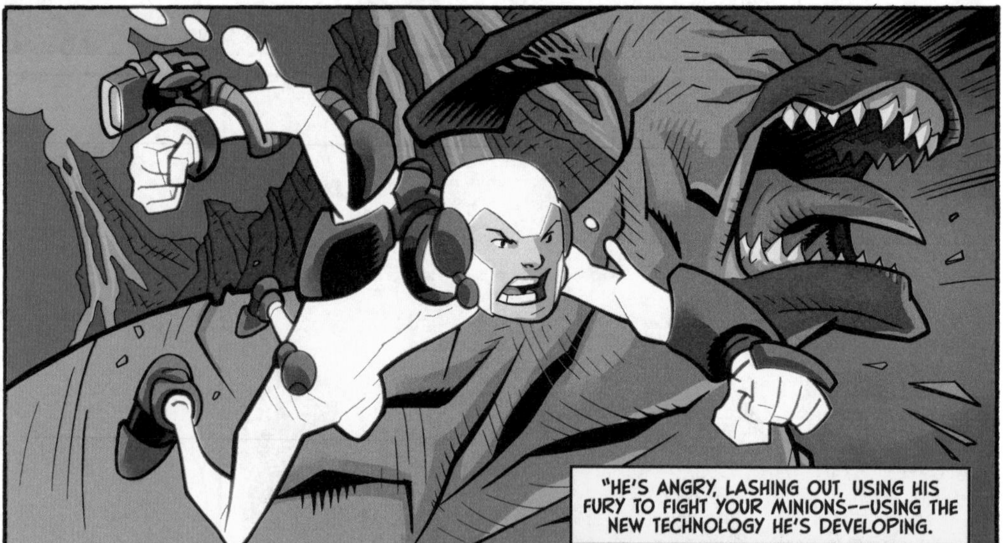
"HE'S ANGRY, LASHING OUT, USING HIS FURY TO FIGHT YOUR MINIONS--USING THE NEW TECHNOLOGY HE'S DEVELOPING.

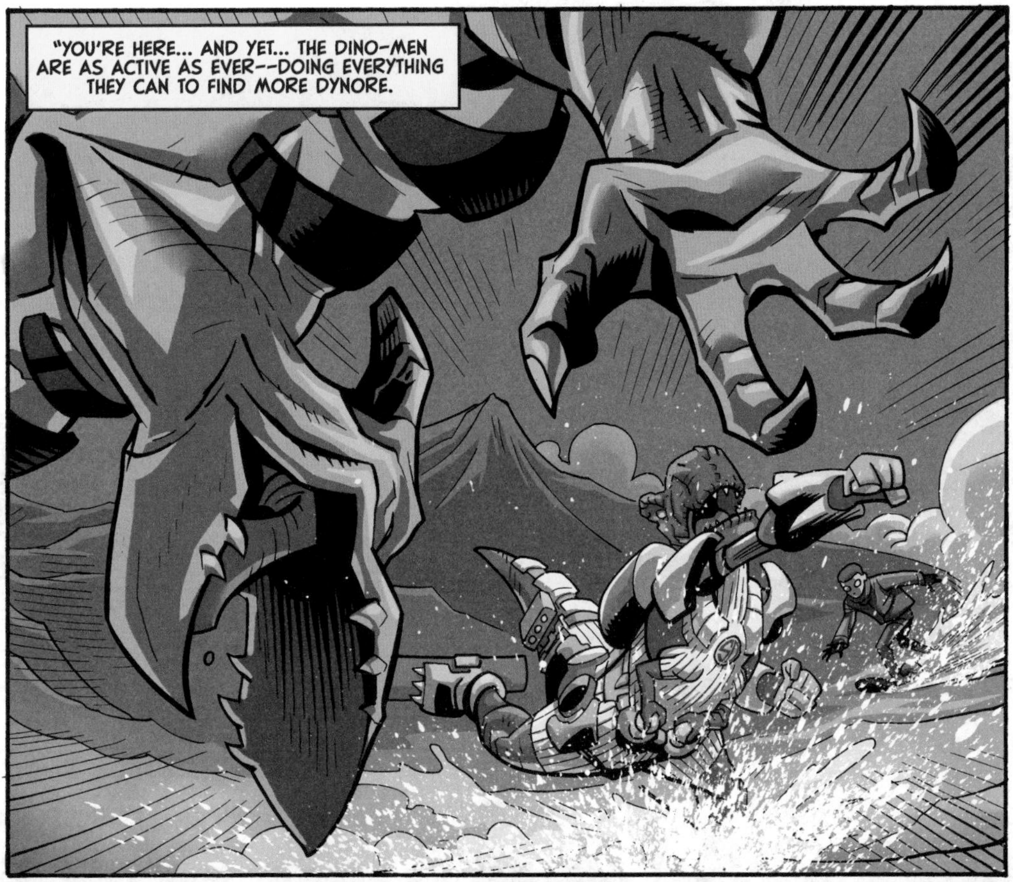
"YOU'RE HERE... AND YET... THE DINO-MEN ARE AS ACTIVE AS EVER--DOING EVERYTHING THEY CAN TO FIND MORE DYNORE.

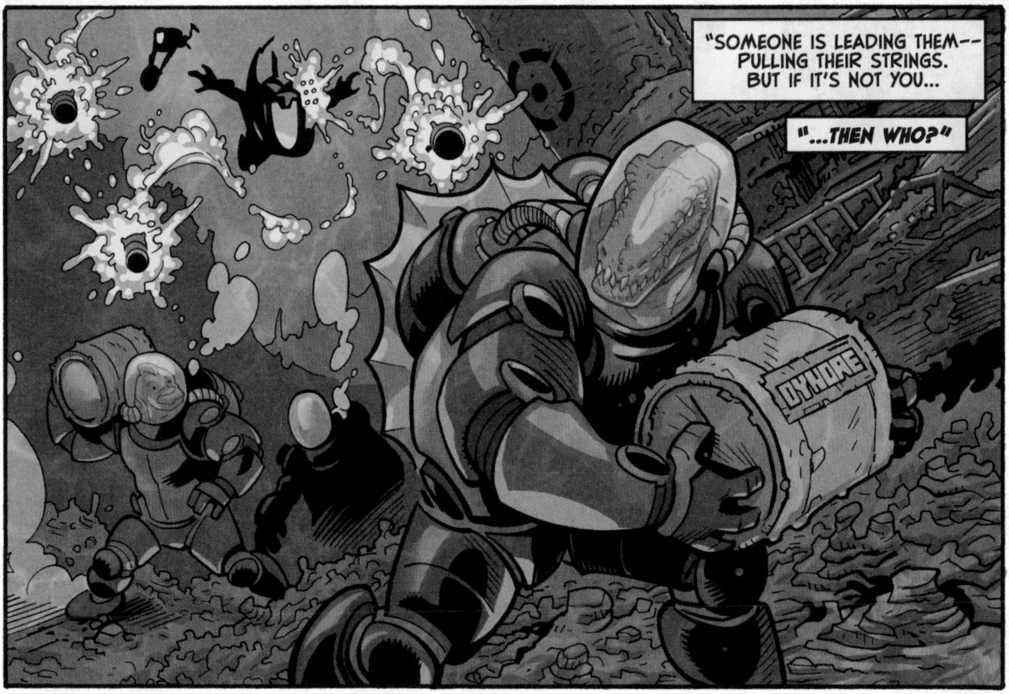
"SOMEONE IS LEADING THEM--PULLING THEIR STRINGS. BUT IF IT'S NOT YOU...
"...THEN WHO?"
DYNORE

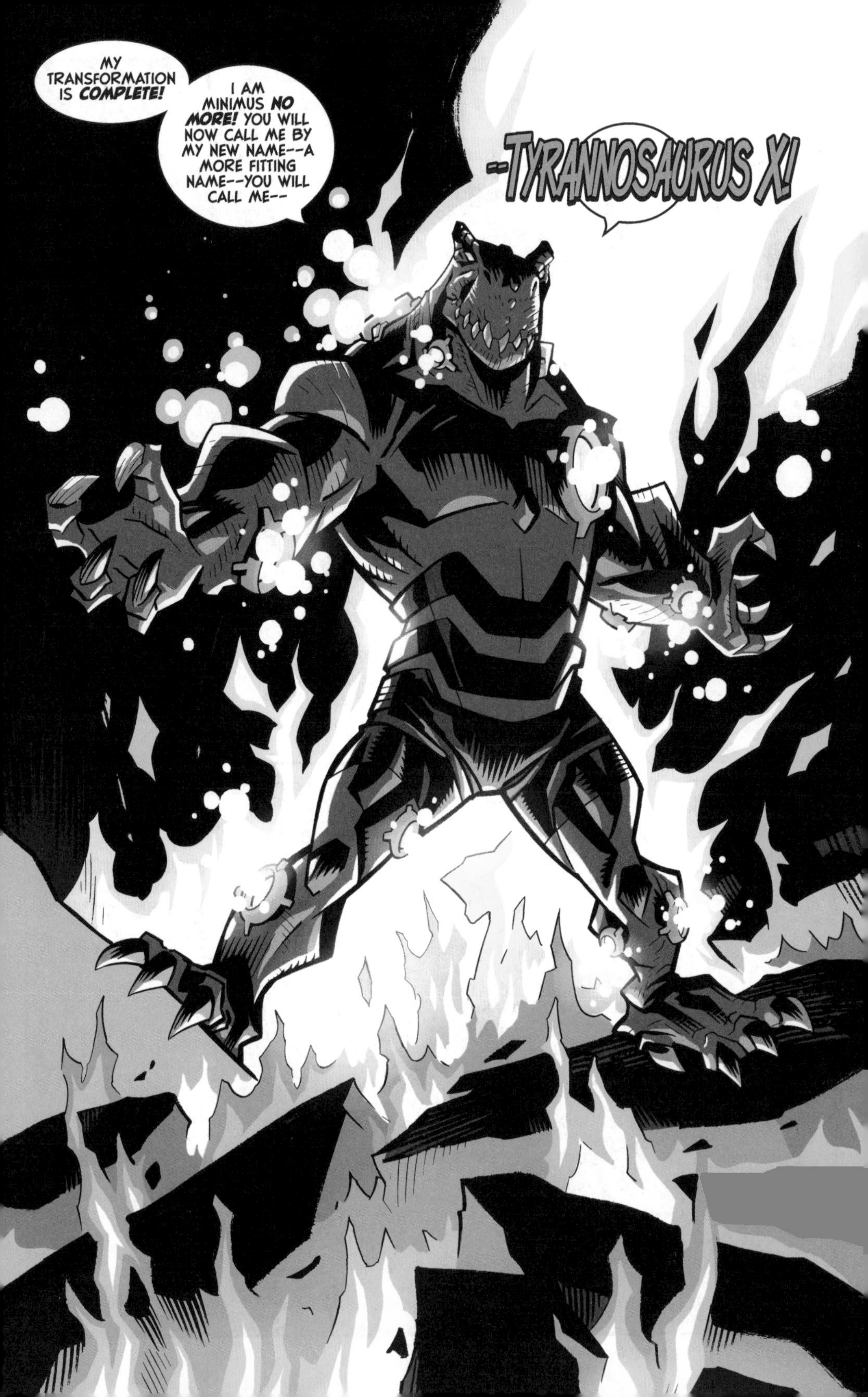
MY TRANSFORMATION IS **COMPLETE!**
I AM MINIMUS **NO MORE!** YOU WILL NOW CALL ME BY MY NEW NAME--A MORE FITTING NAME--YOU WILL CALL ME--
--TYRANNOSAURUS X!

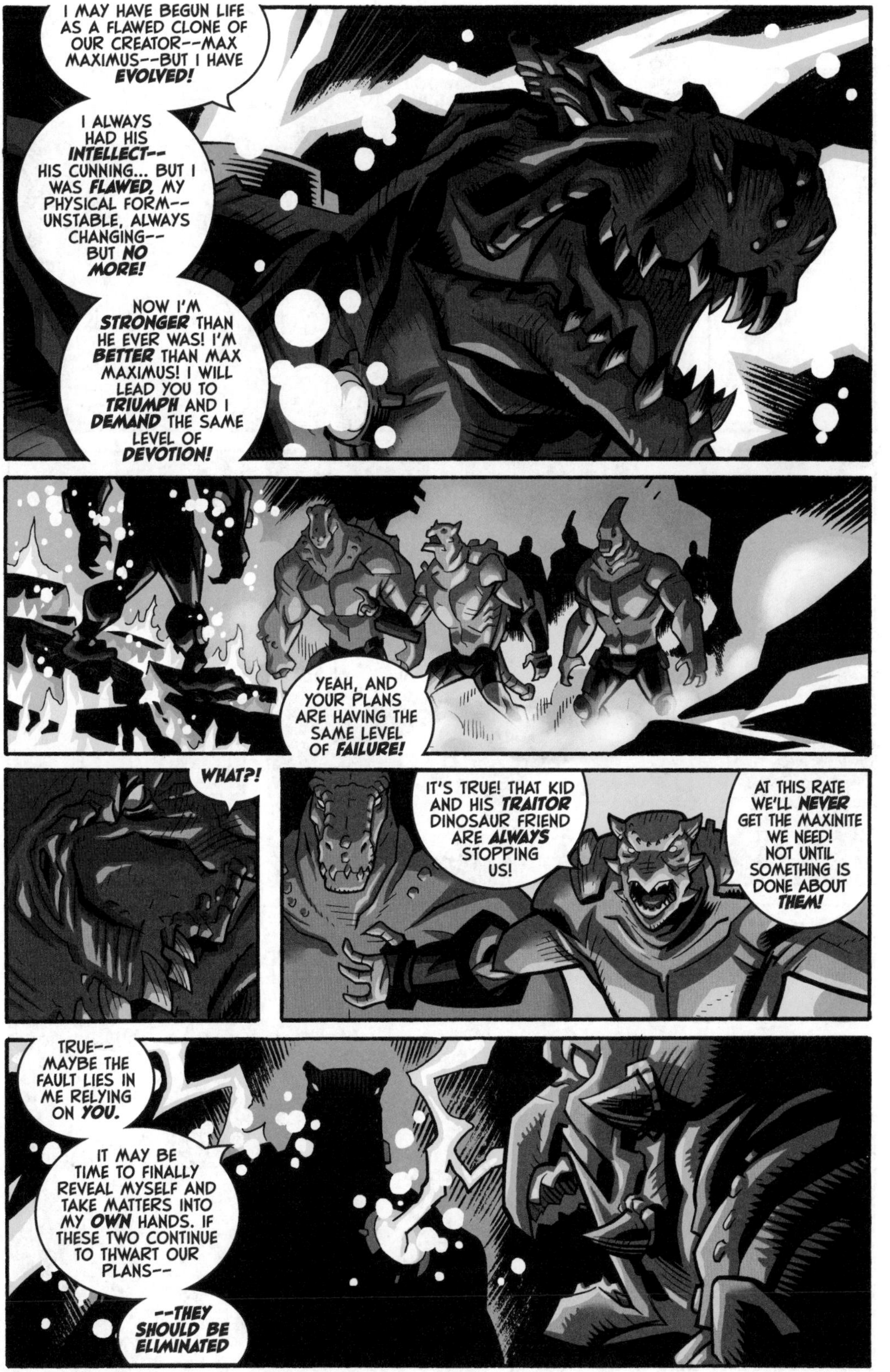

I MAY HAVE BEGUN LIFE AS A FLAWED CLONE OF OUR CREATOR--MAX MAXIMUS--BUT I HAVE EVOLVED!
I ALWAYS HAD HIS INTELLECT-- HIS CUNNING... BUT I WAS FLAWED, MY PHYSICAL FORM-- UNSTABLE, ALWAYS CHANGING-- BUT NO MORE!
NOW I'M STRONGER THAN HE EVER WAS! I'M BETTER THAN MAX MAXIMUS! I WILL LEAD YOU TO TRIUMPH AND I DEMAND THE SAME LEVEL OF DEVOTION!
YEAH, AND YOUR PLANS ARE HAVING THE SAME LEVEL OF FAILURE!
WHAT?!
IT'S TRUE! THAT KID AND HIS TRAITOR DINOSAUR FRIEND ARE ALWAYS STOPPING US!
AT THIS RATE WE'LL NEVER GET THE MAXINITE WE NEED! NOT UNTIL SOMETHING IS DONE ABOUT THEM!
TRUE-- MAYBE THE FAULT LIES IN ME RELYING ON YOU.
IT MAY BE TIME TO FINALLY REVEAL MYSELF AND TAKE MATTERS INTO MY OWN HANDS. IF THESE TWO CONTINUE TO THWART OUR PLANS--
--THEY SHOULD BE ELIMINATED

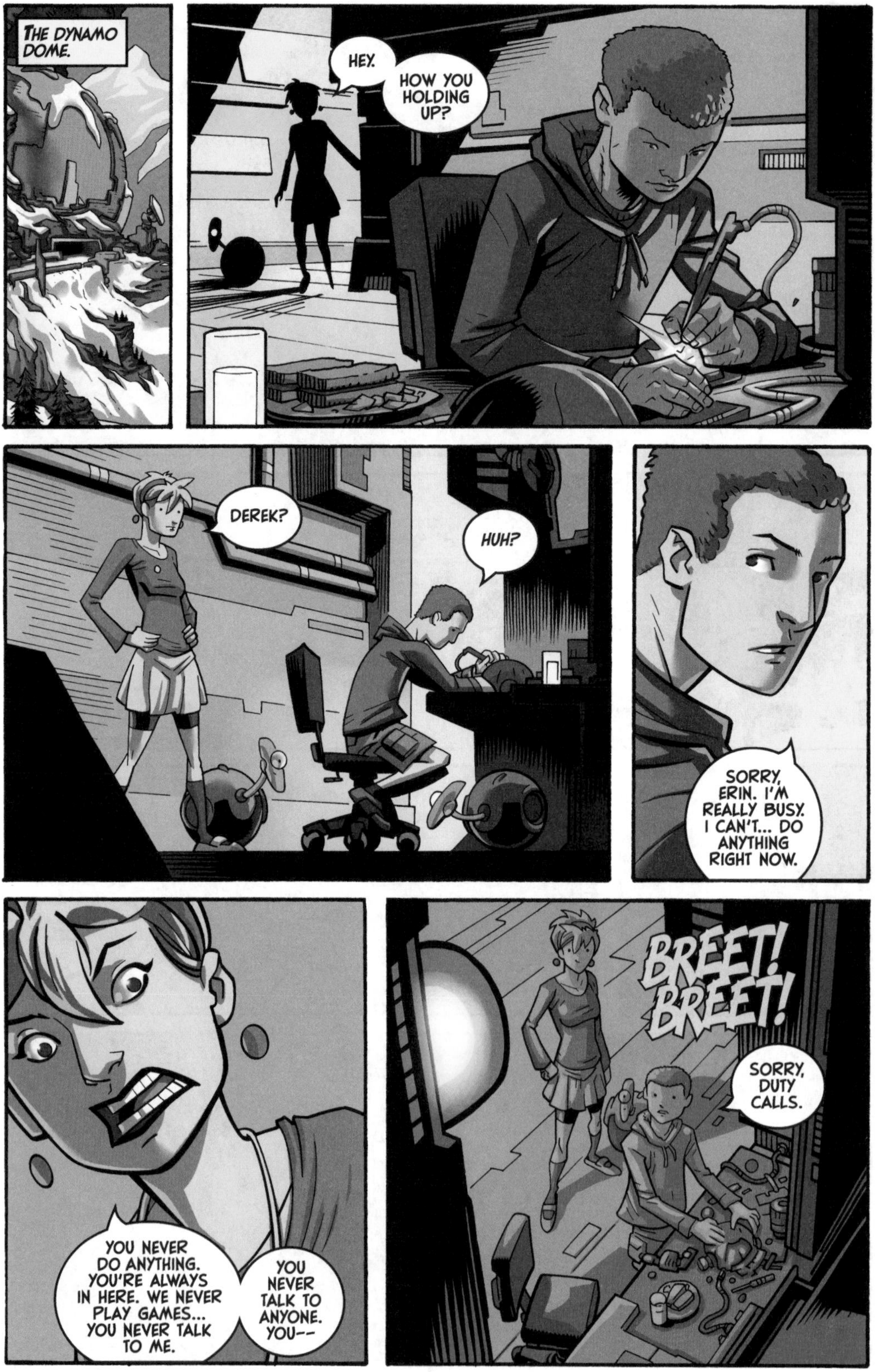

THE DYNAMO DOME.
HEY.
HOW YOU HOLDING UP?
DEREK?
HUH?
SORRY, ERIN. I'M REALLY BUSY. I CAN'T... DO ANYTHING RIGHT NOW.
YOU NEVER DO ANYTHING. YOU'RE ALWAYS IN HERE. WE NEVER PLAY GAMES... YOU NEVER TALK TO ME.
YOU NEVER TALK TO ANYONE. YOU--
BREET! BREET!
SORRY, DUTY CALLS.

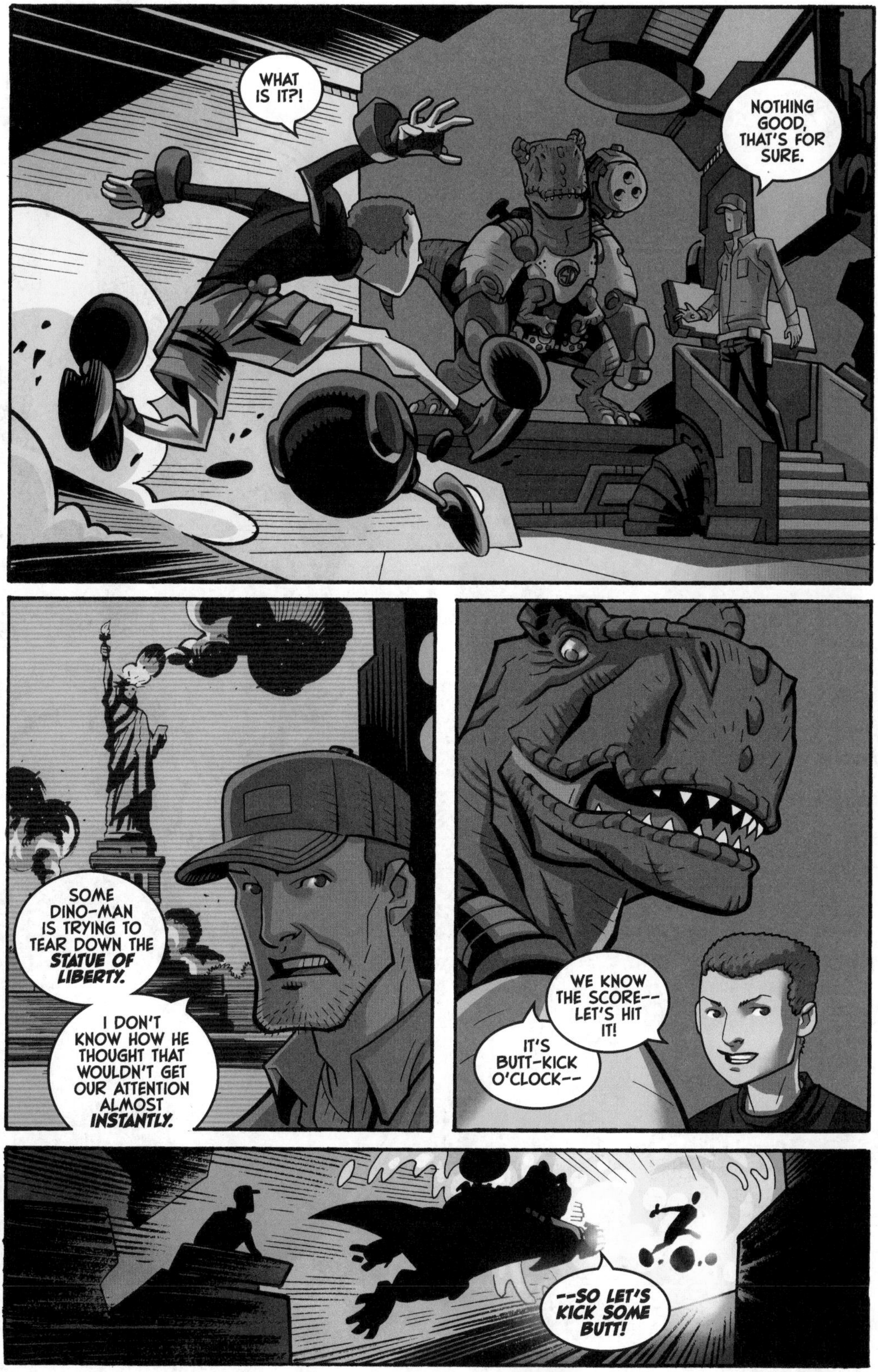
WHAT IS IT?!
NOTHING GOOD, THAT'S FOR SURE.
SOME DINO-MAN IS TRYING TO TEAR DOWN THE STATUE OF LIBERTY.
I DON'T KNOW HOW HE THOUGHT THAT WOULDN'T GET OUR ATTENTION ALMOST INSTANTLY.
WE KNOW THE SCORE--LET'S HIT IT!
IT'S BUTT-KICK O'CLOCK--
--SO LET'S KICK SOME BUTT!

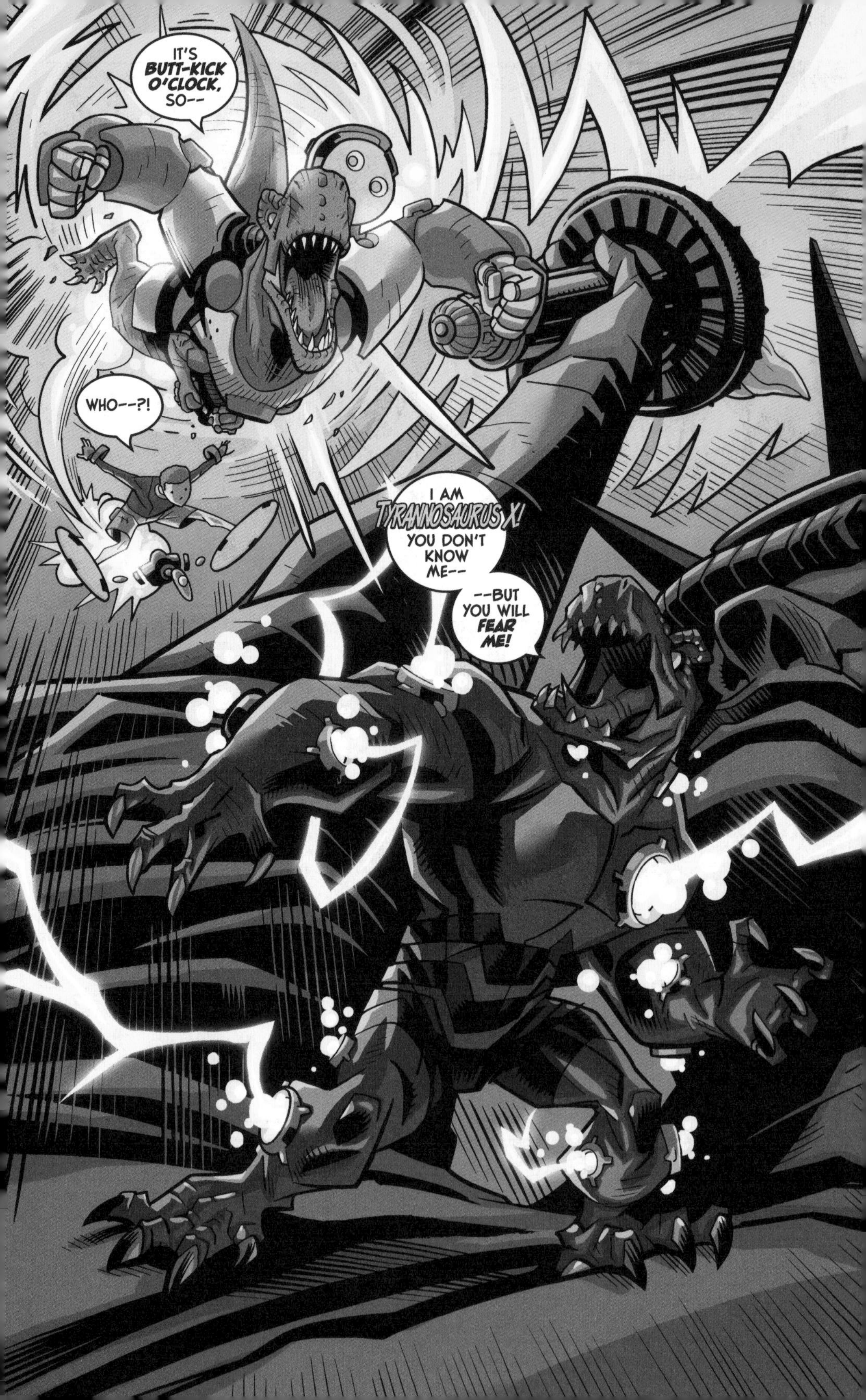
IT'S BUTT-KICK O'CLOCK, SO--
WHO--?!
I AM TYRANNOSAURUS X! YOU DON'T KNOW ME--
--BUT YOU WILL FEAR ME!

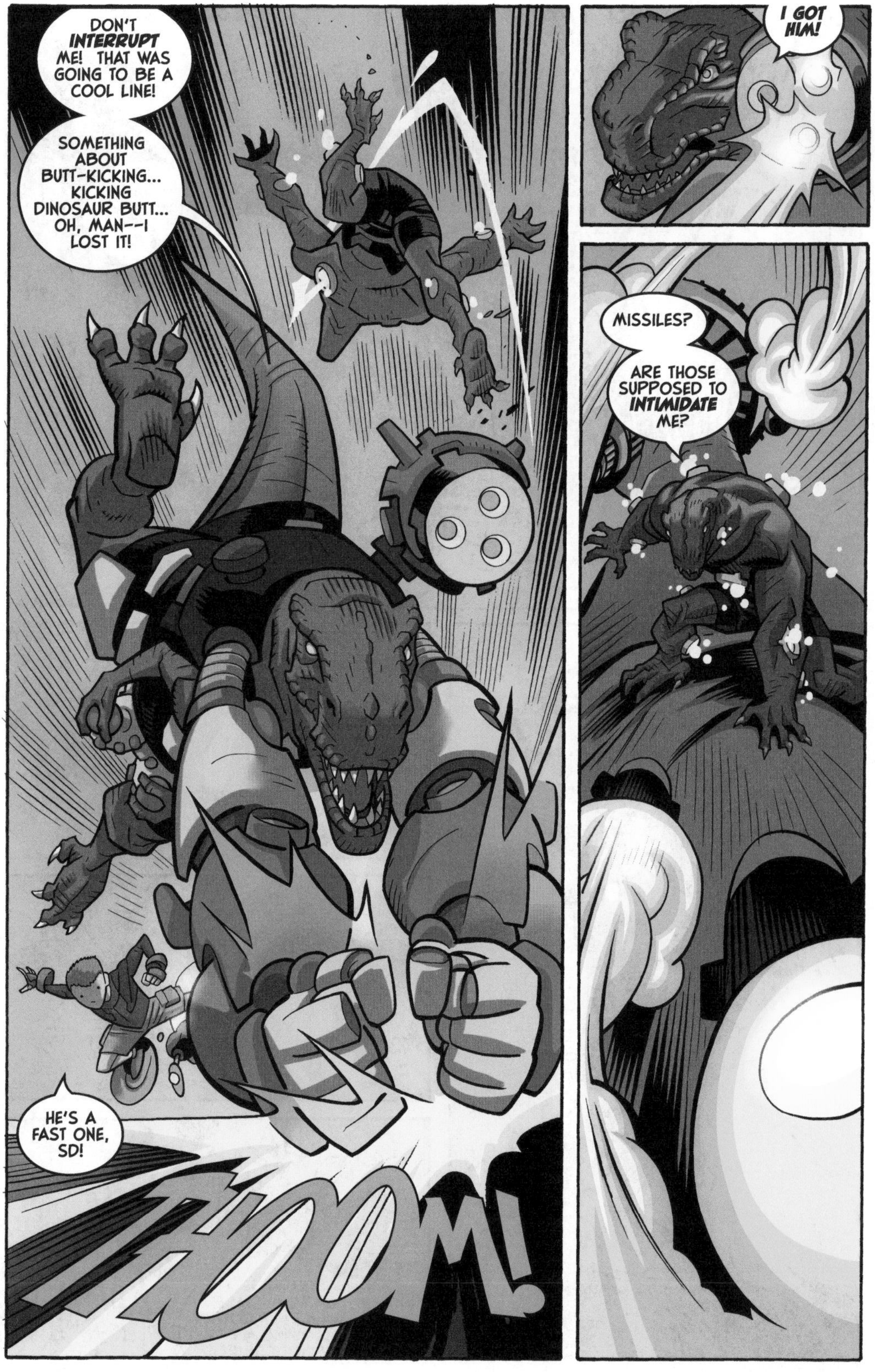
DON'T INTERRUPT ME! THAT WAS GOING TO BE A COOL LINE!
SOMETHING ABOUT BUTT-KICKING... KICKING DINOSAUR BUTT... OH, MAN--I LOST IT!
HE'S A FAST ONE, SD!
THOOOM!
I GOT HIM!
MISSILES?
ARE THOSE SUPPOSED TO INTIMIDATE ME?

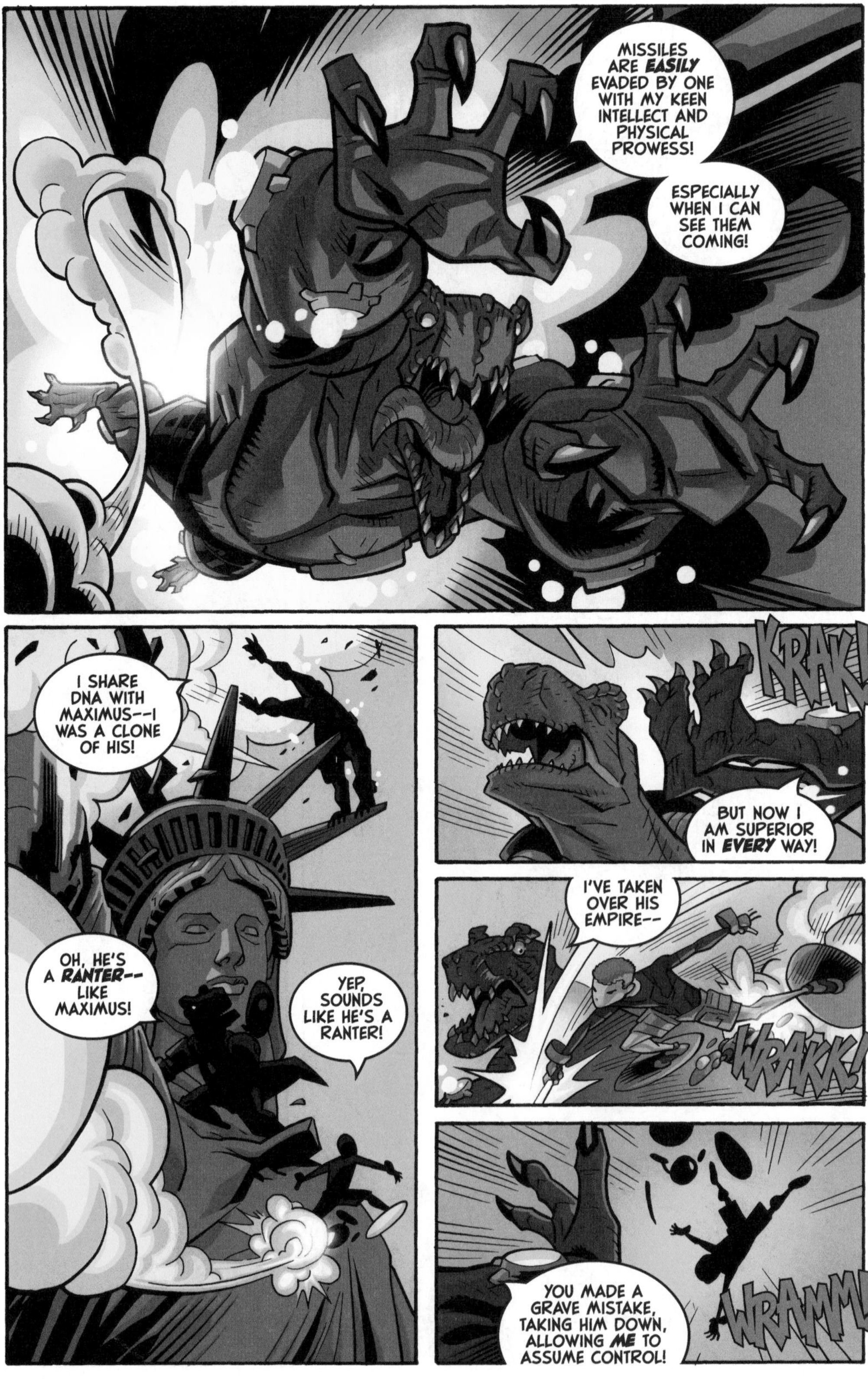
MISSILES ARE EASILY EVADED BY ONE WITH MY KEEN INTELLECT AND PHYSICAL PROWESS!
ESPECIALLY WHEN I CAN SEE THEM COMING!
I SHARE DNA WITH MAXIMUS--I WAS A CLONE OF HIS!
OH, HE'S A RANTER--LIKE MAXIMUS!
YEP, SOUNDS LIKE HE'S A RANTER!
KRAK!
BUT NOW I AM SUPERIOR IN EVERY WAY!
I'VE TAKEN OVER HIS EMPIRE--
WRAKK!
WRAMM!
YOU MADE A GRAVE MISTAKE, TAKING HIM DOWN, ALLOWING ME TO ASSUME CONTROL!

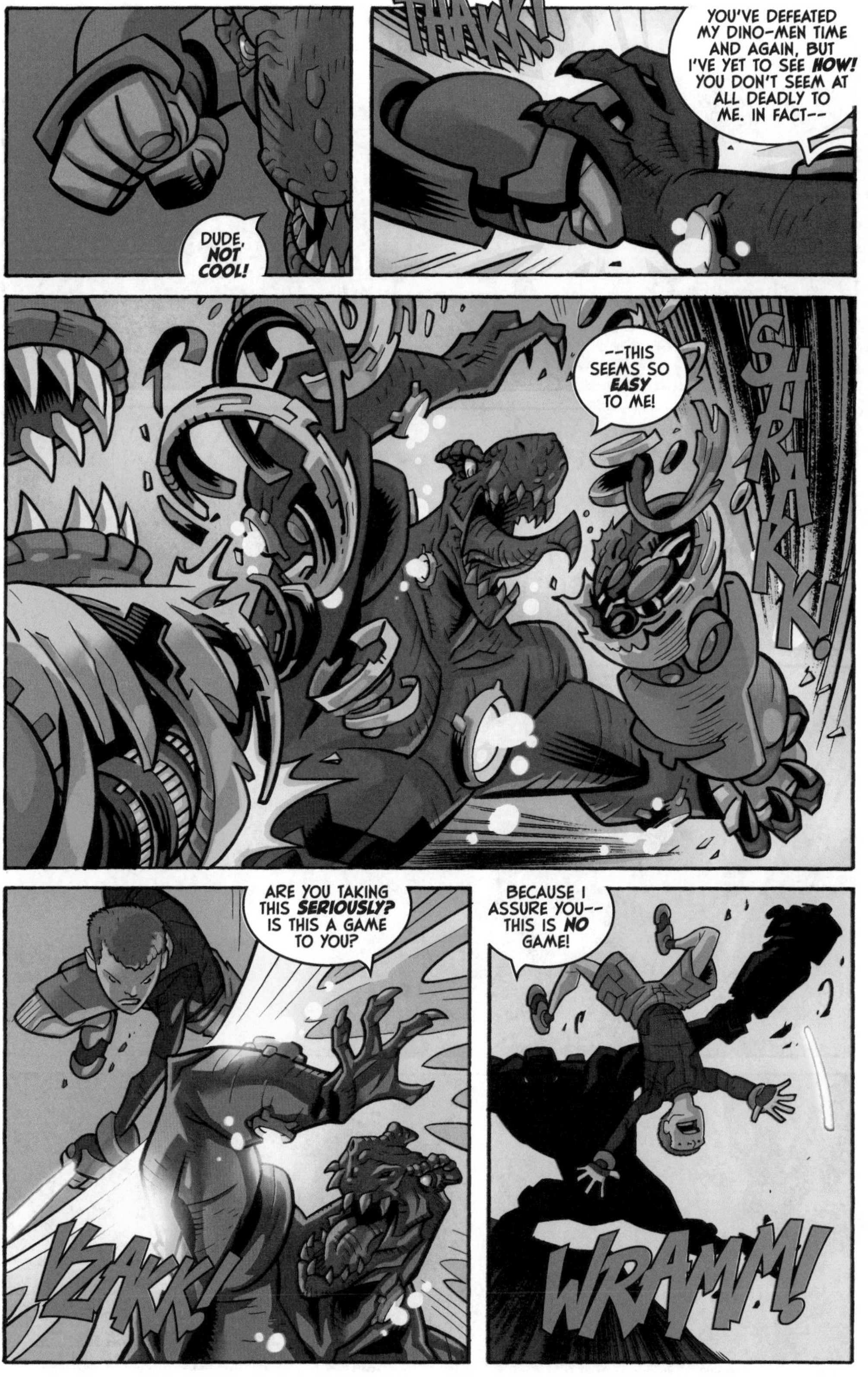

DUDE, NOT COOL!
THAKK!
YOU'VE DEFEATED MY DINO-MEN TIME AND AGAIN, BUT I'VE YET TO SEE HOW! YOU DON'T SEEM AT ALL DEADLY TO ME. IN FACT--
--THIS SEEMS SO EASY TO ME!
SHRAKKK!
ARE YOU TAKING THIS SERIOUSLY? IS THIS A GAME TO YOU?
VZAKK!
BECAUSE I ASSURE YOU-- THIS IS NO GAME!
WRAMM!

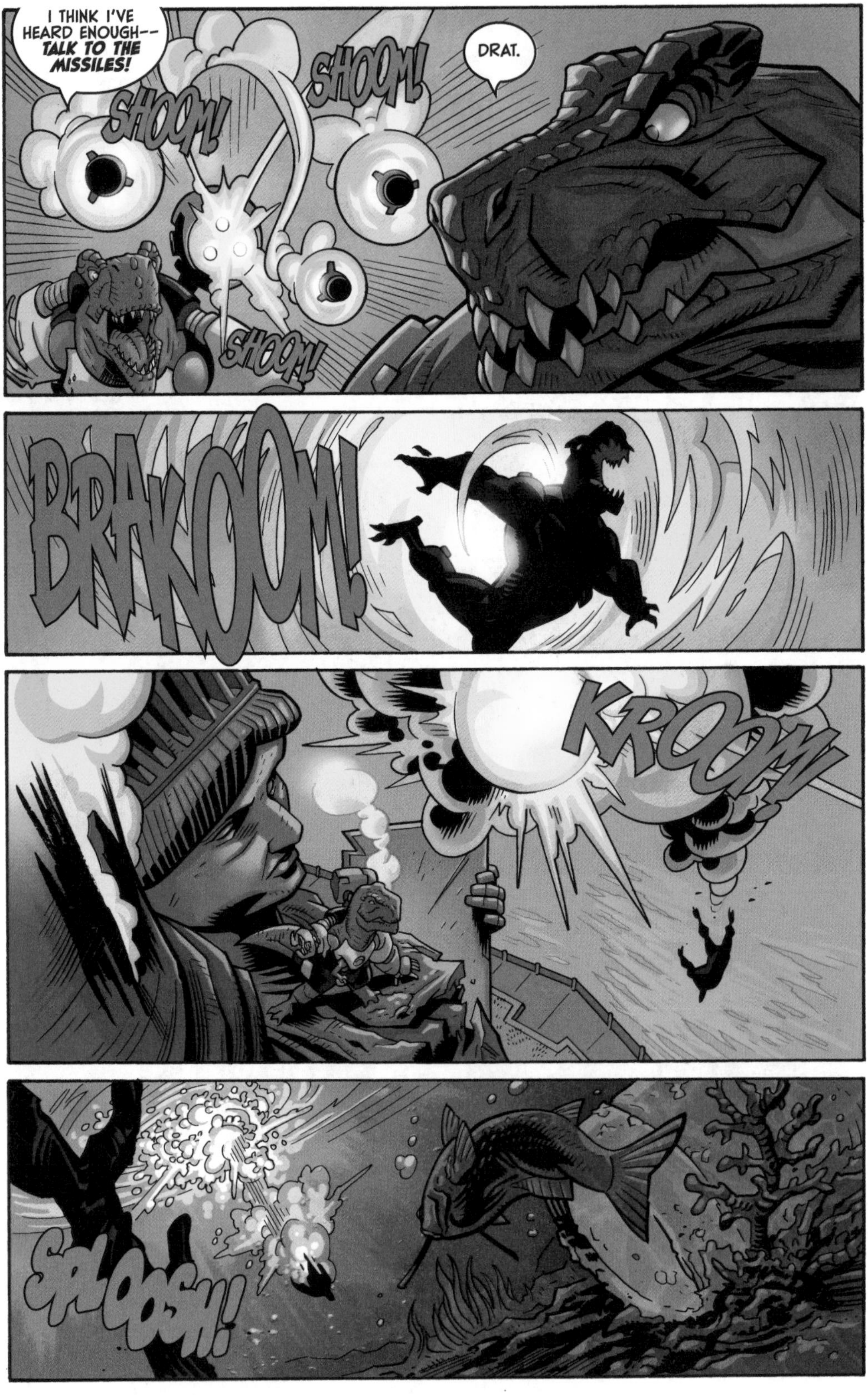

I THINK I'VE HEARD ENOUGH-- TALK TO THE MISSILES!
SHOOM!
SHOOM!
DRAT.
SHOOM!
BRAKOOM!
KROOM!
SPLOOSH!

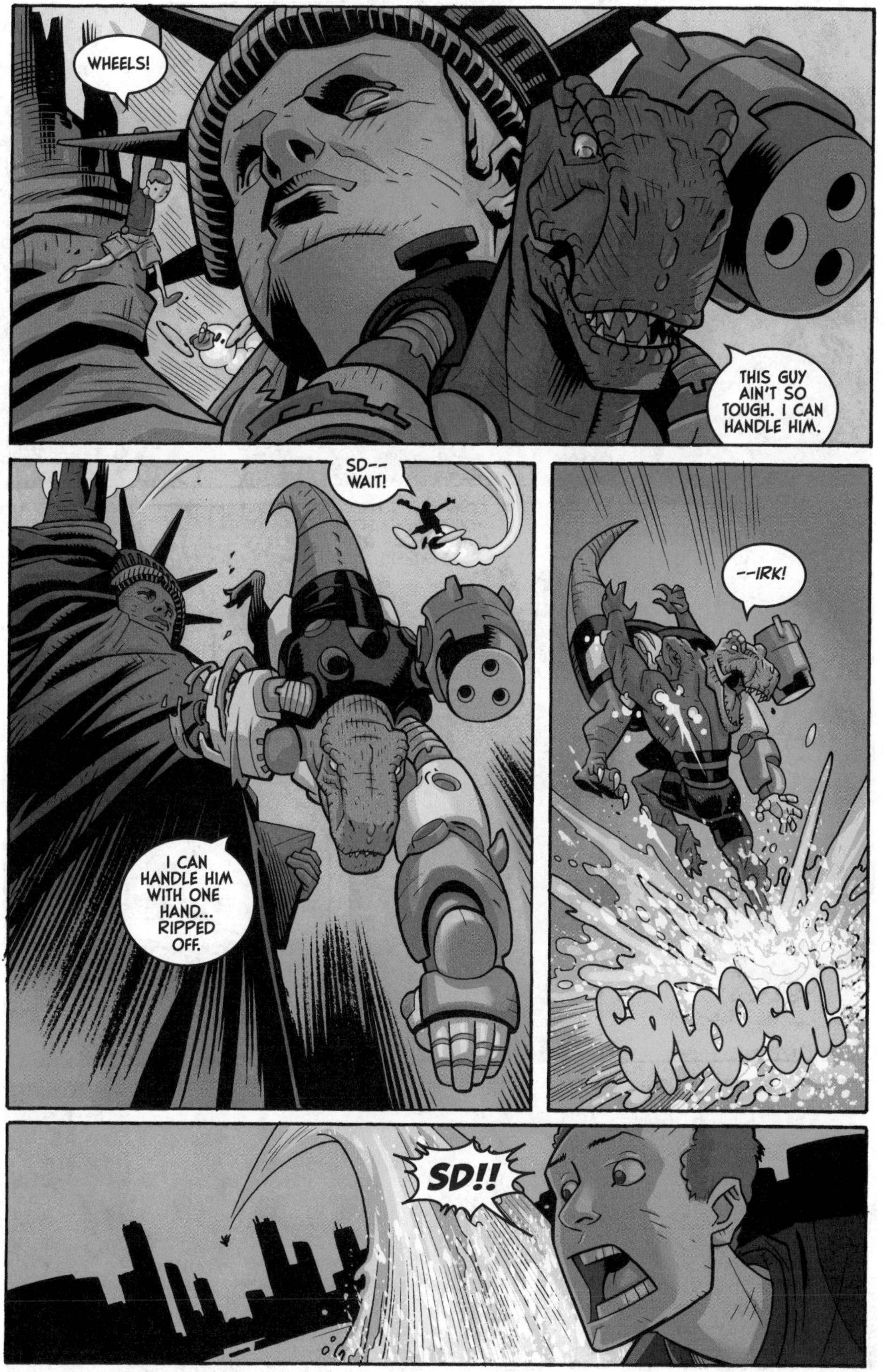
WHEELS!
THIS GUY AIN'T SO TOUGH. I CAN HANDLE HIM.
SD-- WAIT!
I CAN HANDLE HIM WITH ONE HAND... RIPPED OFF.
--IRK!
SPLOOSH!
SD!!

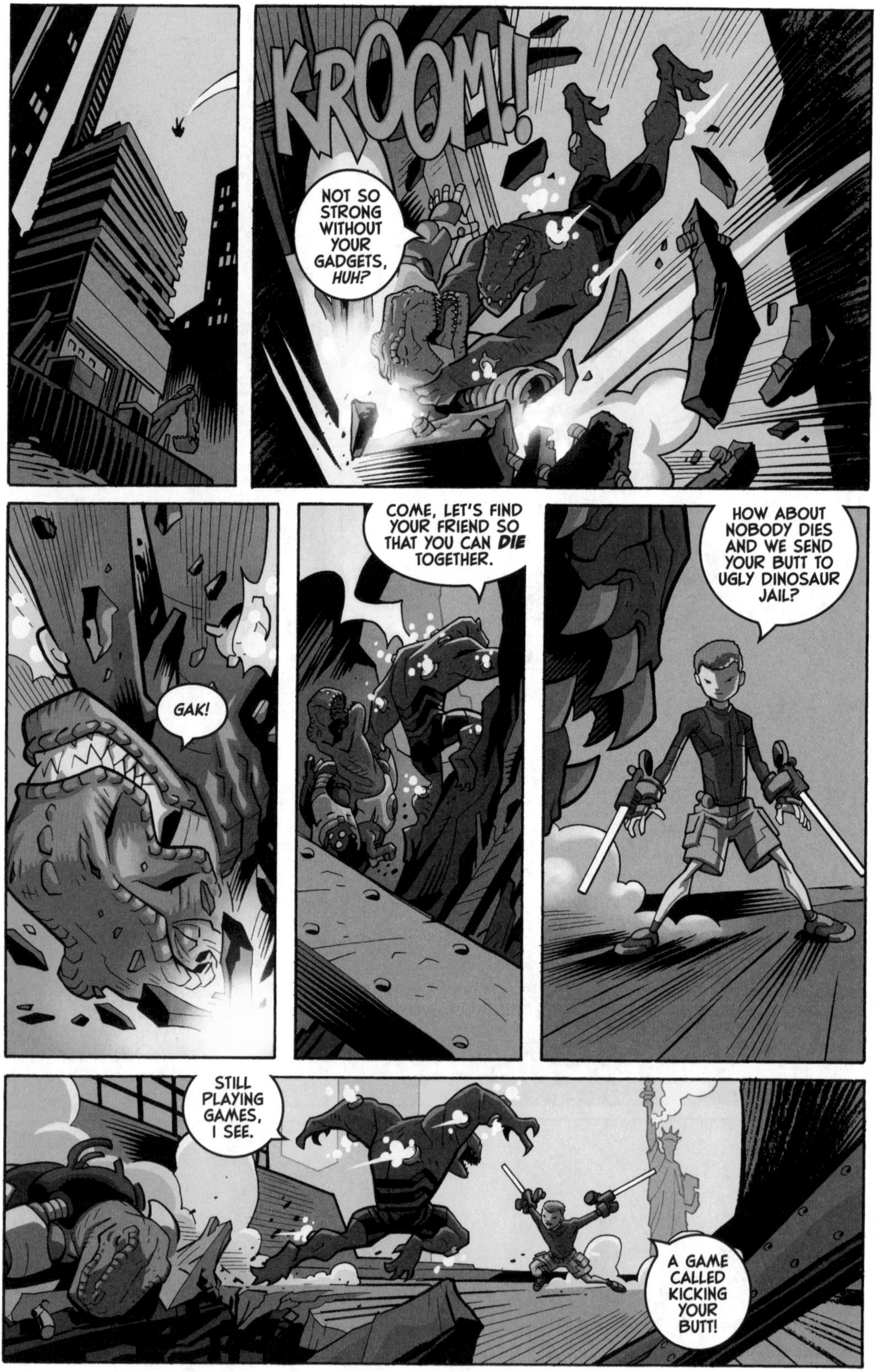
KROOM!!
NOT SO STRONG WITHOUT YOUR GADGETS, HUH?
GAK!
COME, LET'S FIND YOUR FRIEND SO THAT YOU CAN DIE TOGETHER.
HOW ABOUT NOBODY DIES AND WE SEND YOUR BUTT TO UGLY DINOSAUR JAIL?
STILL PLAYING GAMES, I SEE.
A GAME CALLED KICKING YOUR BUTT!

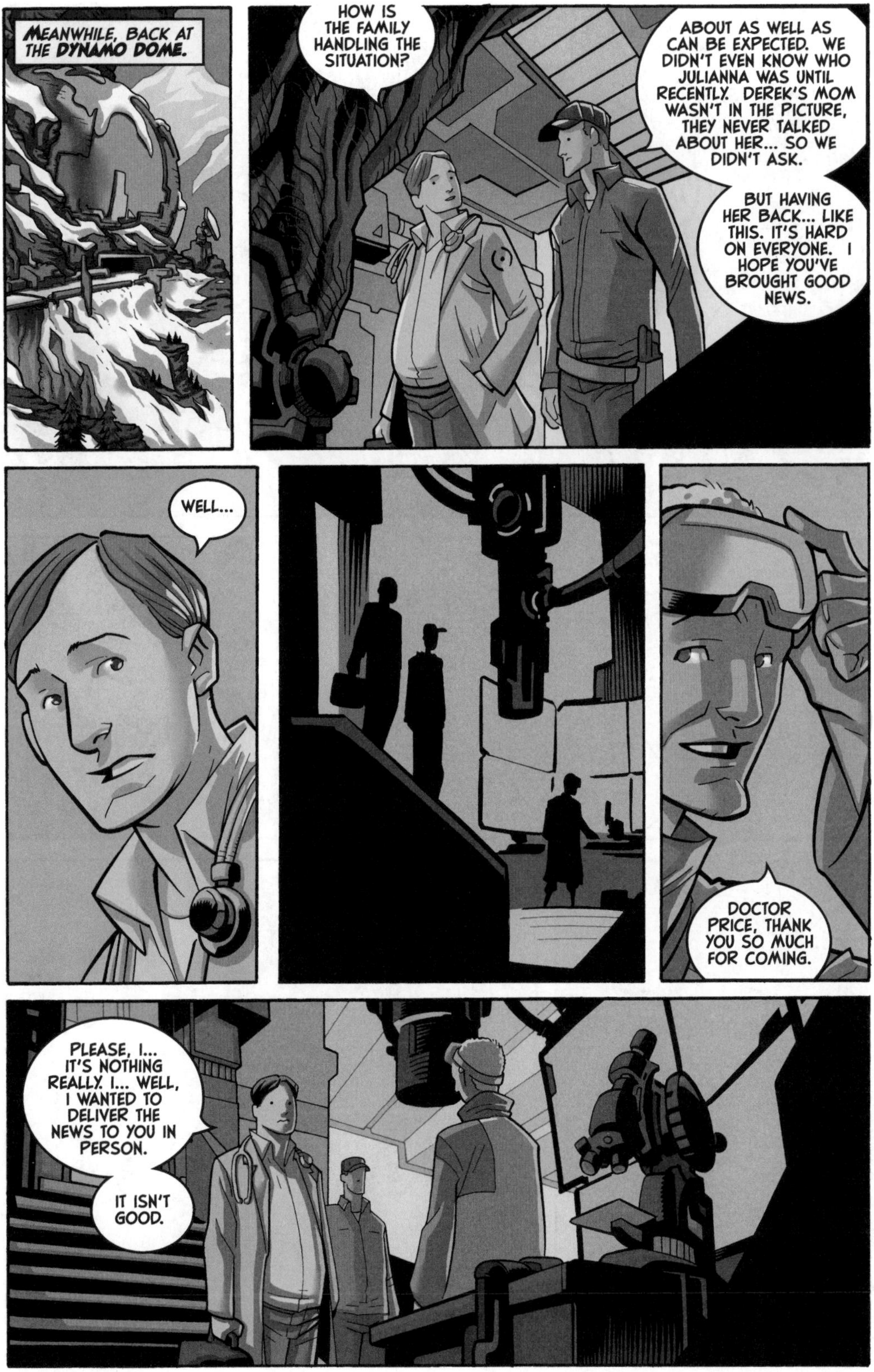
MEANWHILE, BACK AT THE DYNAMO DOME.
HOW IS THE FAMILY HANDLING THE SITUATION?
ABOUT AS WELL AS CAN BE EXPECTED. WE DIDN'T EVEN KNOW WHO JULIANNA WAS UNTIL RECENTLY. DEREK'S MOM WASN'T IN THE PICTURE, THEY NEVER TALKED ABOUT HER... SO WE DIDN'T ASK.
BUT HAVING HER BACK... LIKE THIS. IT'S HARD ON EVERYONE. I HOPE YOU'VE BROUGHT GOOD NEWS.
WELL...
DOCTOR PRICE, THANK YOU SO MUCH FOR COMING.
PLEASE, I... IT'S NOTHING REALLY. I... WELL, I WANTED TO DELIVER THE NEWS TO YOU IN PERSON.
IT ISN'T GOOD.

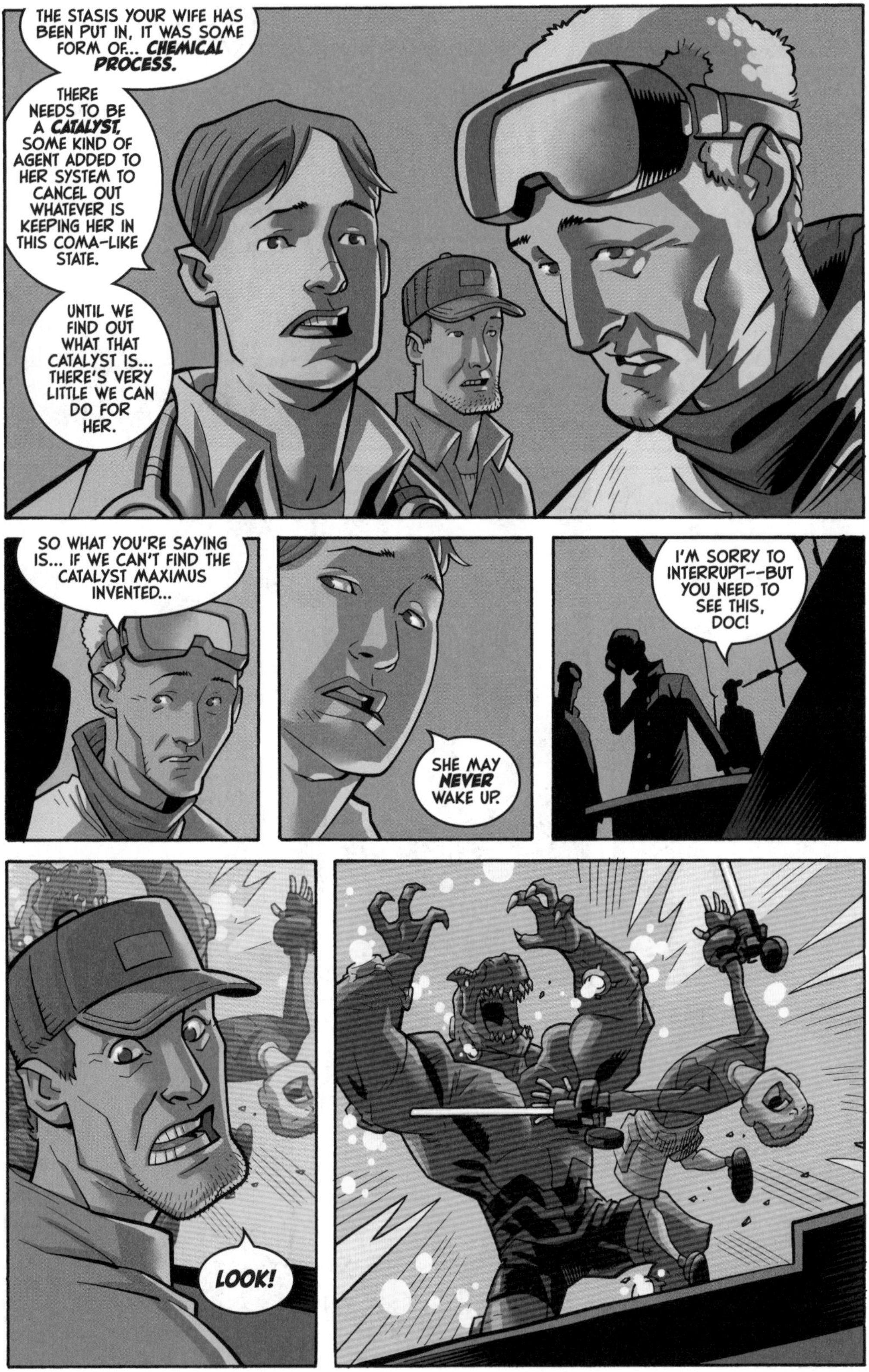
THE STASIS YOUR WIFE HAS BEEN PUT IN, IT WAS SOME FORM OF... CHEMICAL PROCESS.
THERE NEEDS TO BE A CATALYST, SOME KIND OF AGENT ADDED TO HER SYSTEM TO CANCEL OUT WHATEVER IS KEEPING HER IN THIS COMA-LIKE STATE.
UNTIL WE FIND OUT WHAT THAT CATALYST IS... THERE'S VERY LITTLE WE CAN DO FOR HER.
SO WHAT YOU'RE SAYING IS... IF WE CAN'T FIND THE CATALYST MAXIMUS INVENTED...
SHE MAY NEVER WAKE UP.
I'M SORRY TO INTERRUPT--BUT YOU NEED TO SEE THIS, DOC!
LOOK!

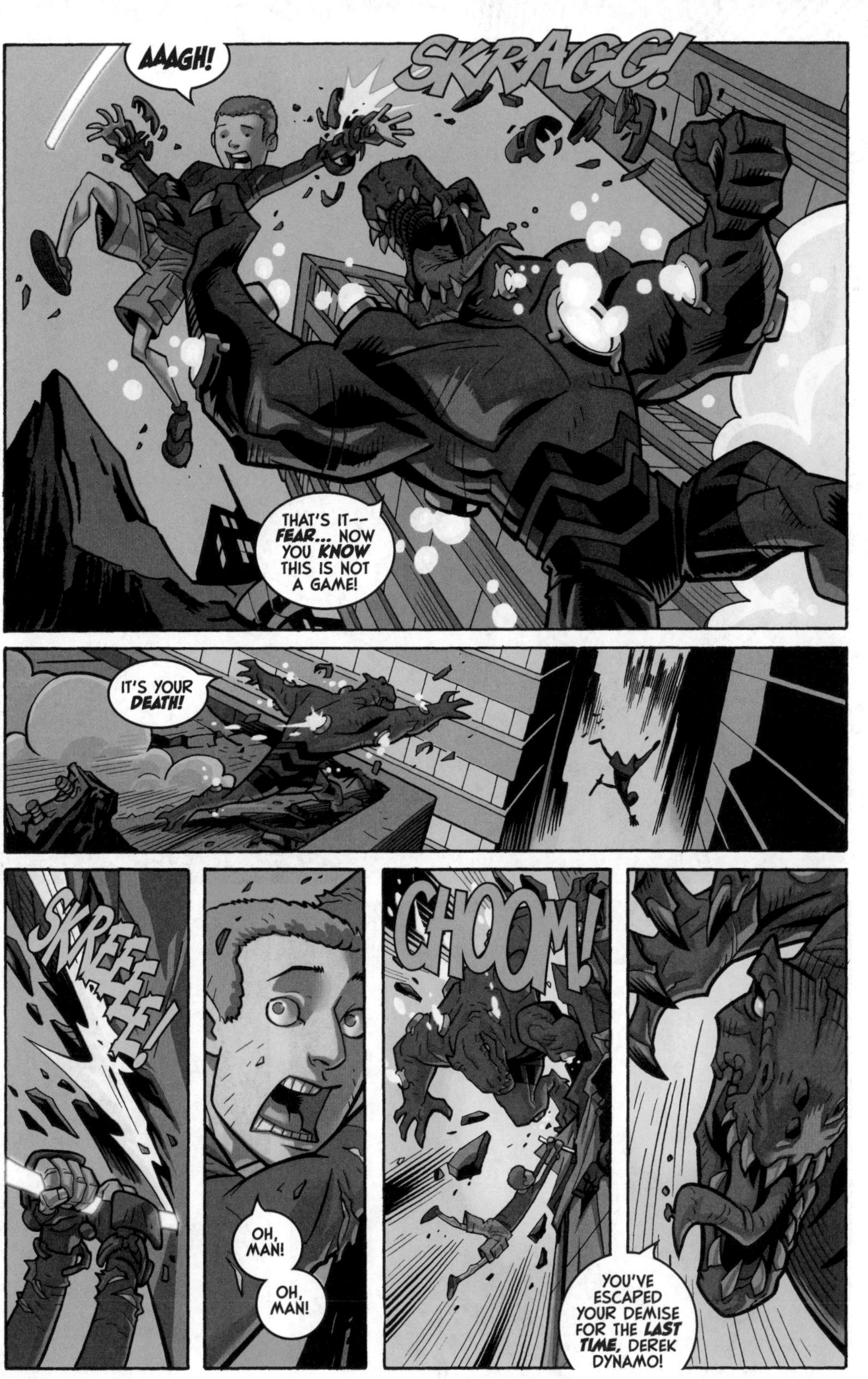
AAAGH!
SKRAGG!
THAT'S IT-- **FEAR...** NOW YOU **KNOW** THIS IS NOT A GAME!
IT'S YOUR **DEATH!**
SKREEEEE!
OH, MAN!
OH, MAN!
CHOOM!
YOU'VE ESCAPED YOUR DEMISE FOR THE **LAST TIME,** DEREK DYNAMO!

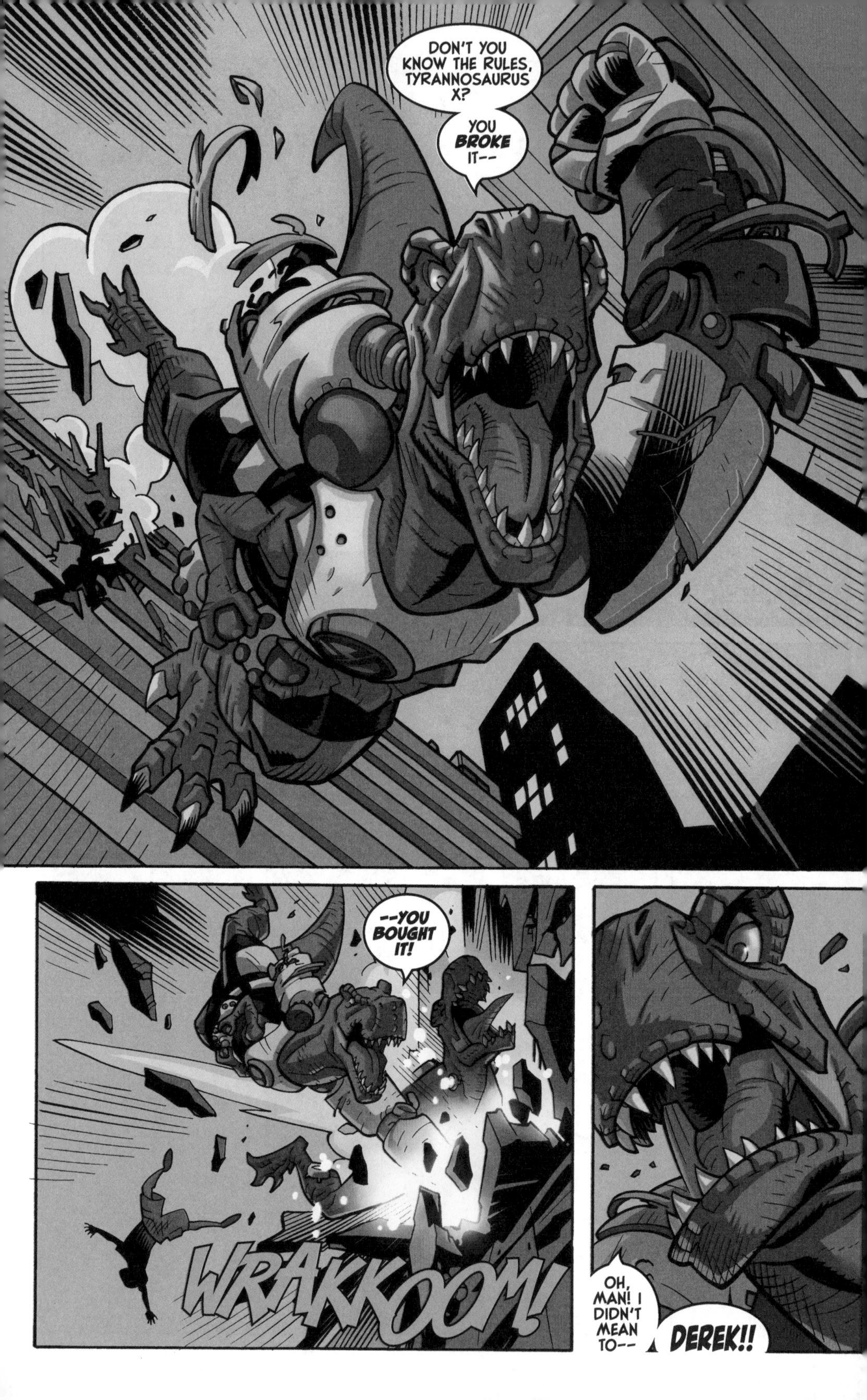
DON'T YOU KNOW THE RULES, TYRANNOSAURUS X?
YOU BROKE IT--
--YOU BOUGHT IT!
WRAKKOOM!
OH, MAN! I DIDN'T MEAN TO--
DEREK!!

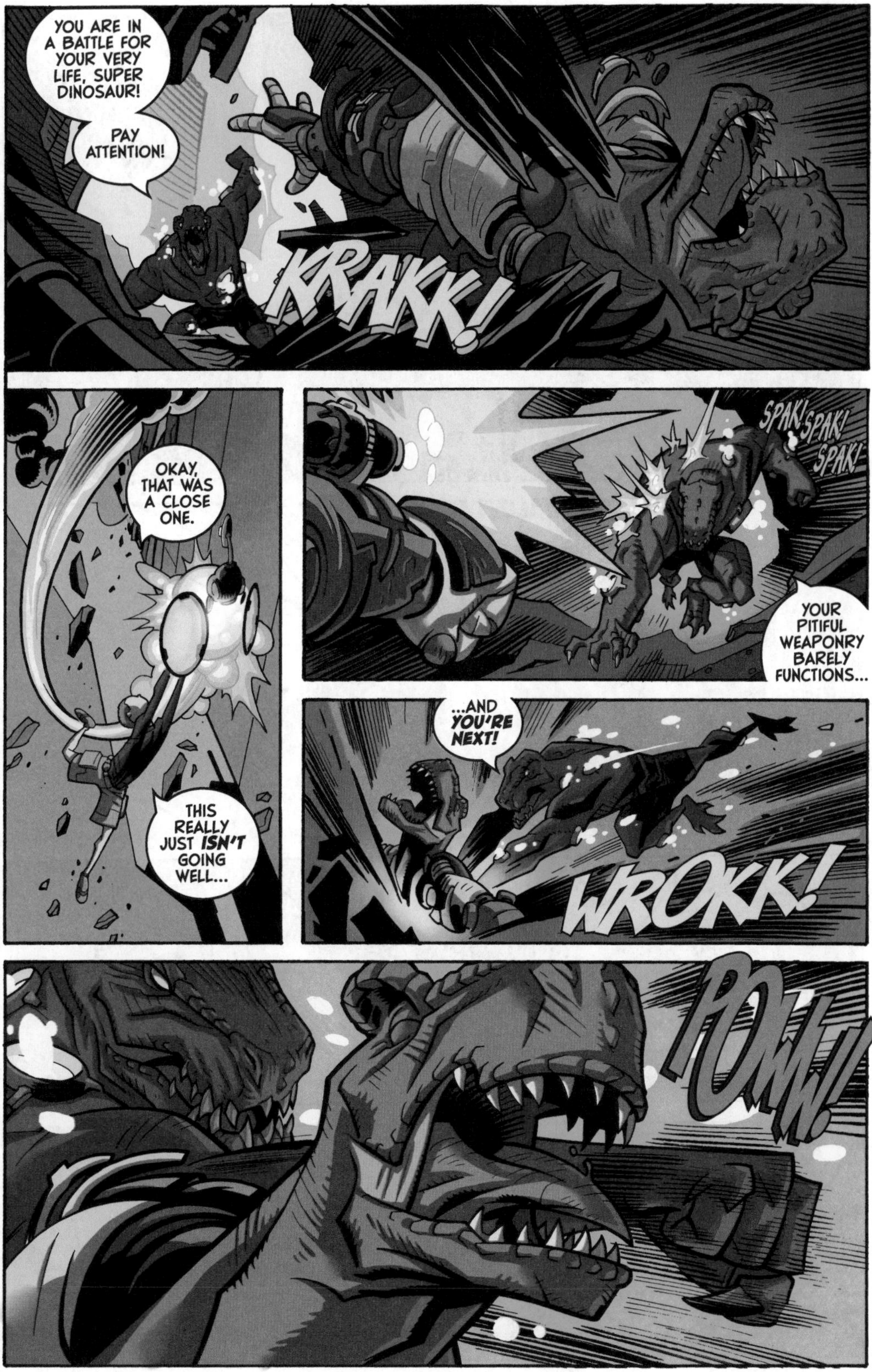
YOU ARE IN A BATTLE FOR YOUR VERY LIFE, SUPER DINOSAUR!
PAY ATTENTION!
KRAKK!
OKAY, THAT WAS A CLOSE ONE.
THIS REALLY JUST ISN'T GOING WELL...
SPAK! SPAK! SPAK!
YOUR PITIFUL WEAPONRY BARELY FUNCTIONS...
...AND YOU'RE NEXT!
WROKK!
POW!

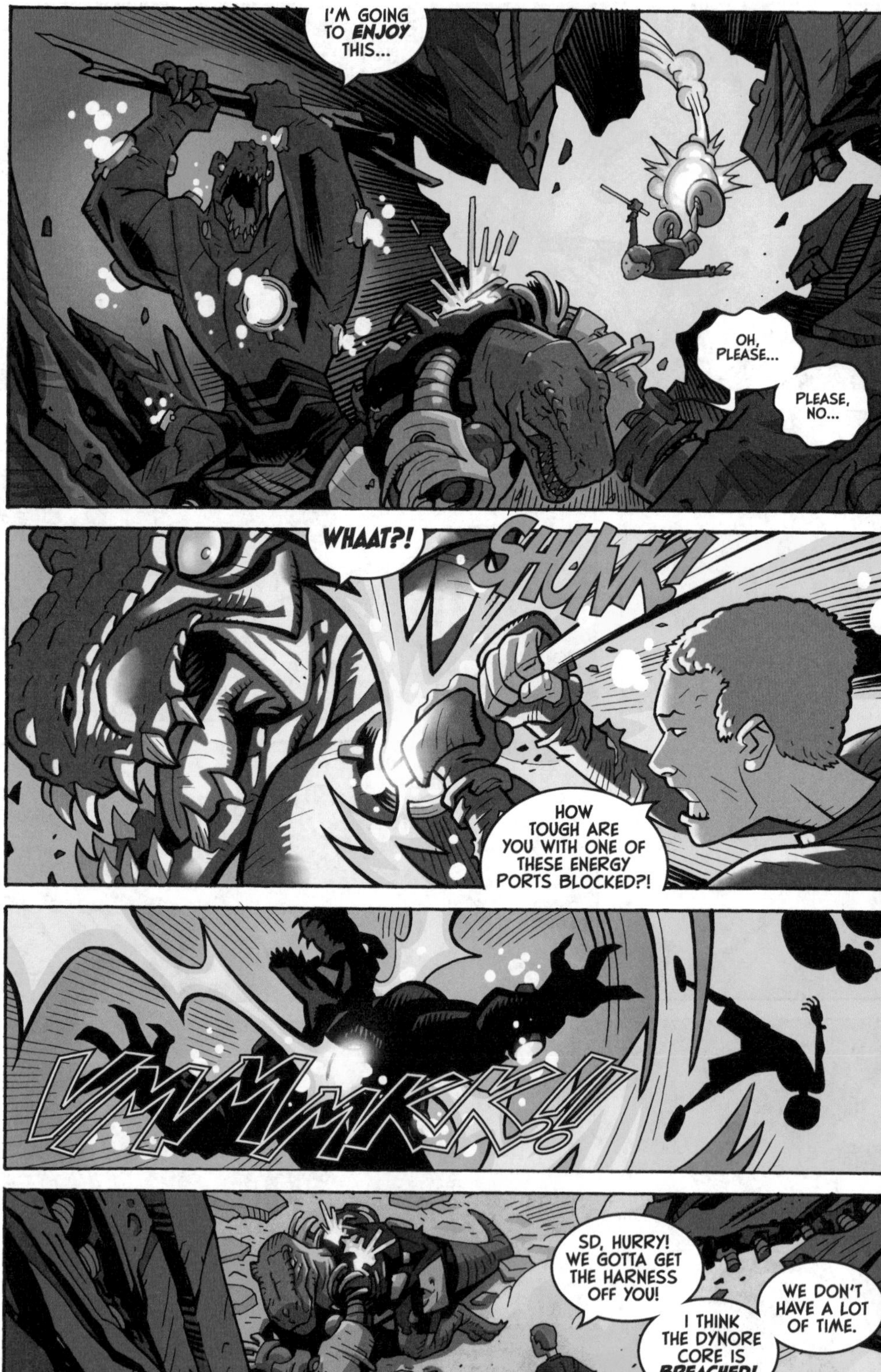
I'M GOING TO ENJOY THIS...
OH, PLEASE...
PLEASE, NO...
WHAAT?!
SHUNK!
HOW TOUGH ARE YOU WITH ONE OF THESE ENERGY PORTS BLOCKED?!
VMMMMKKK!!
SD, HURRY! WE GOTTA GET THE HARNESS OFF YOU!
I THINK THE DYNORE CORE IS BREACHED!
WE DON'T HAVE A LOT OF TIME.

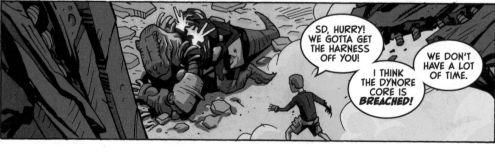

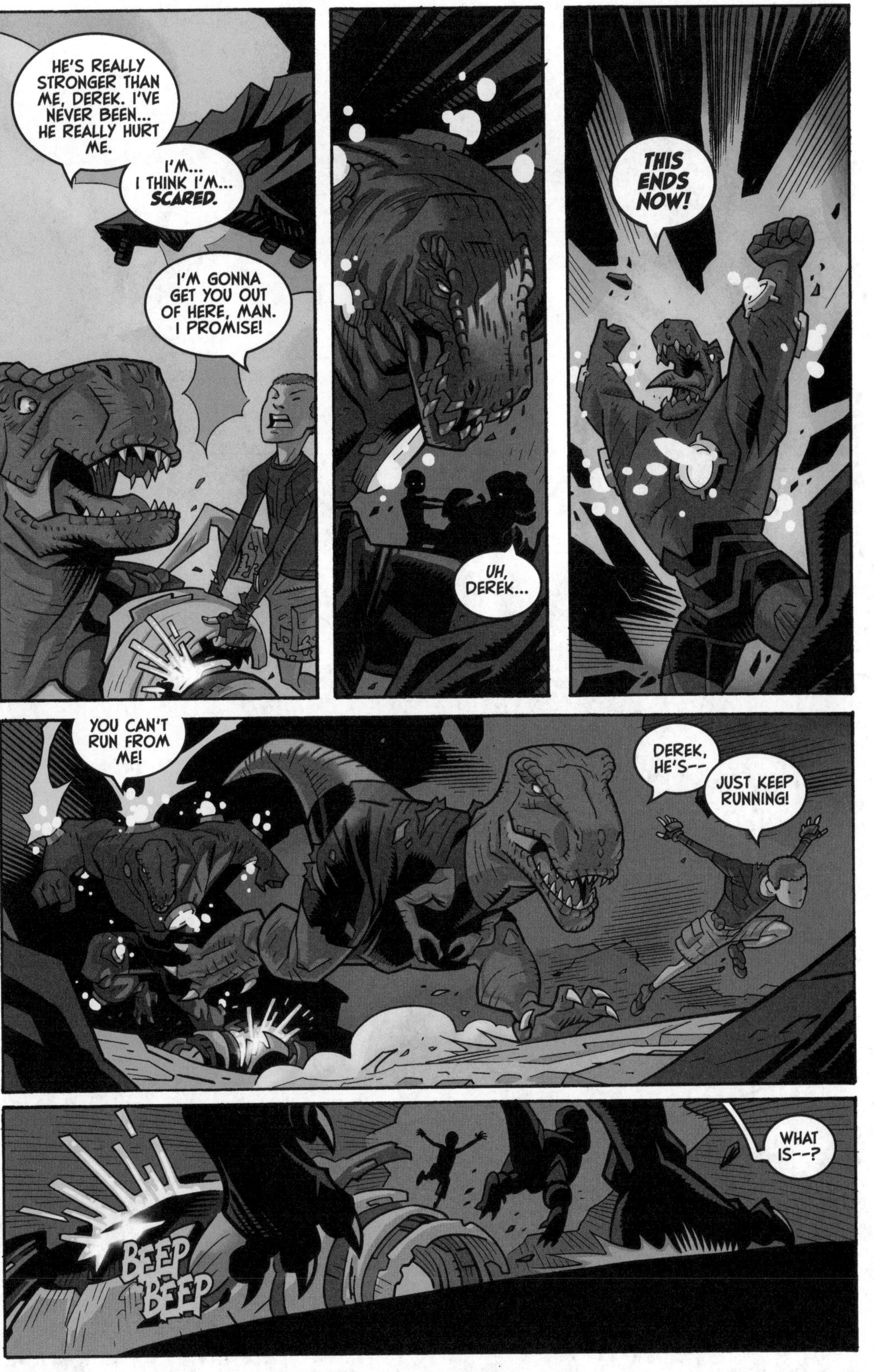
HE'S REALLY STRONGER THAN ME, DEREK. I'VE NEVER BEEN... HE REALLY HURT ME.
I'M... I THINK I'M... SCARED.
I'M GONNA GET YOU OUT OF HERE, MAN. I PROMISE!
UH, DEREK...
THIS ENDS NOW!
YOU CAN'T RUN FROM ME!
DEREK, HE'S--
JUST KEEP RUNNING!
WHAT IS--?
BEEP BEEP

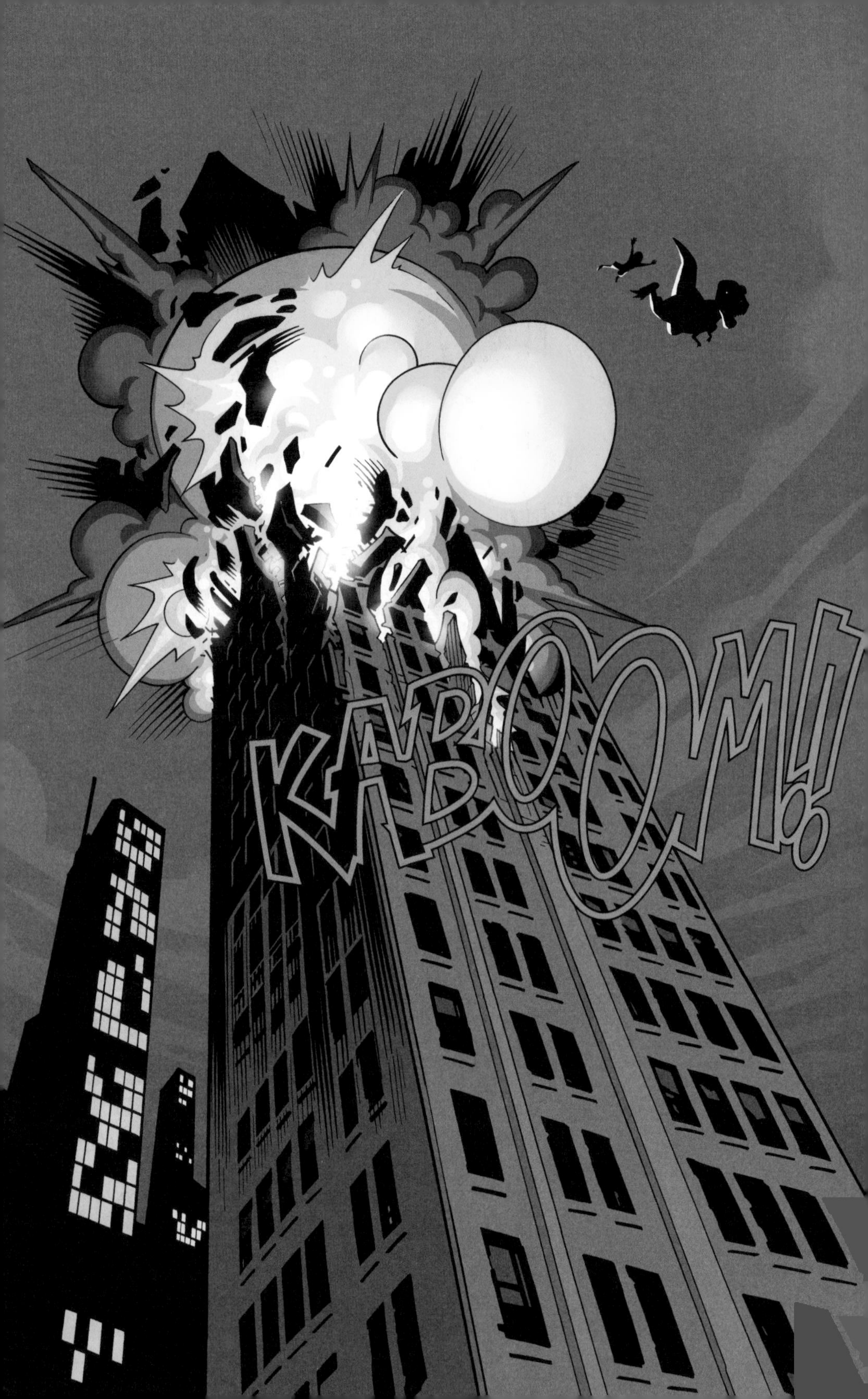
KABOOOM!!

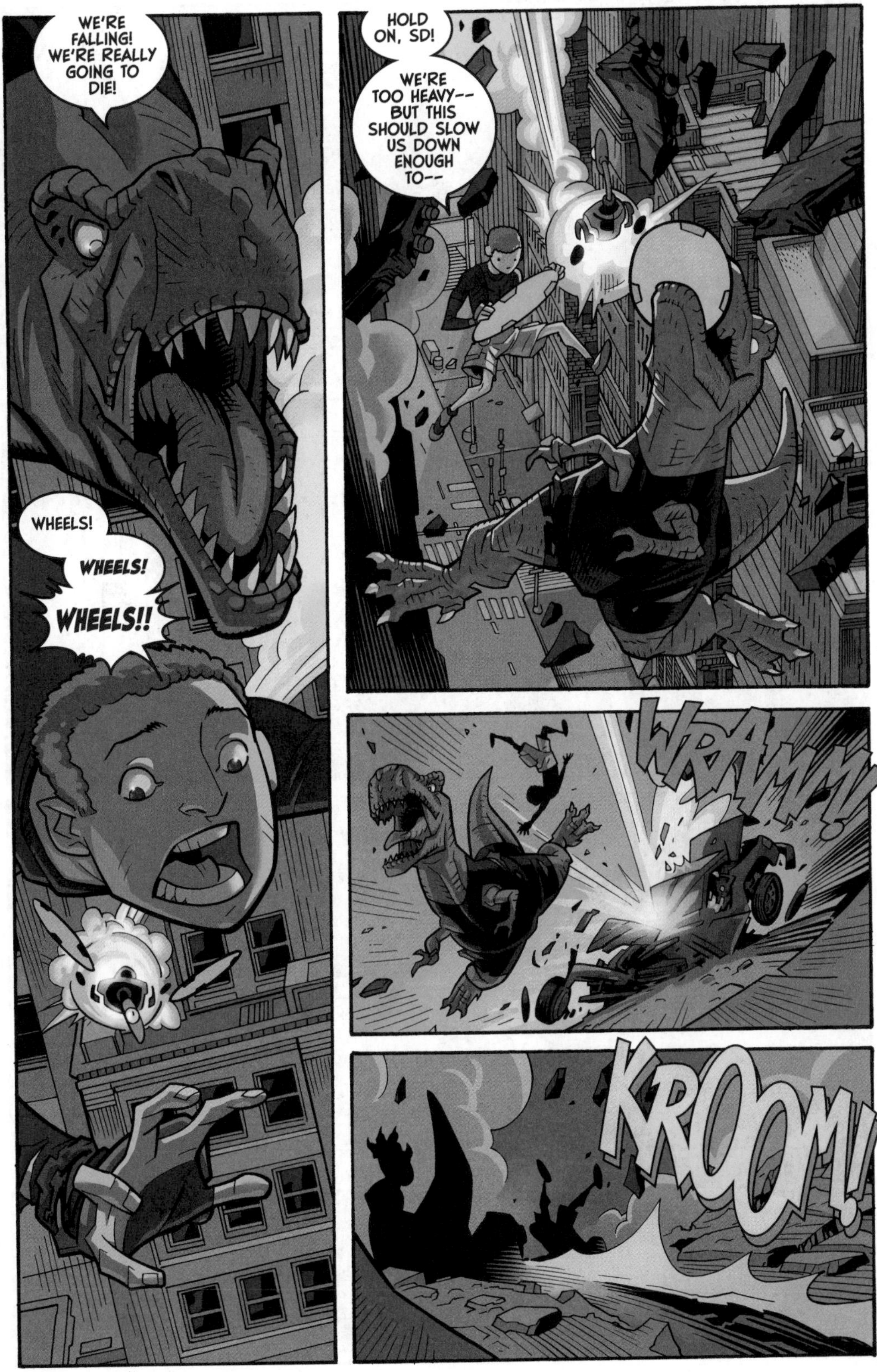
WE'RE FALLING! WE'RE REALLY GOING TO DIE!
WHEELS!
WHEELS!
WHEELS!!
HOLD ON, SD!
WE'RE TOO HEAVY-- BUT THIS SHOULD SLOW US DOWN ENOUGH TO--
WRAMM!
KROOM!

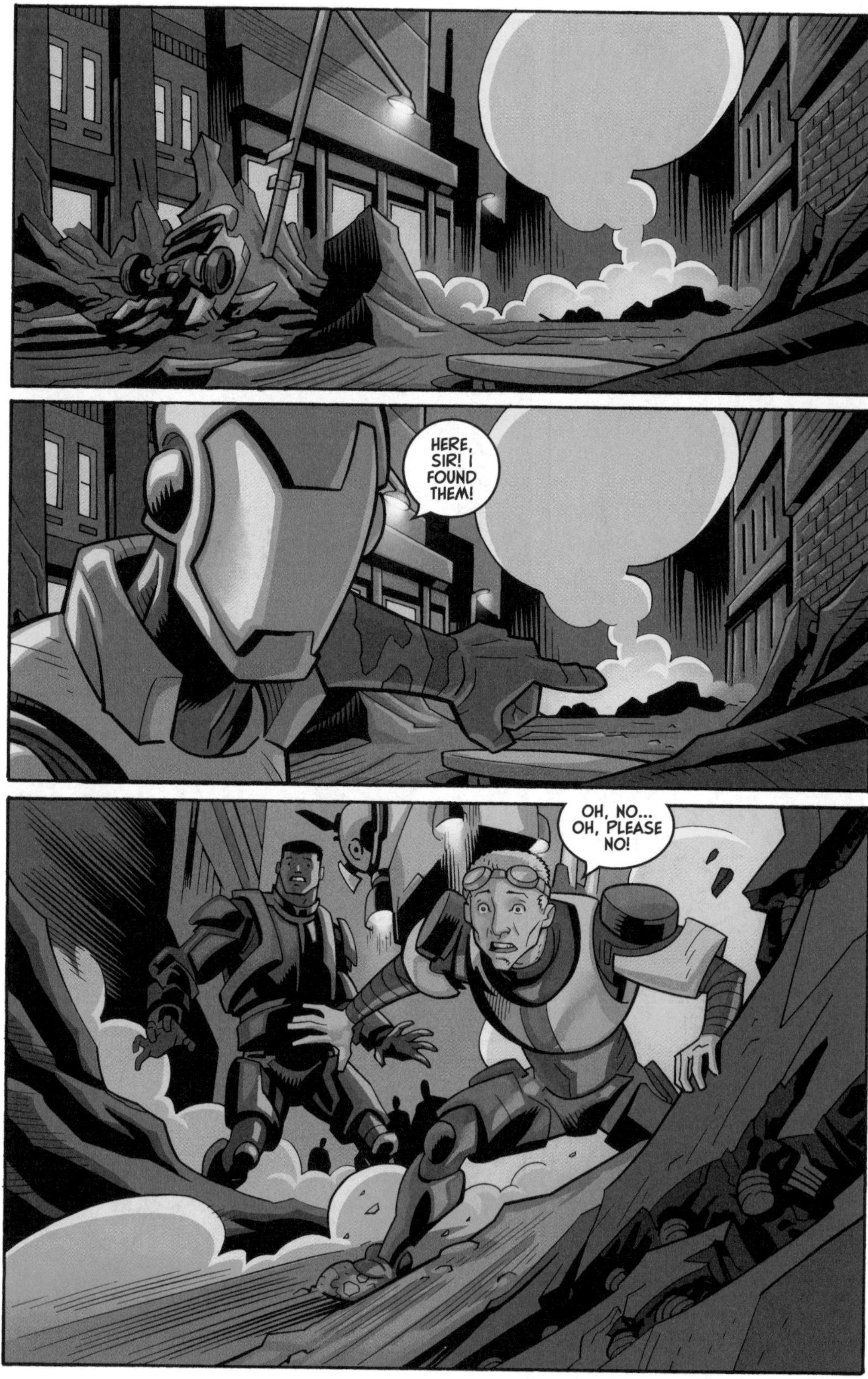
HERE, SIR! I FOUND THEM!
OH, NO... OH, PLEASE NO!

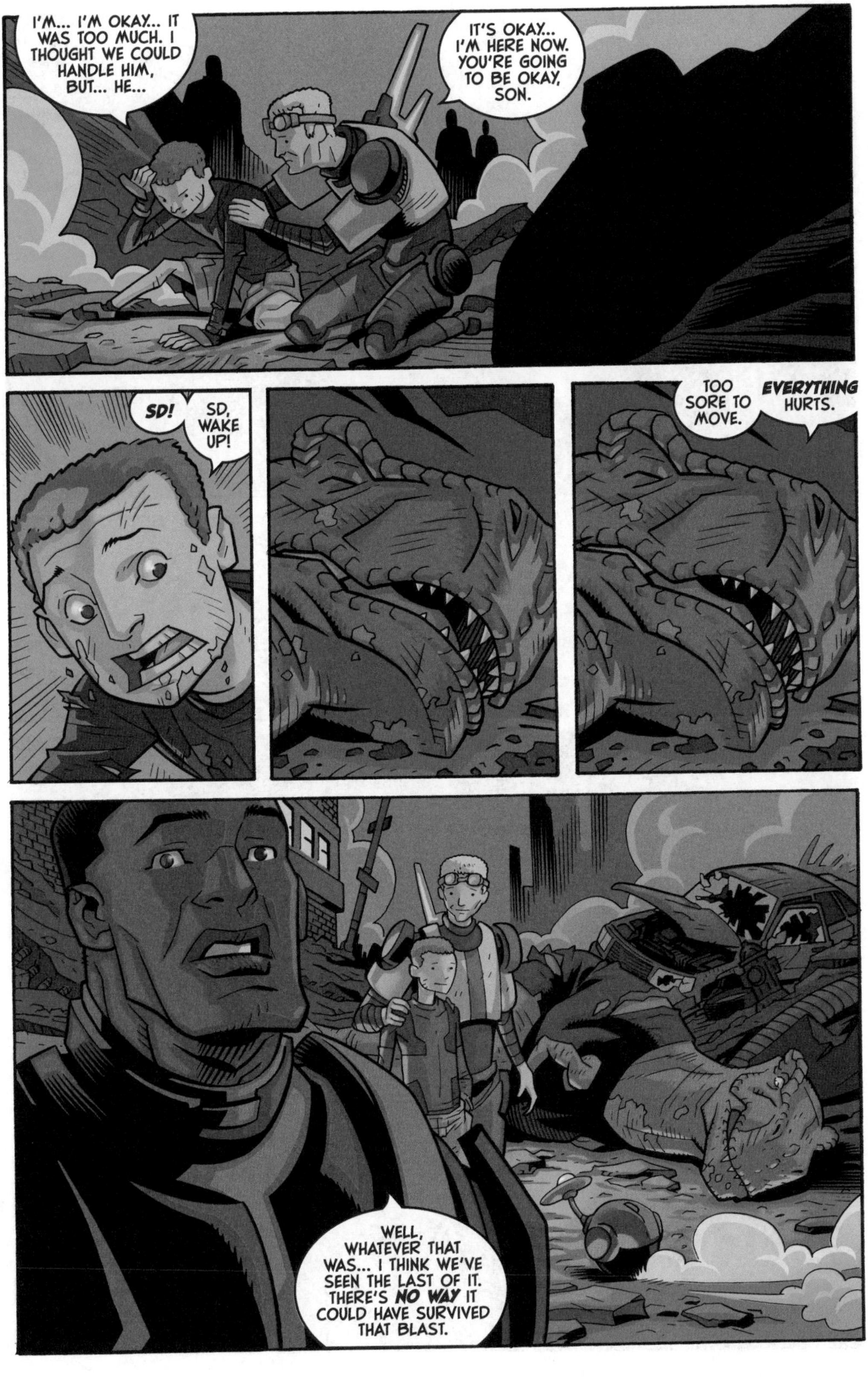

I'M... I'M OKAY... IT WAS TOO MUCH. I THOUGHT WE COULD HANDLE HIM, BUT... HE...
IT'S OKAY... I'M HERE NOW. YOU'RE GOING TO BE OKAY, SON.
SD!
SD, WAKE UP!
TOO SORE TO MOVE.
EVERYTHING HURTS.
WELL, WHATEVER THAT WAS... I THINK WE'VE SEEN THE LAST OF IT. THERE'S NO WAY IT COULD HAVE SURVIVED THAT BLAST.

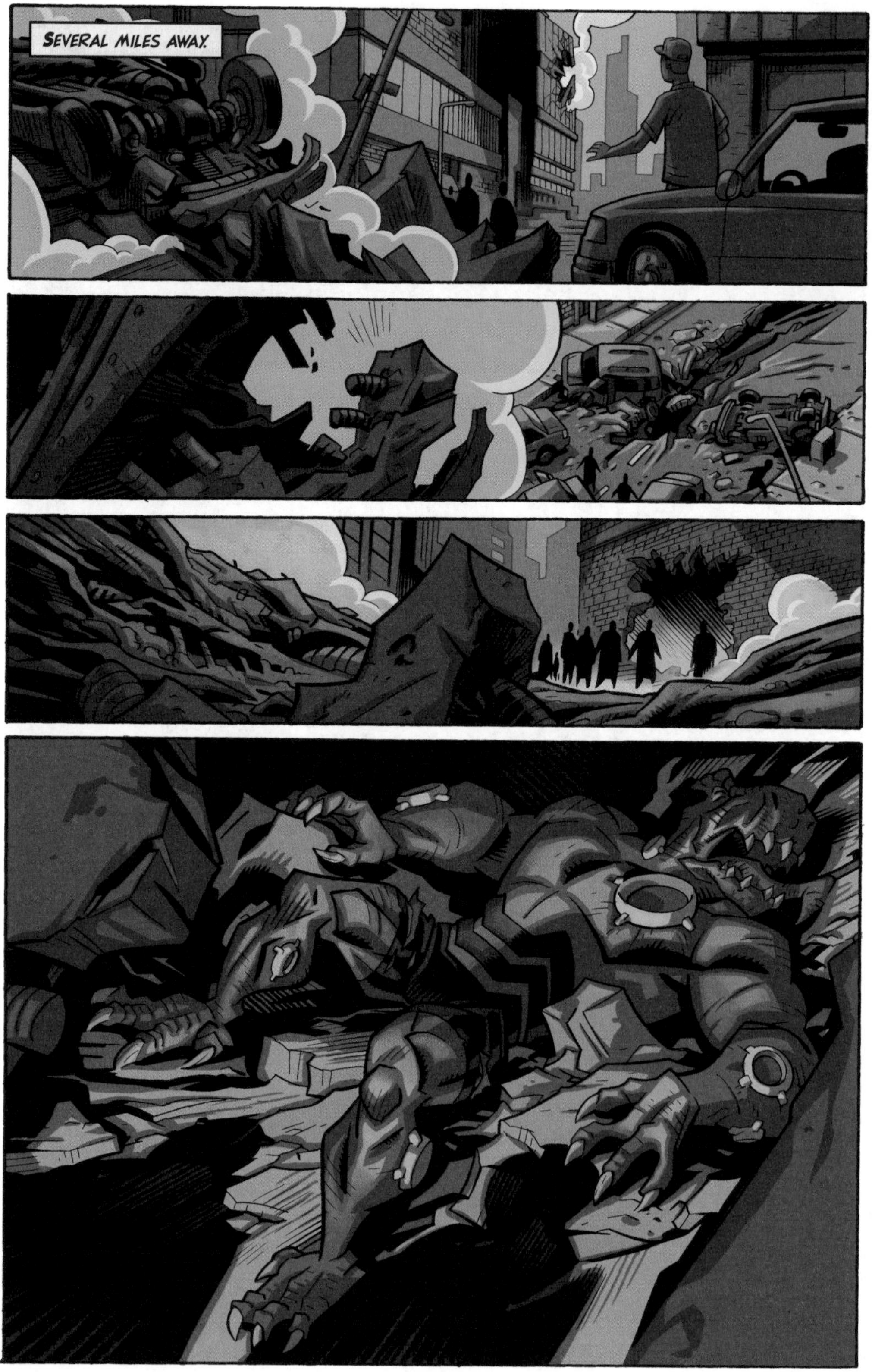
SEVERAL MILES AWAY.

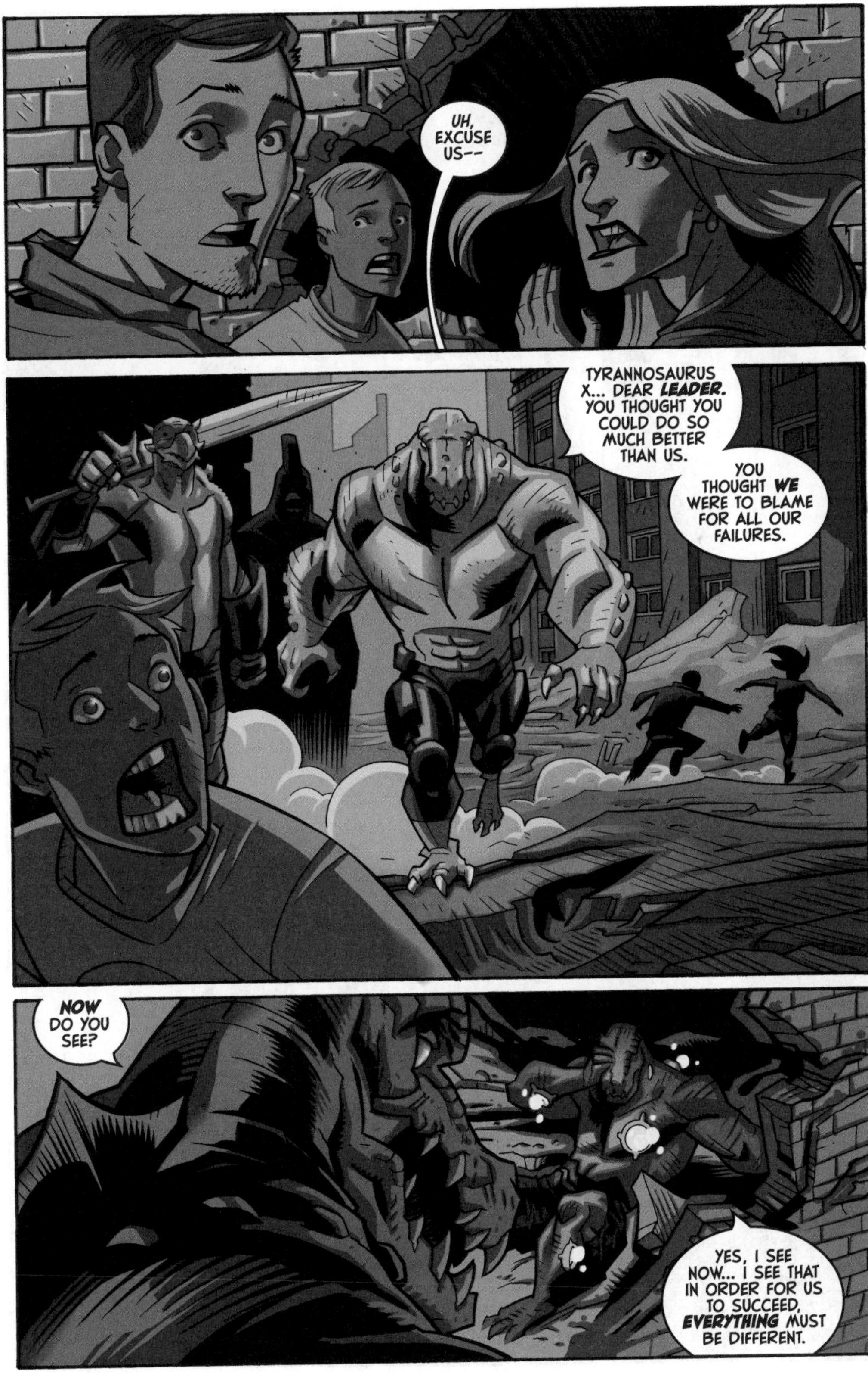
UH, EXCUSE US--
TYRANNOSAURUS X... DEAR LEADER. YOU THOUGHT YOU COULD DO SO MUCH BETTER THAN US.
YOU THOUGHT WE WERE TO BLAME FOR ALL OUR FAILURES.
NOW DO YOU SEE?
YES, I SEE NOW... I SEE THAT IN ORDER FOR US TO SUCCEED, EVERYTHING MUST BE DIFFERENT.

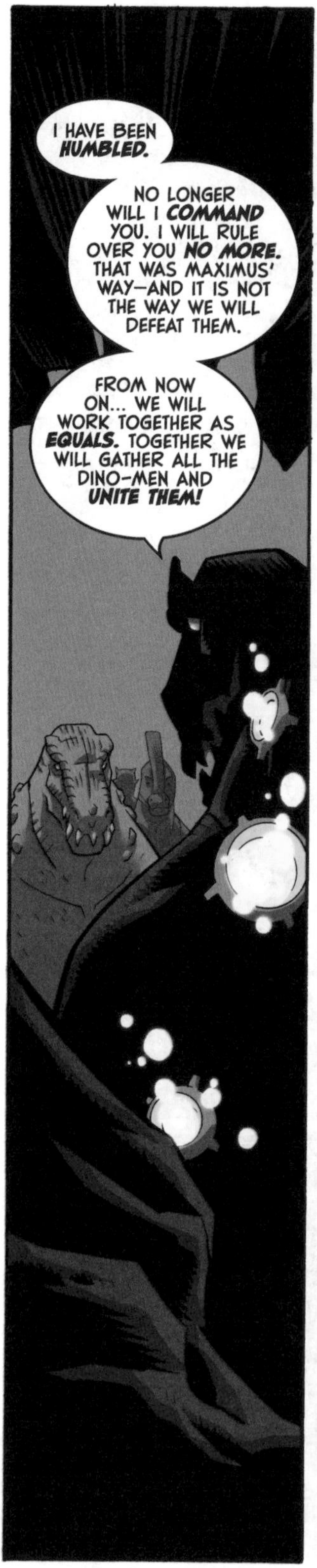
I HAVE BEEN HUMBLED.
NO LONGER WILL I COMMAND YOU. I WILL RULE OVER YOU NO MORE. THAT WAS MAXIMUS' WAY—AND IT IS NOT THE WAY WE WILL DEFEAT THEM.
FROM NOW ON... WE WILL WORK TOGETHER AS EQUALS. TOGETHER WE WILL GATHER ALL THE DINO-MEN AND UNITE THEM!

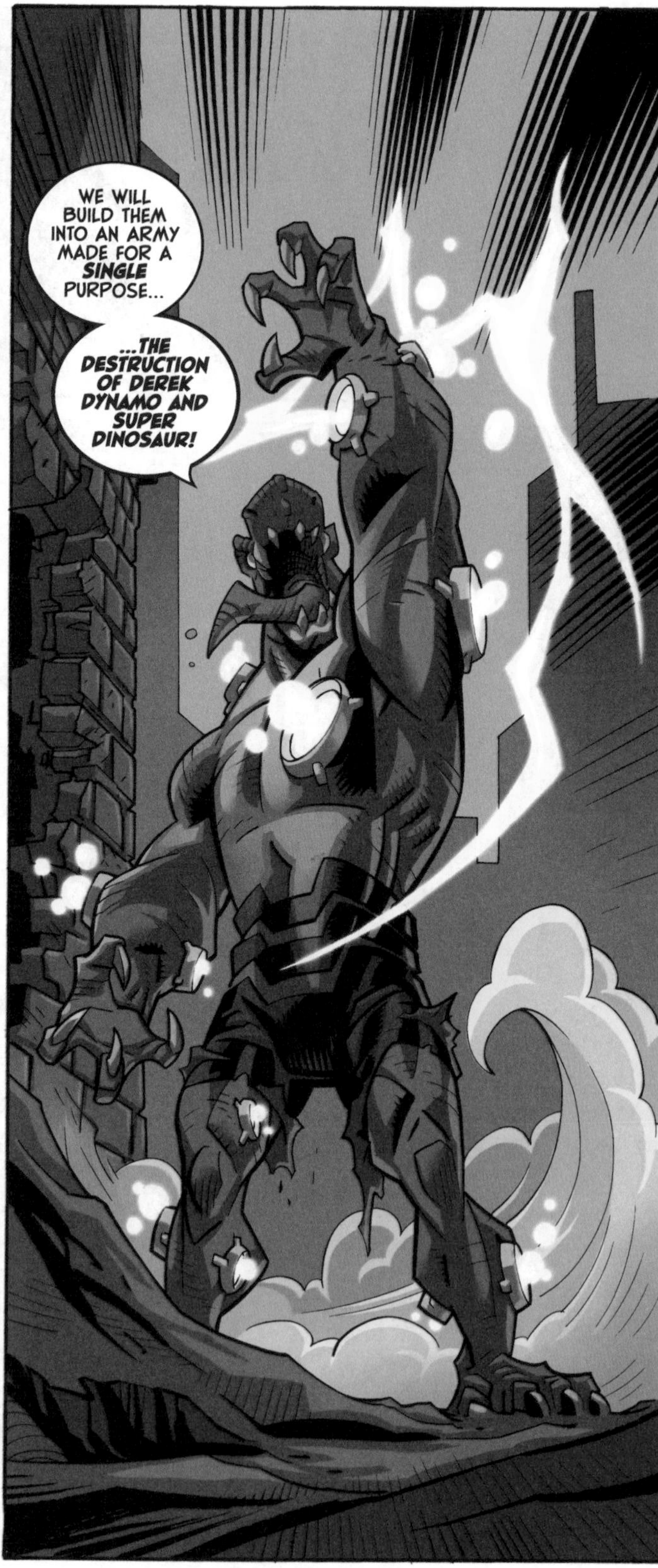
WE WILL BUILD THEM INTO AN ARMY MADE FOR A SINGLE PURPOSE...
...THE DESTRUCTION OF DEREK DYNAMO AND SUPER DINOSAUR!

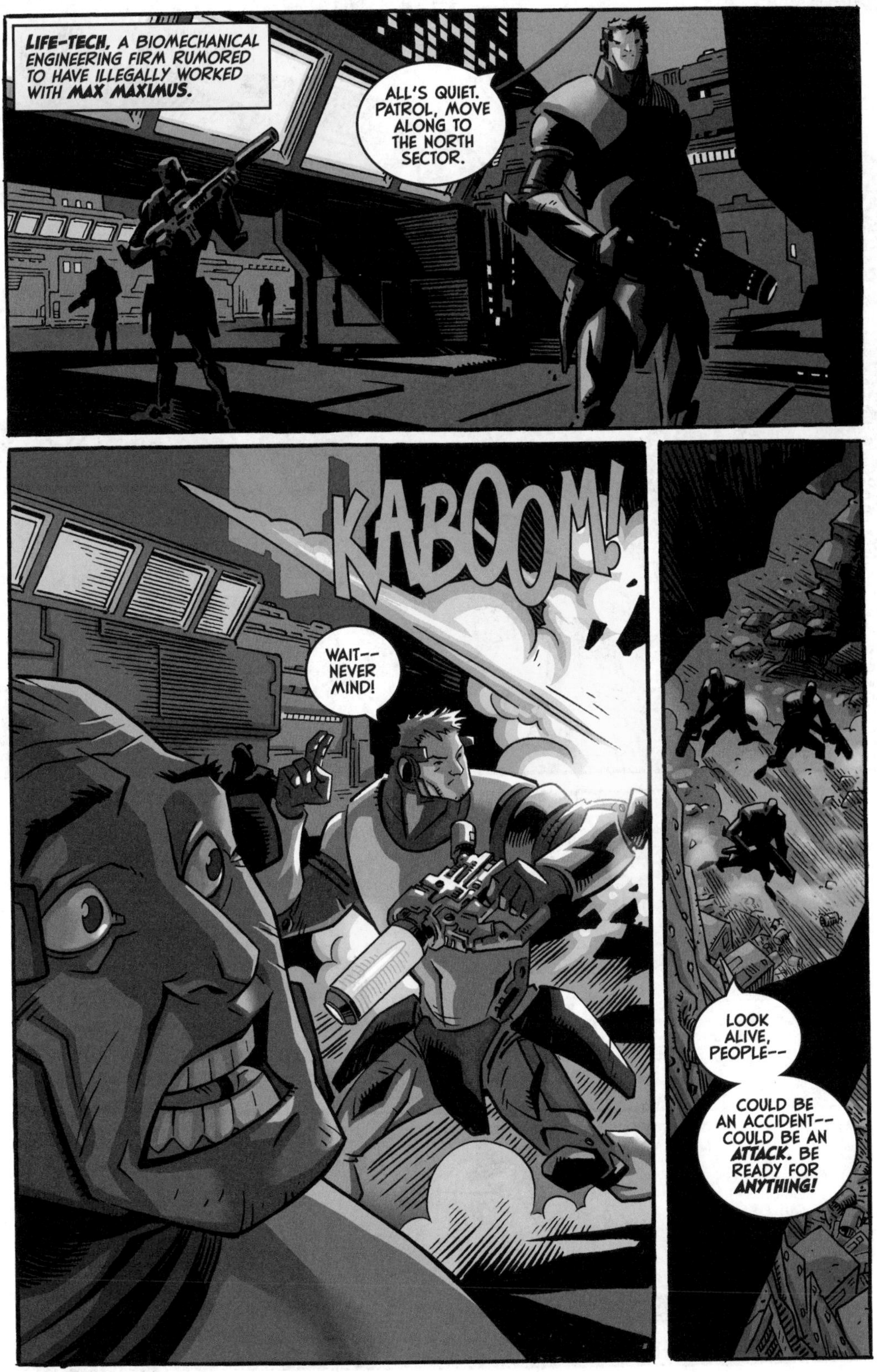
LIFE-TECH, A BIOMECHANICAL ENGINEERING FIRM RUMORED TO HAVE ILLEGALLY WORKED WITH MAX MAXIMUS.
ALL'S QUIET. PATROL, MOVE ALONG TO THE NORTH SECTOR.
KABOOM!
WAIT-- NEVER MIND!
LOOK ALIVE, PEOPLE--
COULD BE AN ACCIDENT-- COULD BE AN ATTACK. BE READY FOR ANYTHING!

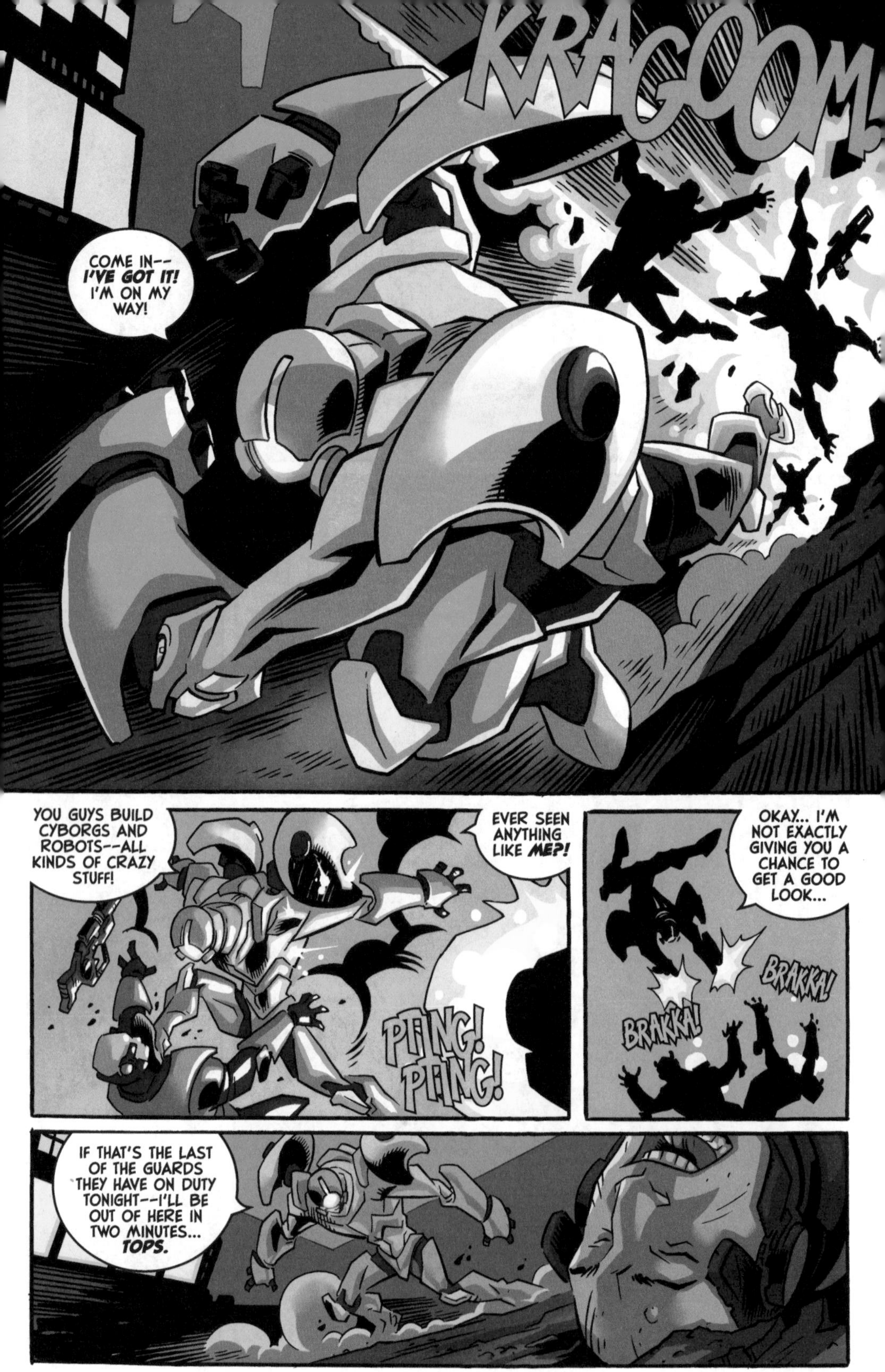
KRAGOOM!
COME IN-- I'VE GOT IT! I'M ON MY WAY!
YOU GUYS BUILD CYBORGS AND ROBOTS--ALL KINDS OF CRAZY STUFF!
EVER SEEN ANYTHING LIKE ME?!
PTING! PTING!
OKAY... I'M NOT EXACTLY GIVING YOU A CHANCE TO GET A GOOD LOOK...
BRAKKA!
BRAKKA!
IF THAT'S THE LAST OF THE GUARDS THEY HAVE ON DUTY TONIGHT--I'LL BE OUT OF HERE IN TWO MINUTES... TOPS.

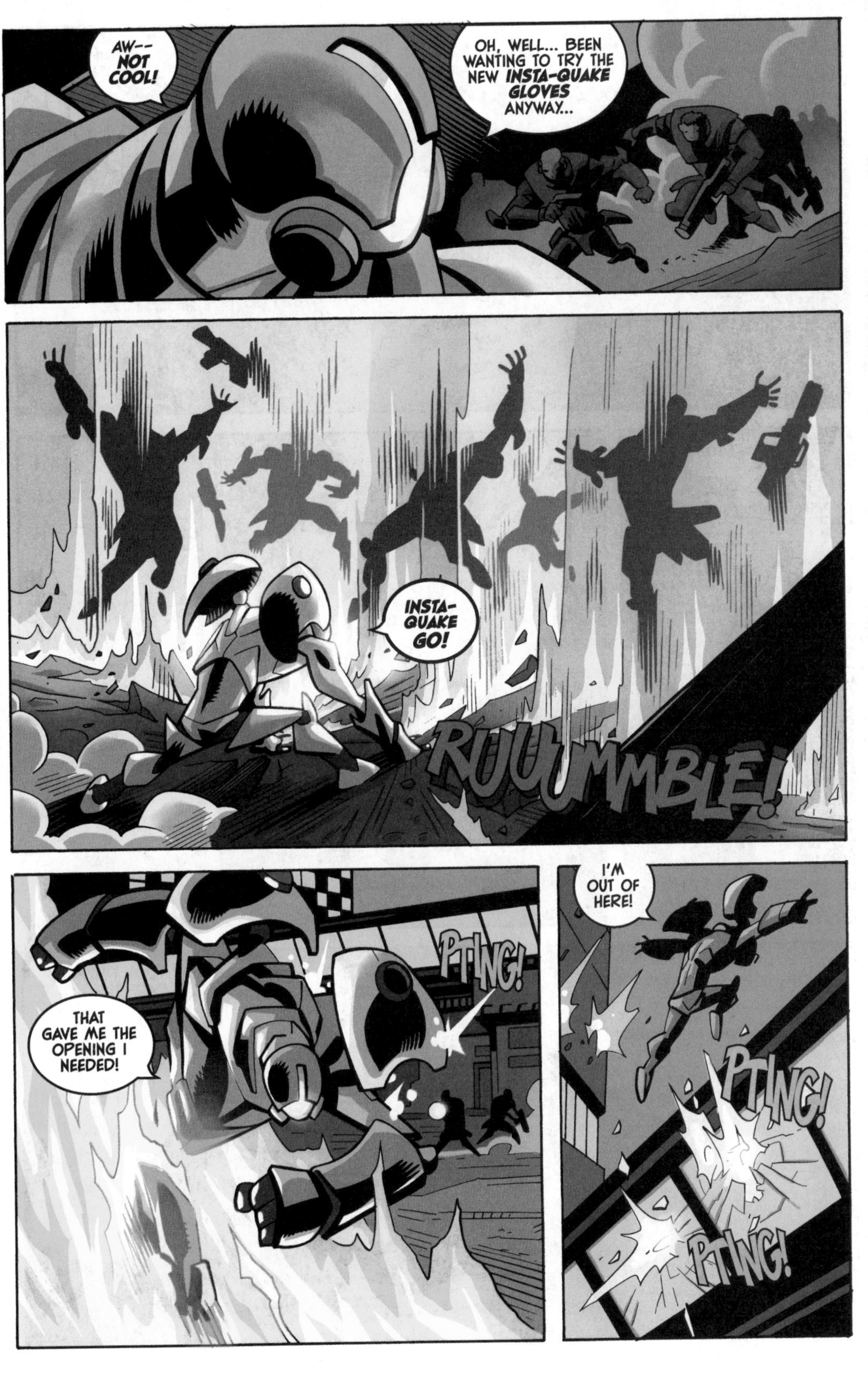
AW-- NOT COOL!
OH, WELL... BEEN WANTING TO TRY THE NEW INSTA-QUAKE GLOVES ANYWAY...
INSTA-QUAKE GO!
RUUUMMBLE!
PTING!
THAT GAVE ME THE OPENING I NEEDED!
I'M OUT OF HERE!
PTING!
PTING!

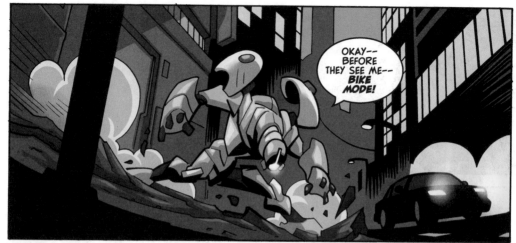

OKAY-- BEFORE THEY SEE ME-- *BIKE MODE!*

THIS IS SO AWESOME.

PSHHH!!

CARGO IN HAND, I'LL BE BACK AT THE DYNAMO DOME IN NO TIME.

MAKE SURE YOU WEREN'T FOLLOWED. THOSE LIFE-TECH GUYS ARE BAD NEWS. IF THEY FIND OUT WE'RE BEHIND THIS...

DON'T WORRY, DAD. I'VE GOT IT COVERED. I ALSO TOOK ENOUGH PHOTOS WHILE I WAS IN THERE THAT WE CAN FINALLY GIVE GENERAL CASEY ENOUGH EVIDENCE TO ARREST THEM.

THESE JERKS WILL BE IN JAIL BY MORNING!

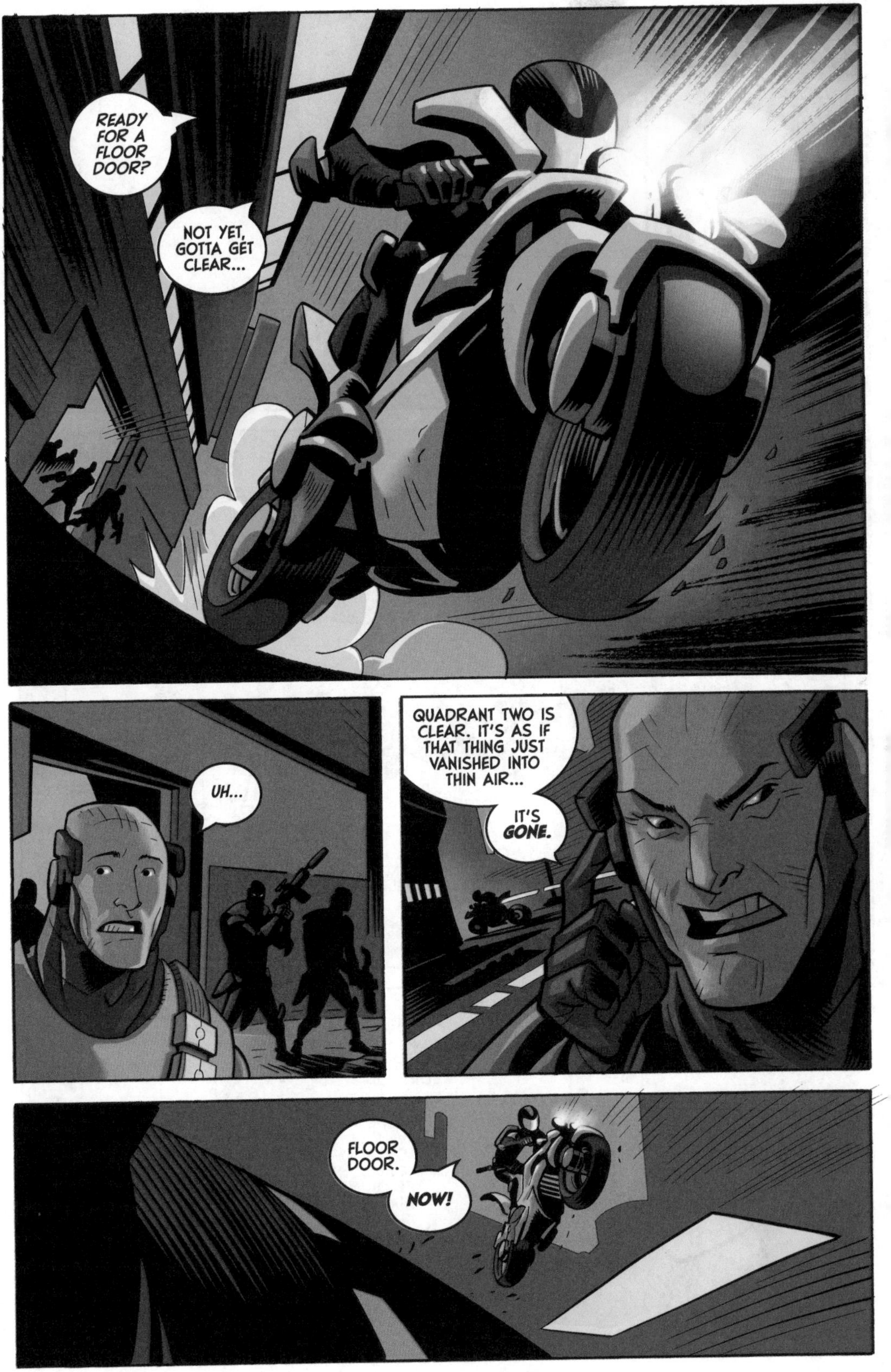
READY FOR A FLOOR DOOR?
NOT YET, GOTTA GET CLEAR...
UH...
QUADRANT TWO IS CLEAR. IT'S AS IF THAT THING JUST VANISHED INTO THIN AIR...
IT'S GONE.
FLOOR DOOR.
NOW!

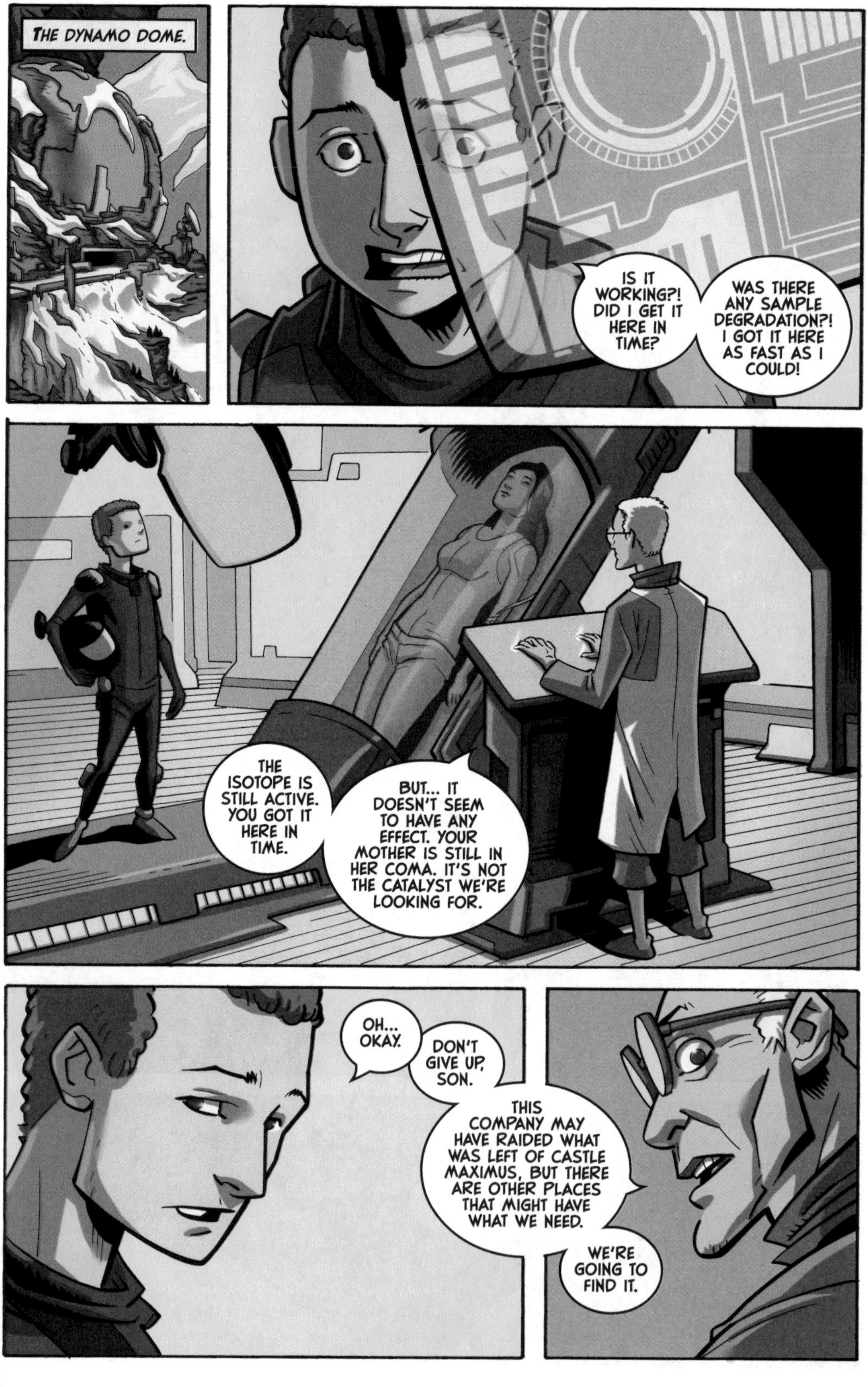
THE DYNAMO DOME.
IS IT WORKING?! DID I GET IT HERE IN TIME?
WAS THERE ANY SAMPLE DEGRADATION?! I GOT IT HERE AS FAST AS I COULD!
THE ISOTOPE IS STILL ACTIVE. YOU GOT IT HERE IN TIME.
BUT... IT DOESN'T SEEM TO HAVE ANY EFFECT. YOUR MOTHER IS STILL IN HER COMA. IT'S NOT THE CATALYST WE'RE LOOKING FOR.
OH... OKAY.
DON'T GIVE UP, SON.
THIS COMPANY MAY HAVE RAIDED WHAT WAS LEFT OF CASTLE MAXIMUS, BUT THERE ARE OTHER PLACES THAT MIGHT HAVE WHAT WE NEED.
WE'RE GOING TO FIND IT.

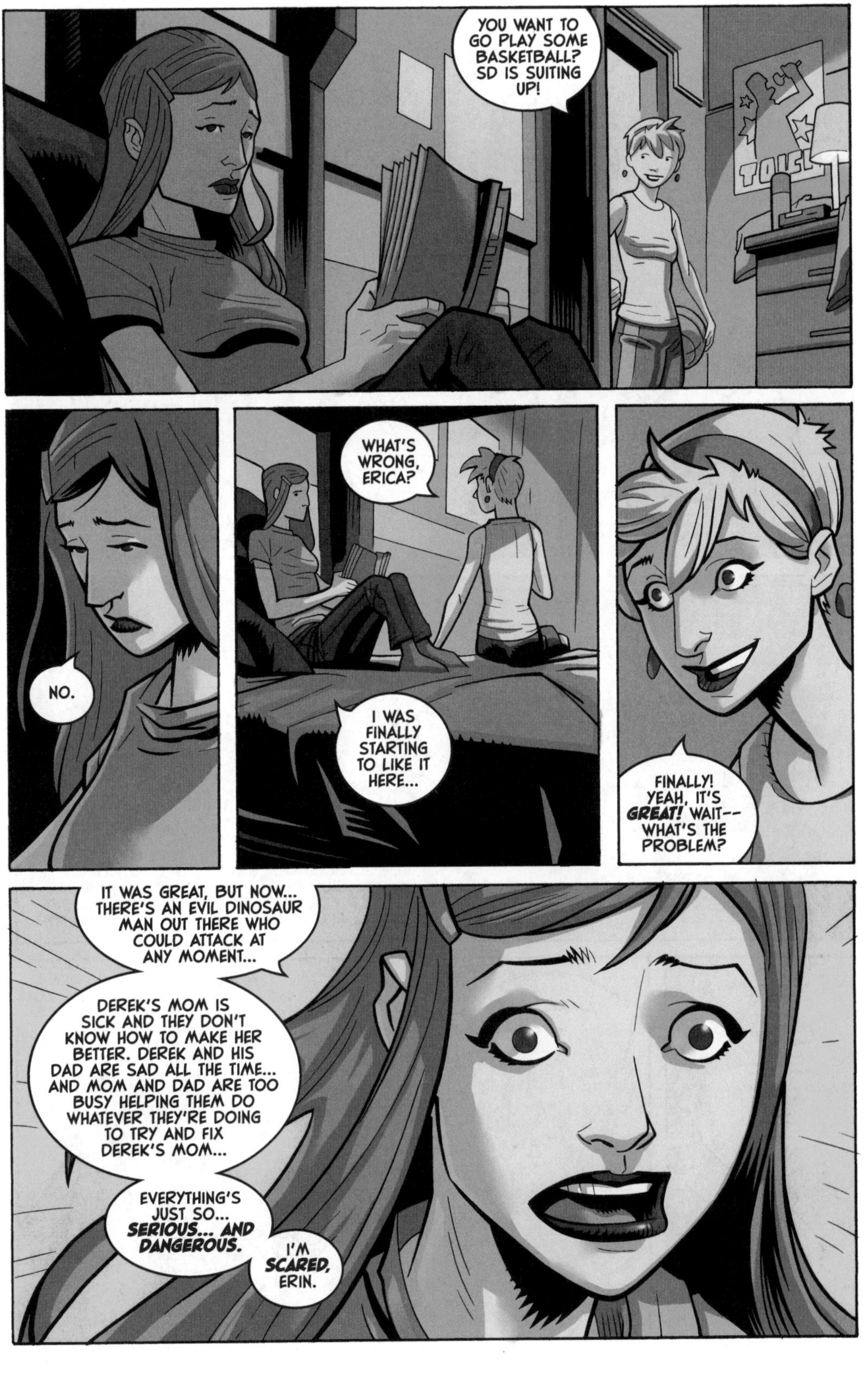
YOU WANT TO GO PLAY SOME BASKETBALL? SD IS SUITING UP!
NO.
WHAT'S WRONG, ERICA?
I WAS FINALLY STARTING TO LIKE IT HERE...
FINALLY! YEAH, IT'S **GREAT!** WAIT-- WHAT'S THE PROBLEM?
IT WAS GREAT, BUT NOW... THERE'S AN EVIL DINOSAUR MAN OUT THERE WHO COULD ATTACK AT ANY MOMENT...
DEREK'S MOM IS SICK AND THEY DON'T KNOW HOW TO MAKE HER BETTER. DEREK AND HIS DAD ARE SAD ALL THE TIME... AND MOM AND DAD ARE TOO BUSY HELPING THEM DO WHATEVER THEY'RE DOING TO TRY AND FIX DEREK'S MOM...
EVERYTHING'S JUST SO... **SERIOUS... AND DANGEROUS.**
I'M **SCARED,** ERIN.

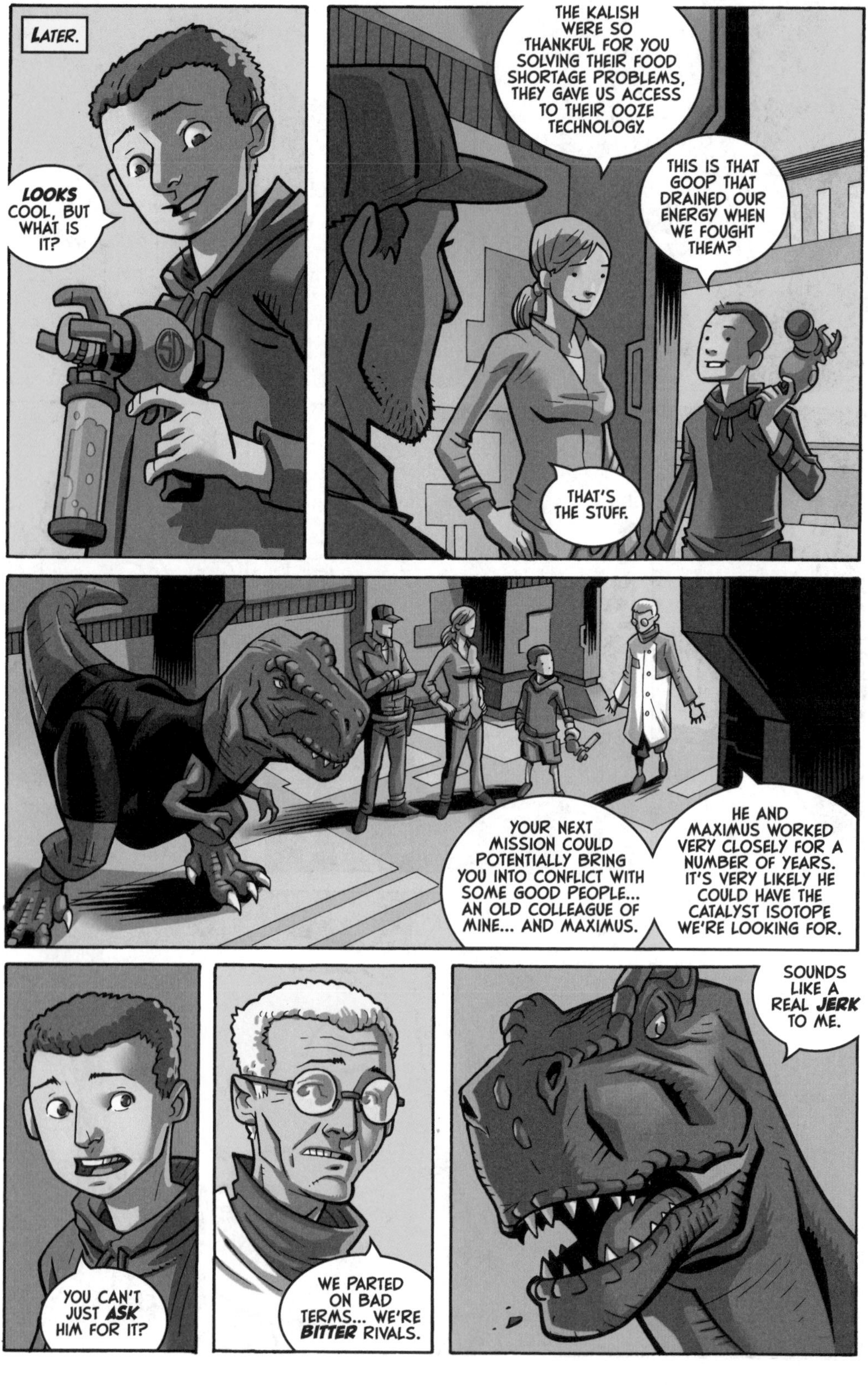
LATER.
LOOKS COOL, BUT WHAT IS IT?
THE KALISH WERE SO THANKFUL FOR YOU SOLVING THEIR FOOD SHORTAGE PROBLEMS, THEY GAVE US ACCESS TO THEIR OOZE TECHNOLOGY.
THIS IS THAT GOOP THAT DRAINED OUR ENERGY WHEN WE FOUGHT THEM?
THAT'S THE STUFF.
YOUR NEXT MISSION COULD POTENTIALLY BRING YOU INTO CONFLICT WITH SOME GOOD PEOPLE... AN OLD COLLEAGUE OF MINE... AND MAXIMUS.
HE AND MAXIMUS WORKED VERY CLOSELY FOR A NUMBER OF YEARS. IT'S VERY LIKELY HE COULD HAVE THE CATALYST ISOTOPE WE'RE LOOKING FOR.
YOU CAN'T JUST ASK HIM FOR IT?
WE PARTED ON BAD TERMS... WE'RE BITTER RIVALS.
SOUNDS LIKE A REAL JERK TO ME.

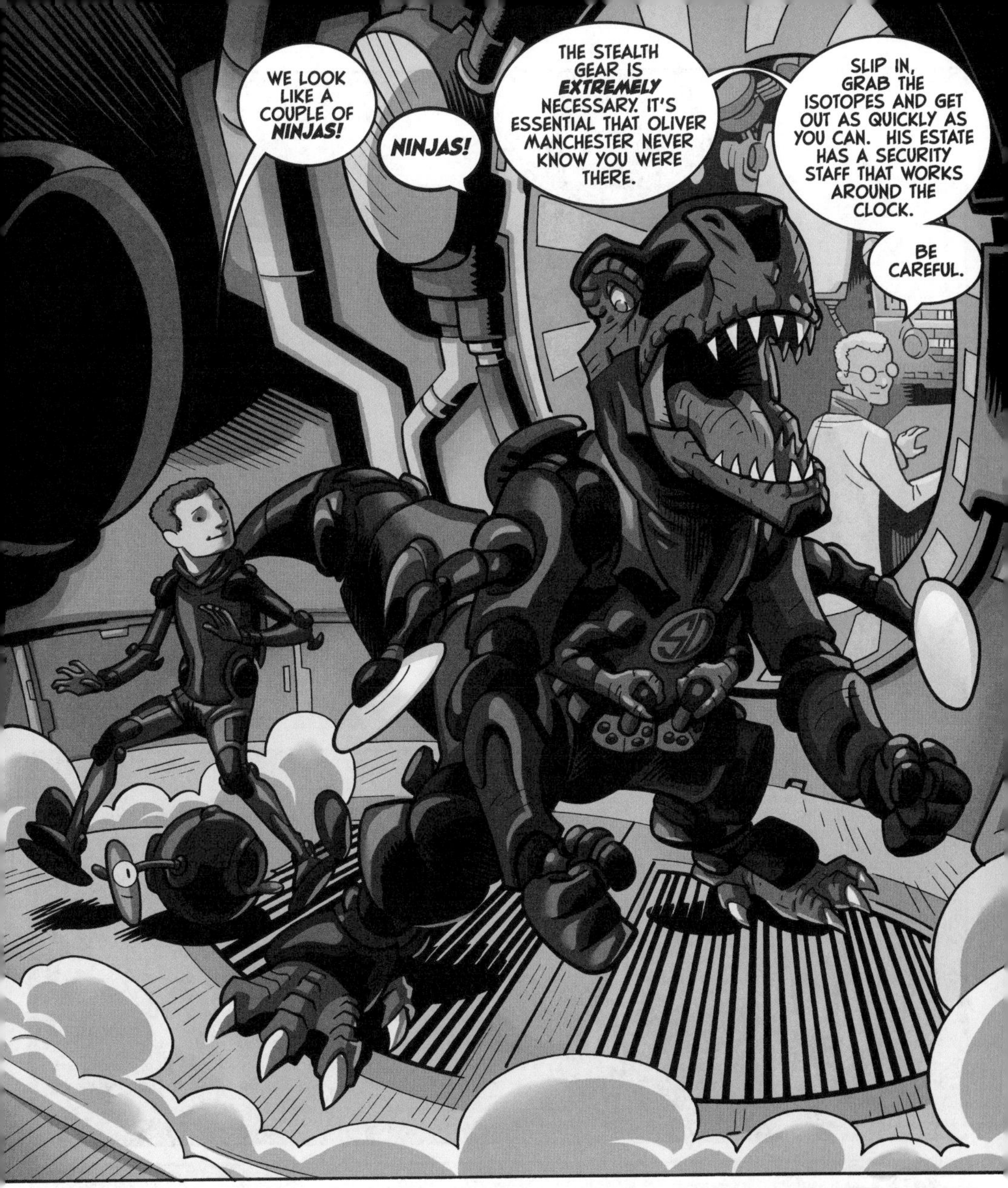
WE LOOK LIKE A COUPLE OF NINJAS!
NINJAS!
THE STEALTH GEAR IS EXTREMELY NECESSARY. IT'S ESSENTIAL THAT OLIVER MANCHESTER NEVER KNOW YOU WERE THERE.
SLIP IN, GRAB THE ISOTOPES AND GET OUT AS QUICKLY AS YOU CAN. HIS ESTATE HAS A SECURITY STAFF THAT WORKS AROUND THE CLOCK.
BE CAREFUL.
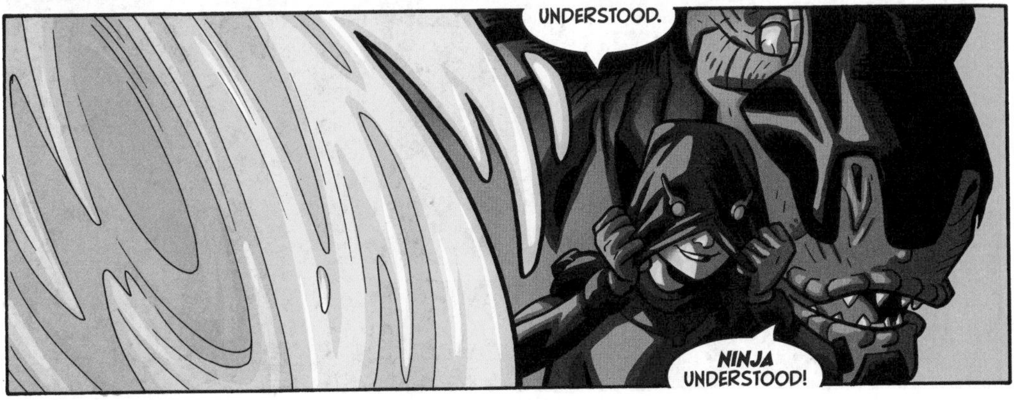
UNDERSTOOD.
NINJA UNDERSTOOD!

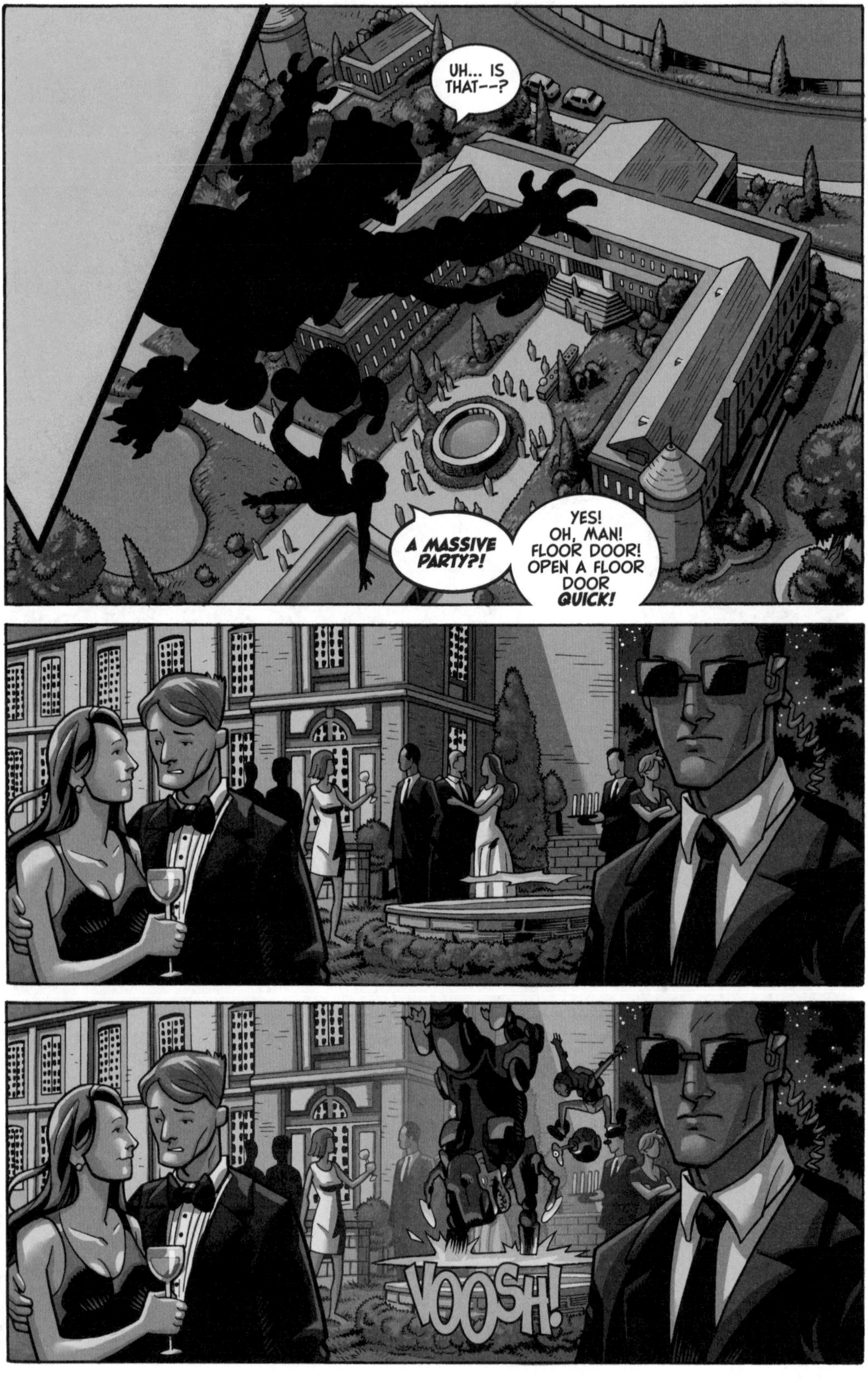
UH... IS THAT--?
A MASSIVE PARTY?!
YES! OH, MAN! FLOOR DOOR! OPEN A FLOOR DOOR QUICK!
VOOSH!

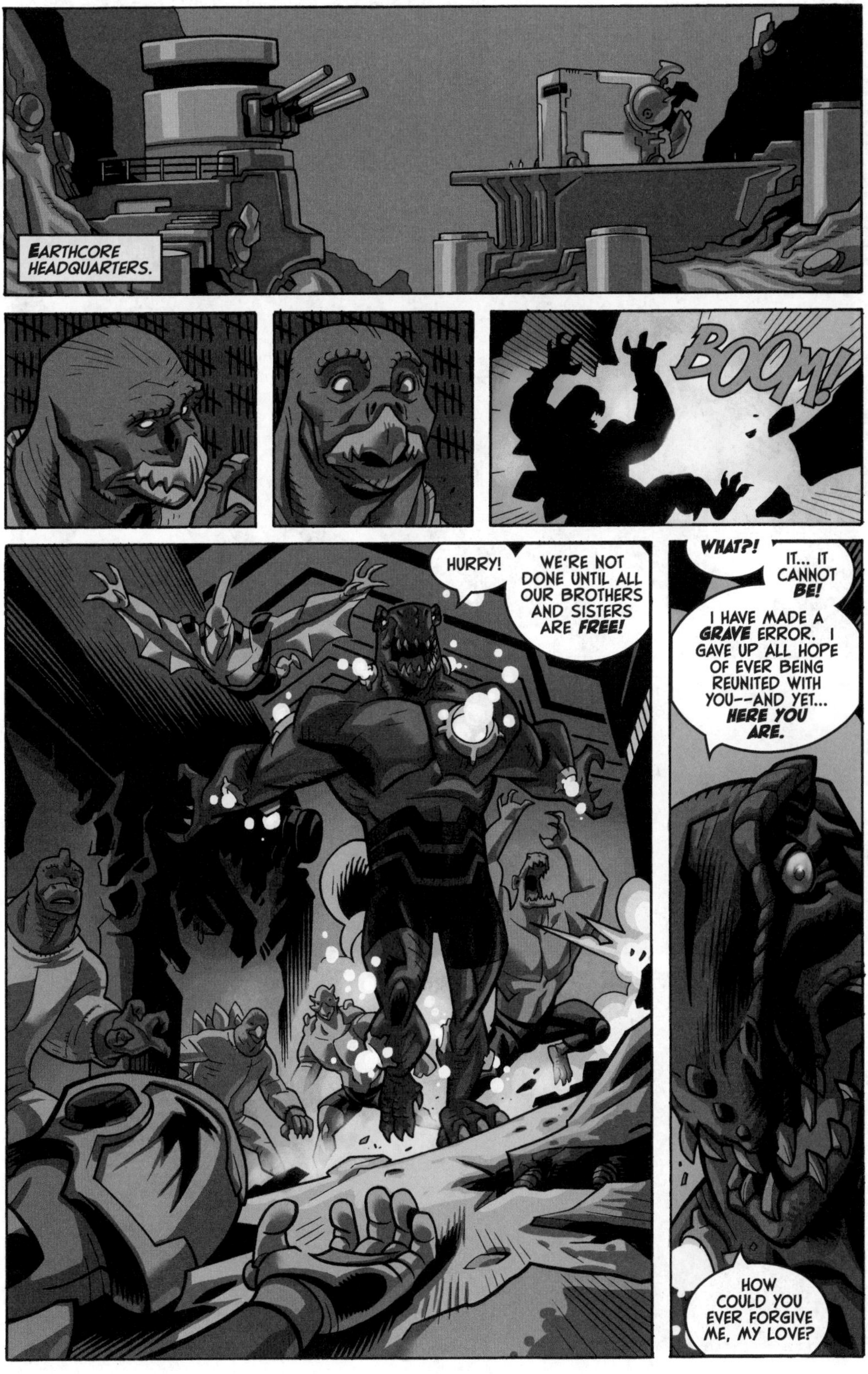
EARTHCORE HEADQUARTERS.
BOOM!
HURRY!
WE'RE NOT DONE UNTIL ALL OUR BROTHERS AND SISTERS ARE FREE!
WHAT?!
IT... IT CANNOT BE!
I HAVE MADE A GRAVE ERROR. I GAVE UP ALL HOPE OF EVER BEING REUNITED WITH YOU--AND YET... HERE YOU ARE.
HOW COULD YOU EVER FORGIVE ME, MY LOVE?

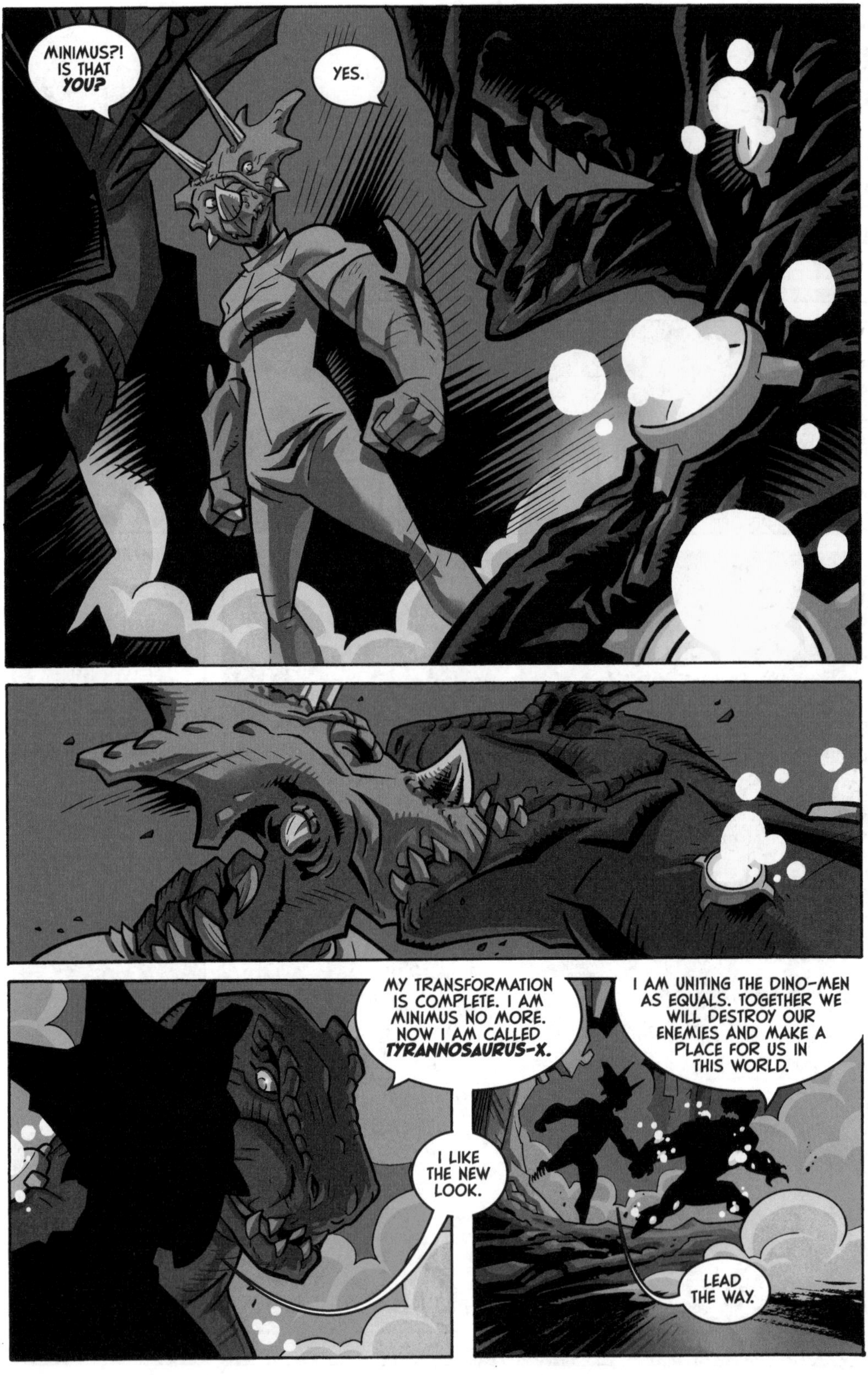
MINIMUS?! IS THAT YOU?
YES.
MY TRANSFORMATION IS COMPLETE. I AM MINIMUS NO MORE. NOW I AM CALLED TYRANNOSAURUS-X.
I LIKE THE NEW LOOK.
I AM UNITING THE DINO-MEN AS EQUALS. TOGETHER WE WILL DESTROY OUR ENEMIES AND MAKE A PLACE FOR US IN THIS WORLD.
LEAD THE WAY.

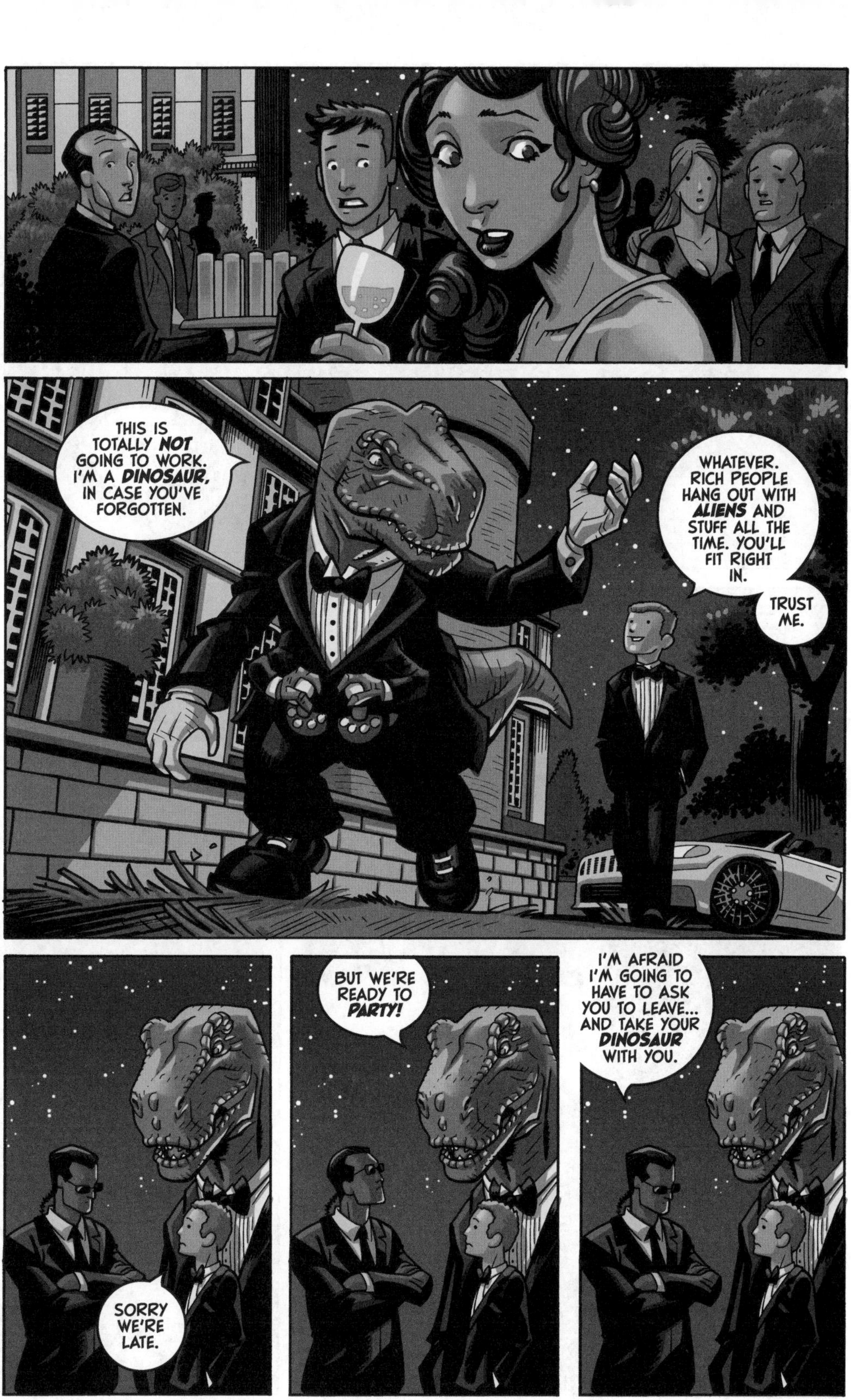
THIS IS TOTALLY NOT GOING TO WORK. I'M A DINOSAUR, IN CASE YOU'VE FORGOTTEN.
WHATEVER. RICH PEOPLE HANG OUT WITH ALIENS AND STUFF ALL THE TIME. YOU'LL FIT RIGHT IN.
TRUST ME.
SORRY WE'RE LATE.
BUT WE'RE READY TO PARTY!
I'M AFRAID I'M GOING TO HAVE TO ASK YOU TO LEAVE... AND TAKE YOUR DINOSAUR WITH YOU.

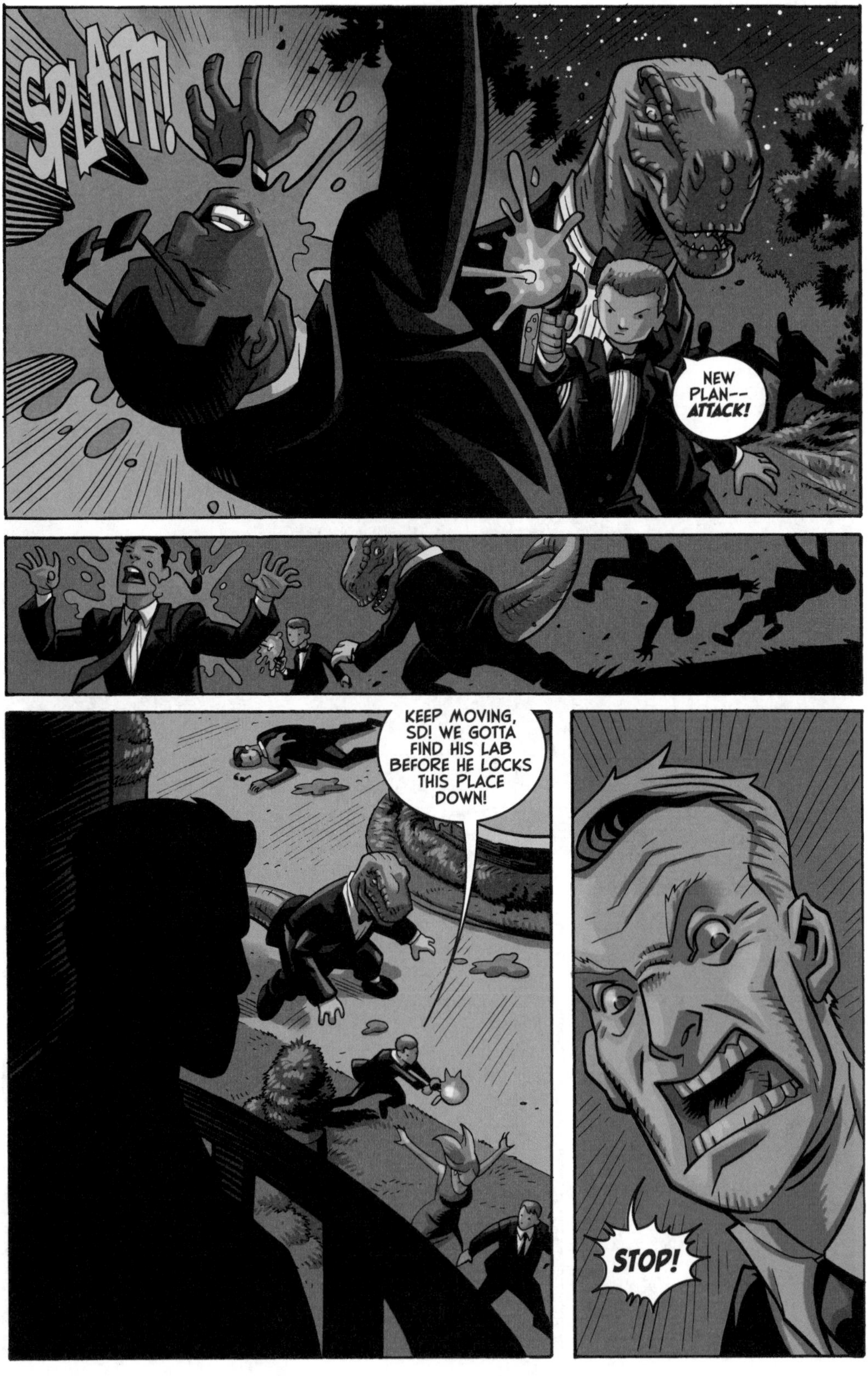
SPLATT!
NEW PLAN-- ATTACK!
KEEP MOVING, SD! WE GOTTA FIND HIS LAB BEFORE HE LOCKS THIS PLACE DOWN!
STOP!

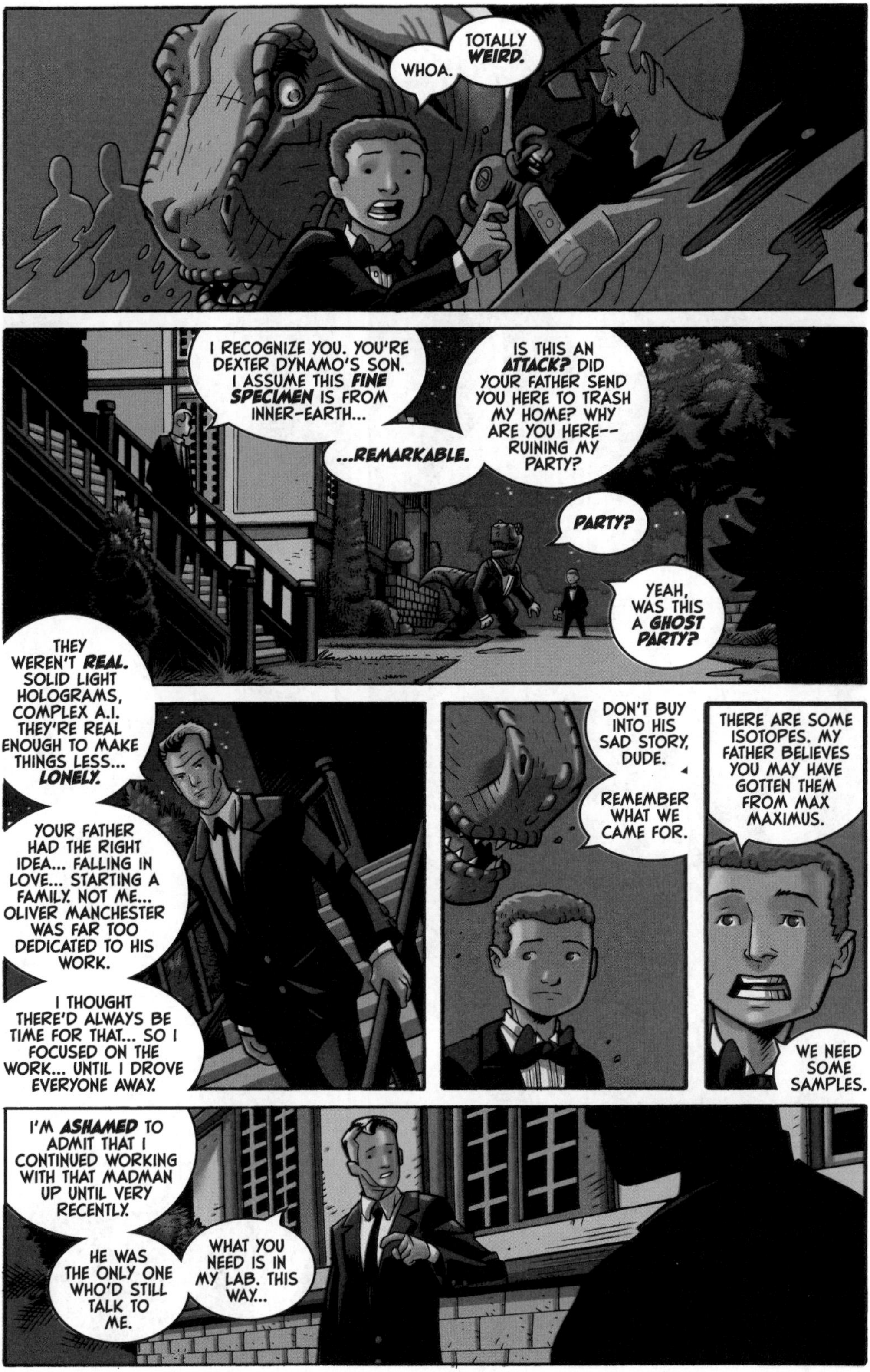
WHOA.
TOTALLY WEIRD.
I RECOGNIZE YOU. YOU'RE DEXTER DYNAMO'S SON. I ASSUME THIS FINE SPECIMEN IS FROM INNER-EARTH...
...REMARKABLE.
IS THIS AN ATTACK? DID YOUR FATHER SEND YOU HERE TO TRASH MY HOME? WHY ARE YOU HERE-- RUINING MY PARTY?
PARTY?
YEAH, WAS THIS A GHOST PARTY?
THEY WEREN'T REAL. SOLID LIGHT HOLOGRAMS, COMPLEX A.I. THEY'RE REAL ENOUGH TO MAKE THINGS LESS... LONELY.
YOUR FATHER HAD THE RIGHT IDEA... FALLING IN LOVE... STARTING A FAMILY. NOT ME... OLIVER MANCHESTER WAS FAR TOO DEDICATED TO HIS WORK.
I THOUGHT THERE'D ALWAYS BE TIME FOR THAT... SO I FOCUSED ON THE WORK... UNTIL I DROVE EVERYONE AWAY.
DON'T BUY INTO HIS SAD STORY, DUDE.
REMEMBER WHAT WE CAME FOR.
THERE ARE SOME ISOTOPES. MY FATHER BELIEVES YOU MAY HAVE GOTTEN THEM FROM MAX MAXIMUS.
WE NEED SOME SAMPLES.
I'M ASHAMED TO ADMIT THAT I CONTINUED WORKING WITH THAT MADMAN UP UNTIL VERY RECENTLY.
HE WAS THE ONLY ONE WHO'D STILL TALK TO ME.
WHAT YOU NEED IS IN MY LAB. THIS WAY...

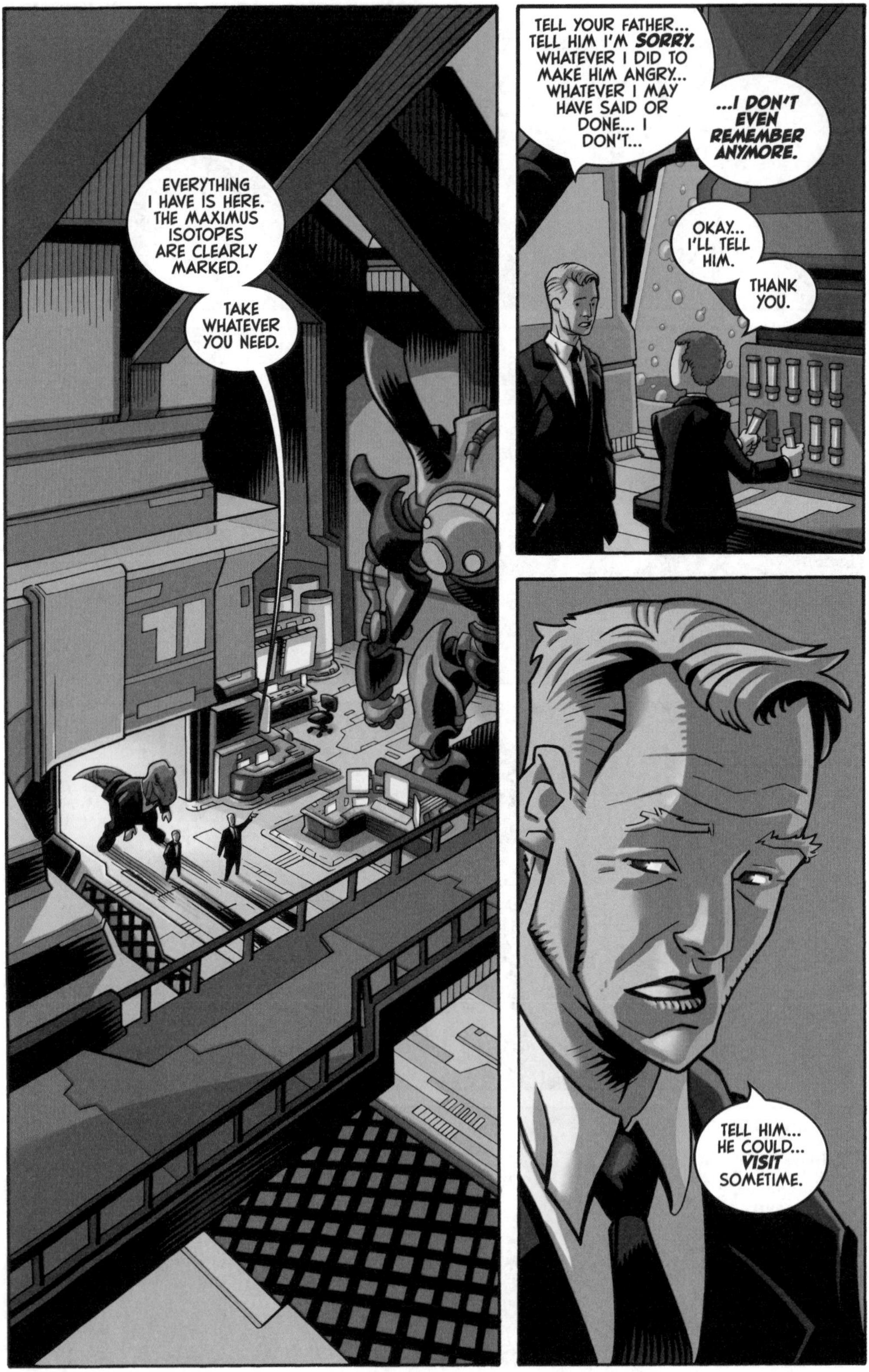
EVERYTHING I HAVE IS HERE. THE MAXIMUS ISOTOPES ARE CLEARLY MARKED.
TAKE WHATEVER YOU NEED.
TELL YOUR FATHER... TELL HIM I'M **SORRY.** WHATEVER I DID TO MAKE HIM ANGRY... WHATEVER I MAY HAVE SAID OR DONE... I DON'T...
...I DON'T EVEN REMEMBER ANYMORE.
OKAY... I'LL TELL HIM.
THANK YOU.
TELL HIM... HE COULD... **VISIT** SOMETIME.

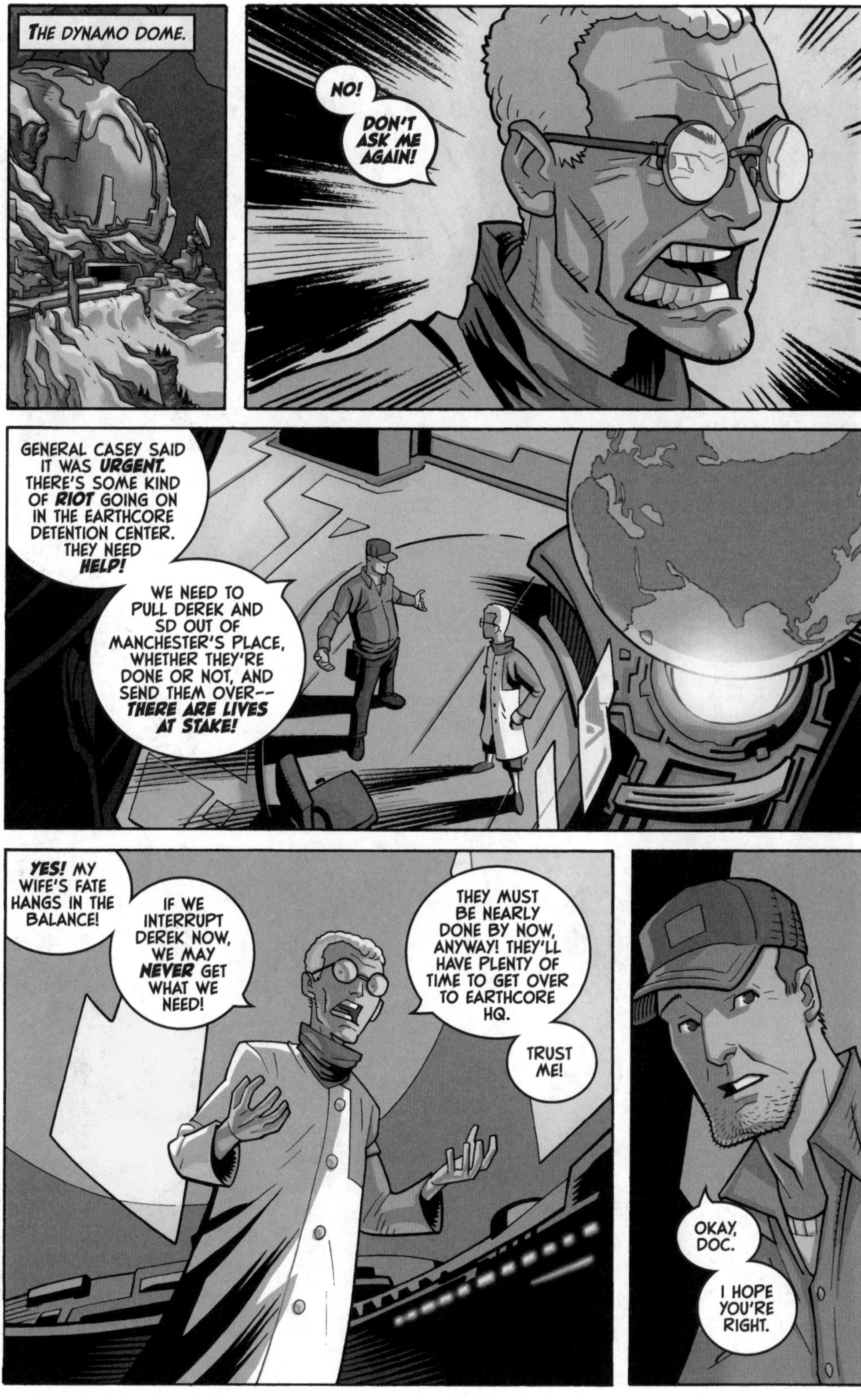
THE DYNAMO DOME.
NO!
DON'T ASK ME AGAIN!
GENERAL CASEY SAID IT WAS URGENT. THERE'S SOME KIND OF RIOT GOING ON IN THE EARTHCORE DETENTION CENTER. THEY NEED HELP!
WE NEED TO PULL DEREK AND SD OUT OF MANCHESTER'S PLACE, WHETHER THEY'RE DONE OR NOT, AND SEND THEM OVER-- THERE ARE LIVES AT STAKE!
YES! MY WIFE'S FATE HANGS IN THE BALANCE!
IF WE INTERRUPT DEREK NOW, WE MAY NEVER GET WHAT WE NEED!
THEY MUST BE NEARLY DONE BY NOW, ANYWAY! THEY'LL HAVE PLENTY OF TIME TO GET OVER TO EARTHCORE HQ.
TRUST ME!
OKAY, DOC.
I HOPE YOU'RE RIGHT.

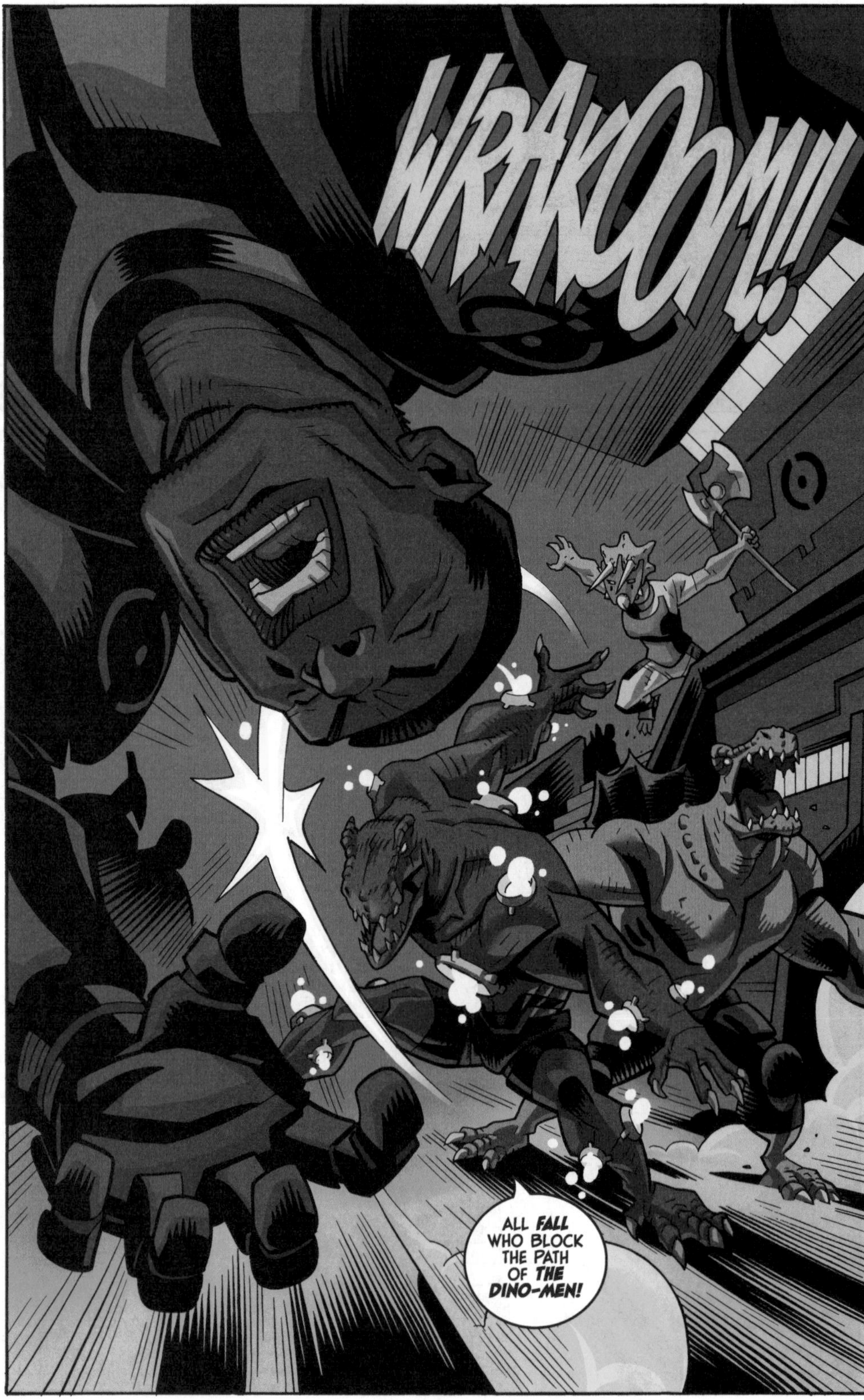
WRAKOOM!!!
ALL FALL WHO BLOCK THE PATH OF THE DINO-MEN!

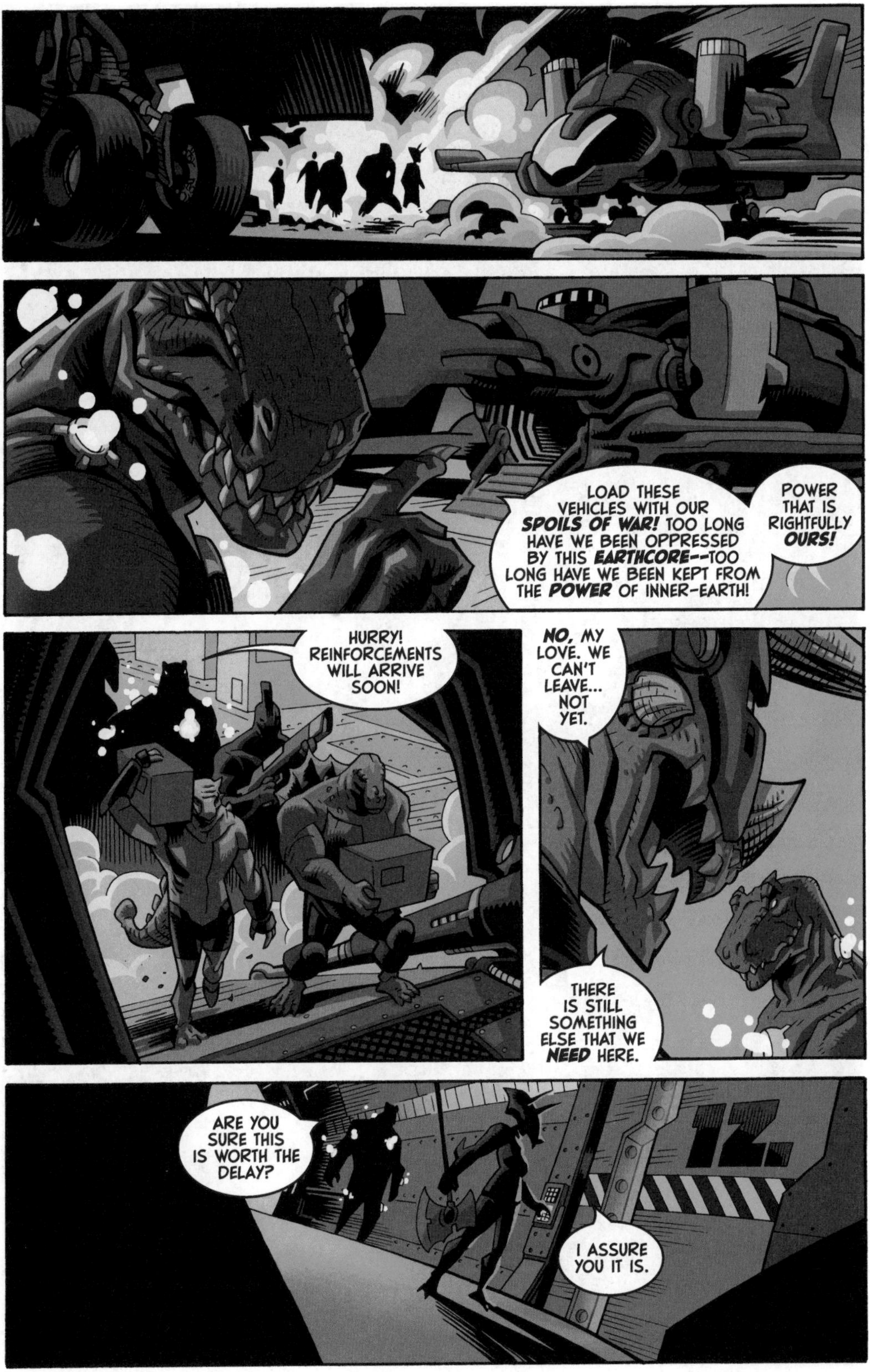
LOAD THESE VEHICLES WITH OUR SPOILS OF WAR! TOO LONG HAVE WE BEEN OPPRESSED BY THIS EARTHCORE--TOO LONG HAVE WE BEEN KEPT FROM THE POWER OF INNER-EARTH!
POWER THAT IS RIGHTFULLY OURS!
HURRY! REINFORCEMENTS WILL ARRIVE SOON!
NO, MY LOVE. WE CAN'T LEAVE... NOT YET.
THERE IS STILL SOMETHING ELSE THAT WE NEED HERE.
ARE YOU SURE THIS IS WORTH THE DELAY?
I ASSURE YOU IT IS.
12

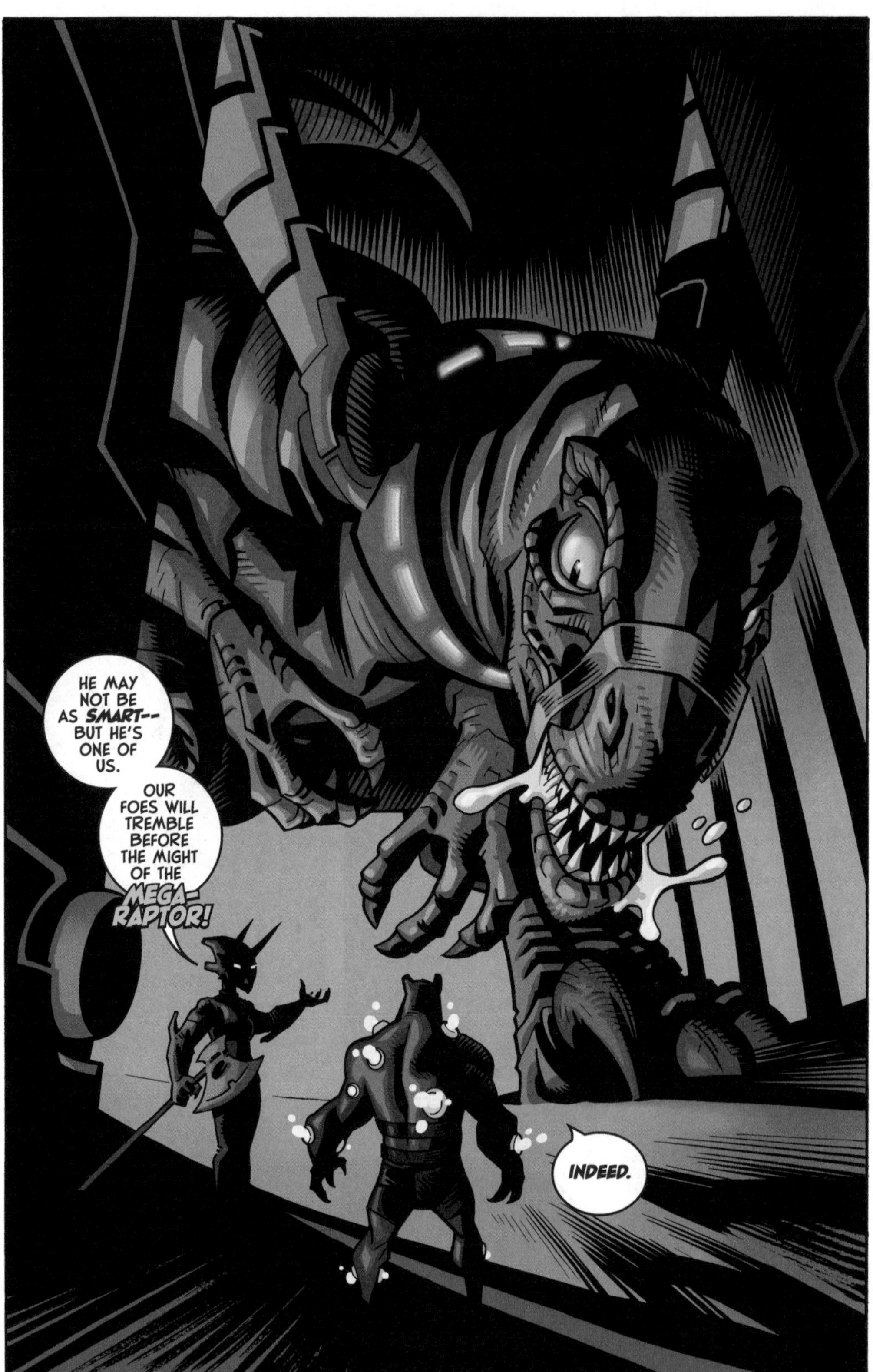
HE MAY NOT BE AS SMART-- BUT HE'S ONE OF US.
OUR FOES WILL TREMBLE BEFORE THE MIGHT OF THE MEGA-RAPTOR!
INDEED.

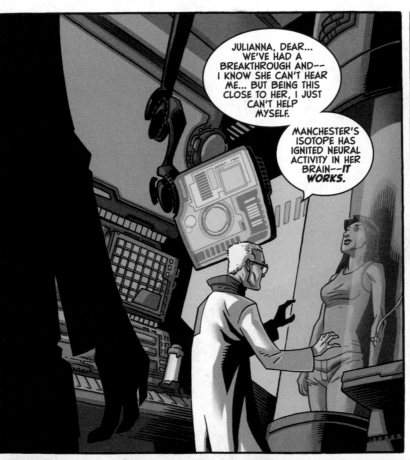

JULIANNA, DEAR... WE'VE HAD A BREAKTHROUGH AND-- I KNOW SHE CAN'T HEAR ME... BUT BEING THIS CLOSE TO HER, I JUST CAN'T HELP MYSELF.

MANCHESTER'S ISOTOPE HAS IGNITED NEURAL ACTIVITY IN HER BRAIN--*IT WORKS.*

THE ONLY PROBLEM IS...

WE DON'T HAVE ENOUGH OF IT. MORE IS NEEDED TO FULLY ACTIVATE HER HIGHER BRAIN FUNCTIONS... TO WAKE HER UP.

BUT I'M *NOT* GIVING UP... NOT AFTER COMING THIS CLOSE.

I WON'T GIVE UP ON YOU, MY LOVE.

"I'VE CONTACTED MANCHESTER. HE'S FAMILIAR WITH THIS ISOTOPE HE GOT FROM MAXIMUS... HE THINKS HE KNOWS WHERE WE CAN FIND MORE.
"DEREK AND SUPER DINOSAUR ARE CURRENTLY EN ROUTE."

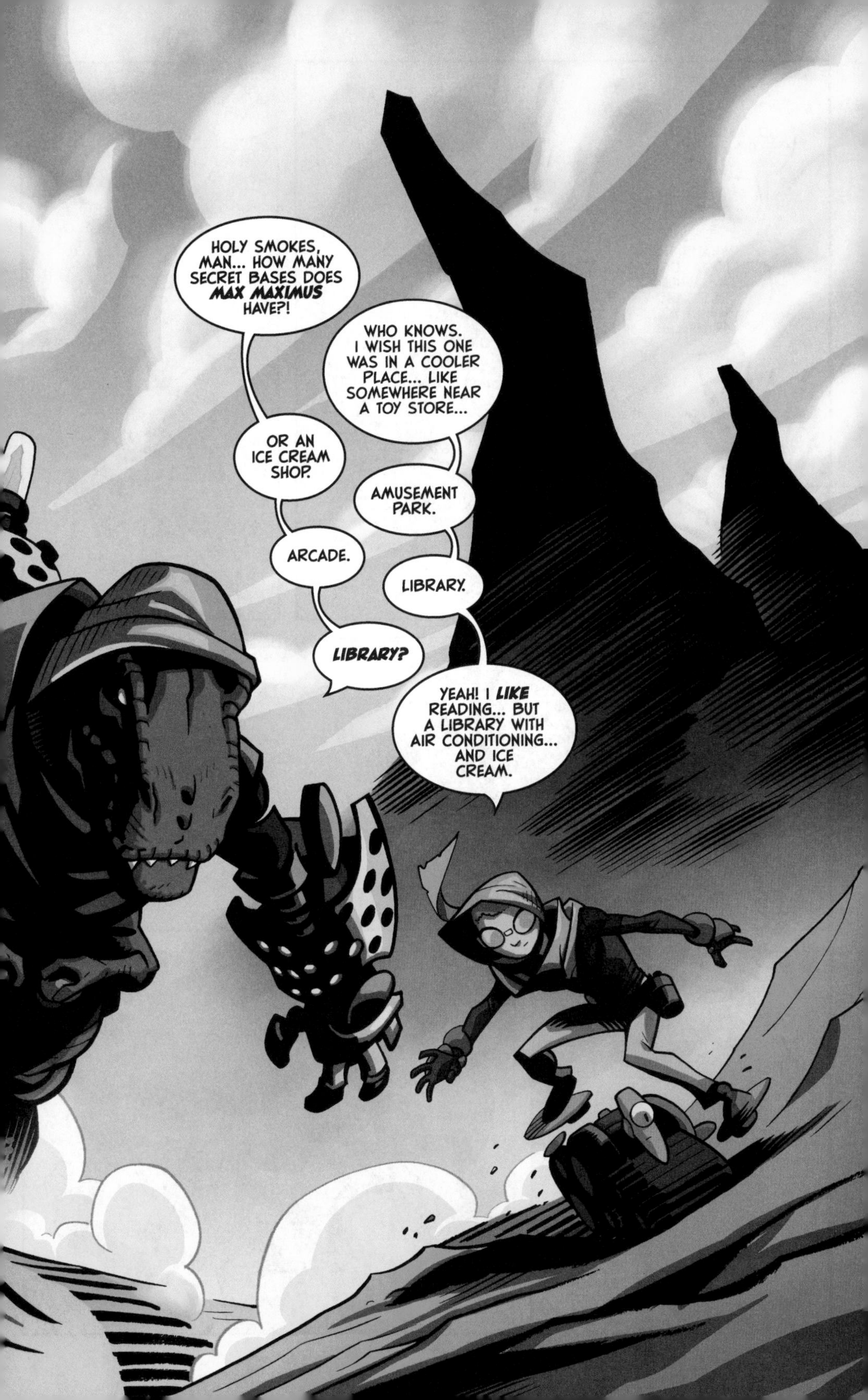
HOLY SMOKES, MAN... HOW MANY SECRET BASES DOES **MAX MAXIMUS** HAVE?!
WHO KNOWS. I WISH THIS ONE WAS IN A COOLER PLACE... LIKE SOMEWHERE NEAR A TOY STORE...
OR AN ICE CREAM SHOP.
AMUSEMENT PARK.
ARCADE.
LIBRARY.
LIBRARY?
YEAH! I **LIKE** READING... BUT A LIBRARY WITH AIR CONDITIONING... AND ICE CREAM.

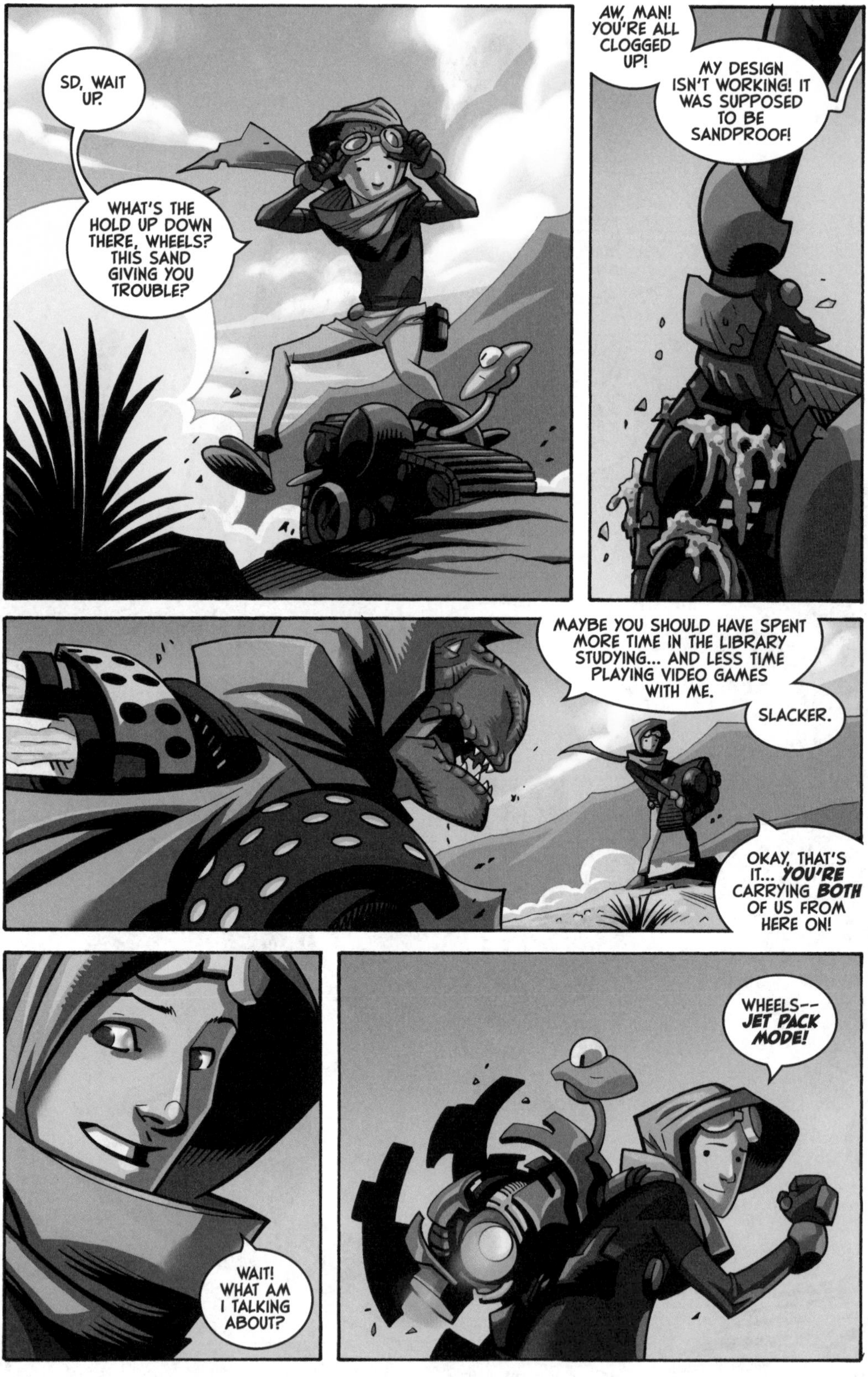
SD, WAIT UP.
WHAT'S THE HOLD UP DOWN THERE, WHEELS? THIS SAND GIVING YOU TROUBLE?
AW, MAN! YOU'RE ALL CLOGGED UP!
MY DESIGN ISN'T WORKING! IT WAS SUPPOSED TO BE SANDPROOF!
MAYBE YOU SHOULD HAVE SPENT MORE TIME IN THE LIBRARY STUDYING... AND LESS TIME PLAYING VIDEO GAMES WITH ME.
SLACKER.
OKAY, THAT'S IT... *YOU'RE* CARRYING *BOTH* OF US FROM HERE ON!
WAIT! WHAT AM I TALKING ABOUT?
WHEELS-- *JET PACK MODE!*

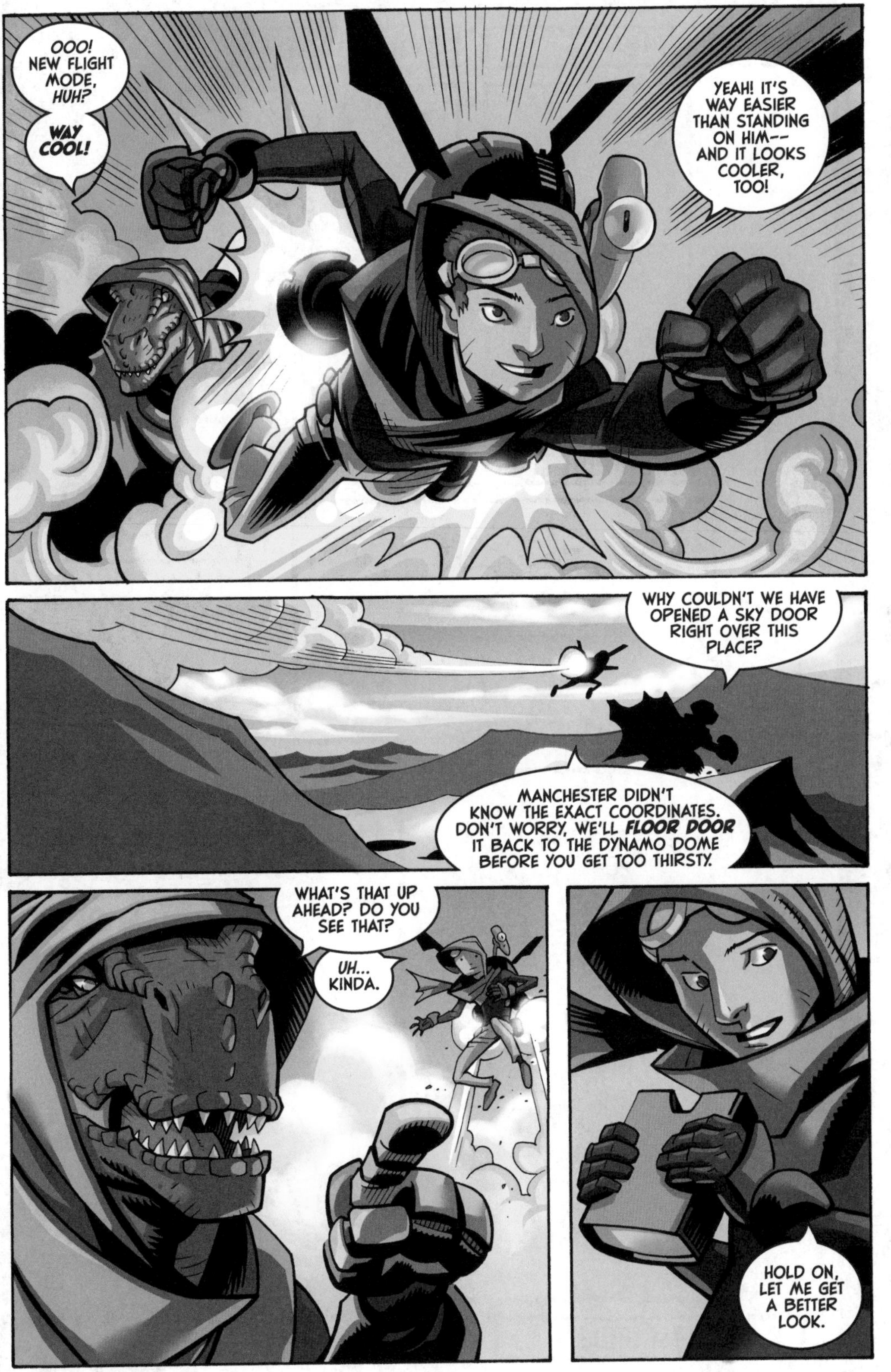
OOO! NEW FLIGHT MODE, HUH?
WAY COOL!
YEAH! IT'S WAY EASIER THAN STANDING ON HIM-- AND IT LOOKS COOLER, TOO!
WHY COULDN'T WE HAVE OPENED A SKY DOOR RIGHT OVER THIS PLACE?
MANCHESTER DIDN'T KNOW THE EXACT COORDINATES. DON'T WORRY, WE'LL FLOOR DOOR IT BACK TO THE DYNAMO DOME BEFORE YOU GET TOO THIRSTY.
WHAT'S THAT UP AHEAD? DO YOU SEE THAT?
UH... KINDA.
HOLD ON, LET ME GET A BETTER LOOK.

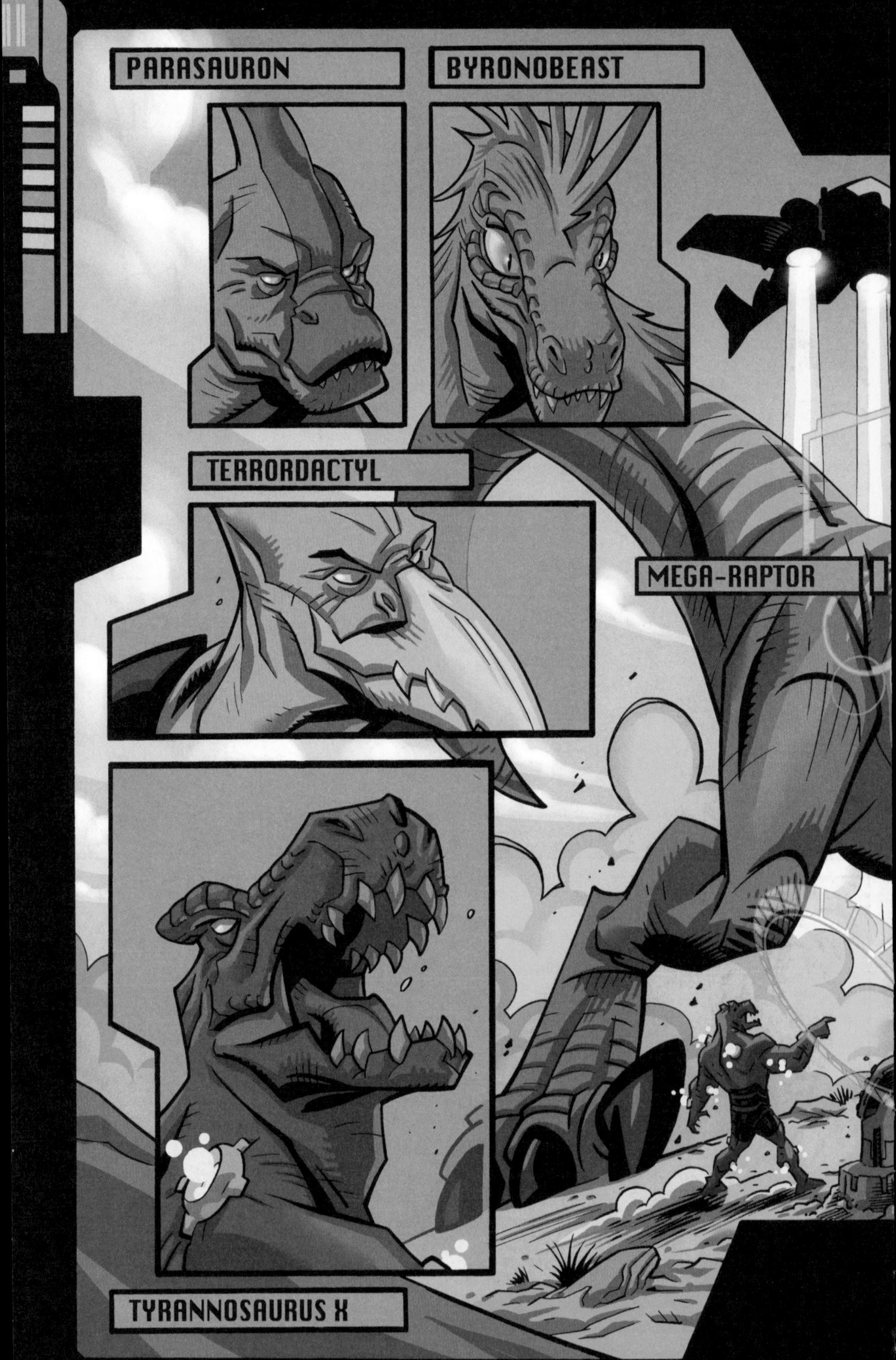
PARASAURON
BYRONOBEAST
TERRORDACTYL
MEGA-RAPTOR
TYRANNOSAURUS X

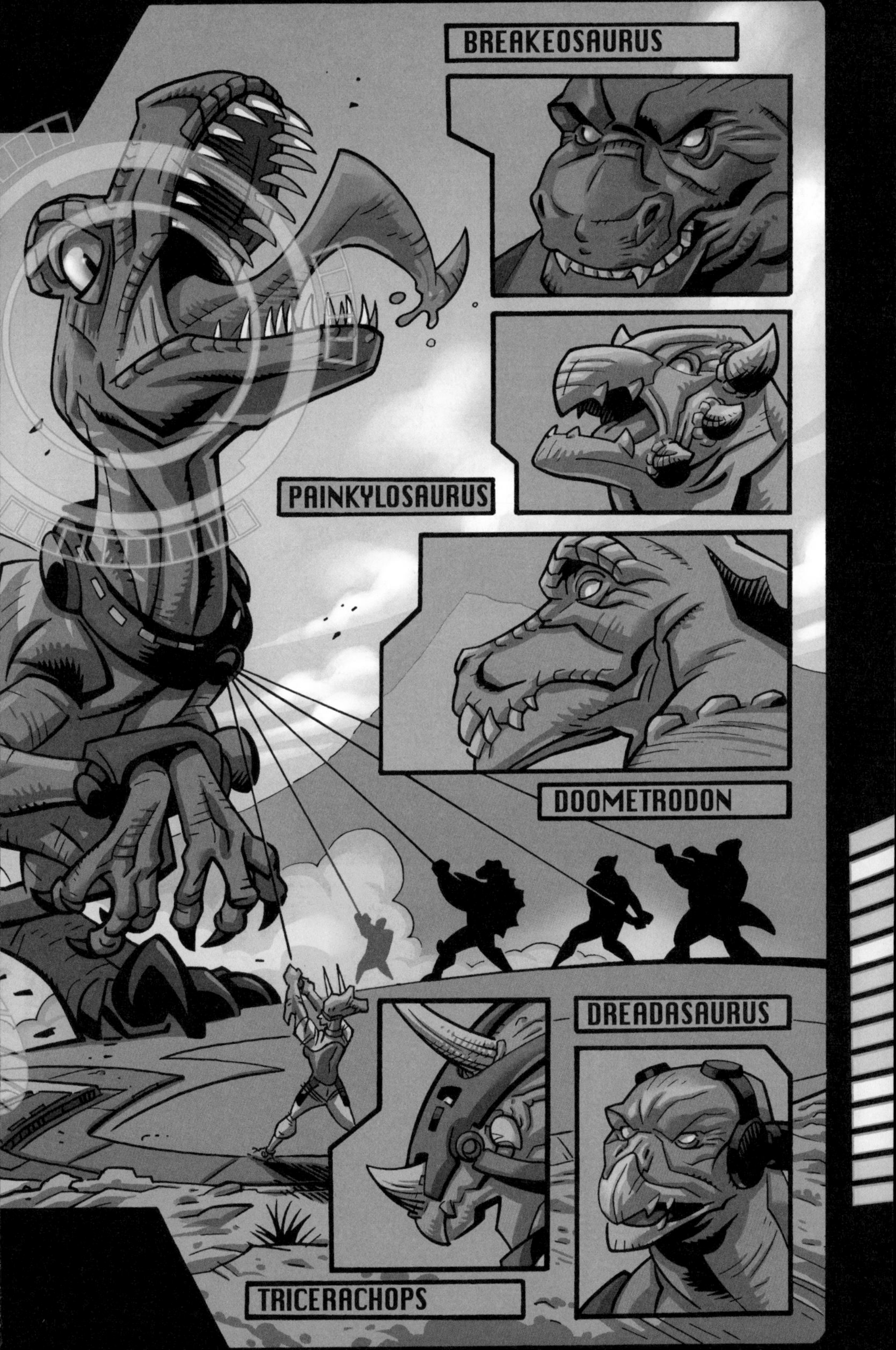
BREAKEOSAURUS
PAINKYLOSAURUS
DOOMETRODON
DREADASAURUS
TRICERACHOPS

WHAT?! WHAT IS IT? **TELL ME!**

IT'S THE BASE! I CAN SEE IT-- BUT ALL THE **DINO-MEN** ARE THERE! AND THEY'RE LEADING THE **MEGA-RAPTOR** INSIDE!

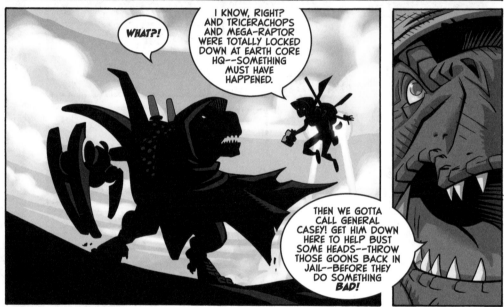

WHAT?!

I KNOW, RIGHT? AND TRICERACHOPS AND MEGA-RAPTOR WERE TOTALLY LOCKED DOWN AT EARTH CORE HQ--SOMETHING MUST HAVE HAPPENED.

THEN WE GOTTA CALL GENERAL CASEY! GET HIM DOWN HERE TO HELP BUST SOME HEADS--THROW THOSE GOONS BACK IN JAIL--BEFORE THEY DO SOMETHING **BAD!**

SO... WHAT ARE WE GOING TO DO?

WE SNEAK IN--GET THE ANTIDOTE ON OUR OWN.

THEN WE CALL IN THE CAVALRY!

RAD!

NO! THE ANTIDOTE FOR **MY MOM** IS IN THERE!

IF THERE WAS A BATTLE-- IT COULD GET DESTROYED-- THE **WHOLE PLACE** COULD!

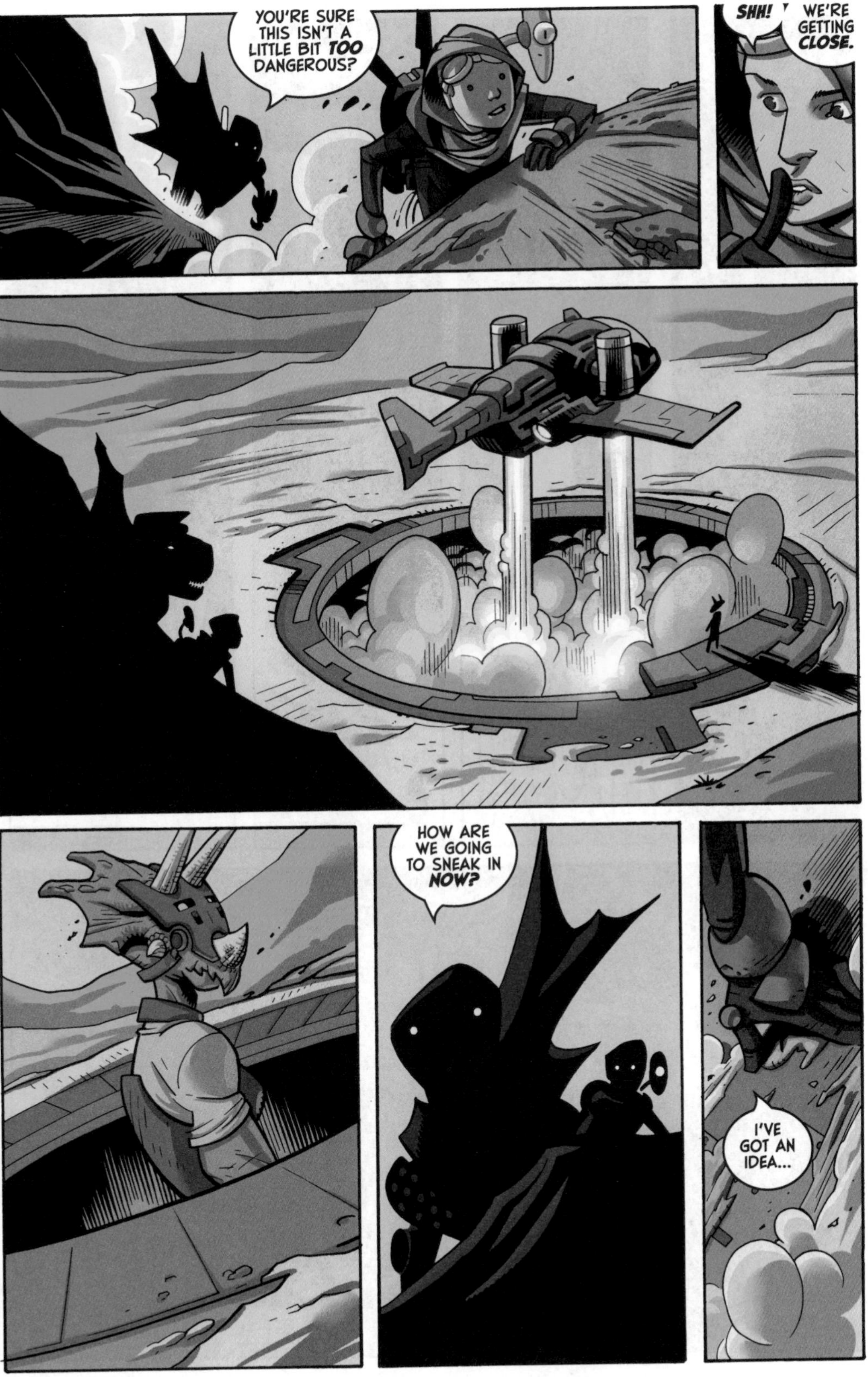
YOU'RE SURE THIS ISN'T A LITTLE BIT TOO DANGEROUS?
SHH!
WE'RE GETTING CLOSE.
HOW ARE WE GOING TO SNEAK IN NOW?
I'VE GOT AN IDEA...

PSSSH!

PSSSSH!

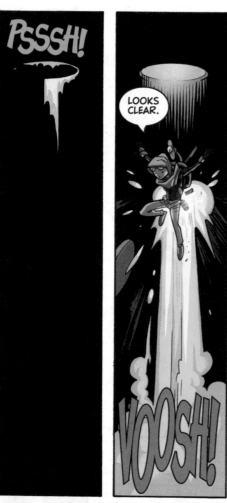

LOOKS CLEAR.

VOOSH!

WHOA!

OKAY!

VOOSH!

OKAY, SMART GUY... WHERE TO?

I DON'T KNOW, UH...

GIVE ME A MINUTE.

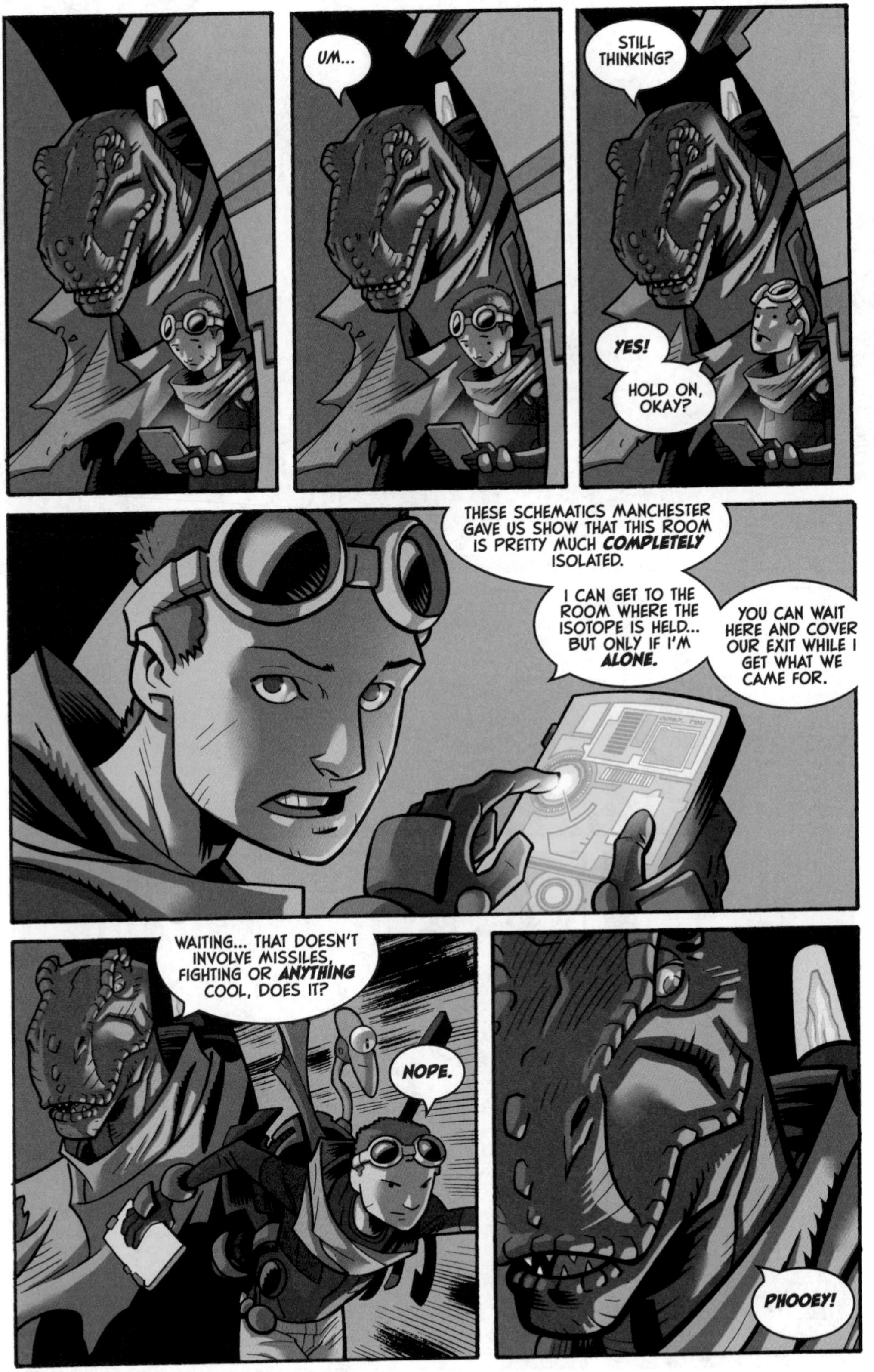
UM...
STILL THINKING?
YES!
HOLD ON, OKAY?
THESE SCHEMATICS MANCHESTER GAVE US SHOW THAT THIS ROOM IS PRETTY MUCH COMPLETELY ISOLATED.
I CAN GET TO THE ROOM WHERE THE ISOTOPE IS HELD... BUT ONLY IF I'M ALONE.
YOU CAN WAIT HERE AND COVER OUR EXIT WHILE I GET WHAT WE CAME FOR.
WAITING... THAT DOESN'T INVOLVE MISSILES, FIGHTING OR ANYTHING COOL, DOES IT?
NOPE.
PHOOEY!

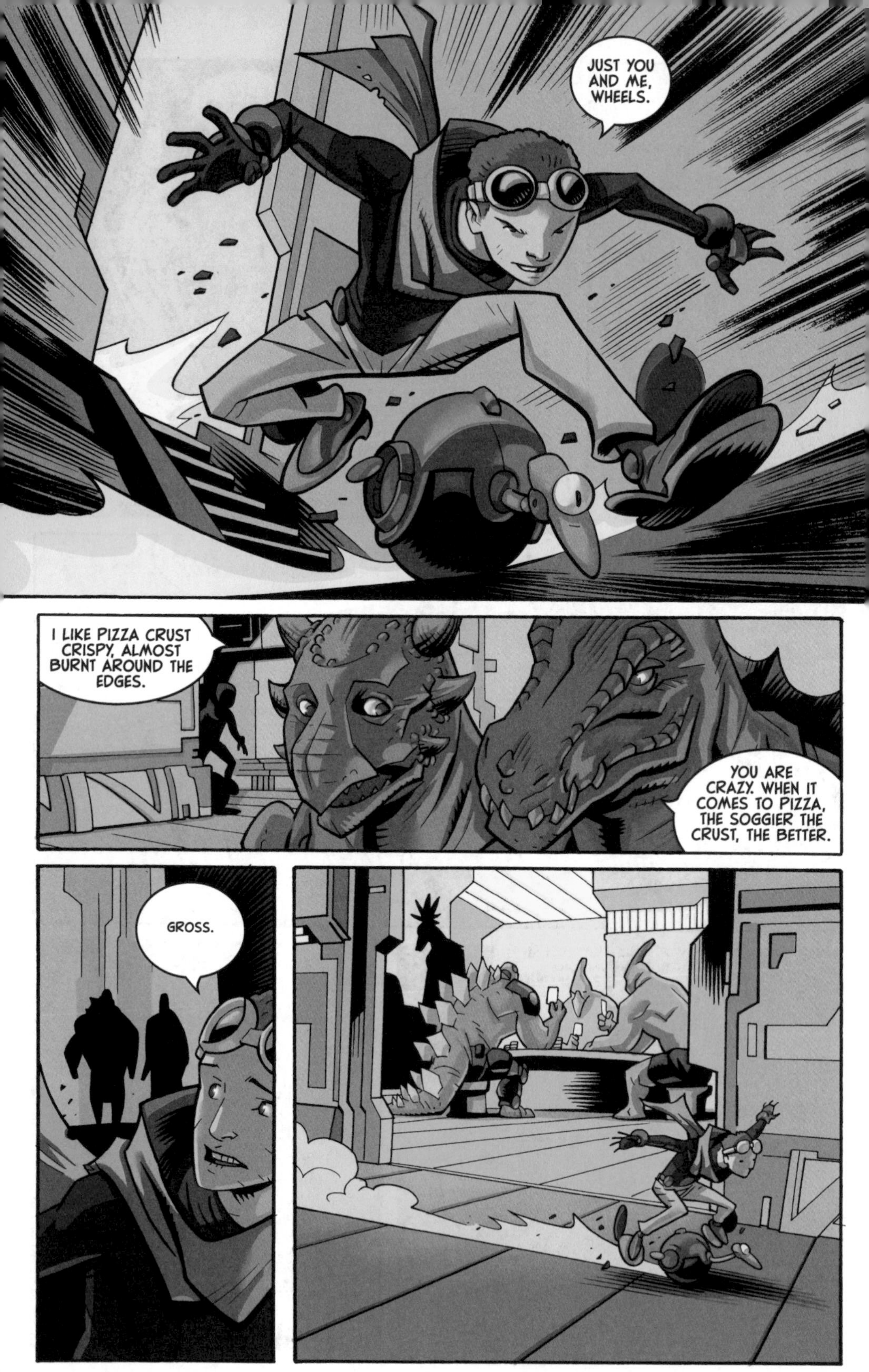
JUST YOU AND ME, WHEELS.
I LIKE PIZZA CRUST CRISPY, ALMOST BURNT AROUND THE EDGES.
YOU ARE CRAZY. WHEN IT COMES TO PIZZA, THE SOGGIER THE CRUST, THE BETTER.
GROSS.

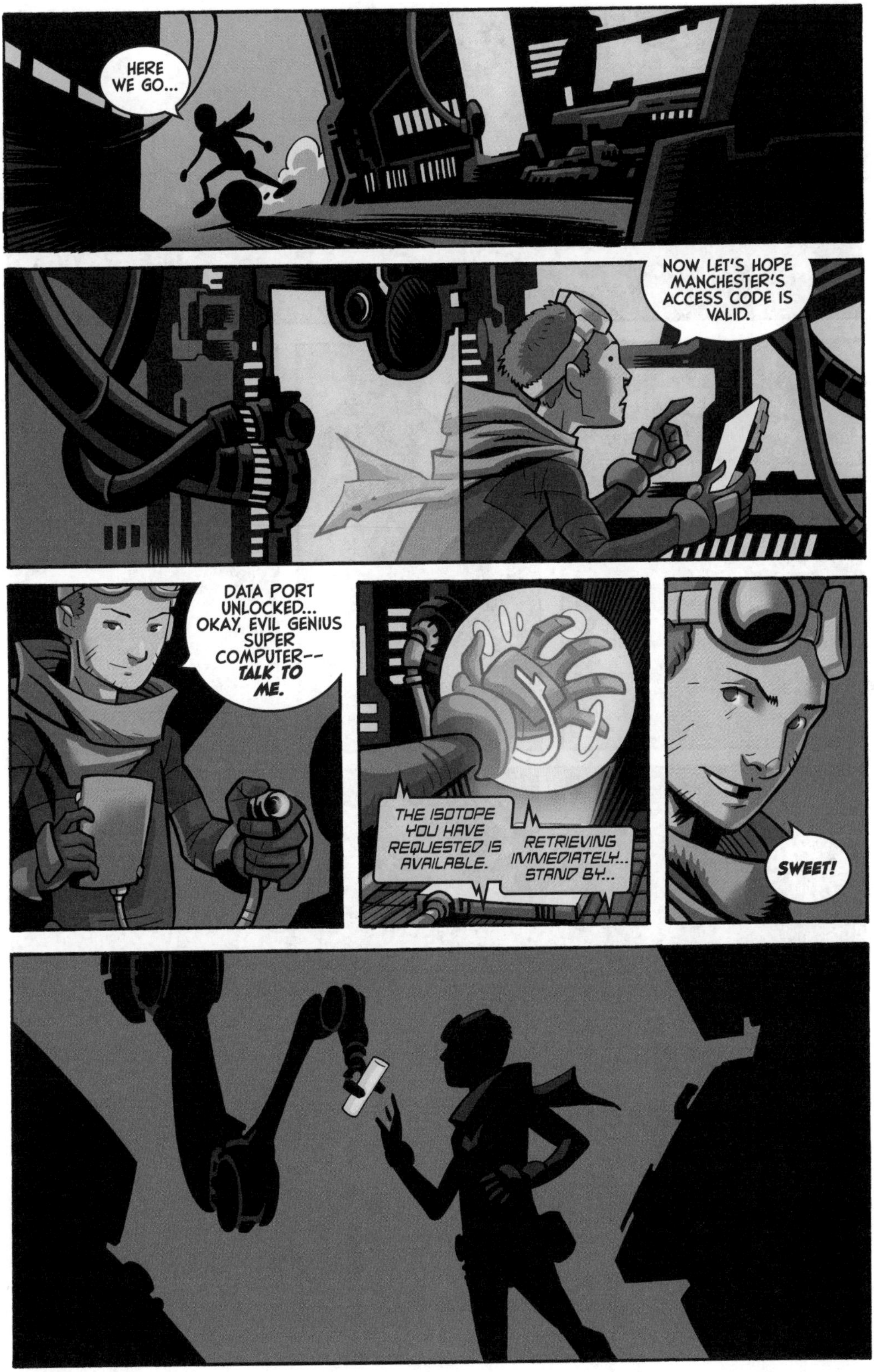
HERE WE GO...
NOW LET'S HOPE MANCHESTER'S ACCESS CODE IS VALID.
DATA PORT UNLOCKED... OKAY, EVIL GENIUS SUPER COMPUTER-- *TALK TO ME.*
THE ISOTOPE YOU HAVE REQUESTED IS AVAILABLE.
RETRIEVING IMMEDIATELY... STAND BY...
SWEET!

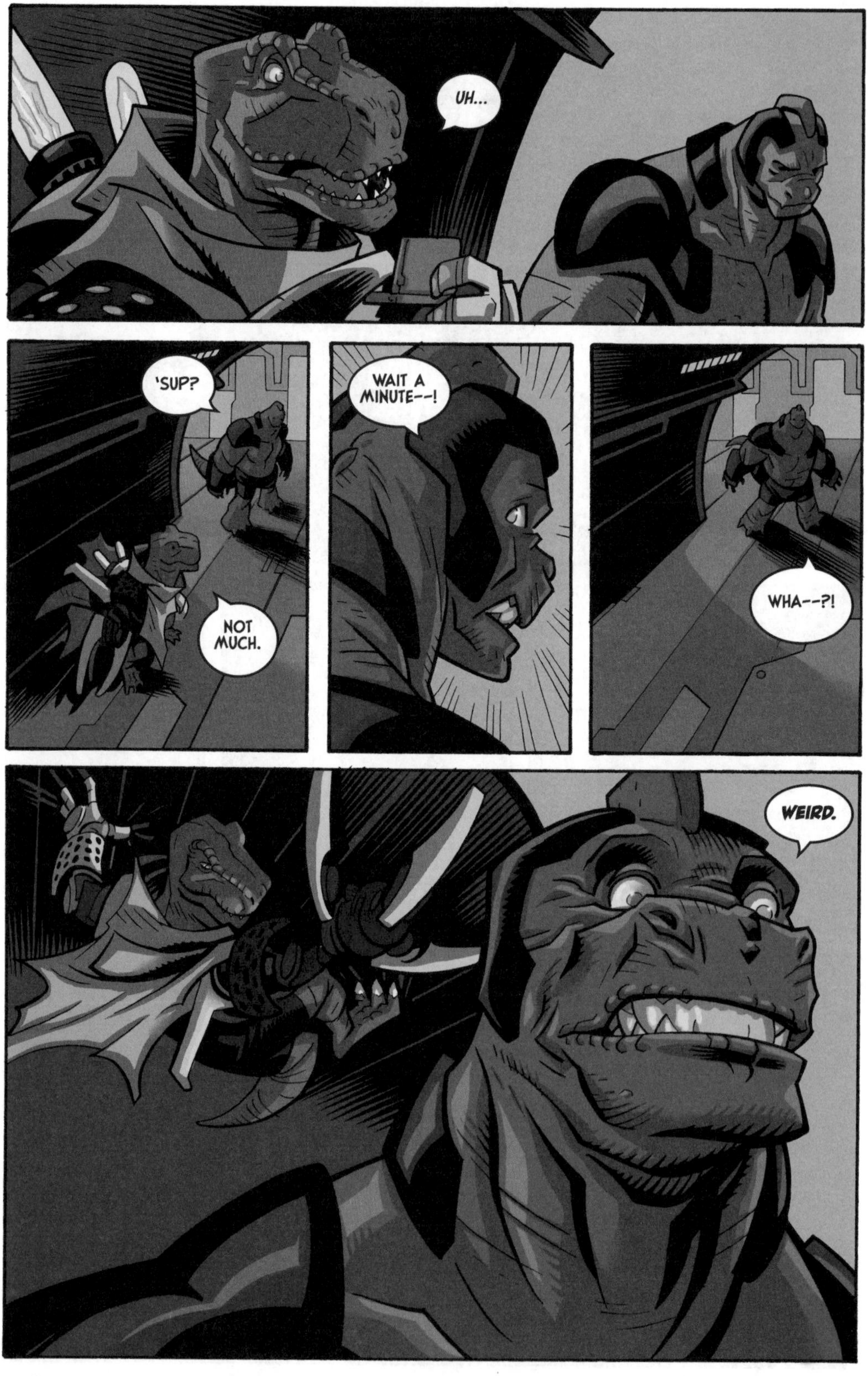
UH...
'SUP?
NOT MUCH.
WAIT A MINUTE--!
WHA--?!
WEIRD.

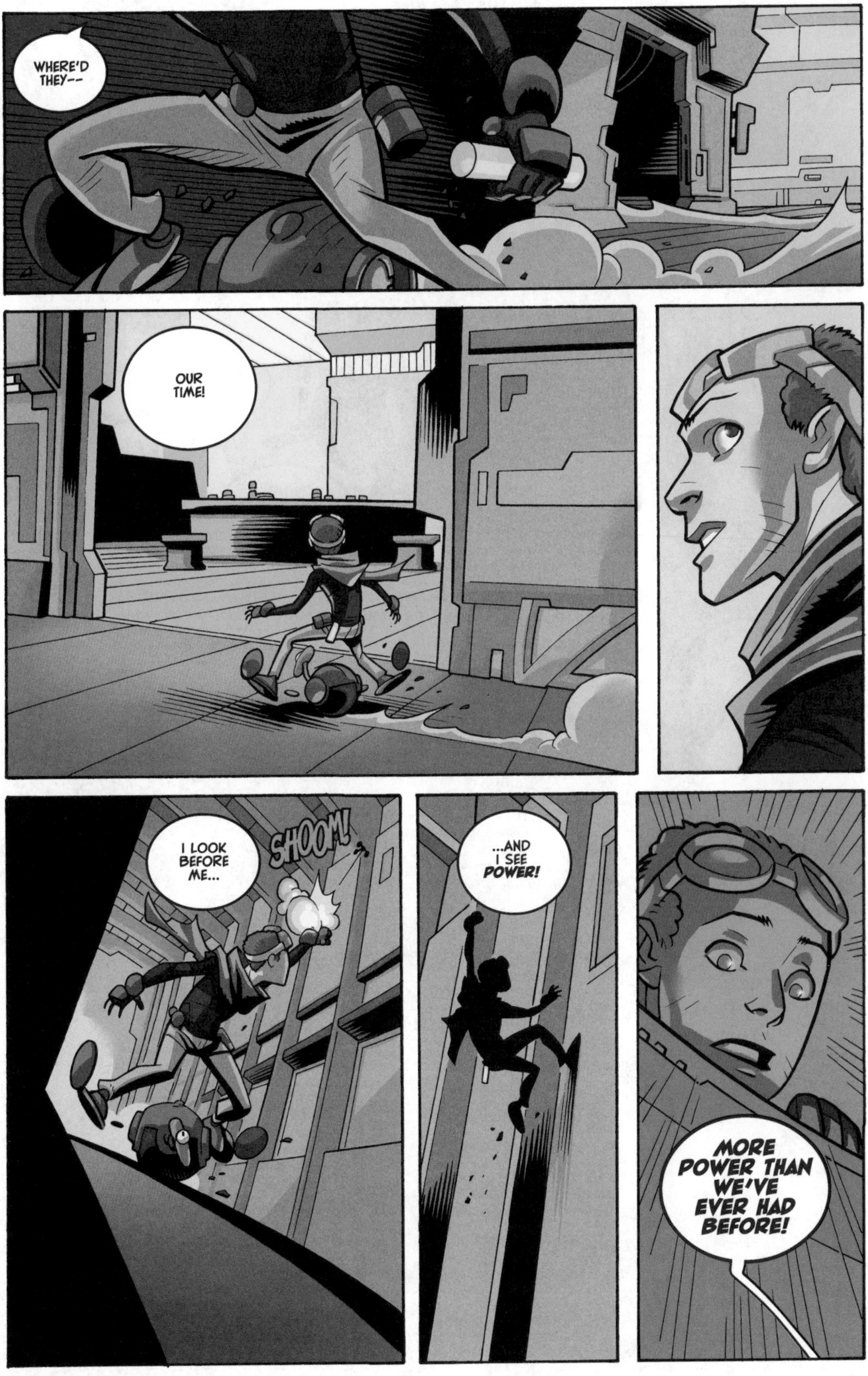
WHERE'D THEY--
OUR TIME!
I LOOK BEFORE ME...
SHOOM!
...AND I SEE POWER!
MORE POWER THAN WE'VE EVER HAD BEFORE!

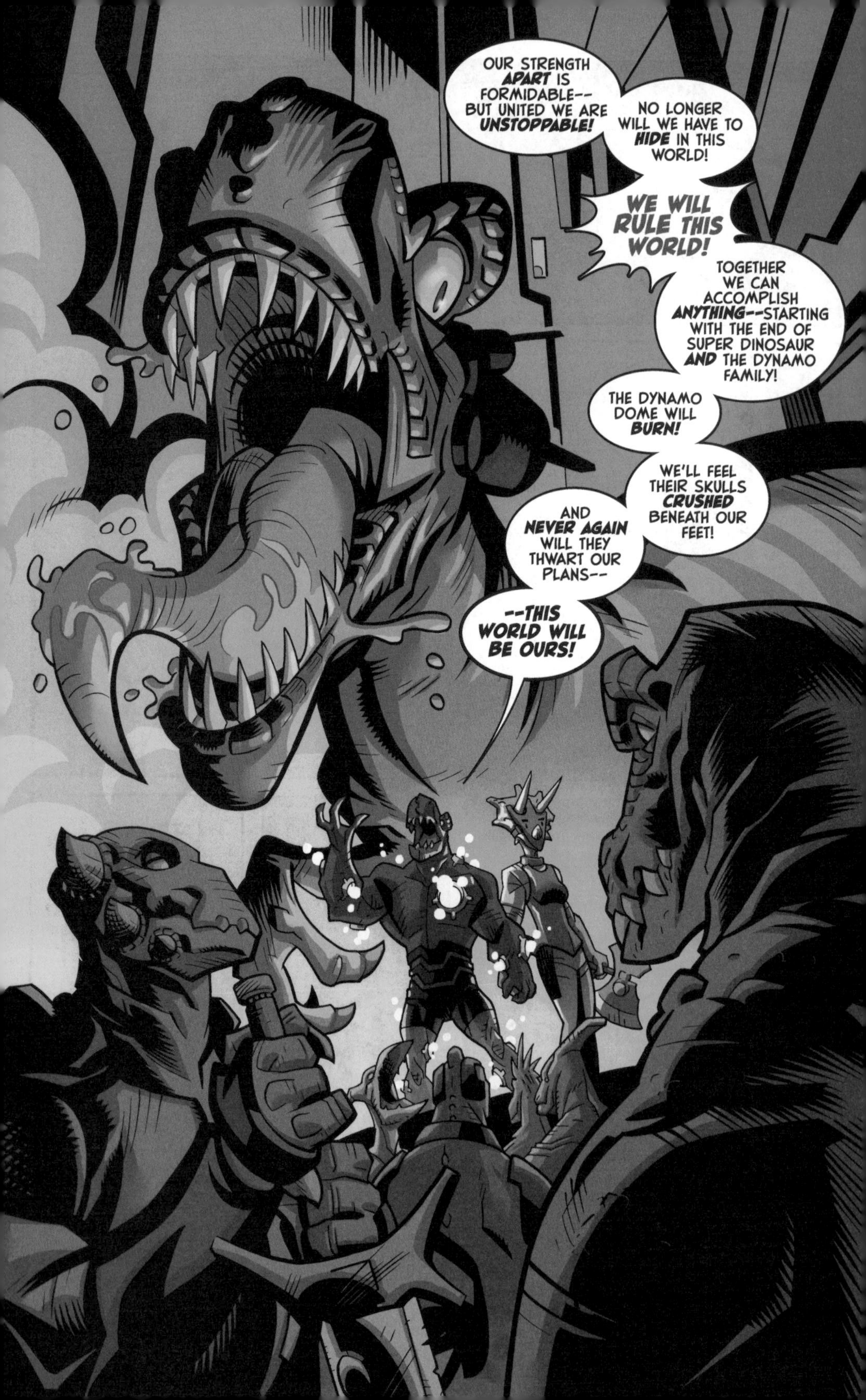
OUR STRENGTH APART IS FORMIDABLE-- BUT UNITED WE ARE UNSTOPPABLE!
NO LONGER WILL WE HAVE TO HIDE IN THIS WORLD!
WE WILL RULE THIS WORLD!
TOGETHER WE CAN ACCOMPLISH ANYTHING--STARTING WITH THE END OF SUPER DINOSAUR AND THE DYNAMO FAMILY!
THE DYNAMO DOME WILL BURN!
WE'LL FEEL THEIR SKULLS CRUSHED BENEATH OUR FEET!
AND NEVER AGAIN WILL THEY THWART OUR PLANS--
--THIS WORLD WILL BE OURS!

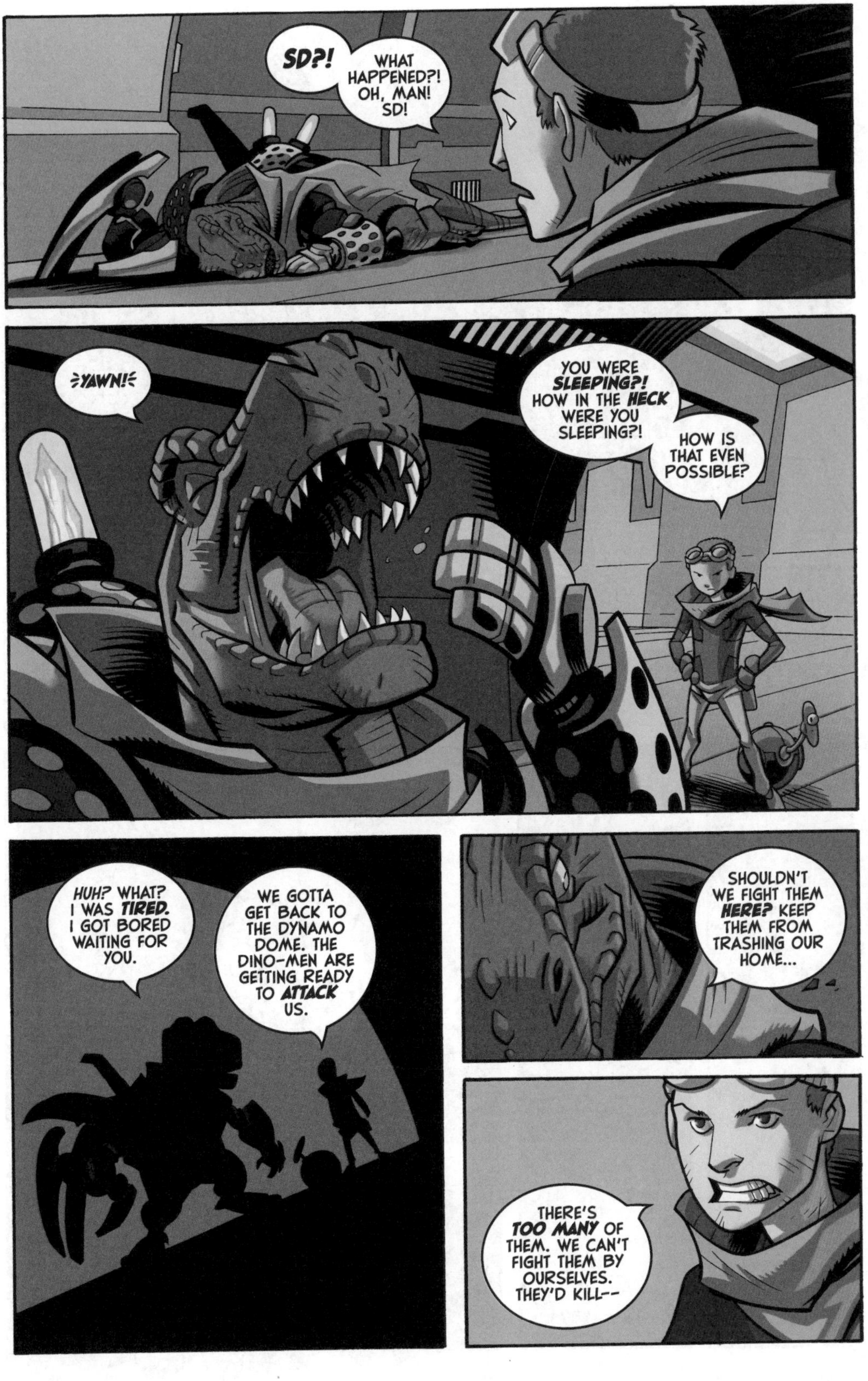

SD?!
WHAT HAPPENED?! OH, MAN! SD!
≷YAWN!≶
YOU WERE SLEEPING?! HOW IN THE HECK WERE YOU SLEEPING?!
HOW IS THAT EVEN POSSIBLE?
HUH? WHAT? I WAS TIRED. I GOT BORED WAITING FOR YOU.
WE GOTTA GET BACK TO THE DYNAMO DOME. THE DINO-MEN ARE GETTING READY TO ATTACK US.
SHOULDN'T WE FIGHT THEM HERE? KEEP THEM FROM TRASHING OUR HOME...
THERE'S TOO MANY OF THEM. WE CAN'T FIGHT THEM BY OURSELVES. THEY'D KILL--

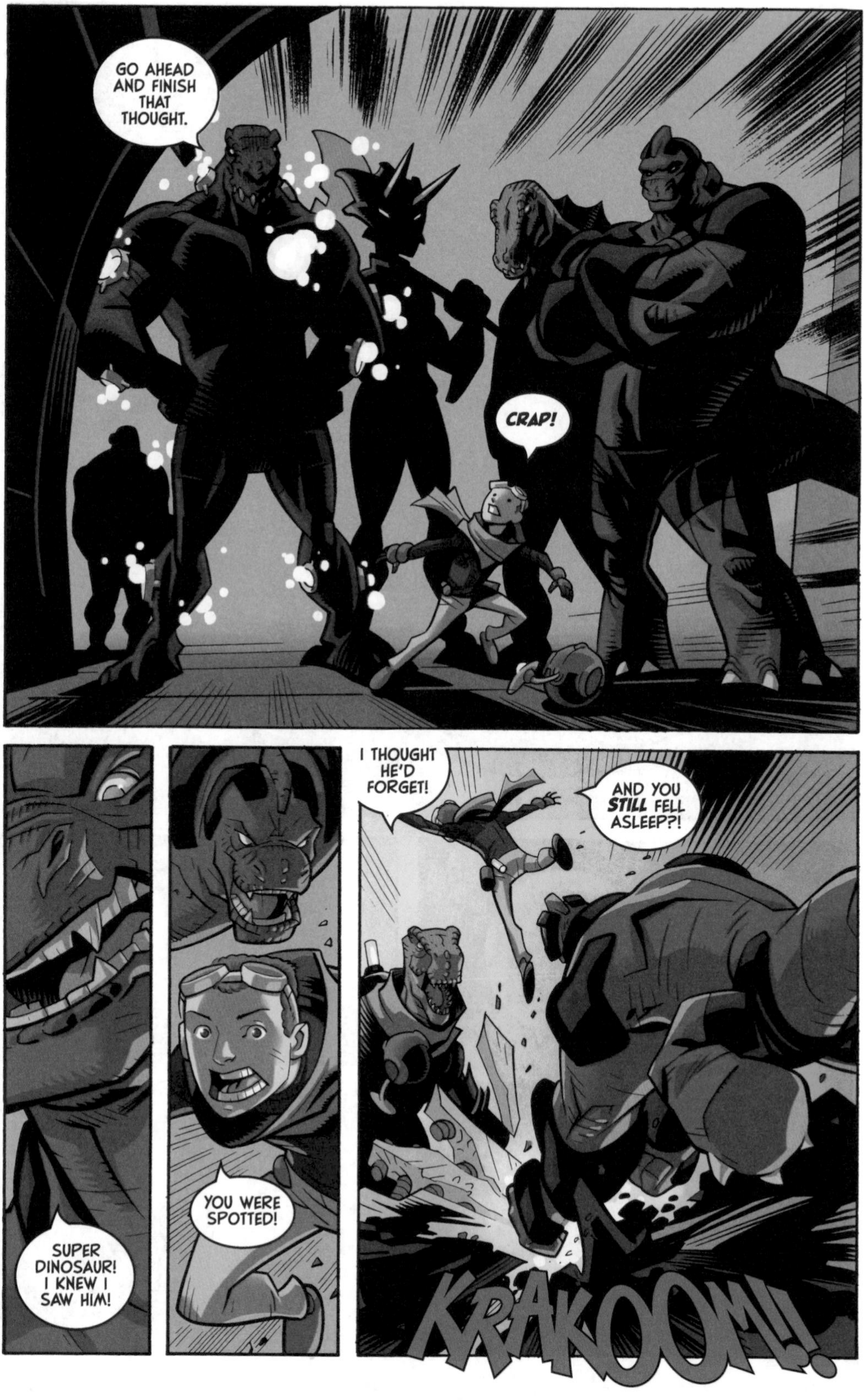
GO AHEAD AND FINISH THAT THOUGHT.
CRAP!
SUPER DINOSAUR! I KNEW I SAW HIM!
YOU WERE SPOTTED!
I THOUGHT HE'D FORGET!
AND YOU STILL FELL ASLEEP?!
KRAKOOM!!

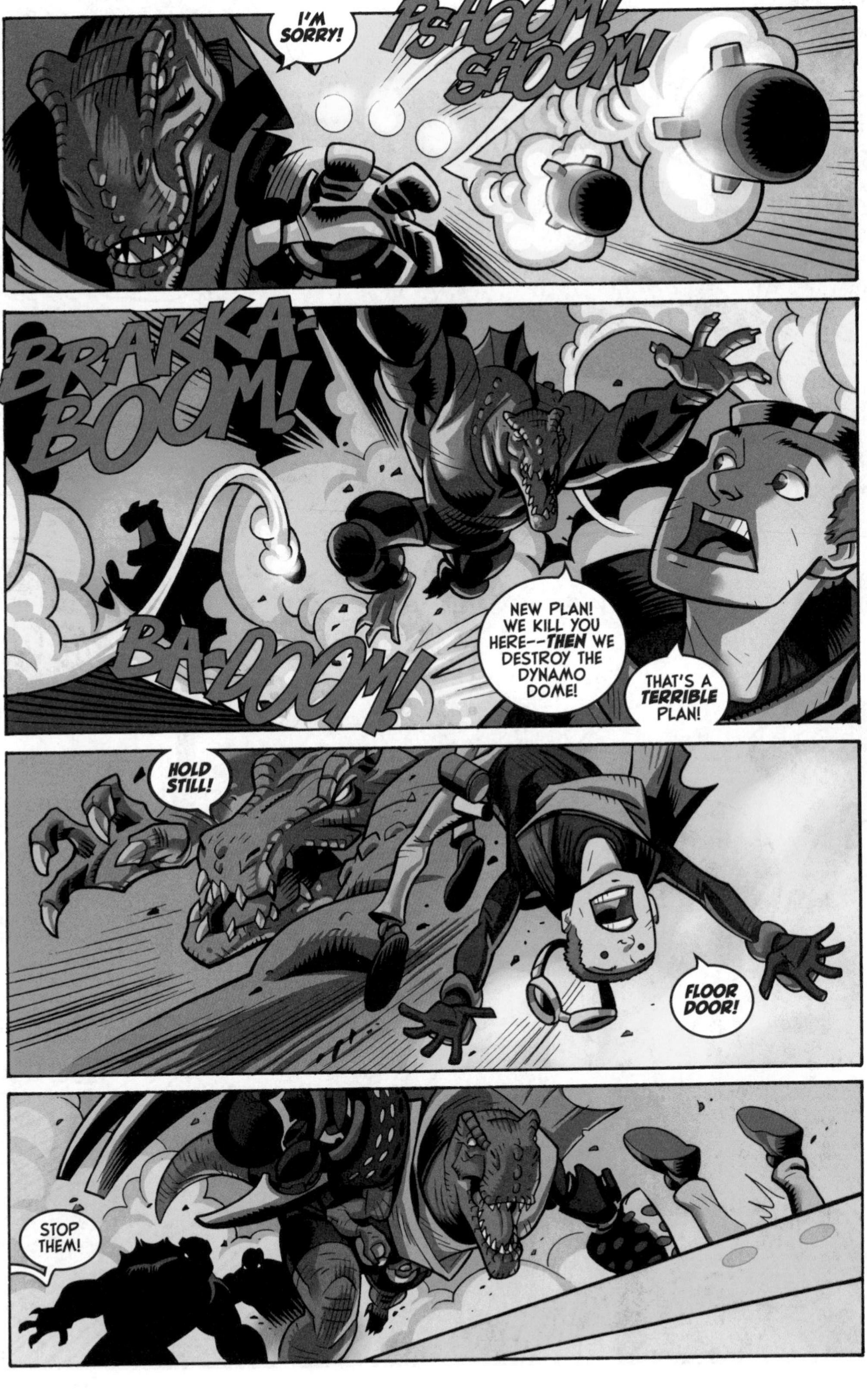
I'M SORRY!
PSHOOM! SHOOM!
BRAKKA-BOOM!
BA-DOOM!
NEW PLAN! WE KILL YOU HERE--THEN WE DESTROY THE DYNAMO DOME!
THAT'S A TERRIBLE PLAN!
HOLD STILL!
FLOOR DOOR!
STOP THEM!

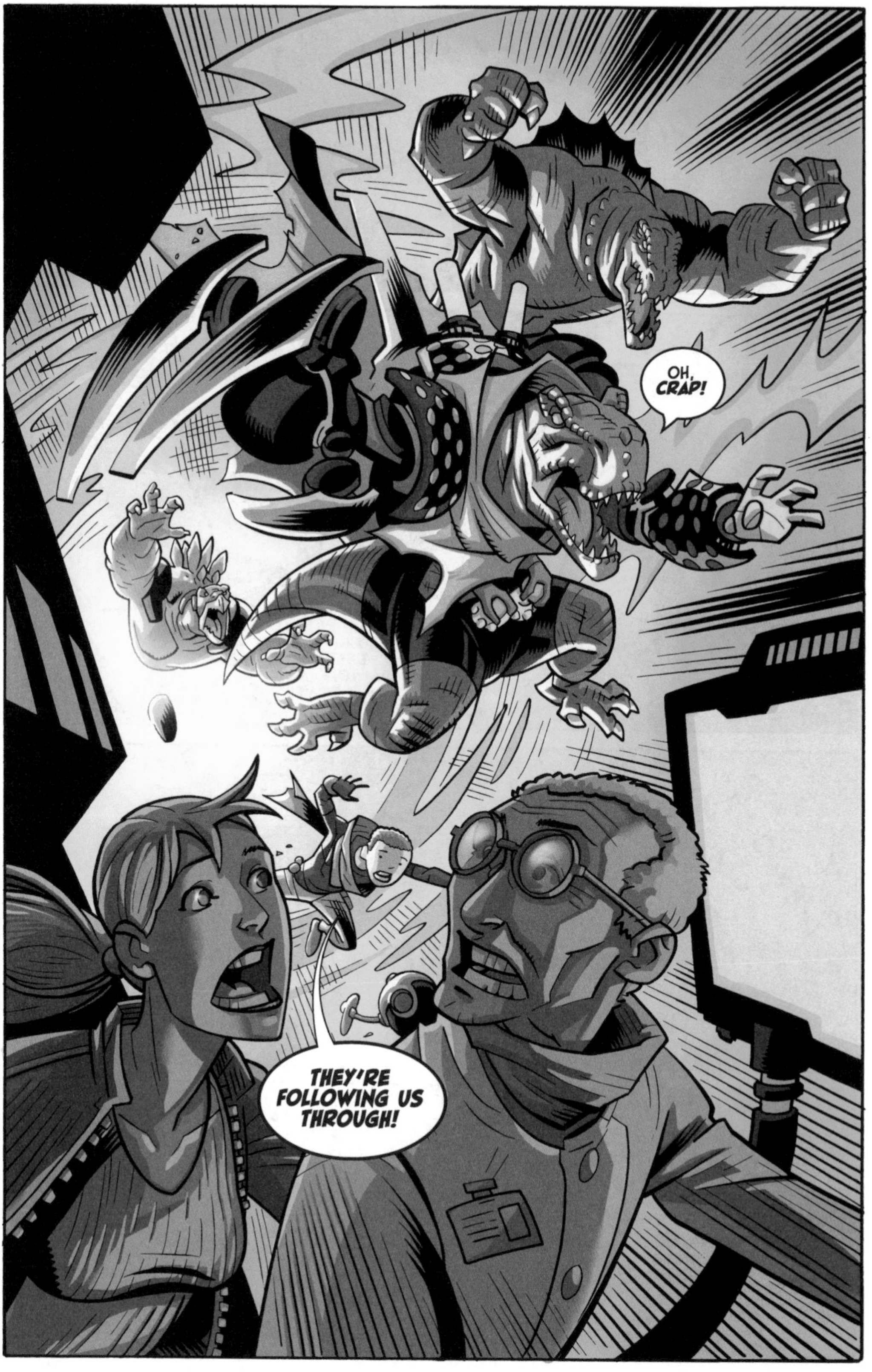
OH, CRAP!
THEY'RE FOLLOWING US THROUGH!

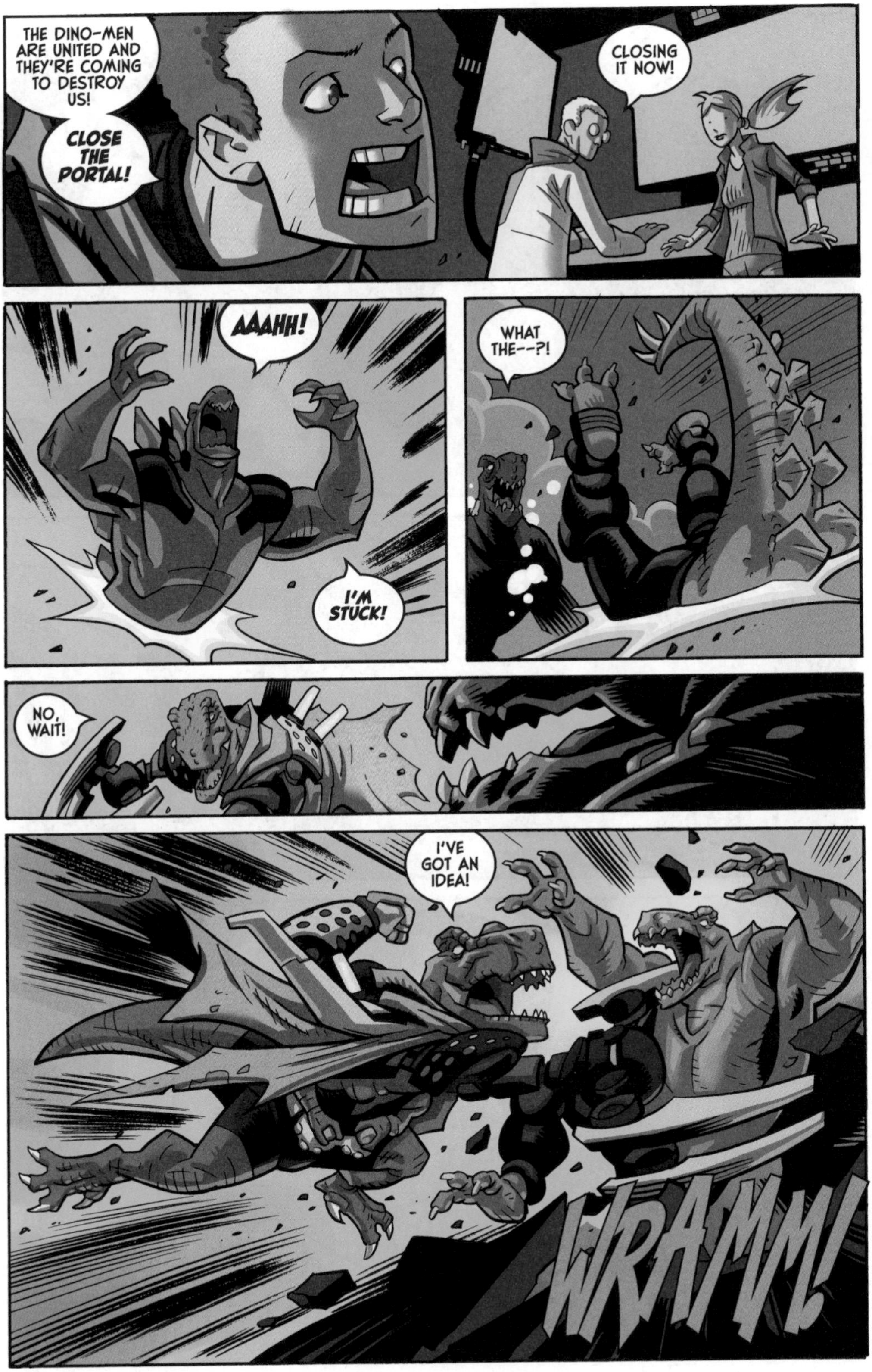
THE DINO-MEN ARE UNITED AND THEY'RE COMING TO DESTROY US!
CLOSE THE PORTAL!
CLOSING IT NOW!
AAAHH!
I'M STUCK!
WHAT THE--?!
NO, WAIT!
I'VE GOT AN IDEA!
WRAMM!

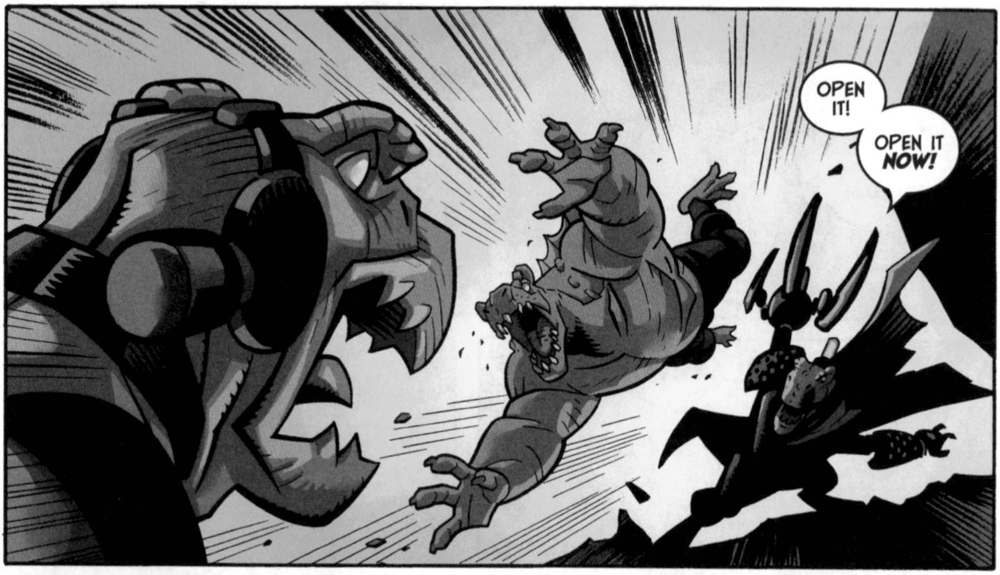
OPEN IT!
OPEN IT NOW!

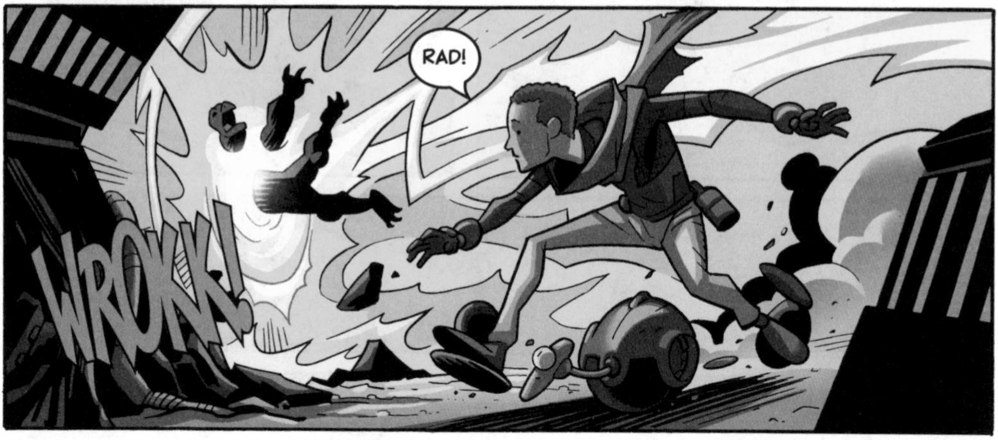
RAD!
WROKK!

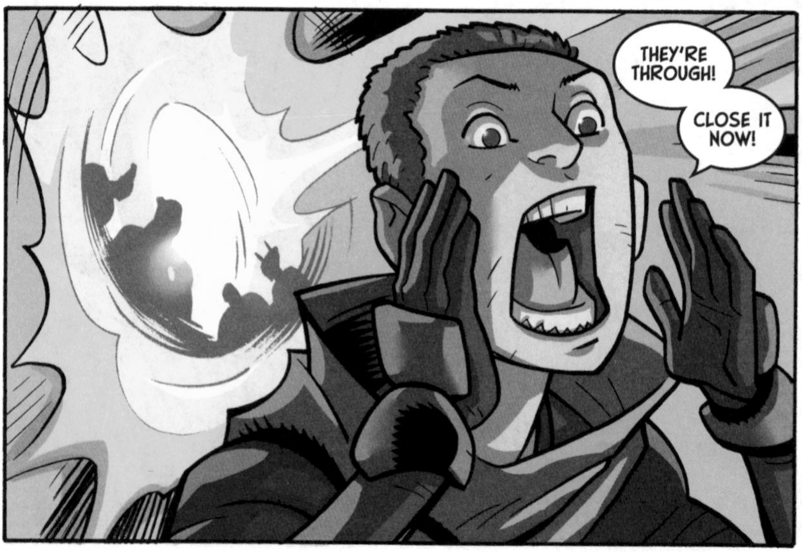
THEY'RE THROUGH!
CLOSE IT NOW!

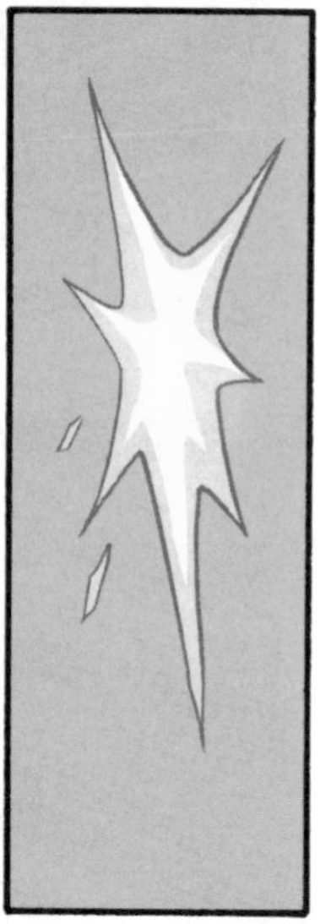

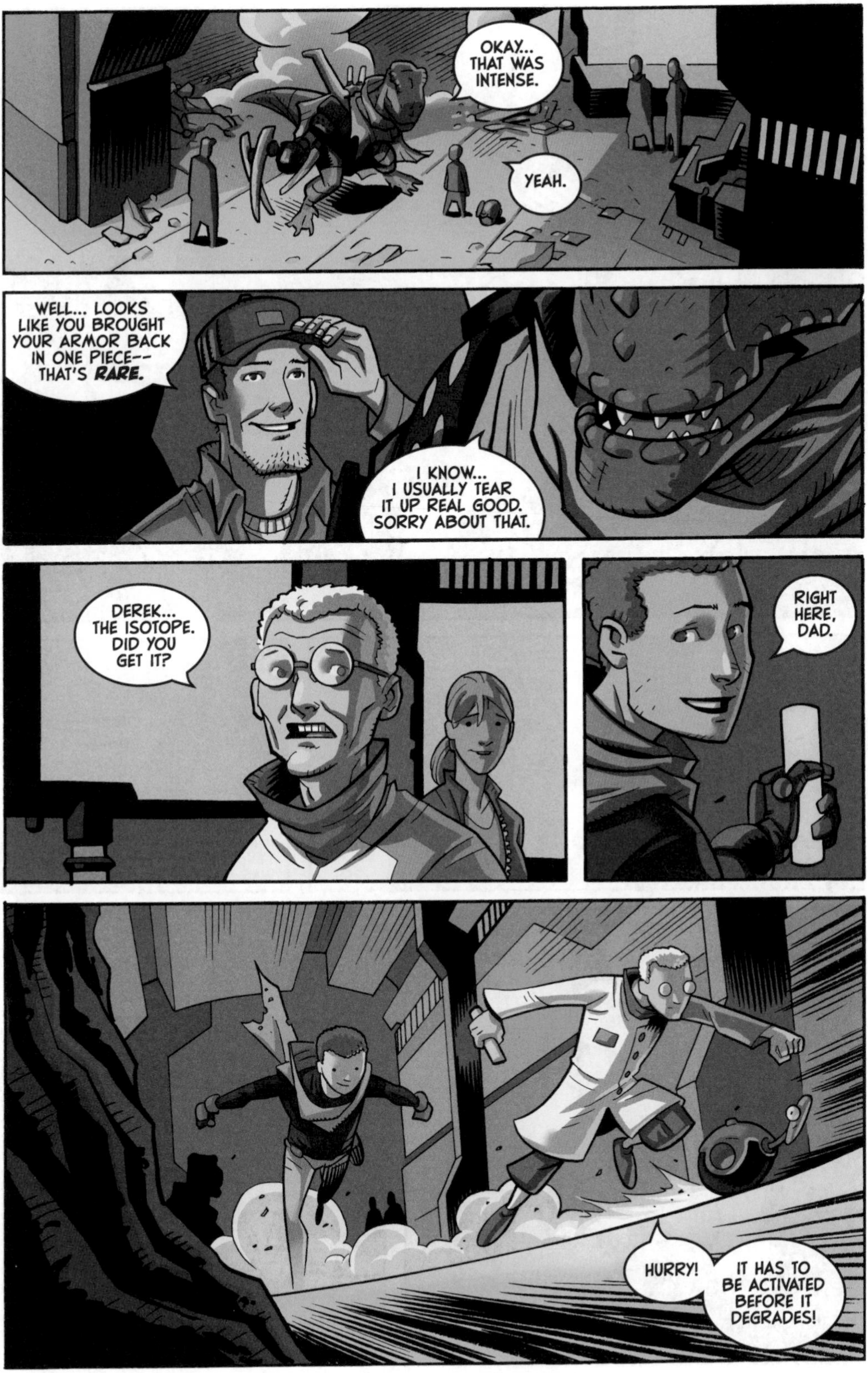
OKAY... THAT WAS INTENSE.
YEAH.
WELL... LOOKS LIKE YOU BROUGHT YOUR ARMOR BACK IN ONE PIECE-- THAT'S RARE.
I KNOW... I USUALLY TEAR IT UP REAL GOOD. SORRY ABOUT THAT.
DEREK... THE ISOTOPE. DID YOU GET IT?
RIGHT HERE, DAD.
HURRY!
IT HAS TO BE ACTIVATED BEFORE IT DEGRADES!

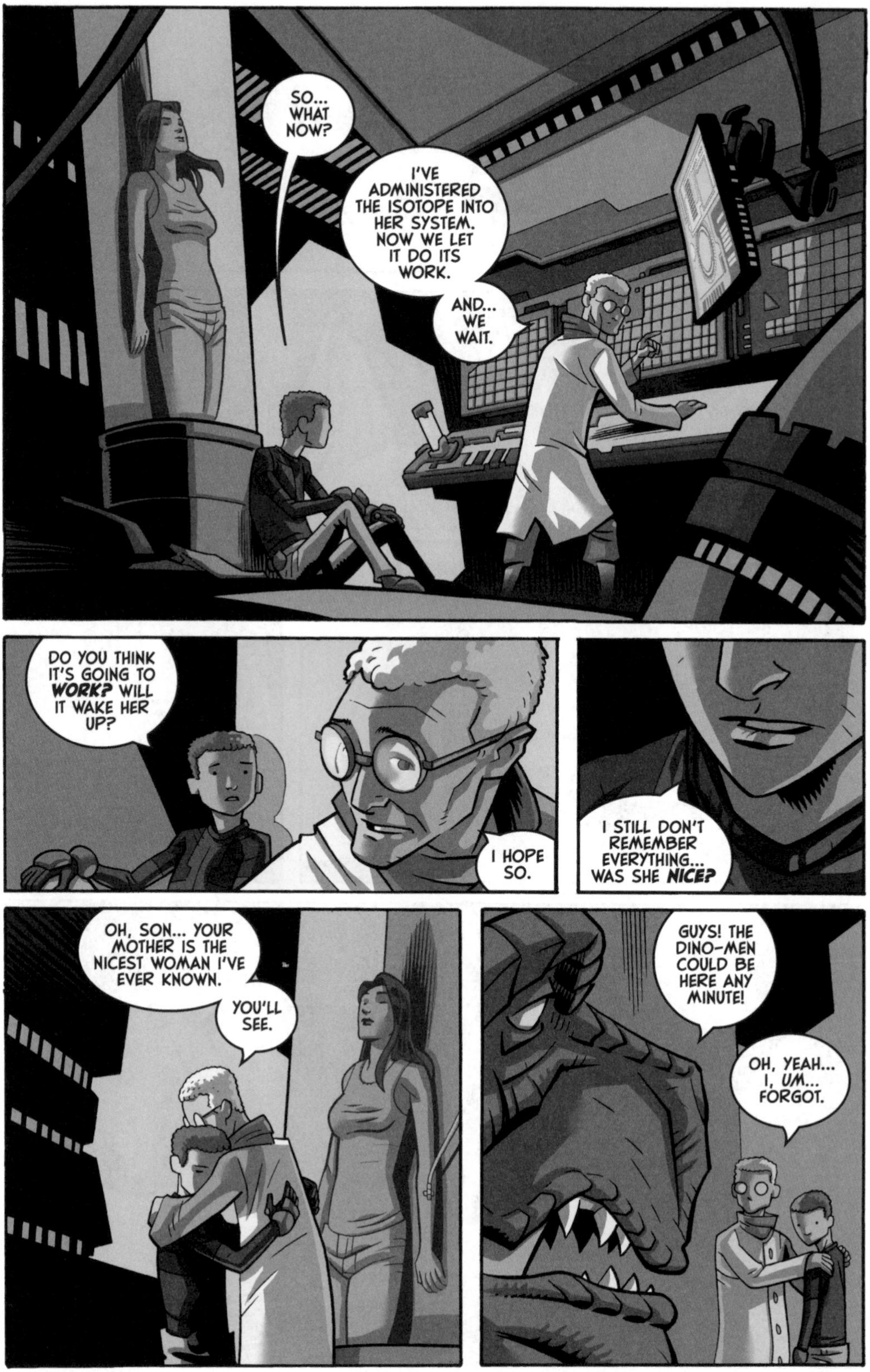
SO... WHAT NOW?
I'VE ADMINISTERED THE ISOTOPE INTO HER SYSTEM. NOW WE LET IT DO ITS WORK.
AND... WE WAIT.
DO YOU THINK IT'S GOING TO *WORK?* WILL IT WAKE HER UP?
I HOPE SO.
I STILL DON'T REMEMBER EVERYTHING... WAS SHE *NICE?*
OH, SON... YOUR MOTHER IS THE NICEST WOMAN I'VE EVER KNOWN.
YOU'LL SEE.
GUYS! THE DINO-MEN COULD BE HERE ANY MINUTE!
OH, YEAH... I, *UM*... FORGOT.

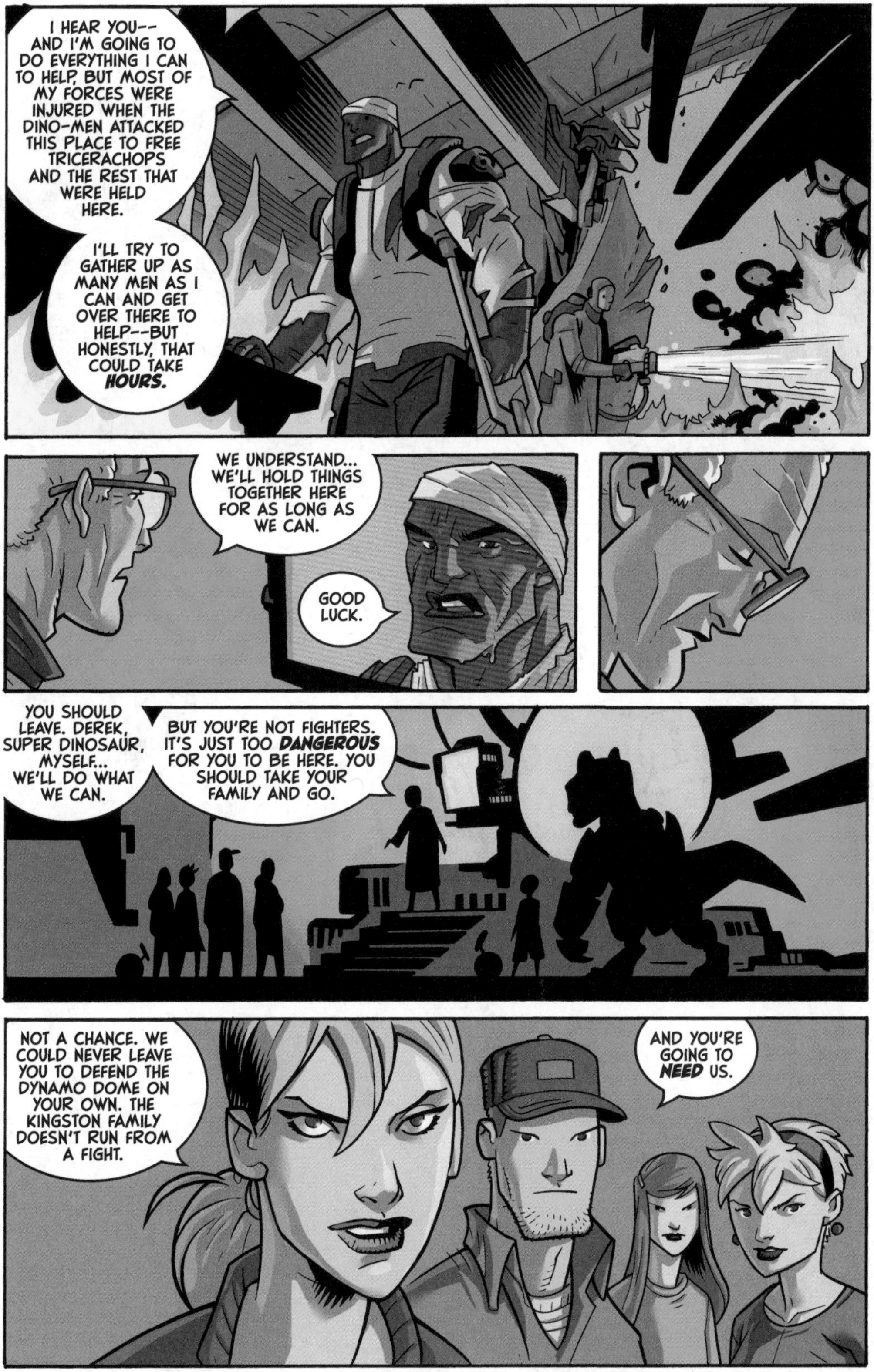
I HEAR YOU-- AND I'M GOING TO DO EVERYTHING I CAN TO HELP, BUT MOST OF MY FORCES WERE INJURED WHEN THE DINO-MEN ATTACKED THIS PLACE TO FREE TRICERACHOPS AND THE REST THAT WERE HELD HERE.
I'LL TRY TO GATHER UP AS MANY MEN AS I CAN AND GET OVER THERE TO HELP--BUT HONESTLY, THAT COULD TAKE *HOURS.*
WE UNDERSTAND... WE'LL HOLD THINGS TOGETHER HERE FOR AS LONG AS WE CAN.
GOOD LUCK.
YOU SHOULD LEAVE. DEREK, SUPER DINOSAUR, MYSELF... WE'LL DO WHAT WE CAN.
BUT YOU'RE NOT FIGHTERS. IT'S JUST TOO *DANGEROUS* FOR YOU TO BE HERE. YOU SHOULD TAKE YOUR FAMILY AND GO.
NOT A CHANCE. WE COULD NEVER LEAVE YOU TO DEFEND THE DYNAMO DOME ON YOUR OWN. THE KINGSTON FAMILY DOESN'T RUN FROM A FIGHT.
AND YOU'RE GOING TO *NEED* US.

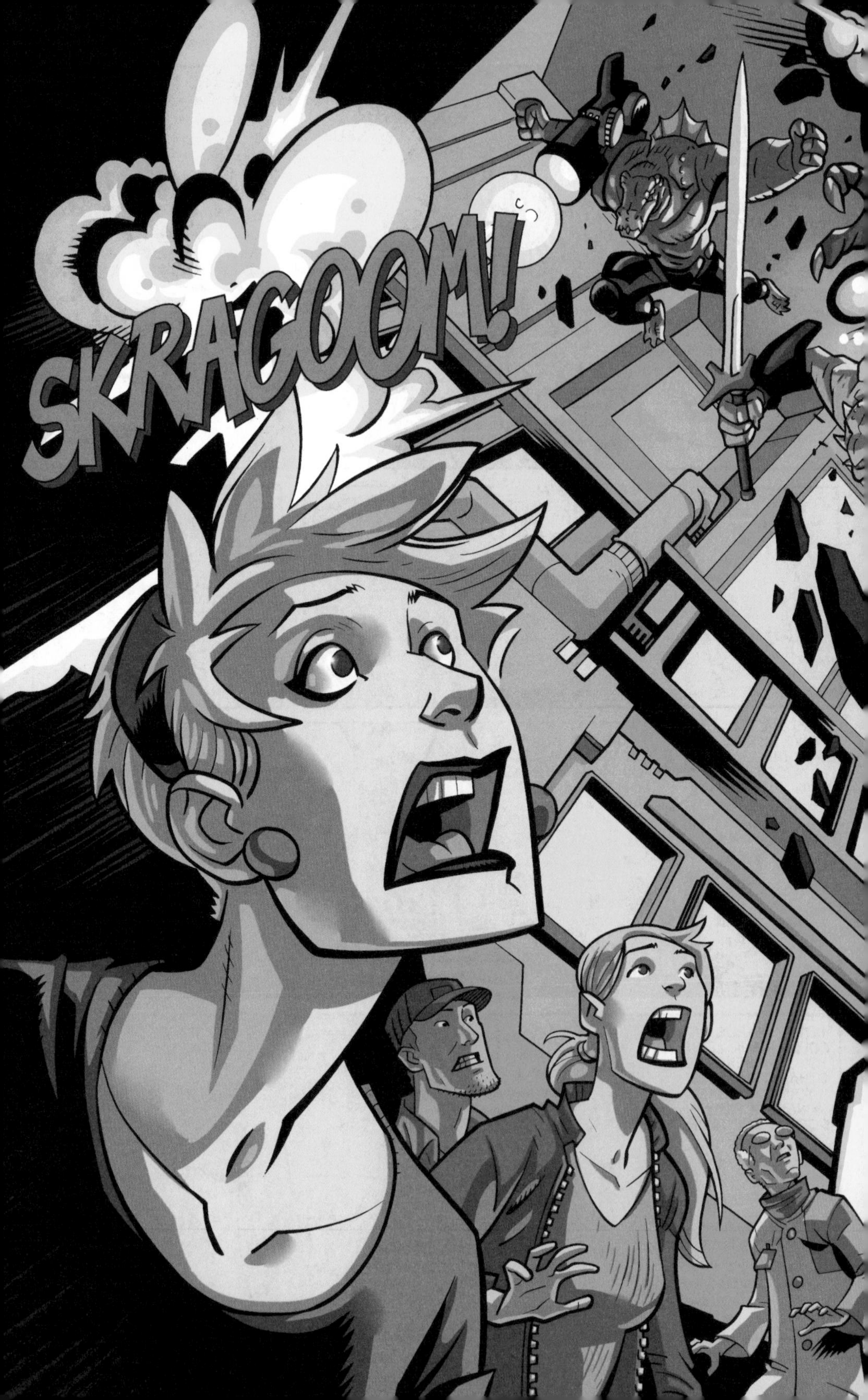
SKRAGOOM!

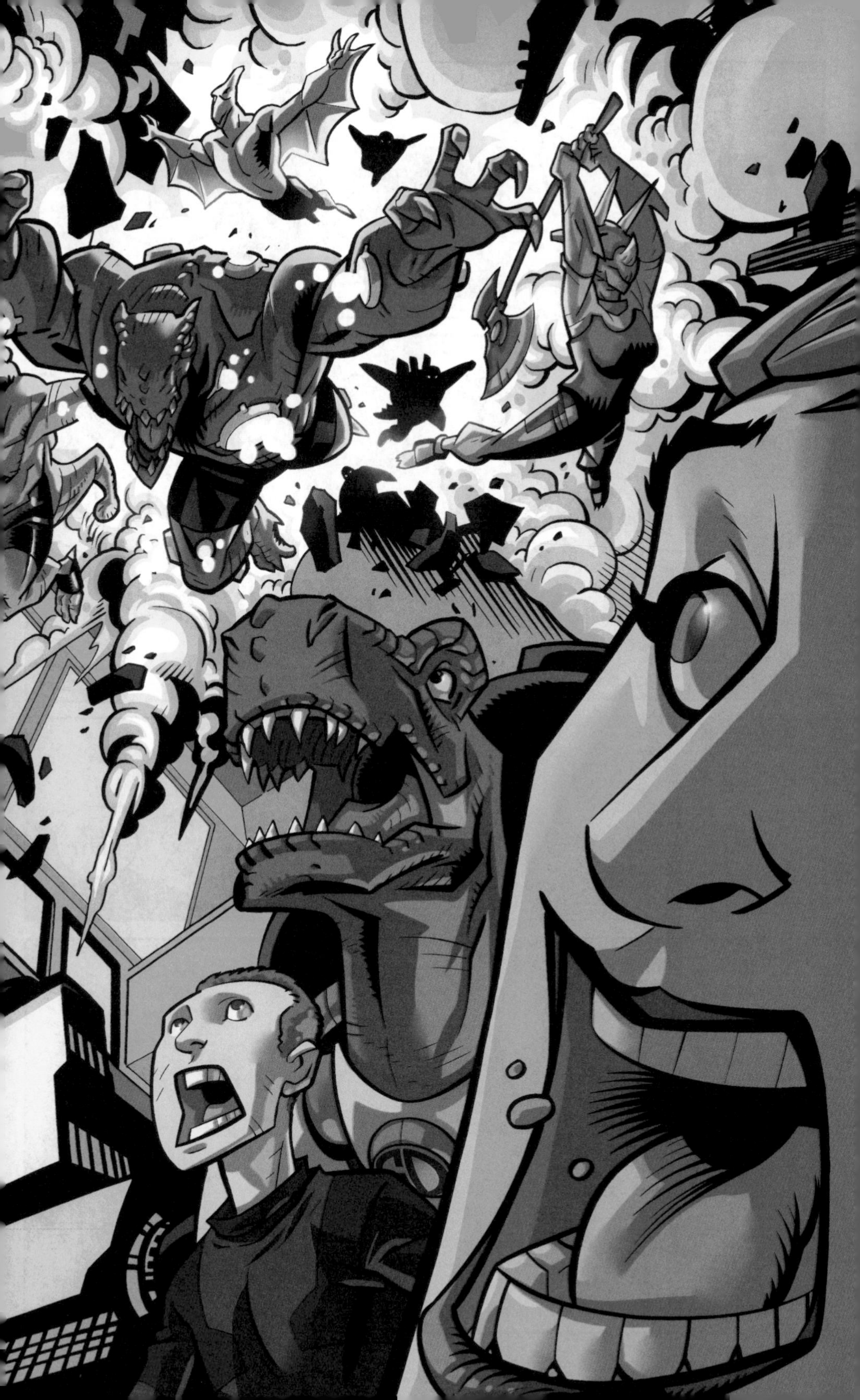

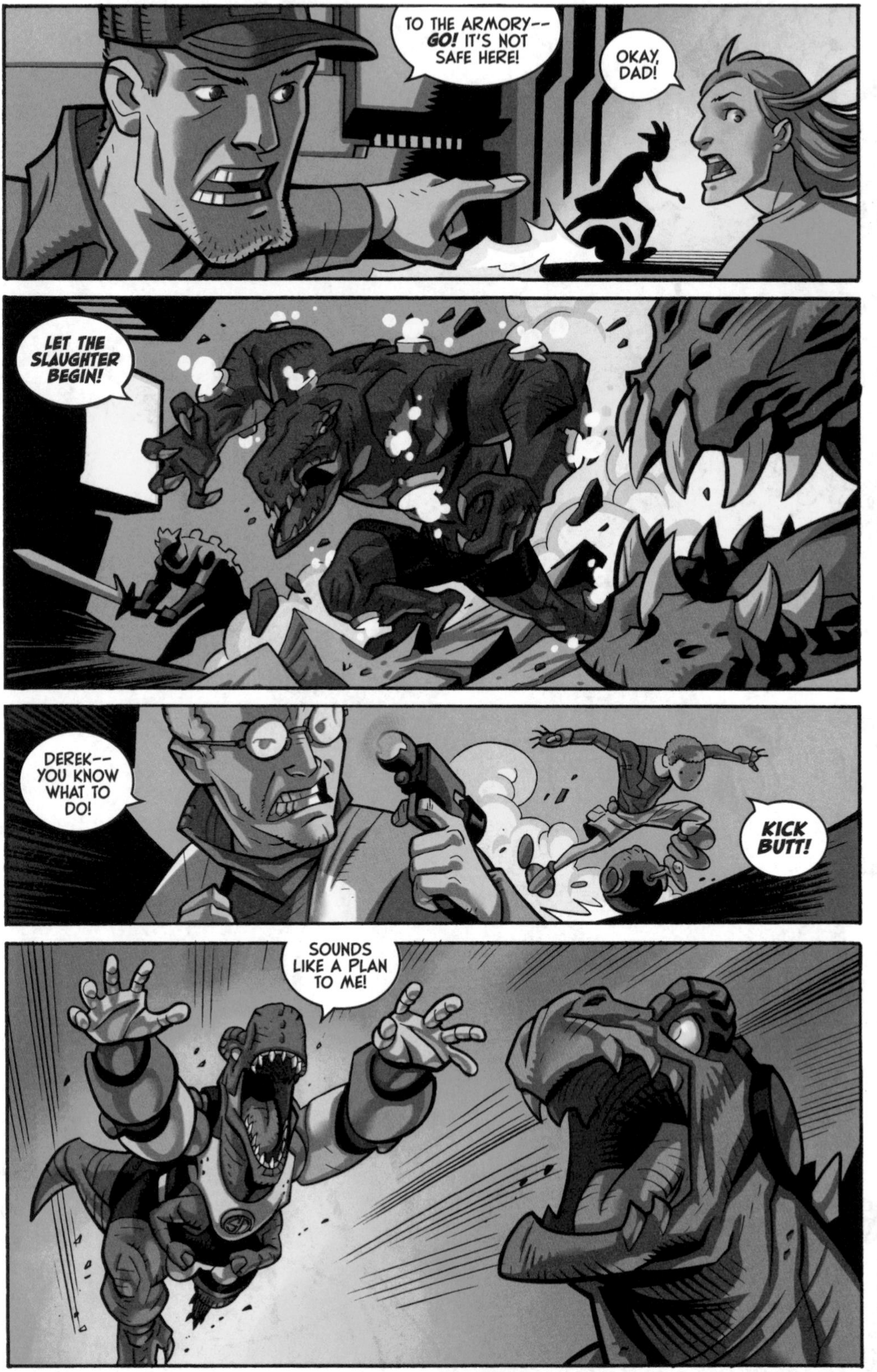
TO THE ARMORY--
GO! IT'S NOT
SAFE HERE!
OKAY,
DAD!
LET THE
SLAUGHTER
BEGIN!
DEREK--
YOU KNOW
WHAT TO
DO!
KICK
BUTT!
SOUNDS
LIKE A PLAN
TO ME!

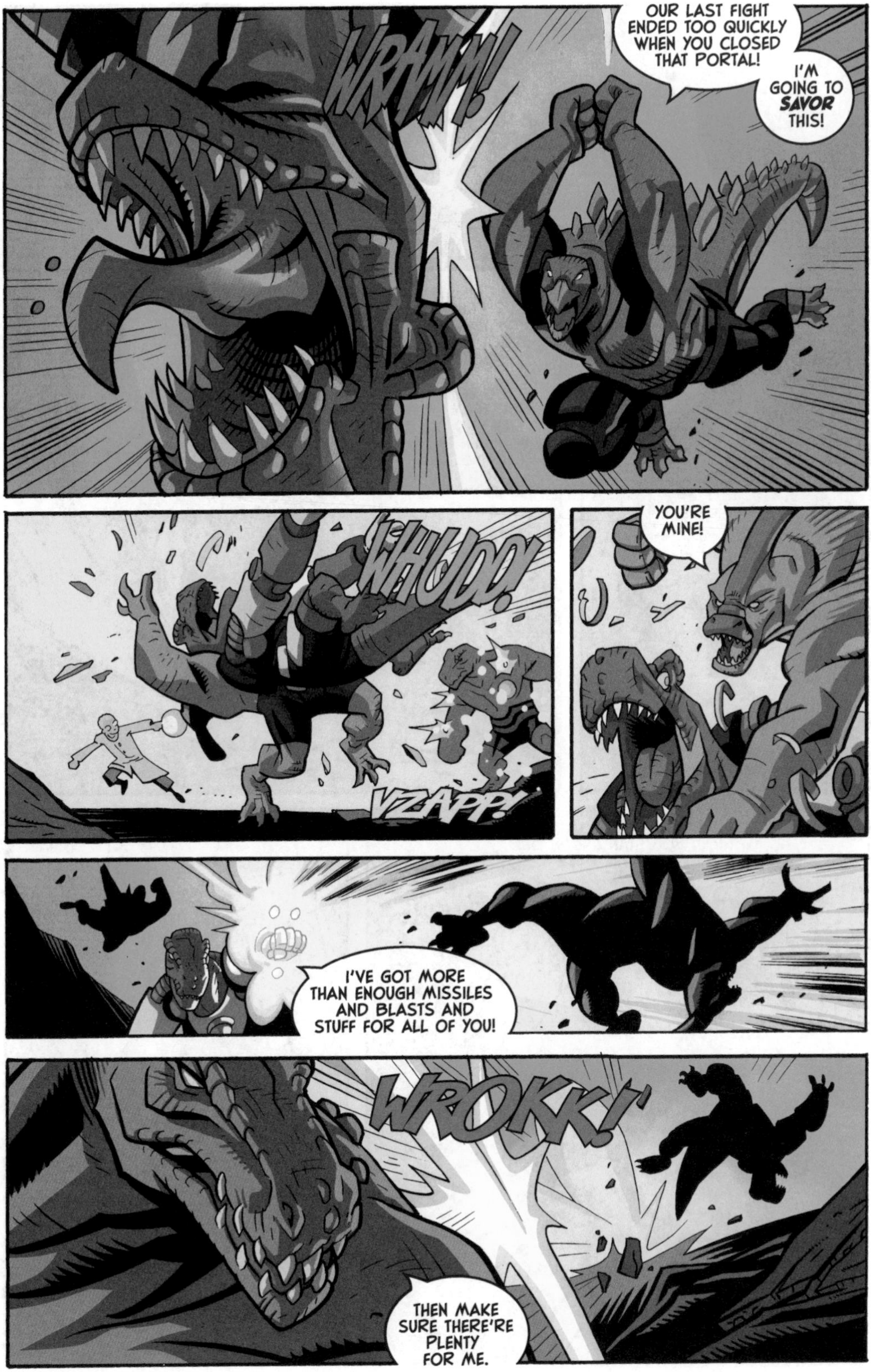
WRAMM!
OUR LAST FIGHT ENDED TOO QUICKLY WHEN YOU CLOSED THAT PORTAL!
I'M GOING TO SAVOR THIS!
WHUDD!
VZAPP!
YOU'RE MINE!
I'VE GOT MORE THAN ENOUGH MISSILES AND BLASTS AND STUFF FOR ALL OF YOU!
WROKK!
THEN MAKE SURE THERE'RE PLENTY FOR ME.

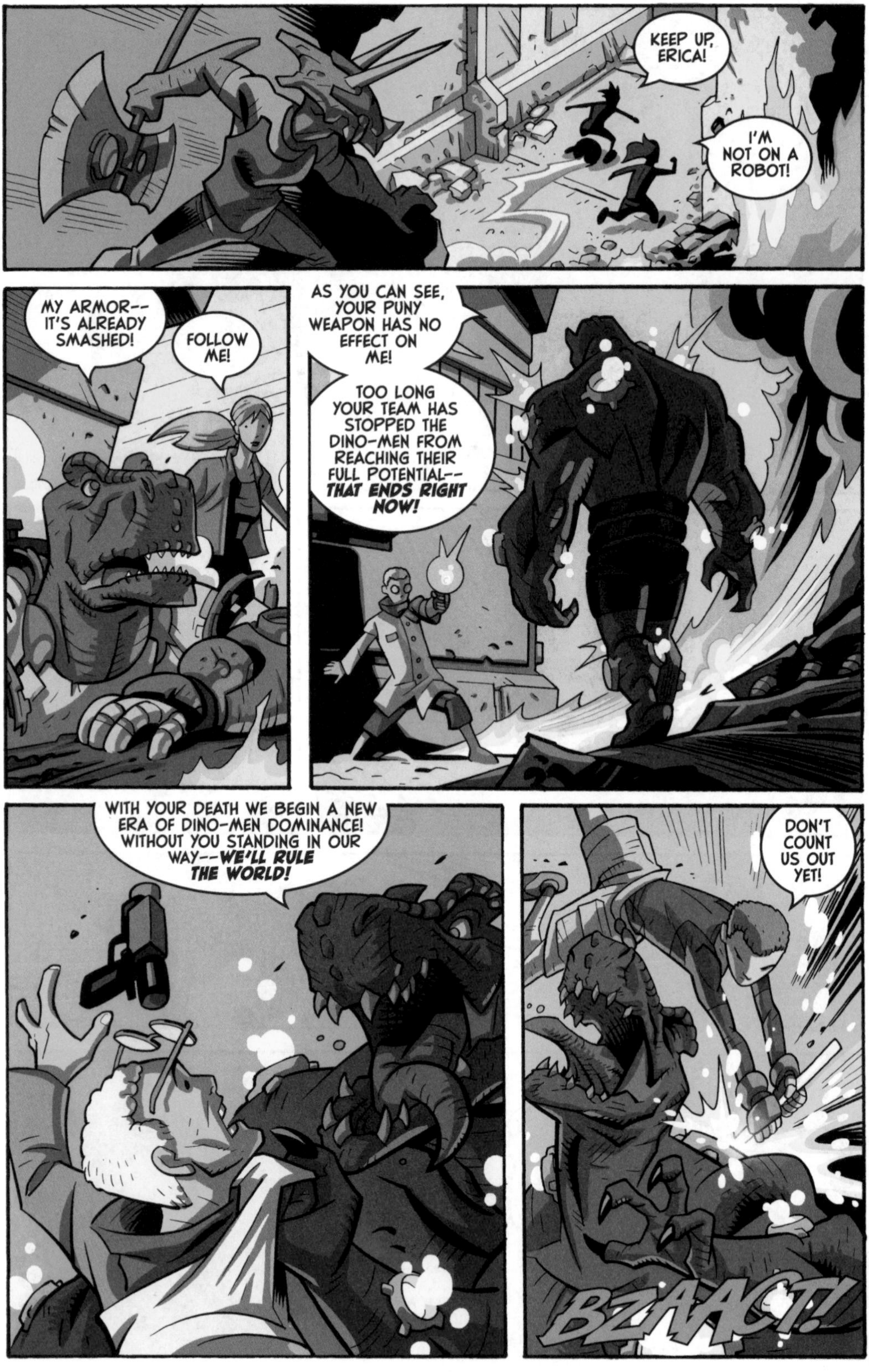
KEEP UP, ERICA!
I'M NOT ON A ROBOT!
MY ARMOR-- IT'S ALREADY SMASHED!
FOLLOW ME!
AS YOU CAN SEE, YOUR PUNY WEAPON HAS NO EFFECT ON ME!
TOO LONG YOUR TEAM HAS STOPPED THE DINO-MEN FROM REACHING THEIR FULL POTENTIAL-- THAT ENDS RIGHT NOW!
WITH YOUR DEATH WE BEGIN A NEW ERA OF DINO-MEN DOMINANCE! WITHOUT YOU STANDING IN OUR WAY--WE'LL RULE THE WORLD!
DON'T COUNT US OUT YET!
BZAACT!

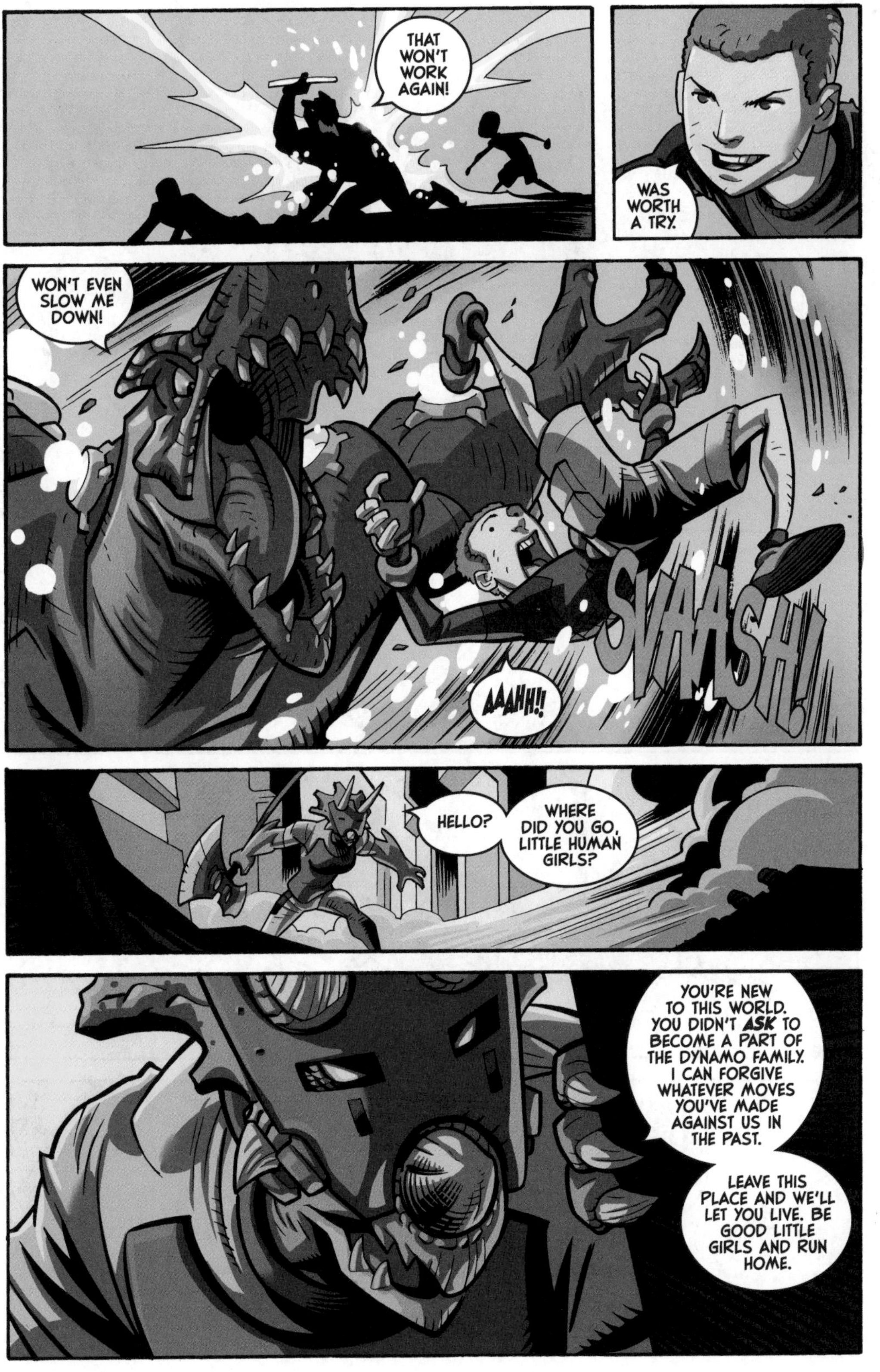
THAT WON'T WORK AGAIN!
WAS WORTH A TRY.
WON'T EVEN SLOW ME DOWN!
SVAASH!
AAAHH!!
HELLO?
WHERE DID YOU GO, LITTLE HUMAN GIRLS?
YOU'RE NEW TO THIS WORLD. YOU DIDN'T ASK TO BECOME A PART OF THE DYNAMO FAMILY. I CAN FORGIVE WHATEVER MOVES YOU'VE MADE AGAINST US IN THE PAST.
LEAVE THIS PLACE AND WE'LL LET YOU LIVE. BE GOOD LITTLE GIRLS AND RUN HOME.

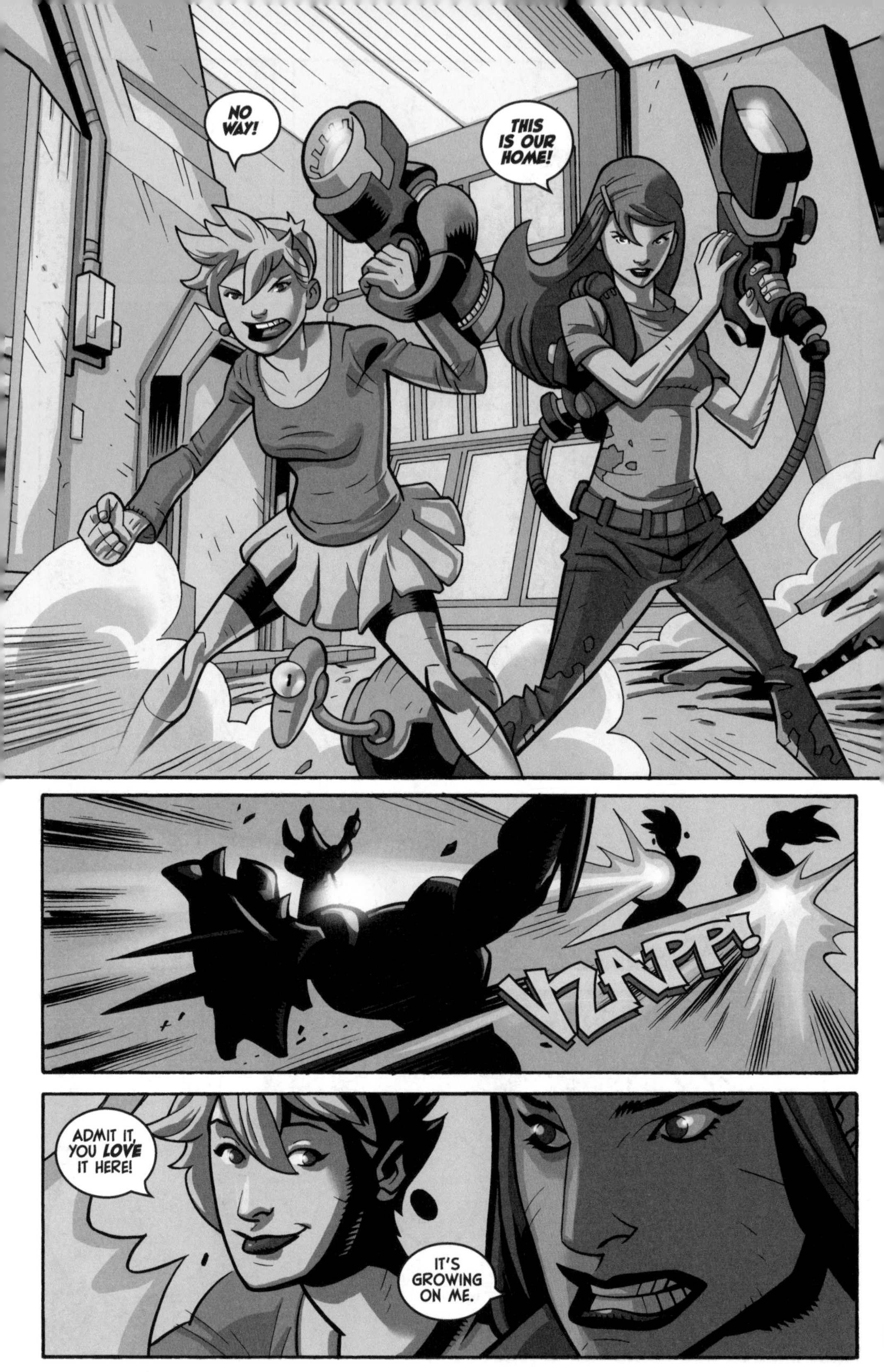
NO WAY!
THIS IS OUR HOME!
VZAPP!
ADMIT IT, YOU **LOVE** IT HERE!
IT'S GROWING ON ME.

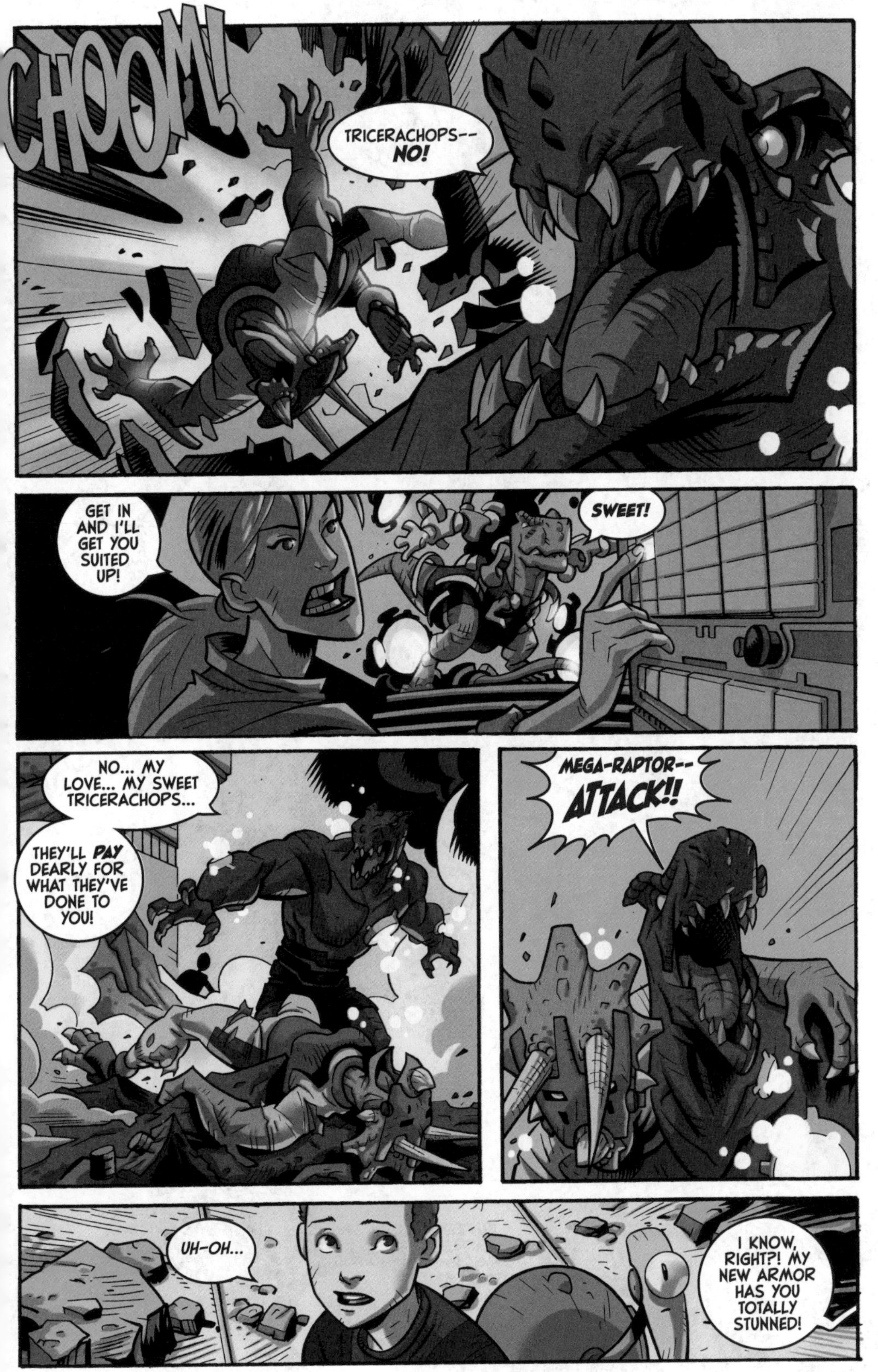
CHOOM!
TRICERACHOPS-- NO!
GET IN AND I'LL GET YOU SUITED UP!
SWEET!
NO... MY LOVE... MY SWEET TRICERACHOPS...
THEY'LL PAY DEARLY FOR WHAT THEY'VE DONE TO YOU!
MEGA-RAPTOR-- ATTACK!!
UH-OH...
I KNOW, RIGHT?! MY NEW ARMOR HAS YOU TOTALLY STUNNED!

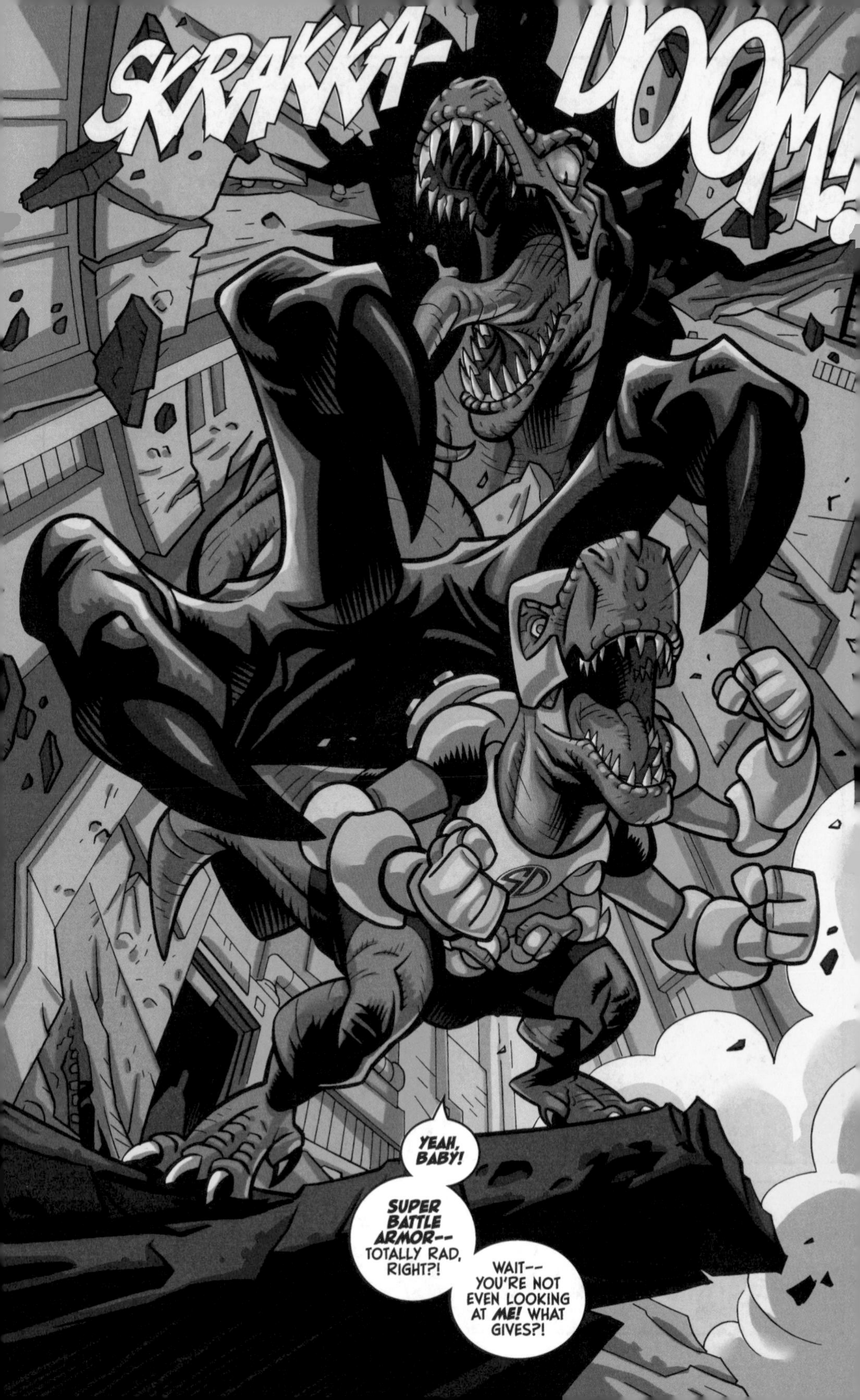
SKRAKKA-
DOOM!!
YEAH, BABY!
SUPER BATTLE ARMOR-- TOTALLY RAD, RIGHT?!
WAIT-- YOU'RE NOT EVEN LOOKING AT ME! WHAT GIVES?!

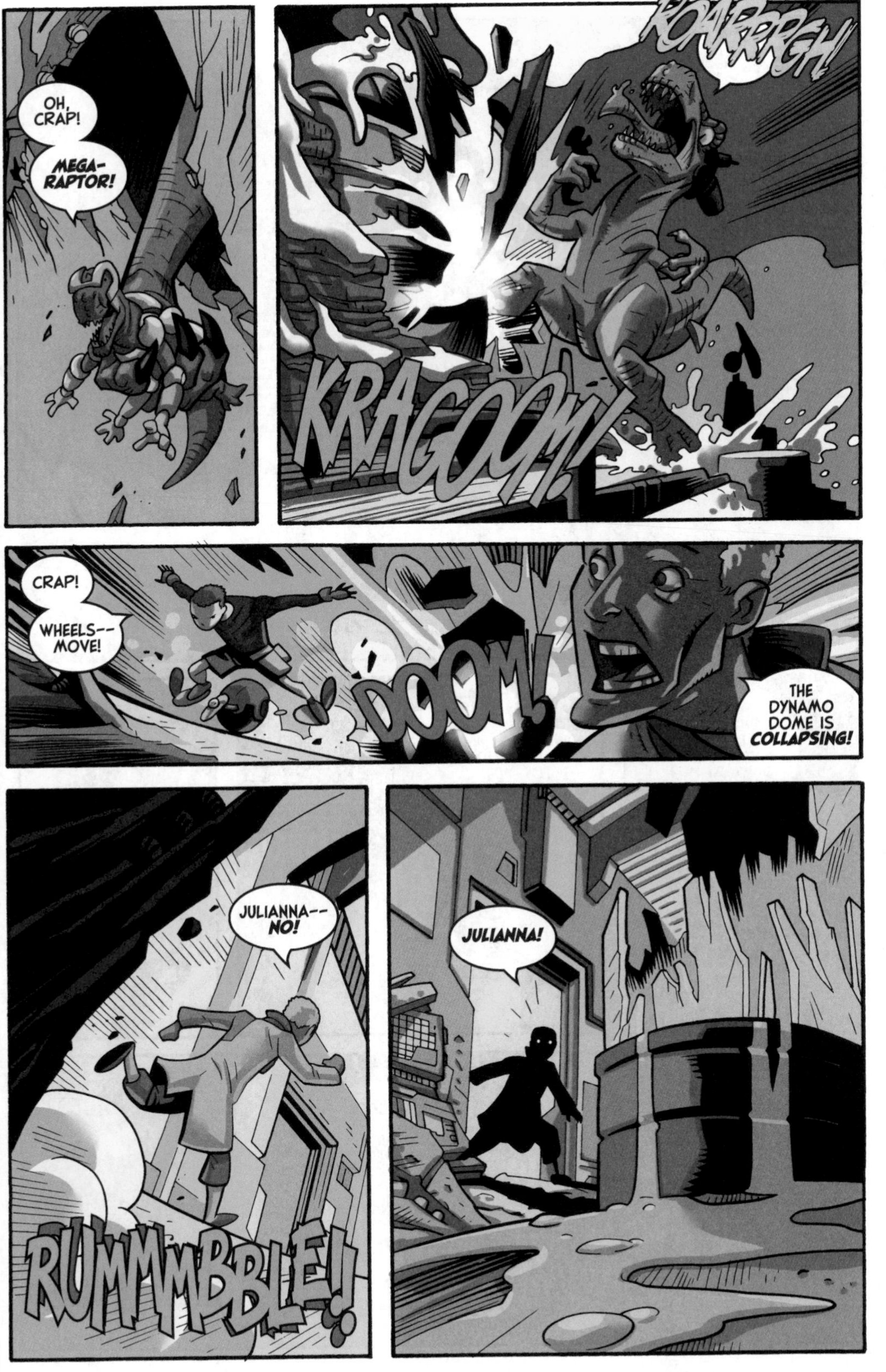
OH, CRAP!
MEGA-RAPTOR!
ROARRRGH!
KRAGOOM!
CRAP!
WHEELS--MOVE!
DOOM!
THE DYNAMO DOME IS COLLAPSING!
JULIANNA--NO!
RUMMMBBLE!!
JULIANNA!

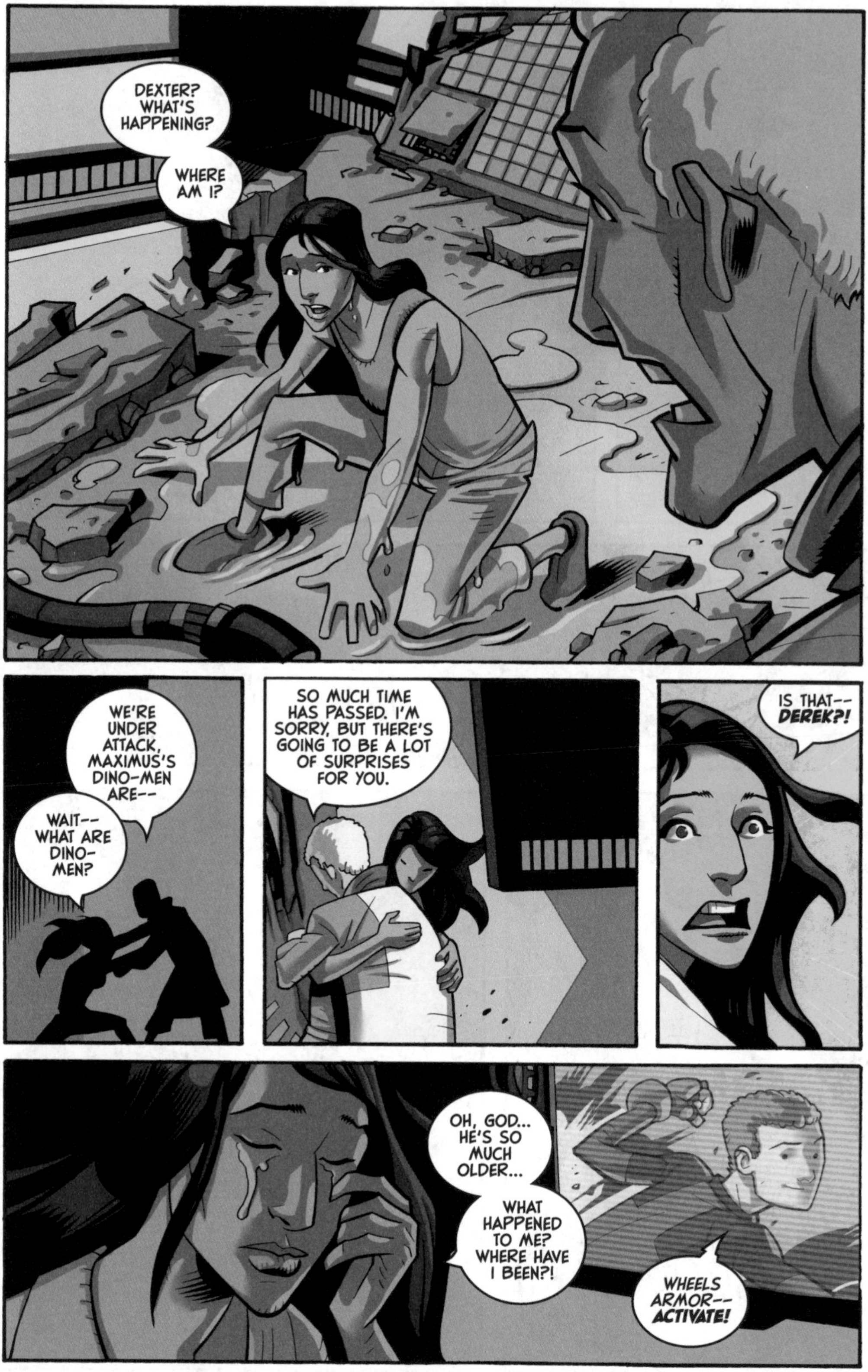
DEXTER? WHAT'S HAPPENING?
WHERE AM I?
WE'RE UNDER ATTACK, MAXIMUS'S DINO-MEN ARE--
WAIT-- WHAT ARE DINO-MEN?
SO MUCH TIME HAS PASSED. I'M SORRY, BUT THERE'S GOING TO BE A LOT OF SURPRISES FOR YOU.
IS THAT-- DEREK?!
OH, GOD... HE'S SO MUCH OLDER...
WHAT HAPPENED TO ME? WHERE HAVE I BEEN?!
WHEELS ARMOR-- ACTIVATE!

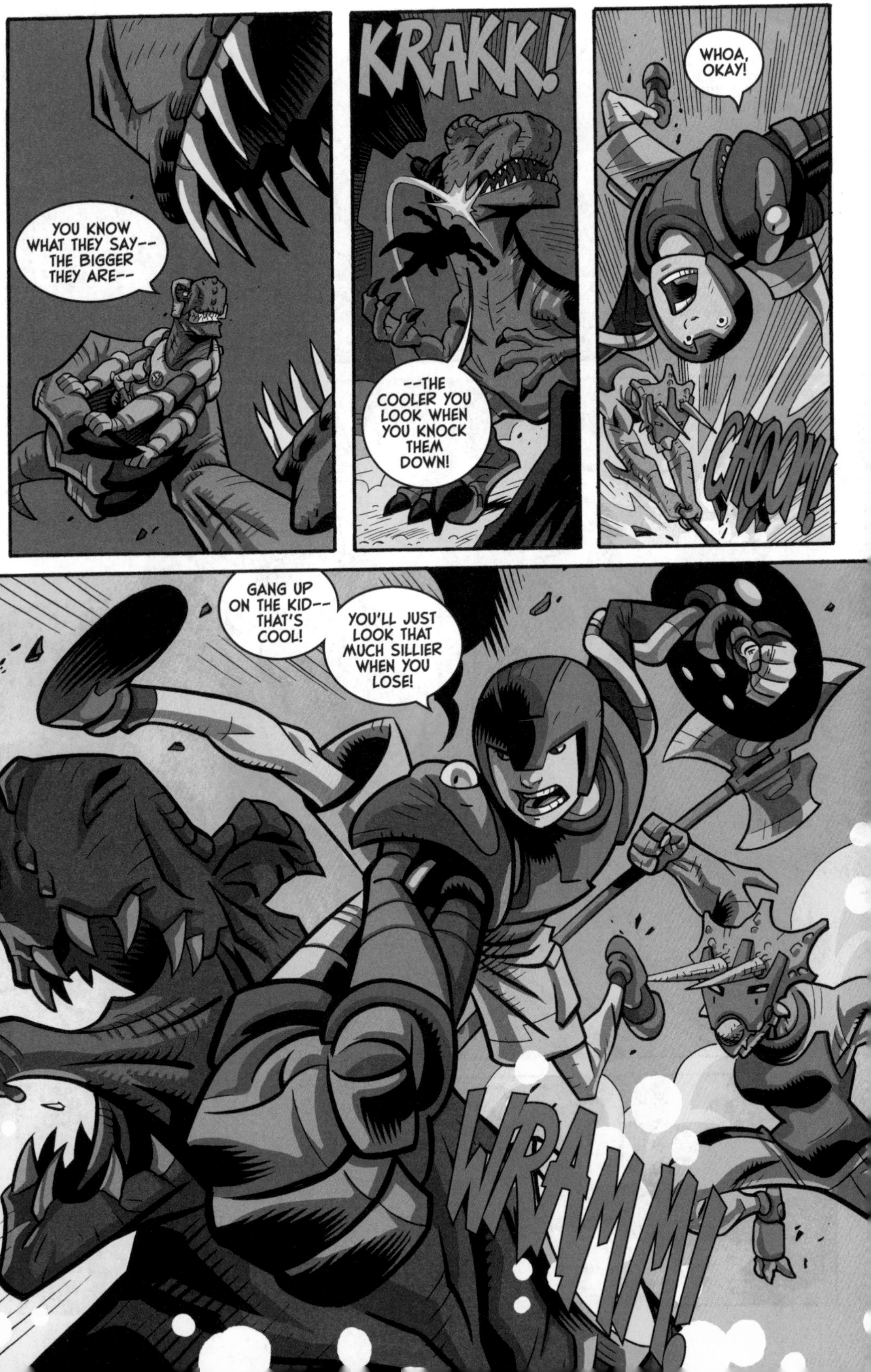
YOU KNOW WHAT THEY SAY-- THE BIGGER THEY ARE--
KRAKK!
--THE COOLER YOU LOOK WHEN YOU KNOCK THEM DOWN!
WHOA, OKAY!
CHOOM!
GANG UP ON THE KID-- THAT'S COOL!
YOU'LL JUST LOOK THAT MUCH SILLIER WHEN YOU LOSE!
WRAMM!

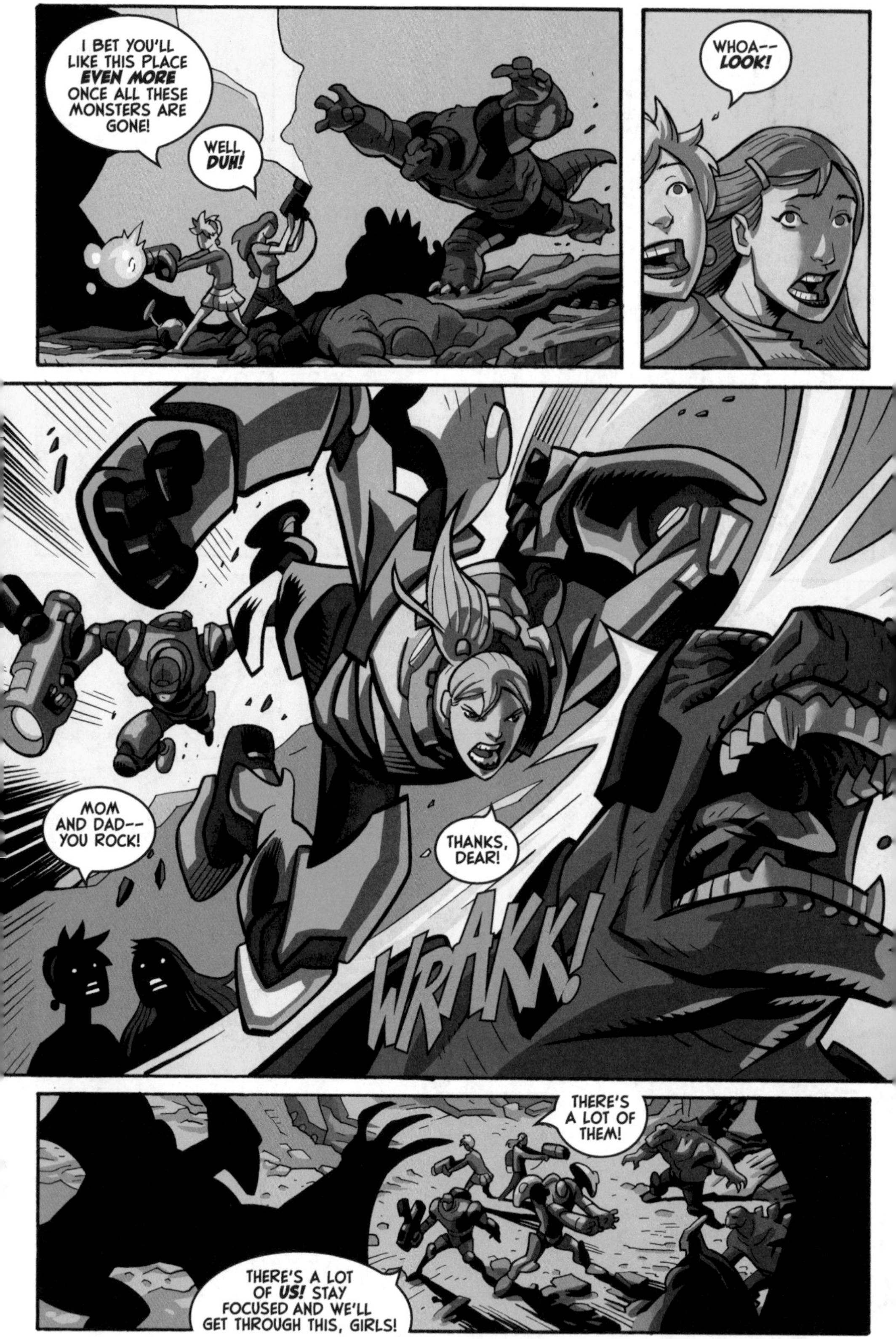
I BET YOU'LL LIKE THIS PLACE ***EVEN MORE*** ONCE ALL THESE MONSTERS ARE GONE!
WELL, ***DUH!***
WHOA-- ***LOOK!***
MOM AND DAD-- YOU ROCK!
THANKS, DEAR!
WRAKK!
THERE'S A LOT OF THEM!
THERE'S A LOT OF ***US!*** STAY FOCUSED AND WE'LL GET THROUGH THIS, GIRLS!

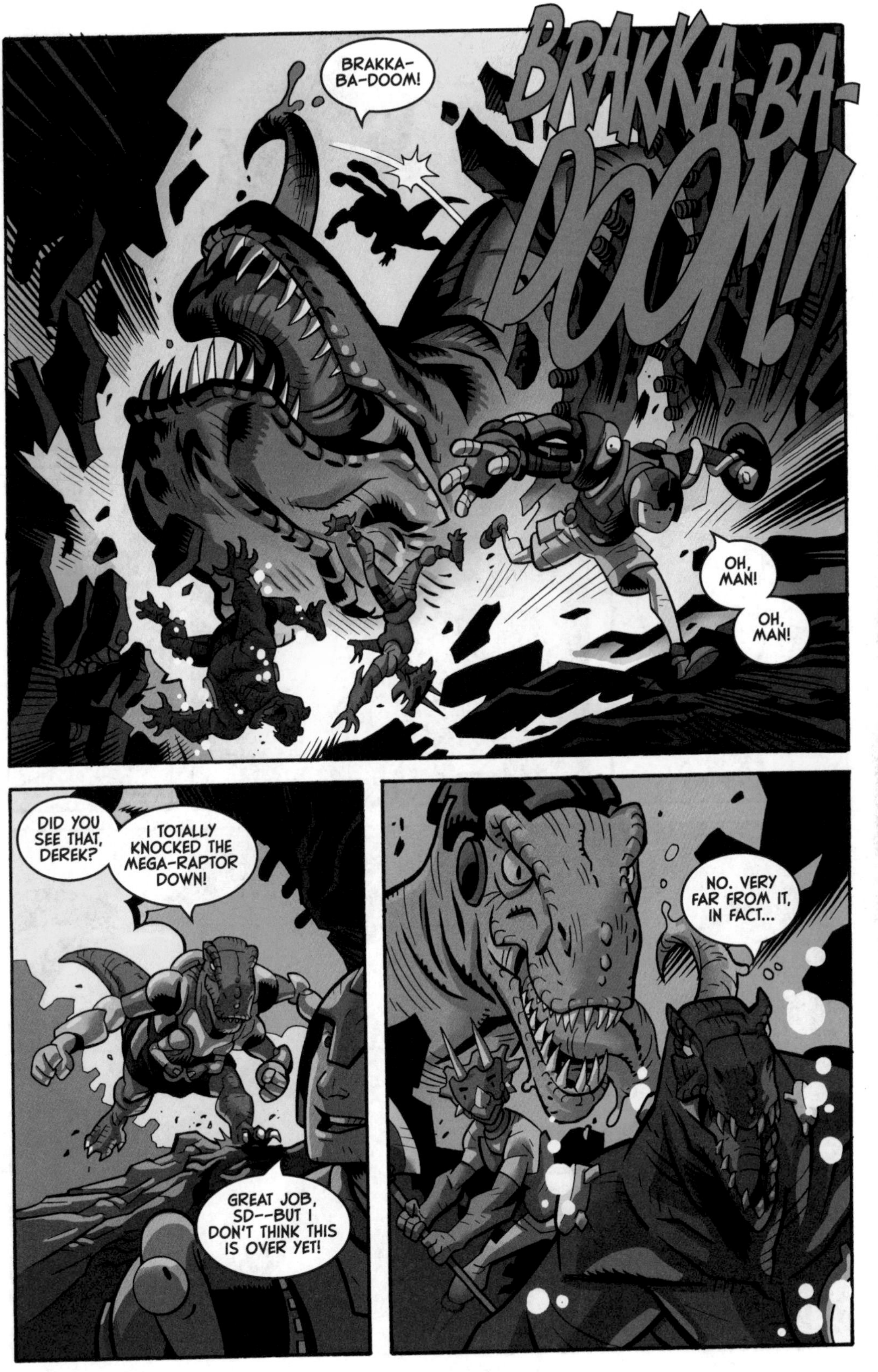
BRAKKA-BA-DOOM!
BRAKKA-BA-DOOM!
OH, MAN!
OH, MAN!
DID YOU SEE THAT, DEREK?
I TOTALLY KNOCKED THE MEGA-RAPTOR DOWN!
GREAT JOB, SD--BUT I DON'T THINK THIS IS OVER YET!
NO. VERY FAR FROM IT, IN FACT...

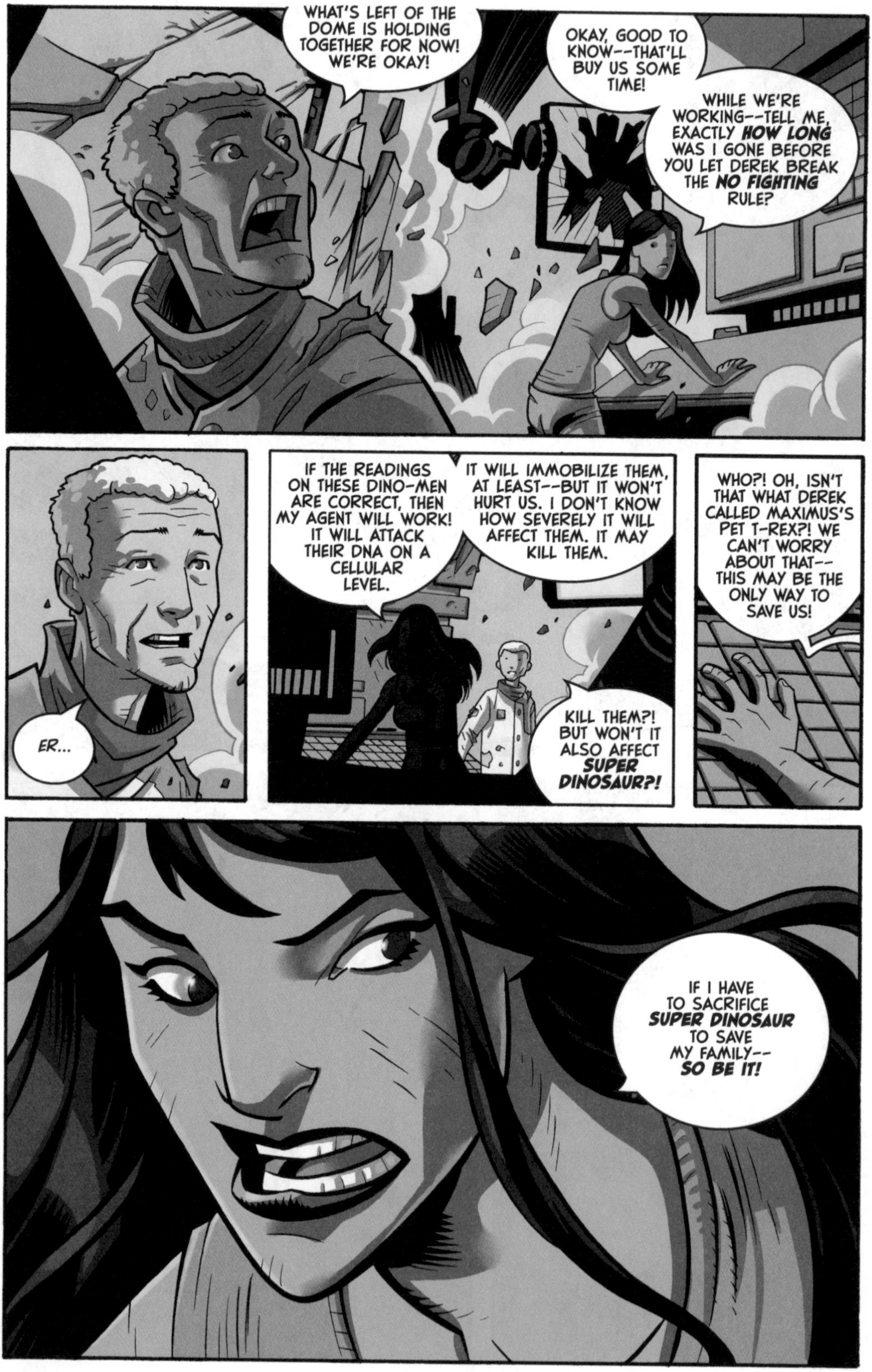
WHAT'S LEFT OF THE DOME IS HOLDING TOGETHER FOR NOW! WE'RE OKAY!
OKAY, GOOD TO KNOW--THAT'LL BUY US SOME TIME!
WHILE WE'RE WORKING--TELL ME, EXACTLY HOW LONG WAS I GONE BEFORE YOU LET DEREK BREAK THE NO FIGHTING RULE?
ER...
IF THE READINGS ON THESE DINO-MEN ARE CORRECT, THEN MY AGENT WILL WORK! IT WILL ATTACK THEIR DNA ON A CELLULAR LEVEL.
IT WILL IMMOBILIZE THEM, AT LEAST--BUT IT WON'T HURT US. I DON'T KNOW HOW SEVERELY IT WILL AFFECT THEM. IT MAY KILL THEM.
KILL THEM?! BUT WON'T IT ALSO AFFECT SUPER DINOSAUR?!
WHO?! OH, ISN'T THAT WHAT DEREK CALLED MAXIMUS'S PET T-REX?! WE CAN'T WORRY ABOUT THAT--THIS MAY BE THE ONLY WAY TO SAVE US!
IF I HAVE TO SACRIFICE SUPER DINOSAUR TO SAVE MY FAMILY--SO BE IT!

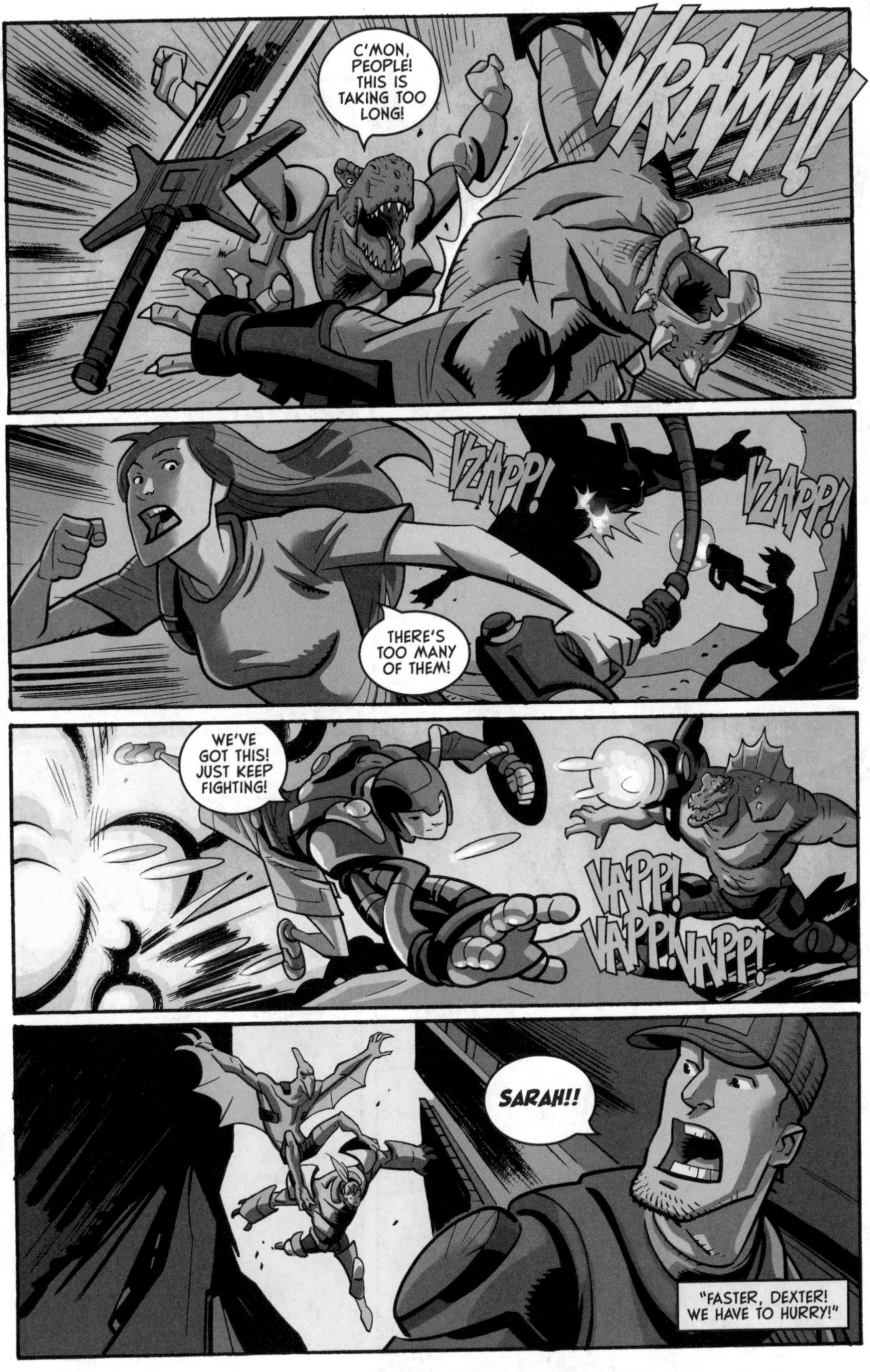
C'MON, PEOPLE! THIS IS TAKING TOO LONG!
WRAMM!
VZAPP!
VZAPP!
THERE'S TOO MANY OF THEM!
WE'VE GOT THIS! JUST KEEP FIGHTING!
VAPP! VAPP! VAPP!
SARAH!!
"FASTER, DEXTER! WE HAVE TO HURRY!"

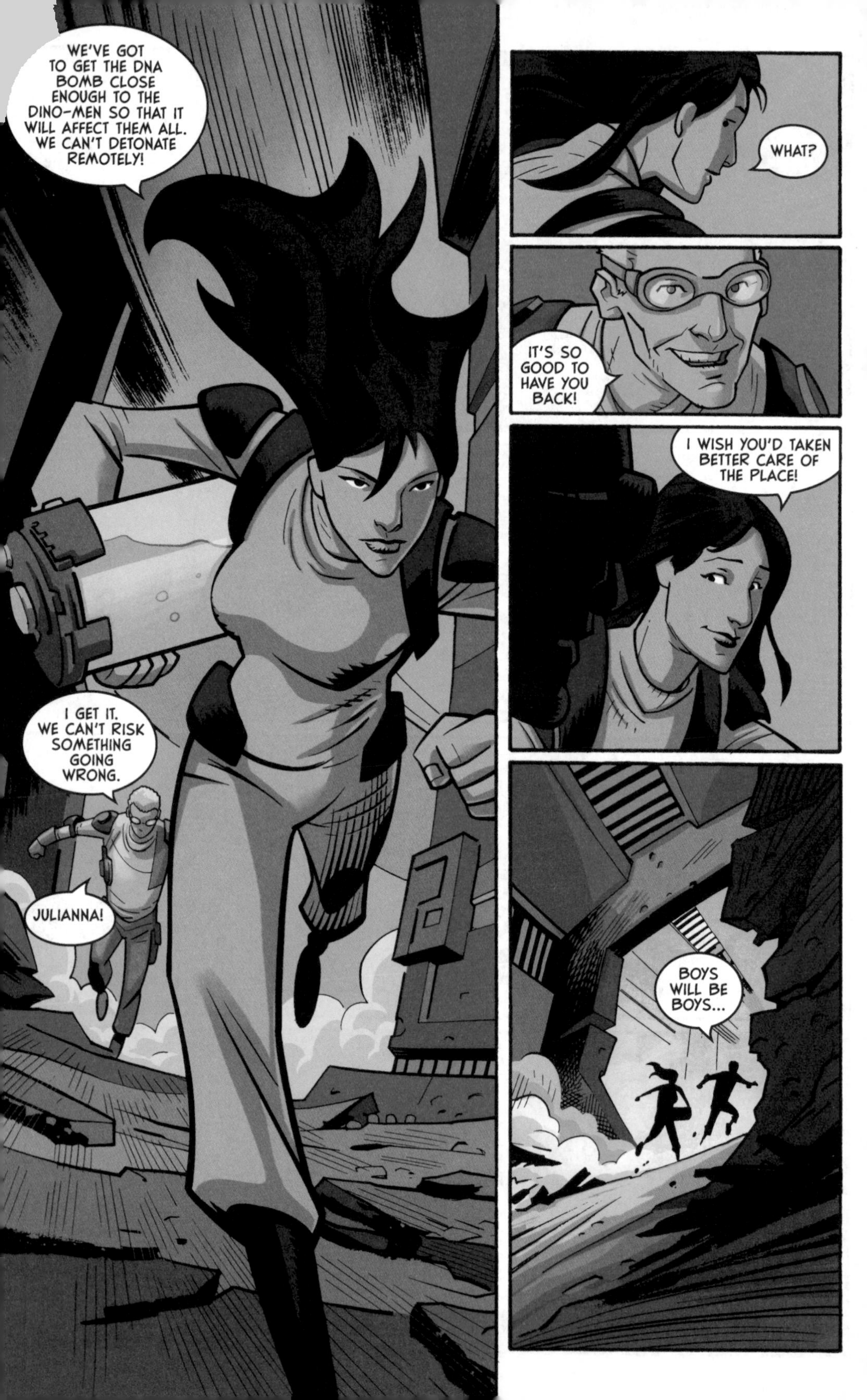
WE'VE GOT TO GET THE DNA BOMB CLOSE ENOUGH TO THE DINO-MEN SO THAT IT WILL AFFECT THEM ALL. WE CAN'T DETONATE REMOTELY!
I GET IT. WE CAN'T RISK SOMETHING GOING WRONG.
JULIANNA!
WHAT?
IT'S SO GOOD TO HAVE YOU BACK!
I WISH YOU'D TAKEN BETTER CARE OF THE PLACE!
BOYS WILL BE BOYS...

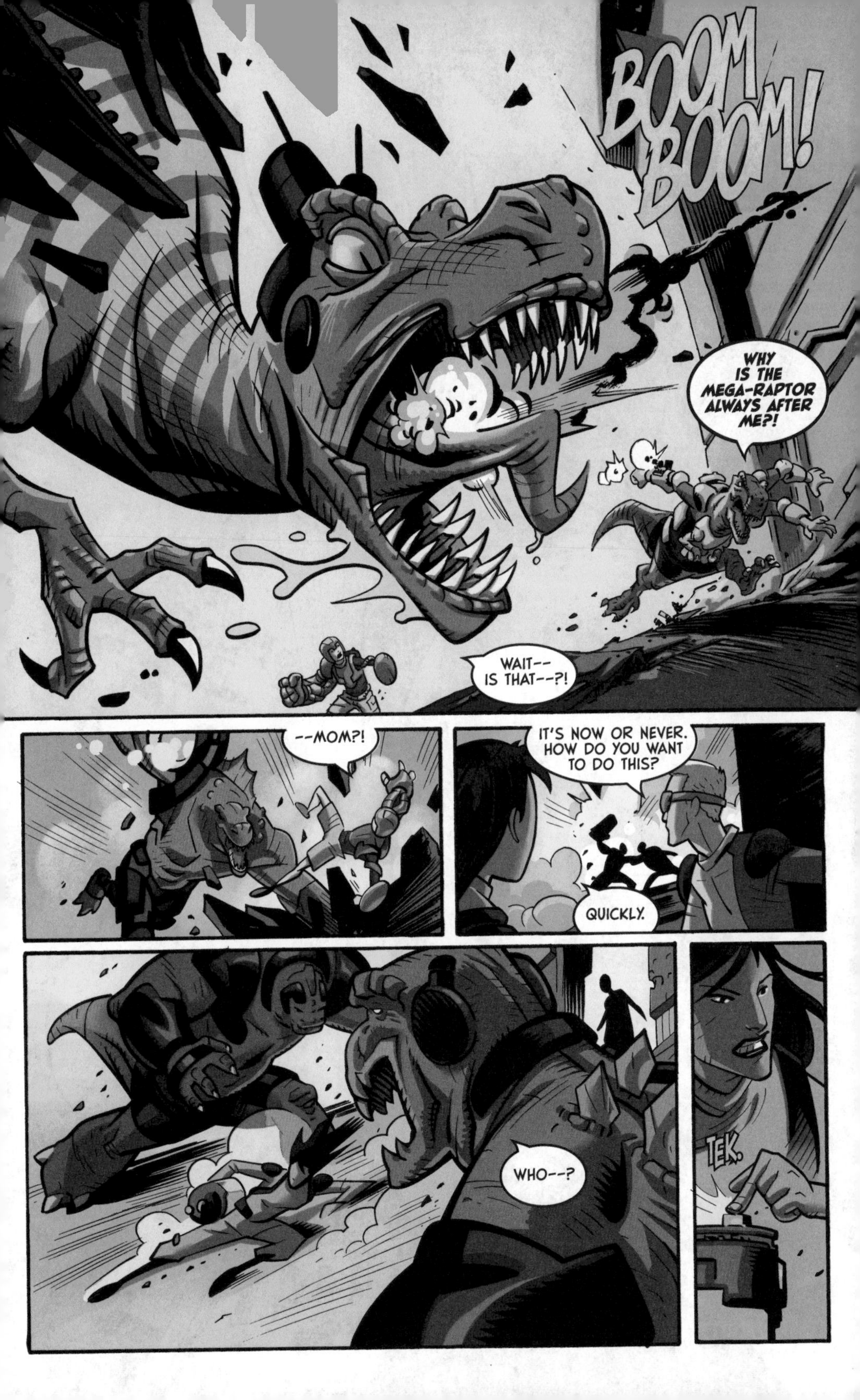
BOOM BOOM!
WHY IS THE MEGA-RAPTOR ALWAYS AFTER ME?!
WAIT-- IS THAT--?!
--MOM?!
IT'S NOW OR NEVER. HOW DO YOU WANT TO DO THIS?
QUICKLY.
WHO--?
TEK.

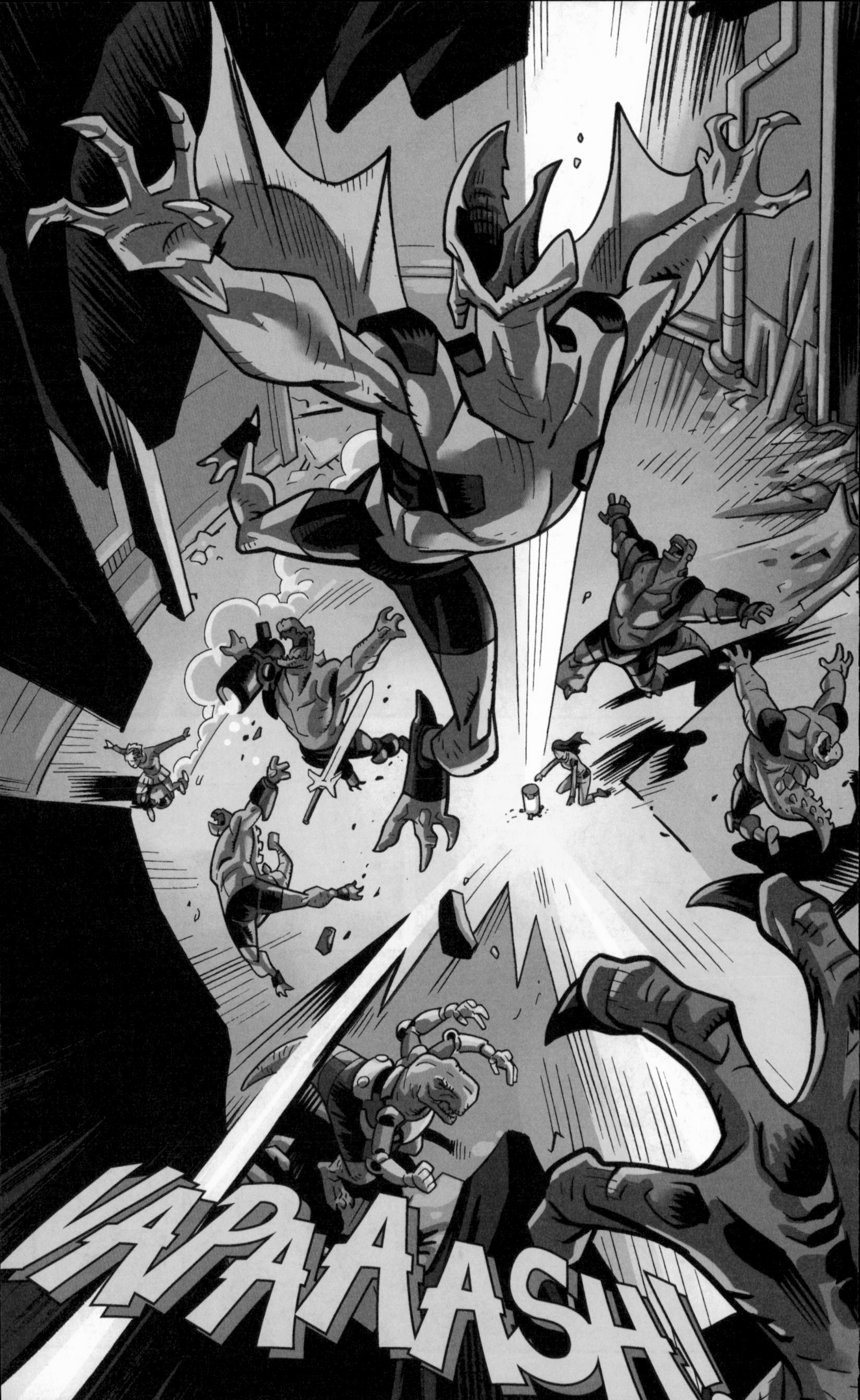
VRAAASH!

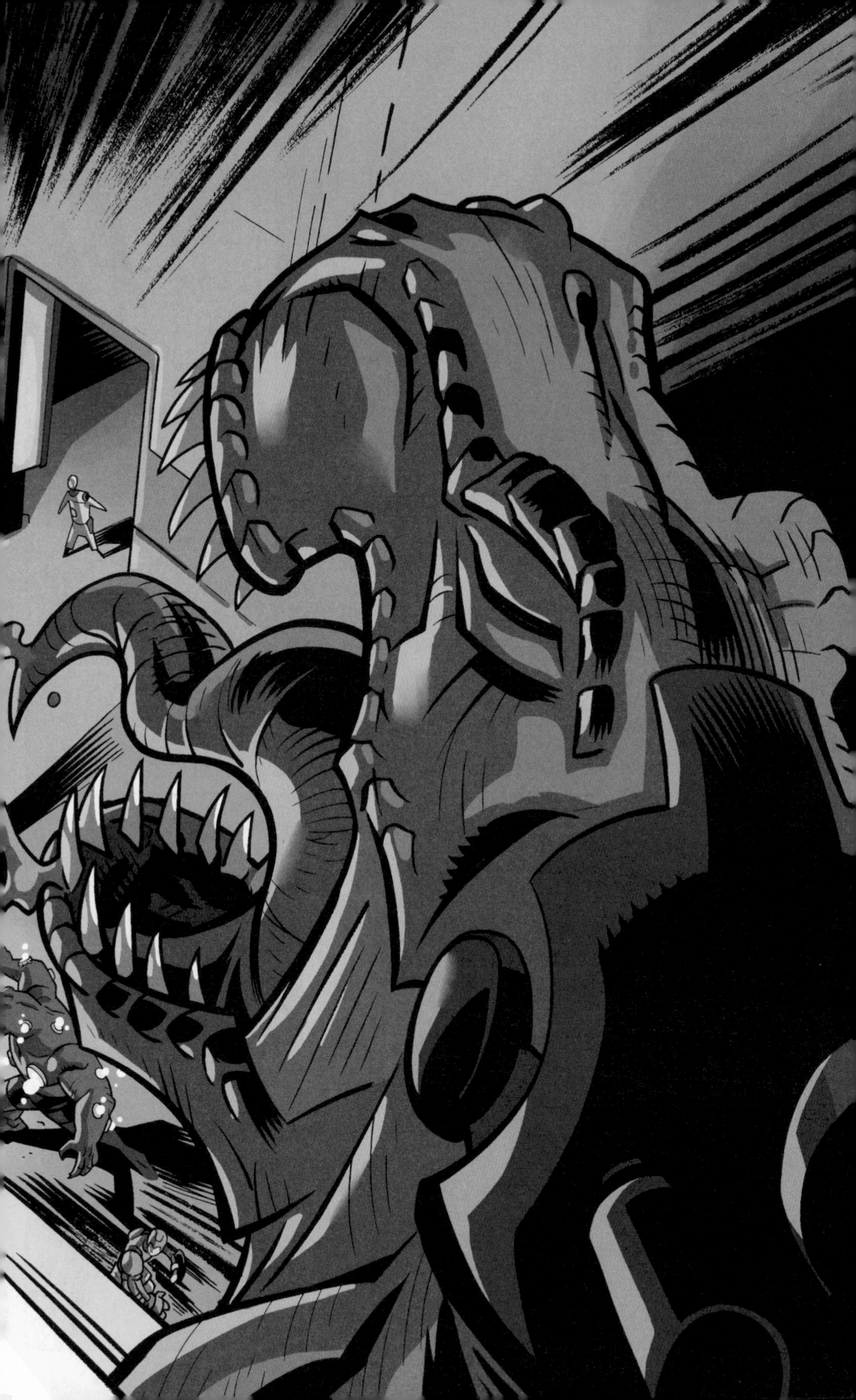

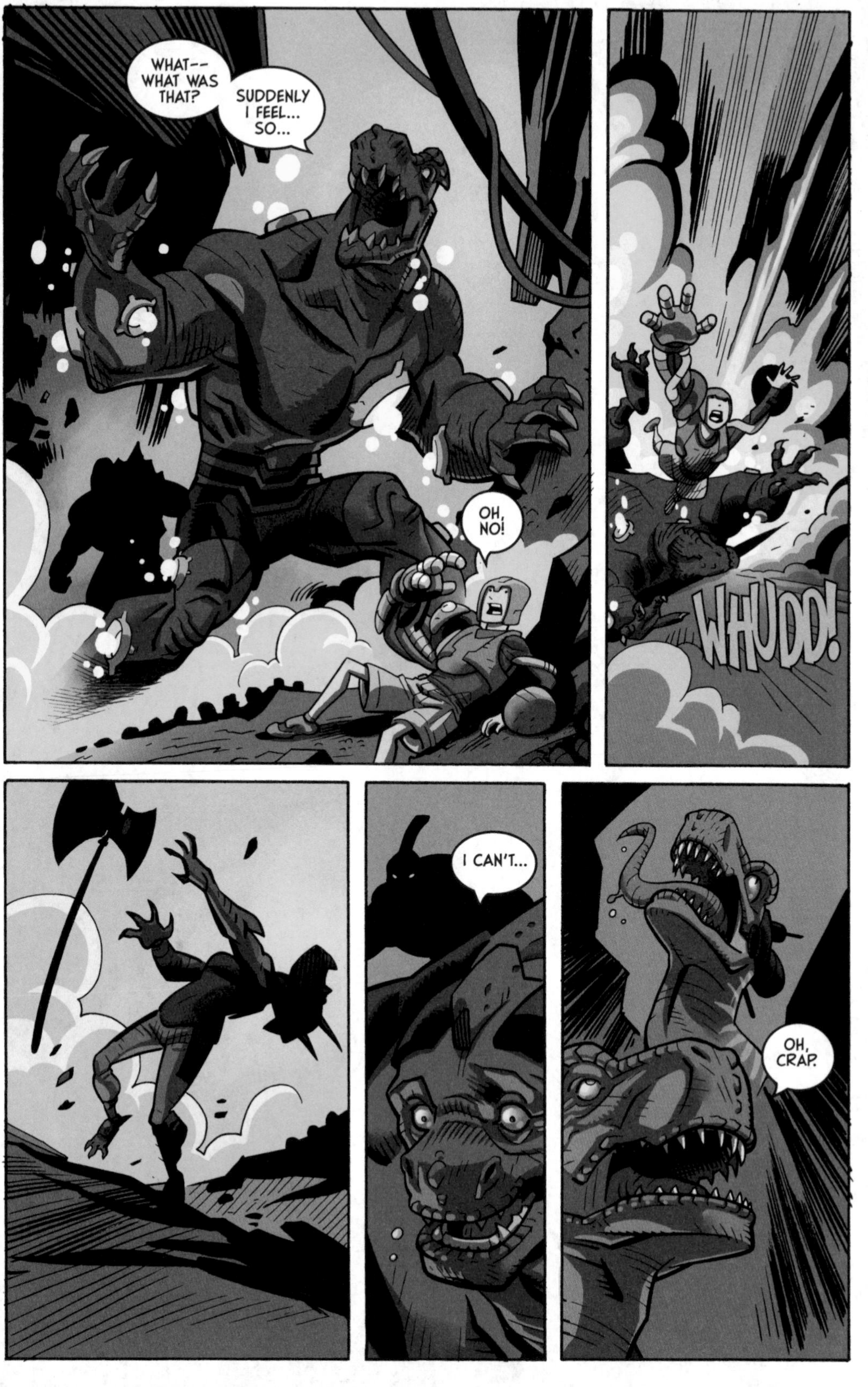
WHAT--
WHAT WAS
THAT?
SUDDENLY
I FEEL...
SO...
OH,
NO!
WHUDD!
I CAN'T...
OH,
CRAP.

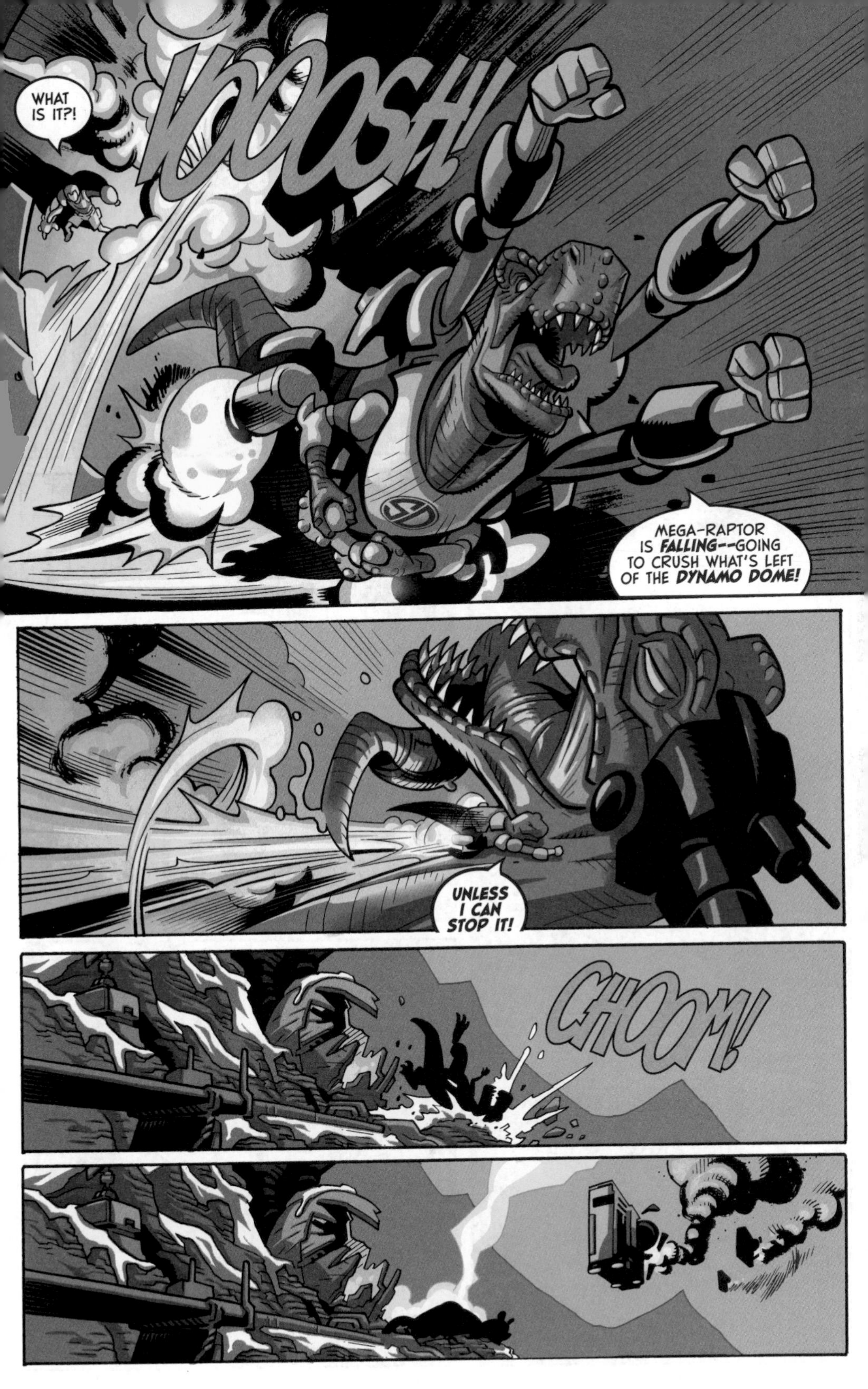
WHAT IS IT?!
VOOOSH!
MEGA-RAPTOR IS FALLING--GOING TO CRUSH WHAT'S LEFT OF THE DYNAMO DOME!
UNLESS I CAN STOP IT!
CHOOM!

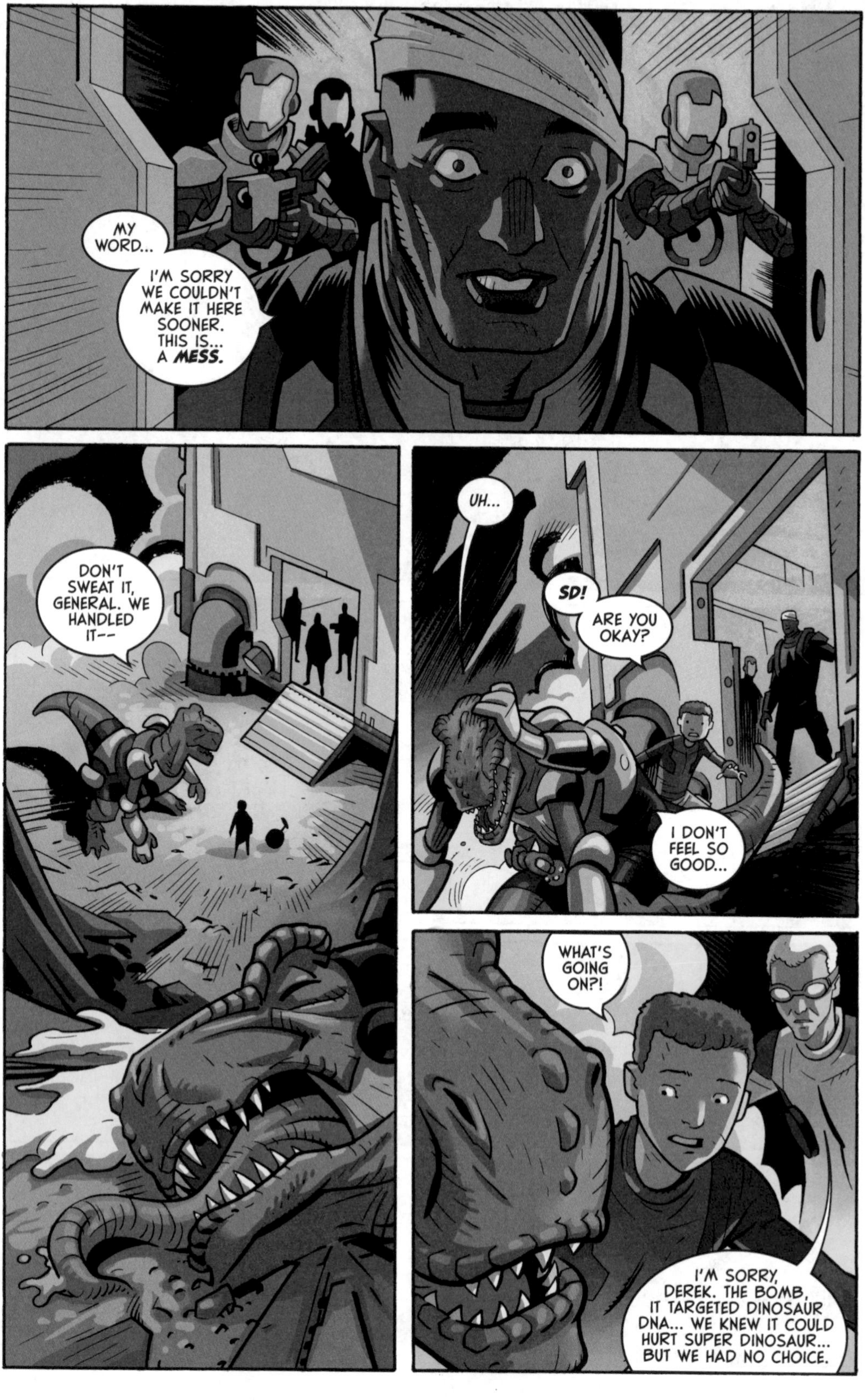
MY WORD...
I'M SORRY WE COULDN'T MAKE IT HERE SOONER. THIS IS... A MESS.
DON'T SWEAT IT, GENERAL. WE HANDLED IT--
UH...
SD!
ARE YOU OKAY?
I DON'T FEEL SO GOOD...
WHAT'S GOING ON?!
I'M SORRY, DEREK. THE BOMB, IT TARGETED DINOSAUR DNA... WE KNEW IT COULD HURT SUPER DINOSAUR... BUT WE HAD NO CHOICE.

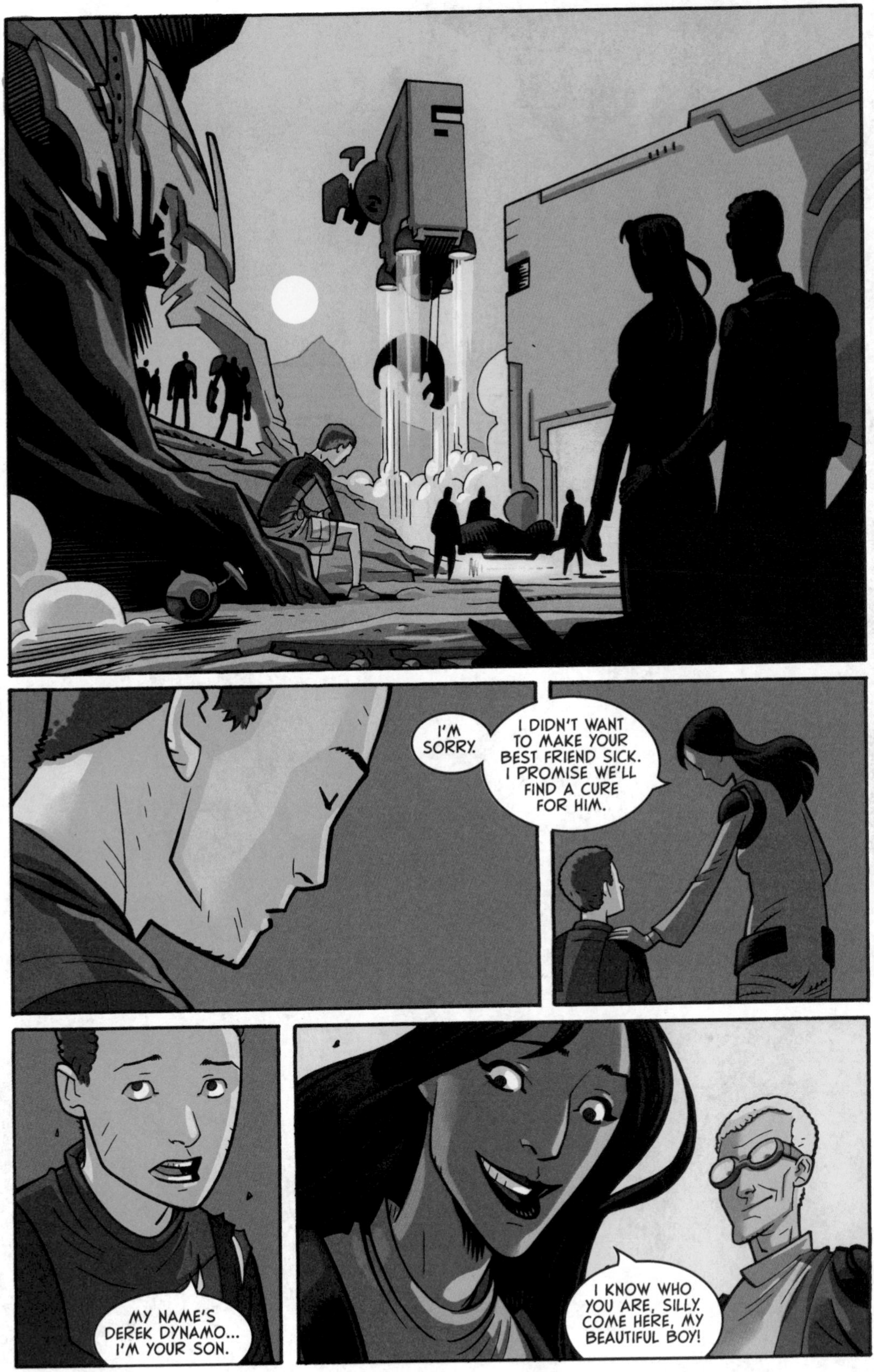
I'M SORRY.
I DIDN'T WANT TO MAKE YOUR BEST FRIEND SICK. I PROMISE WE'LL FIND A CURE FOR HIM.
MY NAME'S DEREK DYNAMO... I'M YOUR SON.
I KNOW WHO YOU ARE, SILLY. COME HERE, MY BEAUTIFUL BOY!

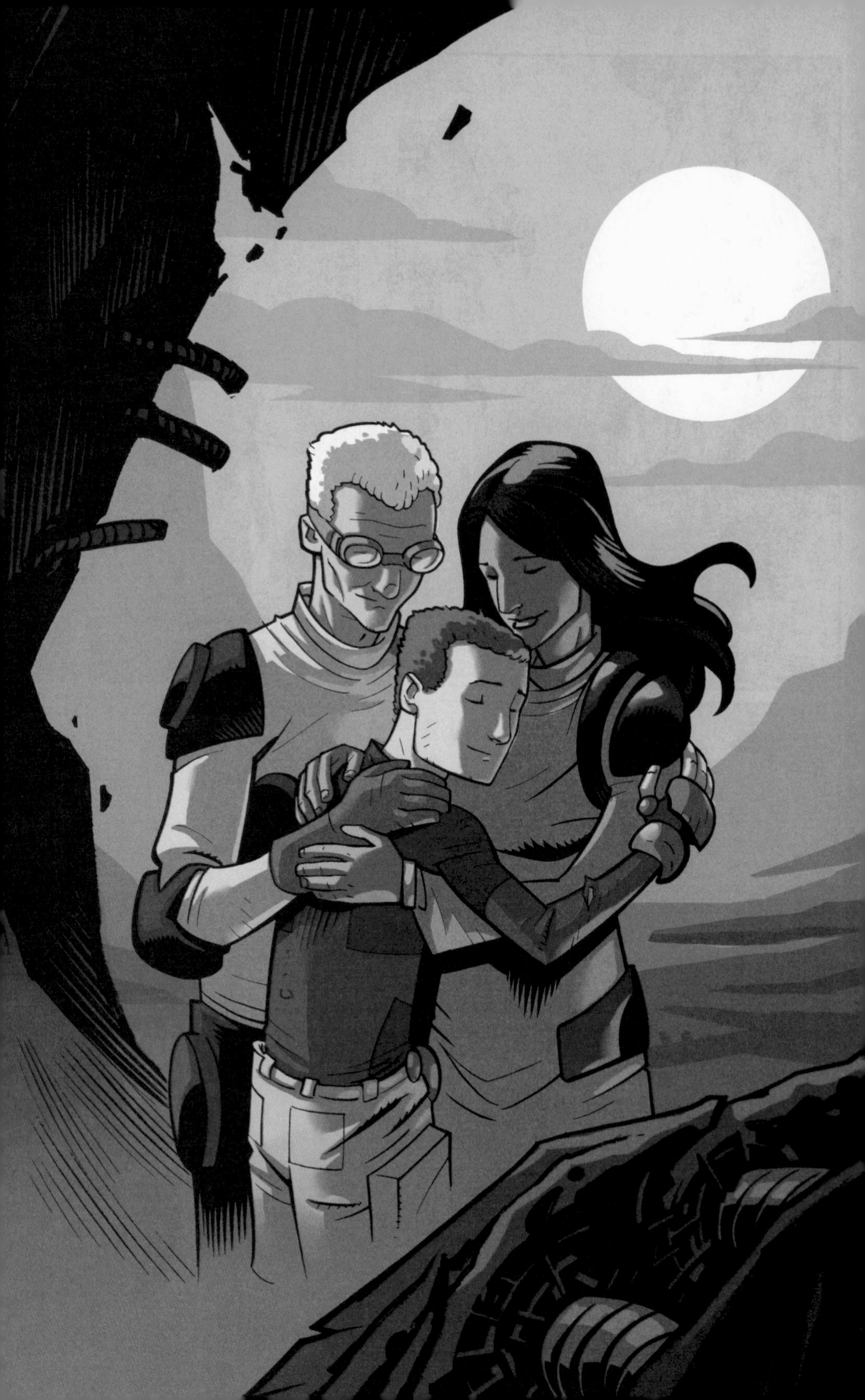

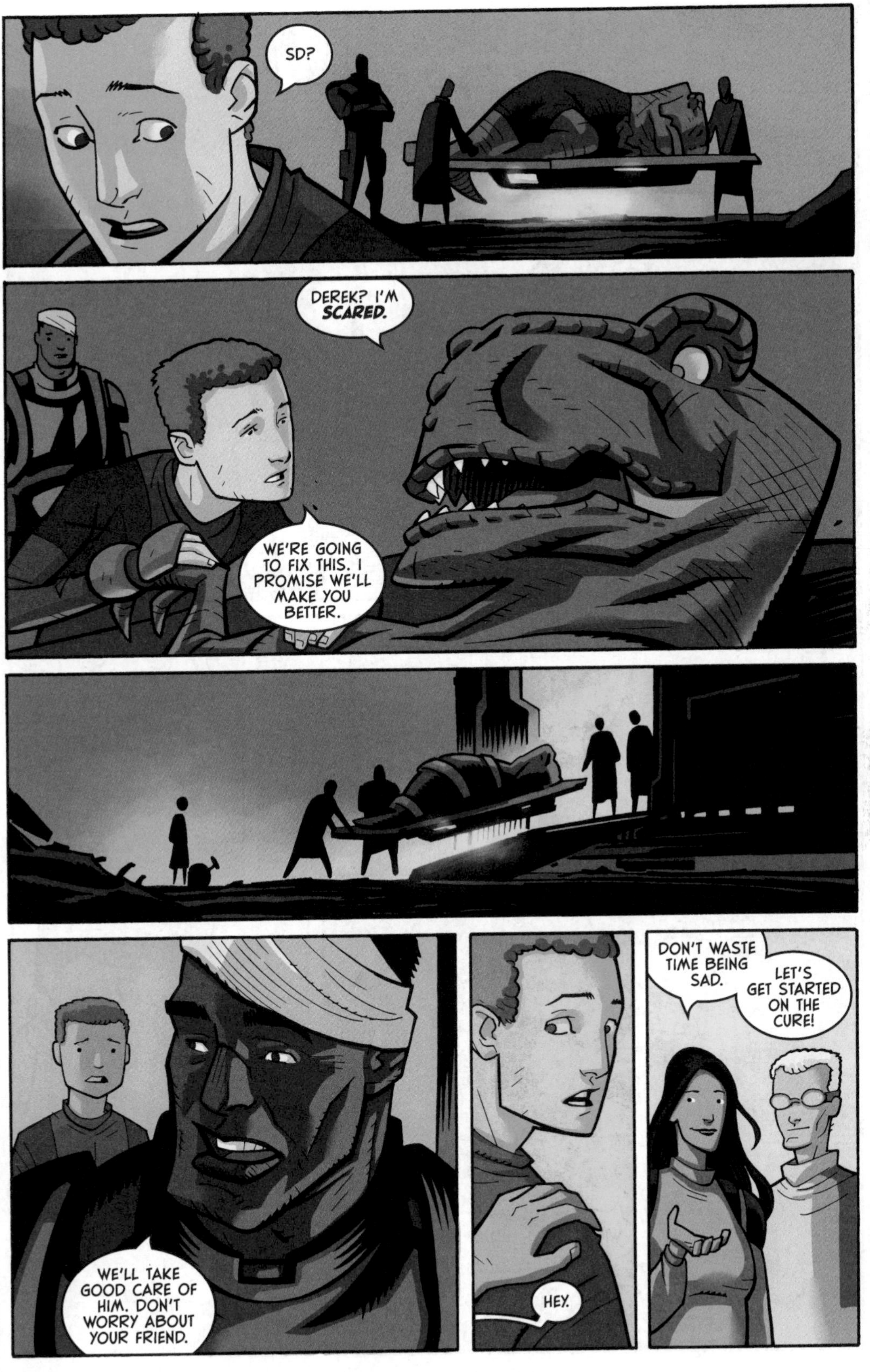
SD?
DEREK? I'M SCARED.
WE'RE GOING TO FIX THIS. I PROMISE WE'LL MAKE YOU BETTER.
WE'LL TAKE GOOD CARE OF HIM. DON'T WORRY ABOUT YOUR FRIEND.
HEY.
DON'T WASTE TIME BEING SAD.
LET'S GET STARTED ON THE CURE!

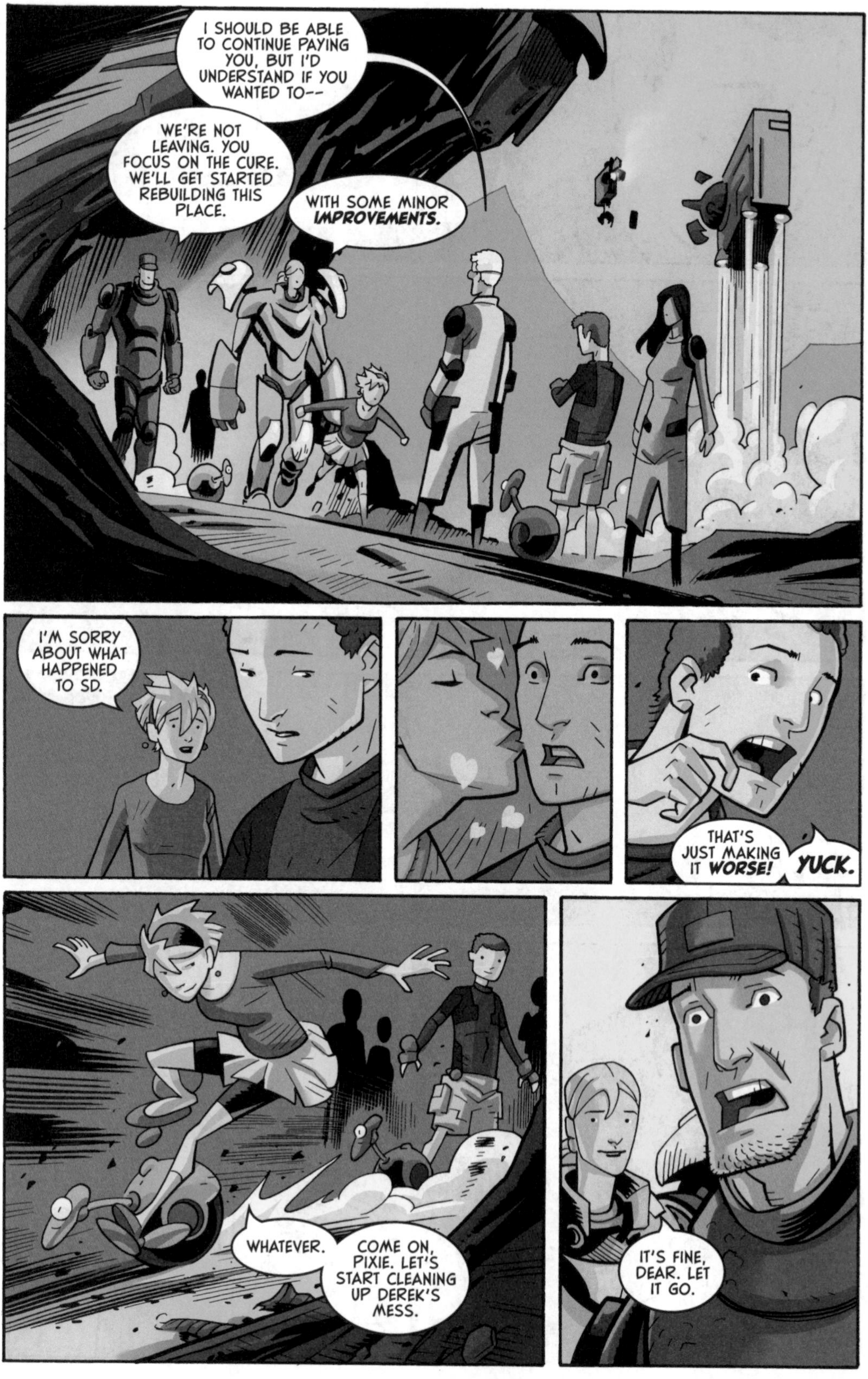
I SHOULD BE ABLE TO CONTINUE PAYING YOU, BUT I'D UNDERSTAND IF YOU WANTED TO--
WE'RE NOT LEAVING. YOU FOCUS ON THE CURE. WE'LL GET STARTED REBUILDING THIS PLACE.
WITH SOME MINOR **IMPROVEMENTS.**
I'M SORRY ABOUT WHAT HAPPENED TO SD.
THAT'S JUST MAKING IT **WORSE!**
YUCK.
WHATEVER.
COME ON, PIXIE. LET'S START CLEANING UP DEREK'S MESS.
IT'S FINE, DEAR. LET IT GO.

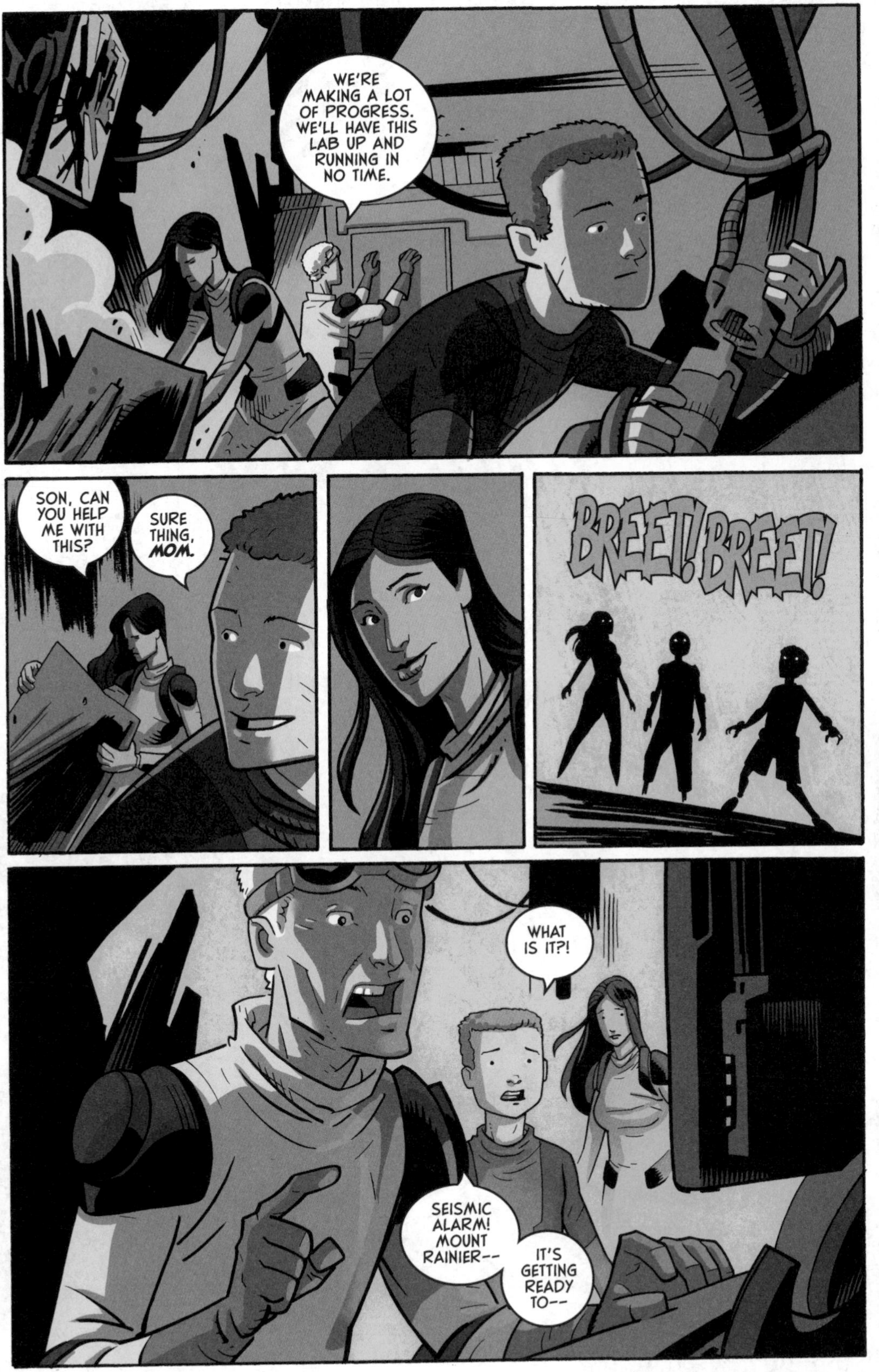
WE'RE MAKING A LOT OF PROGRESS. WE'LL HAVE THIS LAB UP AND RUNNING IN NO TIME.
SON, CAN YOU HELP ME WITH THIS?
SURE THING, MOM.
BREET! BREET!
WHAT IS IT?!
SEISMIC ALARM! MOUNT RAINIER--
IT'S GETTING READY TO--

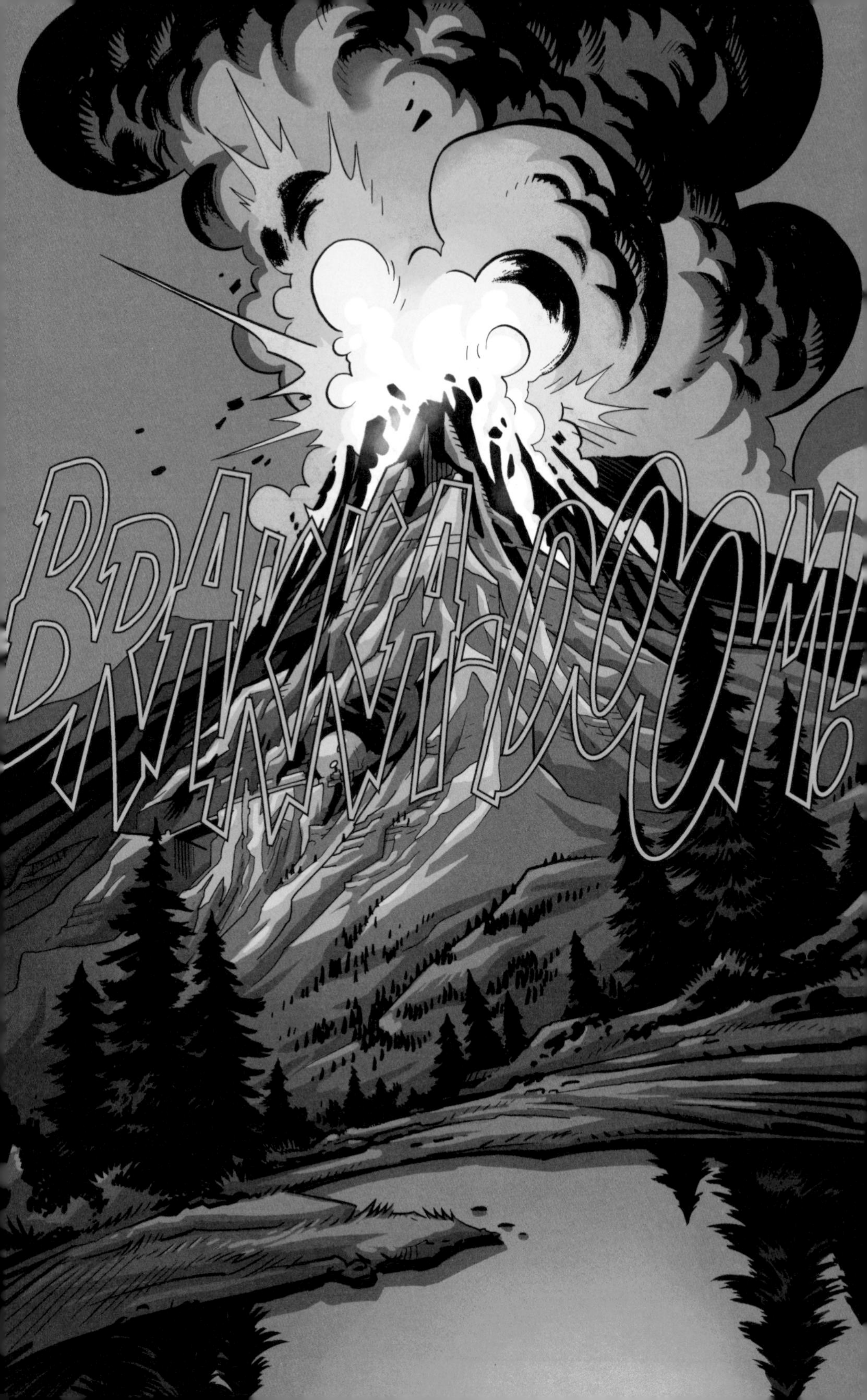

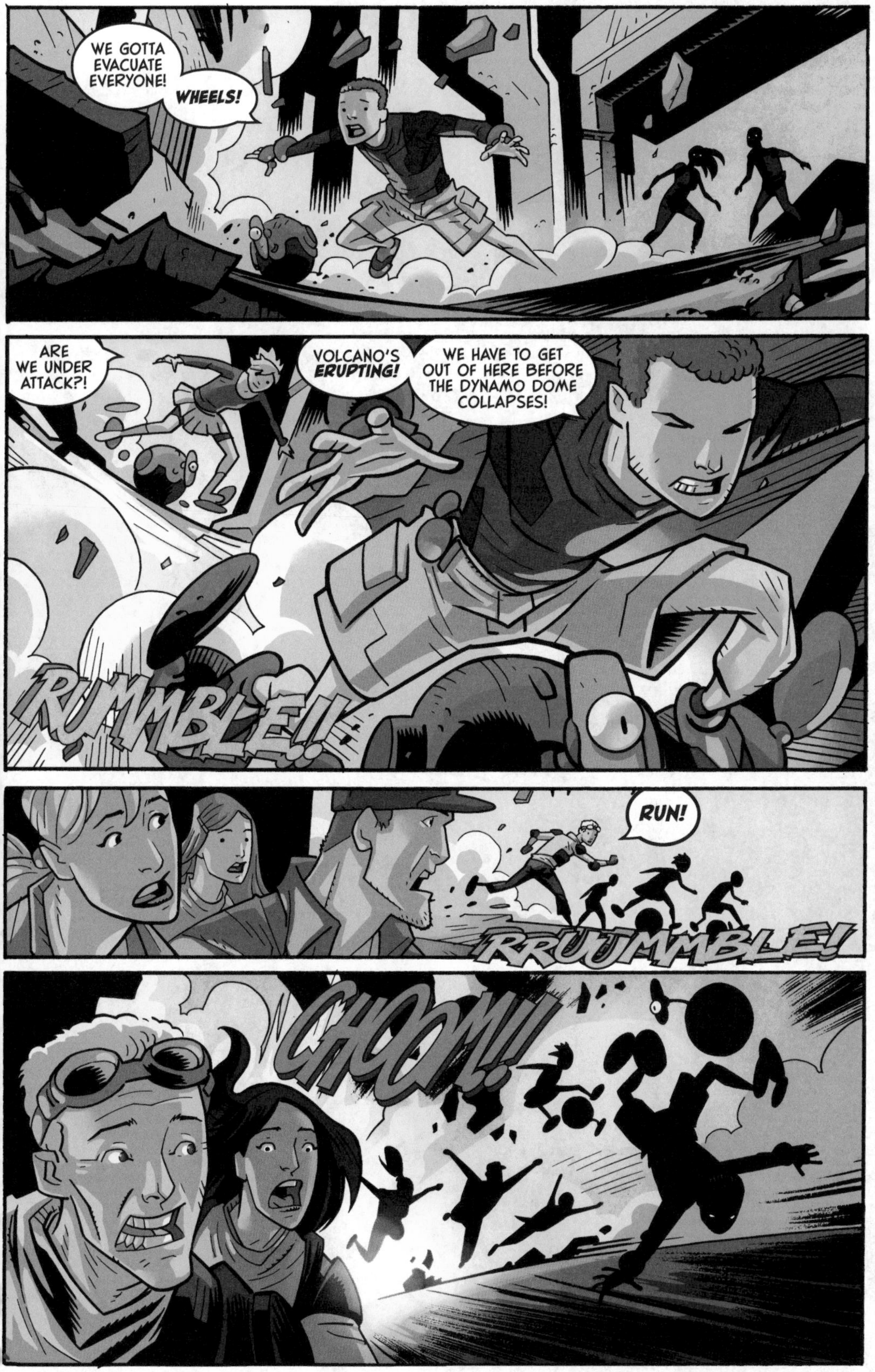
WE GOTTA EVACUATE EVERYONE!
WHEELS!
ARE WE UNDER ATTACK?!
VOLCANO'S ERUPTING!
WE HAVE TO GET OUT OF HERE BEFORE THE DYNAMO DOME COLLAPSES!
RUMMBLE!!
RUN!
RRUUMMBLE!
CHOOM!!

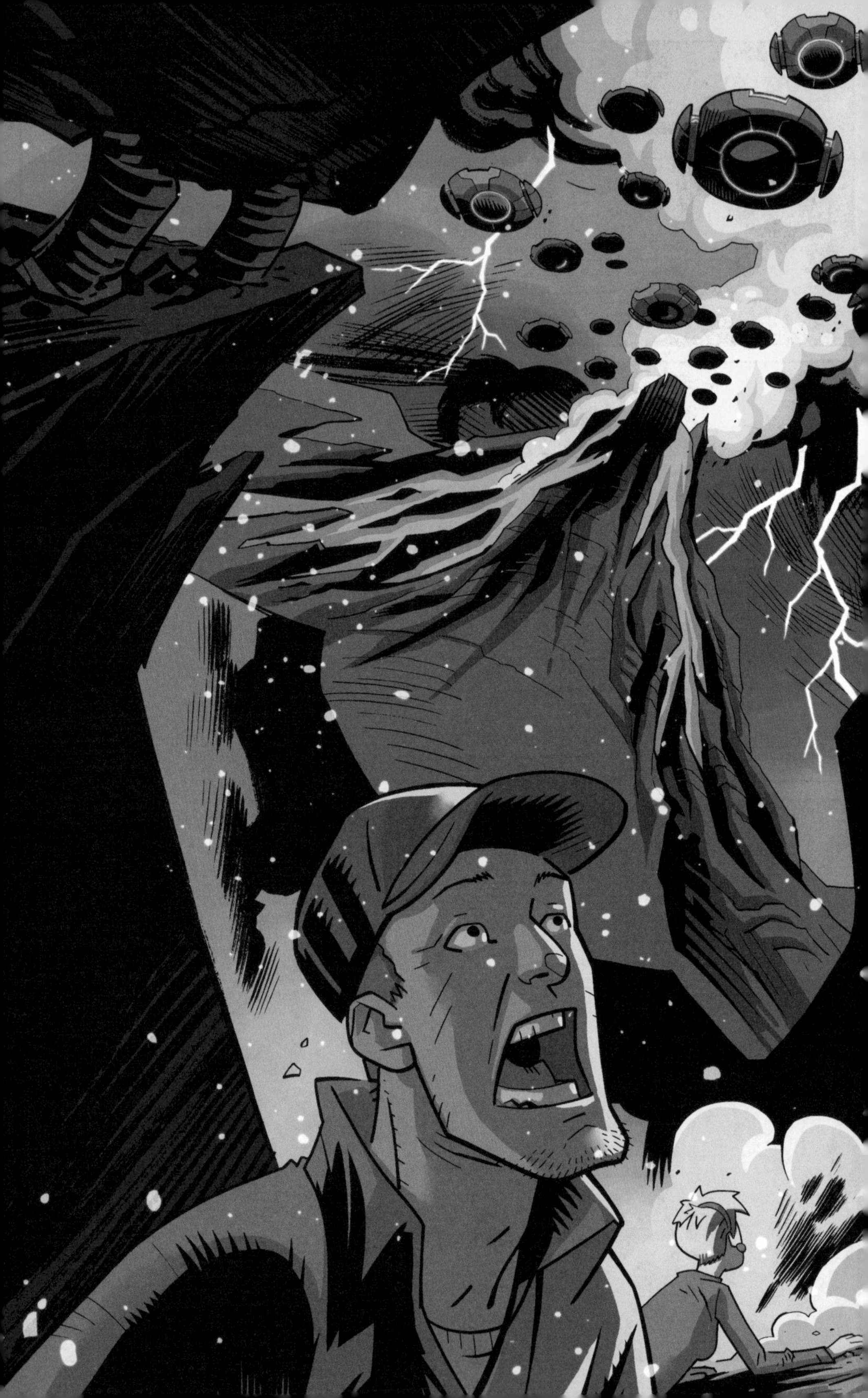

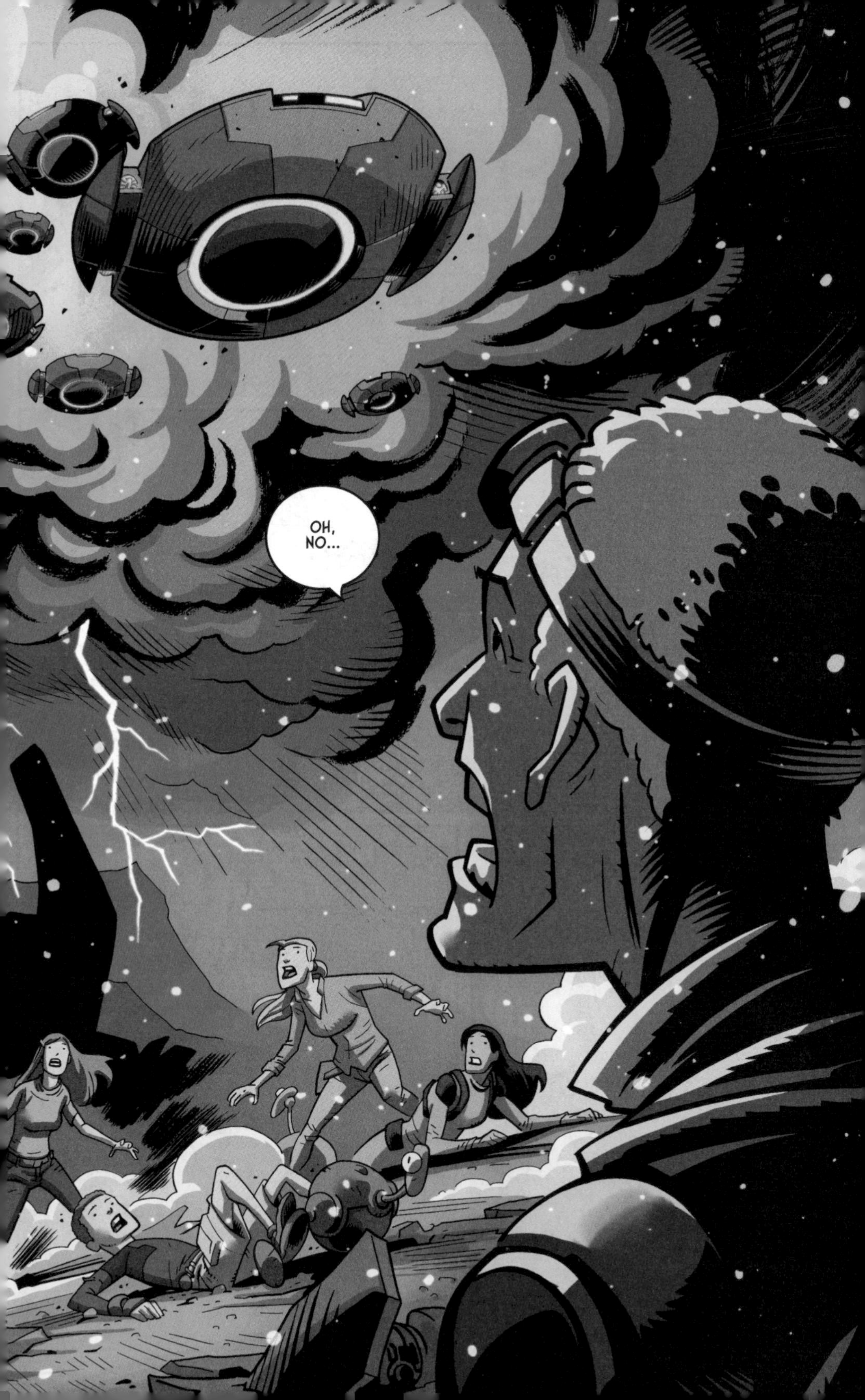
OH, NO...

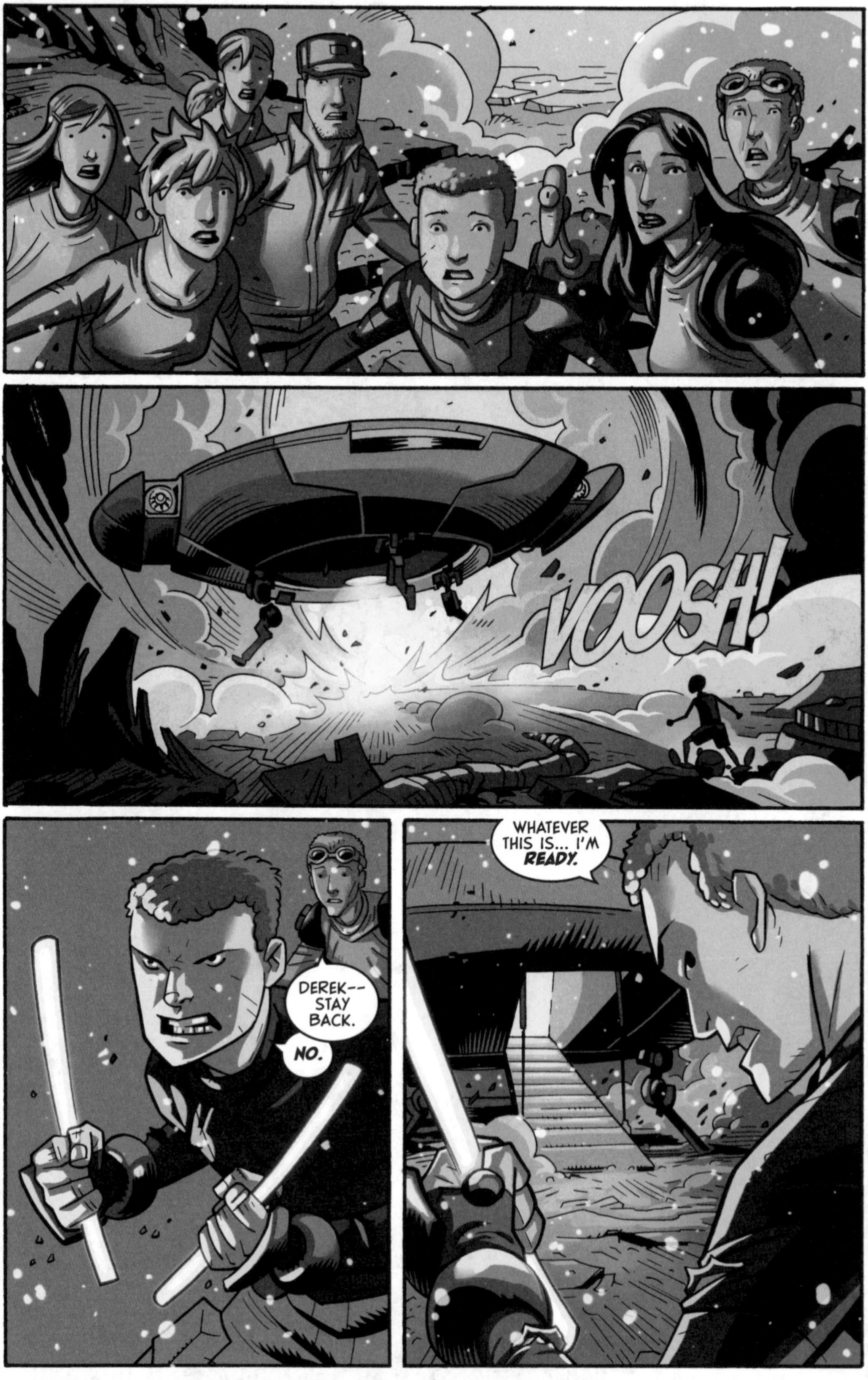
VOOSH!
DEREK--
STAY
BACK.
NO.
WHATEVER
THIS IS... I'M
READY.

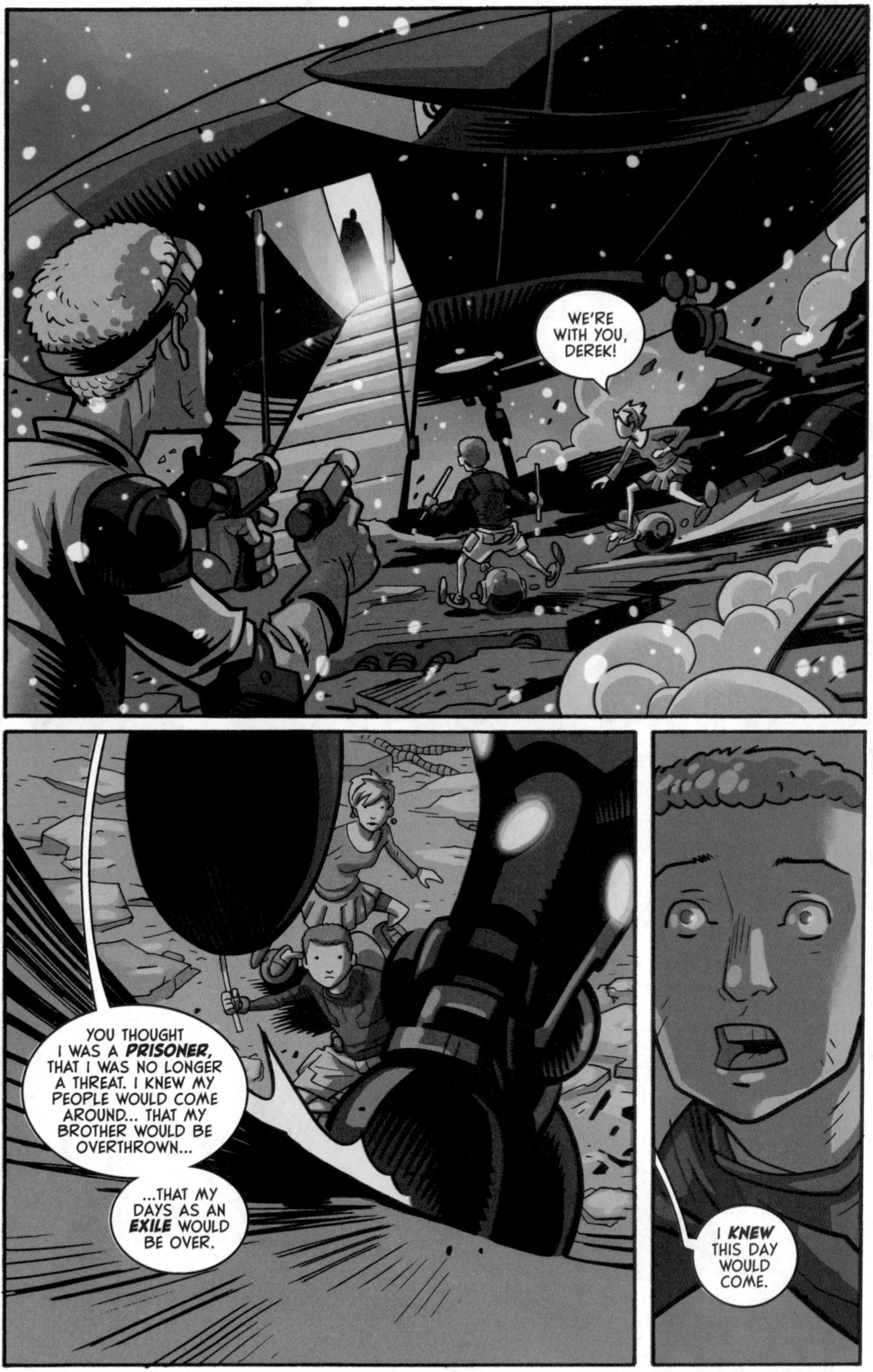
WE'RE WITH YOU, DEREK!
YOU THOUGHT I WAS A PRISONER, THAT I WAS NO LONGER A THREAT. I KNEW MY PEOPLE WOULD COME AROUND... THAT MY BROTHER WOULD BE OVERTHROWN...
...THAT MY DAYS AS AN EXILE WOULD BE OVER.
I KNEW THIS DAY WOULD COME.

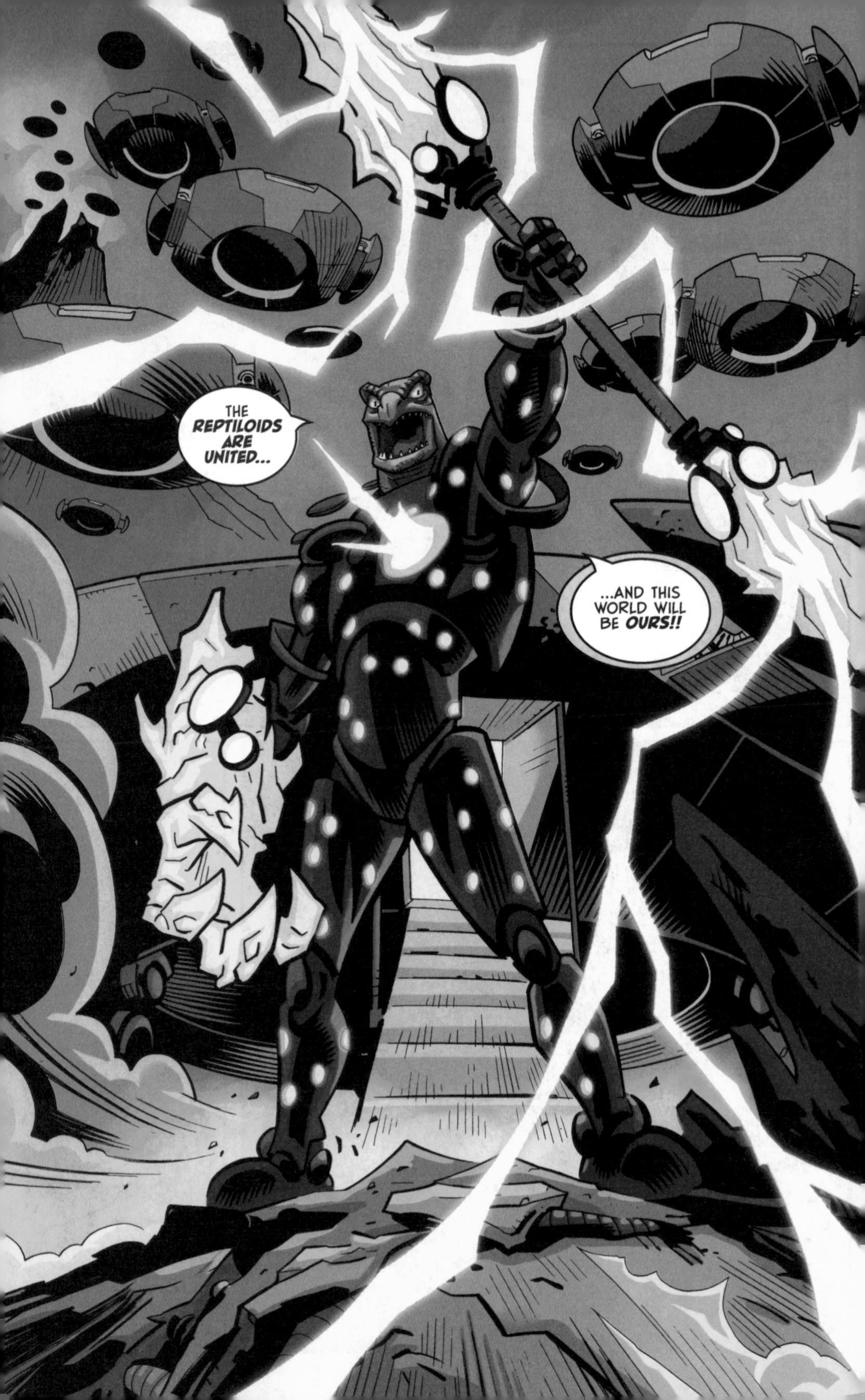
THE REPTILOIDS ARE UNITED...
...AND THIS WORLD WILL BE OURS!!

TO BE CONTINUED....